Phil Robinson

Noah's Ark, or, Mornings in the Zoo

Phil Robinson

Noah's Ark, or, Mornings in the Zoo

ISBN/EAN: 9783337030568

Printed in Europe, USA, Canada, Australia, Japan

Cover: Foto ©Andreas Hilbeck / pixelio.de

More available books at **www.hansebooks.com**

NOAH'S ARK;

OR,

"MORNINGS IN THE ZOO."

BEING

A CONTRIBUTION TO THE STUDY OF UNNATURAL HISTORY.

BY

PHIL ROBINSON,

AUTHOR OF "IN MY INDIAN GARDEN," "UNDER THE PUNKAH,"
ETC., ETC.
LATE PROFESSOR OF LITERATURE AND LOGIC, ALLAHABAD, INDIA.

London :

SAMPSON LOW, MARSTON, SEARLE, & RIVINGTON,
CROWN BUILDINGS, 188, FLEET STREET.
1882.

NOTE TO PREFACE.

~~~~~~~

I AM of opinion that no one living can be considered
a greater authority upon the subject of Noah's
Ark than my daughter Edith, for on the occasion
of her second birthday (last Thursday), we gave
her a Noah's Ark, and her life ever since has been
devoted to original researches into the properties
of its various inhabitants. Not only does she
bathe and feed each individual of the menagerie
every day, but she puts Noah and all his family,
and as many of the Beasts as she can find, under
her pillow every night. Moreover, she approaches
her subject quite unprejudiced by previous information, and with a grasp that is both bold and
comprehensive. This free, generous handling of
the persons and animals that have come under her
notice, convinces me, therefore, that the contents of

this volume will receive from her a fairer introduc-
tion to the Public than I could expect from a
more precisely critical pen.

Phil Robinson.

———

PREFACE.

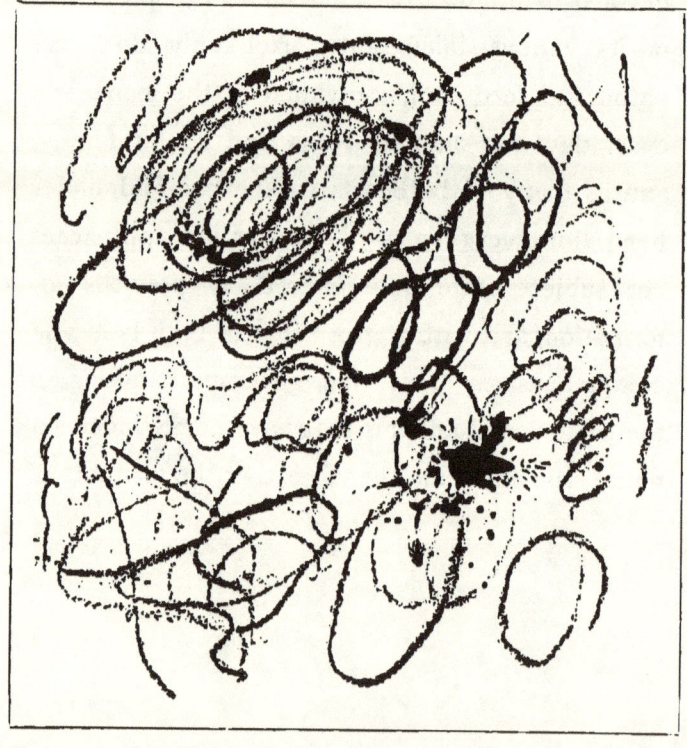

A PRELIMINARY WARNING

OF

THE CONTENTS OF THIS BOOK.

The radical mistake in all our writing and painting of animals from very early ages has been the semi-serious effort to *see human nature* in the brute and bird, and to describe it as, in fact, a Man in fur or in feathers. The process, though at first sight similar to the true method, is in reality the very converse of it, and beginning at the wrong end, diverges wider from the truth at every step. The more elaborate the story or the picture so constructed, and the more wire-drawn the parallel, the further it inevitably departs from the veracity of nature. Not by starting with the resolution to find human character in animals, but by studying them carefully and dispassionately till we come down to the ground of common feeling where they and we are alike, and where Nature is neither Human nor bestial, can we hope to obtain a real knowledge of them."— *Frances Power Cobbe.*

NOAH'S ARK.

A CONTRIBUTION TO THE STUDY OF UNNATURAL HISTORY.

CHAPTER I.

THE WORLD'S GREAT BEAST-GATHERINGS.

WHAT THE DODO SAID TO KING SOLOMON : AND WHAT CAME
OF IT——UNTIMELY DEATH OF THE WELL-MEANING KING
AND DISPERSION OF HIS MENAGERIE——THE GREAT BEAST-
GATHERINGS——MAN'S OPPORTUNITIES IN EDEN AND IN THE
ARK——ADAM NAMES THE ANIMALS——NOAH SAVES THEM
——MODERN CHANCES OF CONCILIATION FRUSTRATED BY
ROMAN CRUELTY——BUT A BETTER UNDERSTANDING POS-
SIBLE—— DANGER OF MISCONSTRUCTION —— HOW SOME
GEESE GOT DRUNK AND WERE PLUCKED AS BEING DEAD——
DEMORALIZATION OF BEASTS BY MAN —— KEEPERS THE
NATURAL FOOD OF LIONS——ENNOBLING INFLUENCES OF
MAN ON BEASTS——PRIZE PIGS AND POULTRY.

"IT is worth your Majesty's noting," said the
Dodo to King Solomon, " that Man was not
created until the last of the six days ; that he
is, in fact, the Junior of the Animals.

" Earth was sufficiently complete without him, and

B

already populated before he came. · He was, at best, a splendid afterthought.

"Yet he, Man—this appendix to creation, this supplement as it were, a mere addendum or postscript—has disorganized the whole. He found us all living together happily in one spot, and was the cause of our miserable dispersion over the world. To quote the poet of the future Romans—

> ' Tum vero infelix viris exterrita, Dodo
> Mortem oravi.'

"I have no doubt," replied the King, "that you are right—from a Dodo's point of view—

> ' Infelix Dodo, nunc te facta impia tangunt'

—and so forth. But has it not occurred to you, madam, that if it had not been for this same Man, you would all have come rather badly off in that matter of Noah's Ark ?"

Solomon's good intentions.

I confess I am inclined to suspect the above as being apocryphal.[1] But let that be as it may, the fact remains (and I now move from the firm ground of pure invention to the quagmire of Rabbinical conjecture) that King Solomon seems to have done his best to repair the mischief worked by his ancestors. For he tried to

---

[1] My suspicion receives some confirmation from the circumstance that I never read the above passage until I had written it. Yet the quotations seem to me to be from the Æneid.—P. R.

bring all the beasts together again by opening Zoological Gardens near Jerusalem, and, knowing the languages of animals, he established, so to speak, a thorough understanding with them.

But before he was able to make good the original breach between man and the other creatures, King Solomon unfortunately died, and, as neither Rehoboam nor Jeroboam inherited their father's scientific tastes, the contents of the Gardens escaped from Jerusalem at the earliest opportunity, and went back to their respective homes more discontented than ever.

Thus collapsed one of the most stupendous enterprises for the world's welfare ever undertaken by a human being. Indeed, imagination fails one to form any adequate idea of the benefits that might have resulted to humanity, if Solomon had only succeeded in securing for man the cordial co-operation of all the beasts, birds, reptiles, fishes, and insects. We should have known everything, possessed everything, done everything. As it is, however, the opportunity has gone. It is too late now to think of a universal confederation. We have had our chances. Adam's opportunity in Eden was full of possibilities, and Noah's in the Ark was not far behind it.

Since then circumstances have changed, and for us at the present day the project is virtually impracticable, owing, if to nothing else, to the complete destruction of the beasts' confidence in man by two centuries of Roman cruelty.

These, then, have been the World's Great Beast-Gatherings for—putting on one side such inconsiderable collections as those of Solomon or Orpheus, or those conventions referred to in myth, or Thierfabel, or Kalandar's tale—we find that four times only in history have men ever seen the beast-world adequately represented in assembly: in the Garden of Eden; in the Ark; in the Roman arena; in the Zoological Gardens.

One of the very few positive facts we have about Adam is that he gave names to all the living things in Eden: not of course those by which even antiquity knew them, but names such as Primitive Man, wherever he still exists, distinguishes the creatures about him by. To him, for instance, the squirrel is "the thing that sits in the shadow of its tail," and in Accadian nomenclature there is no lion, but only "the great-voiced one." We have only to see how the Boers in Africa have individualized their fauna, their "earth-wolves" and "sea-cows," to understand the nature of Adam's names, or indeed to look round in the rural districts of England, where "wind-hovers," and "flitter-mice," and "sheep-stares," still do duty for kestrels, bats, and starlings.

But to be able to name the creatures, furred and feathered, with such picturesque appropriateness argues a knowledge of their habits founded upon personal observation, and the legend therefore that tells us how the Angels failed to execute the orders of the Creator is not

at all an absurd one. Allah, it is said, told the Angels—
who were sneering at man—to name the animals, and
they tried to do so, but could not. So then he turned to
Adam, and the Angels stood listening, ashamed, as the
patriarch drew a picture of each creature in a word.
The angelic host of course had no sympathy with
them. Indeed, perhaps, they had no knowledge whatever
of the earth and its things; for it is possible, as Milton
supposes, that the Angels never left the upper sky,
except on special missions. With Adam it was different.
In his habits of daily life he was in the closest sympathy
with other animals, and virtually one of themselves.
Each beast and bird therefore, as it passed before him,
suggested to him at once some distinguishing epithet, and
he found no difficulty in assigning to every individual
an appropriate name, and appointing each his proper
place in the system of creation.

It is generally supposed that this system has now *Political
and Social*
developed into an unconstitutional monarchy, but *Systems of
the Beasts.*
there is much more to be said on the side of its being an
Oligarchy. The beasts, like everything else in nature,
"move violently to their places, but quietly in their
places," and even their very revolutions seem, by the
tranquillity of the process, to be rather the result of the
mere lapse of time than of the sudden outgrowth of new
necessities.

Thus in the beginning of days all power was in the
hands of the Titans, the mammoths and the mastodons

of antiquity, but in time a more vigorous race of beasts was gradually developed, and the Saturn and Tellus, Ops and Typhon of the primeval earth were one by one unseated and dispossessed of power by the younger creatures, the eagles of Jupiter and the tigers of Bacchus, the serpents of Athene and the wolves of Mars.

The elder rulers of the wild world accepted at their hands the dignity of extinction, but nevertheless they loom out to-day from the background of time as the " dead but sceptred sovereigns, that still rule us from their urns,"—the mammoth caves of Kentucky, the elephant pits of Essex, the mastodon ice-drifts of the Russian coast and the dinornis beds of the Austral sea.

Next, there came a period of calm transition, during which our modern oceans were brimming up into their present basins, and our modern continents were taking shape. But in spite of the august deliberateness of these stupendous changes, the revolution when eventually complete was found to have been radical. Instead of a few Behemoths lording it among the vast commonwealth of the earth, there were many nations of lesser things, all divided into their tribes and clans, and transacting, each within their own countries, all the duties of life, exercising the high functions of authority, and carrying on the work of an orderly world.

On land, the tiger and the lion, the python, the polar bear, and the grizzly, gradually rose to the acknowledged dignity of crowned heads. In the air there was the

royal condor and the eagle, with a peerage of falcons.
In the mysterious empire of the sea there was but one
supreme authority, the sea · serpent, with its terrible
lieutenants, the octopus and the devil-fish.

Yet none of these are absolute autocrats beyond the *Penalties* immediate territory they reside in.   They have all to *of Extended Dominion.*
pay in vexed boundaries the penalty of extended domi-
nion.   Thus, though the tiger may be supreme in the
jungles of the Himalayan Terai, he finds upon his wild
Naga frontier the irreconcilable rhinoceros, and in
the fierce Guzerati country there is the maneless lion.
Up among the hills are the fearless Ghoorkha leopards,
and in the broken lowlands along the river that stout old
Rohilla thakoor, the wild boar, resents all royal interference.   The lion, again, they say, is King in Africa, yet
the gorilla Zulus it over the forests within the lion's territory ; the ostrich on the plain despises all his mandates,
and in the earldom of the rivers the crocodile cares nothing
for his favour or his wrath.   The lion, indeed, claims to
be King of the Beasts ; but, loud as his roar is, it does
not quite reach across the Atlantic, and we find the puma
not only asserting leonine authority, but actually usurping
the royal title as " the American lion," just as in Africa,
under the lion's very nose, the leopard claims an equality
of power by calling itself " the tiger."   The polar bear
can command no homage from the walrus, nor the
grizzly bear levy taxes from the bison. The python, "the
emperor" of Mexican folk-lore, has none to attack him,

but on the other hand, he does not venture to treat the jaguar as a serf.

Among the birds " of the air," though eagles be Kings, the raven asserts a melancholy supremacy over the solitudes of wildernesses, and the albatross is monarch of the waves. · No one will deny the aristocracy of the flamingo, the bustard, or the swan, or dispute the nobility of the ibis on the Nile, or of the birds of Paradise in their leafy Edens of the Eastern Seas. For pretenders to high place we have the peacock and the vulture, and as democrats, to incite the proletariat of fowldom to disaffection, and even turbulence, we need not search further than the crows.

In the sea, the Kraken is king. It is the hierophant of the oceanic mysteries, secret as a Prince of the Assassins, or veiled Prophet, and sacred from its very secrecy like the Lama of Thibet or the Unseen God of the Tartars. Yet there are those who dispute the weird majesty of the hidden potentate, for the whales, to north and south, enjoy a limited sovereignty, while all along the belt of the tropics the pirate sharks scourge the sea-folk as they will.

*   *   *   *   *

Even this, after all, is too narrow a view of the wild world. And I find myself, catholic as I am in my regard for the things in fur and feathers, falling very often into the same offence against the dignity of beasts and birds, that the over-scientific naturalist on the one hand, and the indifferent visitor to the Gardens on the other, seem to me to commit. How easy it is, for instance, to misunderstand the animals ; to think ill of the bear for sulking, when it is only weary of seeking explanation for its captivity ; to laugh at the meaningless rage of the buffalo, when in reality it sniffs the tainted air from the lion-house ; to quarrel with the dulness of the osprey that sits dreaming of spring-time among the crags that overlook Lake Erie. Remember, reader, the geese of Apfel, and take the moral of their story to heart.

A farmer's wife had been making some cherry brandy ; *How some Geese got drunk and What came of it.* but as she found, during the process, that the fruit was unsound, she threw the whole mess out into the yard, and, without looking to see what followed, shut down the window.

Now, as it fell out, a party of geese, good fellows all of them, happened to be waddling by at the time, and, seeing the cherries trundling about, at once investigated them. The preliminary inquiry proving satisfactory, these misguided poultry set to and swallowed the whole lot. "No heeltaps" was the order of the carouse, and so they finished all the cherries off at one sitting, so to speak.

The effect of the spirituous fruit was soon apparent, for on trying to make the gate which led from the scene of the debauch to the horsepond, they found everything against them. Whether a high wind had got up, or what had happened, they could not tell, but it seemed to the geese as if there was an uncommonly high sea running, and the ground set in towards them with a strong steady swell that was most embarrassing to progress. To escape these difficulties some lashed their rudders and hove to, others tried to run before the wind, while the rest tacked for the pigstye. But there was no living in such weather, and one by one the craft lurched over and went down all standing.

Meanwhile the dame, the unconscious cause of this disaster, was attracted by the noise in the fowl-yard, and looking out saw all her ten geese behaving as if they were mad. The gander himself, usually so solemn and decorous, was balancing himself on his beak, and spinning round the while, in a prodigious flurry of feathers and dust, while the old grey goose, remarkable even among her kind for the circumspection of her conduct, was lying stomach upwards in the gutter, feebly gesticulating with her legs. Others of the party were no less conspicuous for the extravagance of their attitudes and gestures, while the remainder were to be seen lying in a helpless confusion of feathers in the lee scuppers, that is to say, in the gutter by the pigstye.

Perplexed by the spectacle, the dame called in her neighbours, and after careful investigation it was decided in council that the birds *had died of poison*. Under these circumstances their carcases were worth nothing for food, but, as the neighbours said, their feathers were not poisoned, and so, the next day being market-day, they

set to work then and there and plucked the ten geese
bare. Not a feather did they leave on the gander, not
a tuft of down on the old grey goose, and, the job com-
pleted, they left the dame with her bag full of plumage
and her ten plucked geese, not without assuring her, we
may be certain, of their sympathy with her in her loss.

Next morning the good woman got up as usual, and,
remembering the feathers downstairs, dressed betimes,
for she hoped, thrifty soul, to get them off her hands
that very day, at market. And then she bethought her
of the ten plucked bodies lying out under the porch,
and resolved that they should be buried before she went.
But as she approached the door, on these decent rites
intent, and was turning the key, there fell on her ears
the sound of a familiar voice—and then another—and
another—until at last the astonished dame heard in full
chorus the well-known accents of all her plucked and
poisoned geese ! The throat of the old gander sounded,
no doubt, a trifle husky, and the grey goose spoke in
muffled tones suggestive of a chastening headache ; but
there was no mistaking those voices, and the dame,
fumbling at the door, wondered what it all might mean.

Has a goose a ghost ? Did any one ever read or hear
of the spectre of a gander ?

The key turned at last ; the door opened, and there,
quacking in subdued tones, suppliant and shivering,
stood all her flock ! There they stood, the ten miserable
birds, with splitting headaches and parched tongues

contrite and dejected, asking to have their feathers back
again. The situation was painful to both parties. The
forlorn geese saw in each other's persons the humiliating
reflection of their own condition, while the dame, guiltily
conscious of that bag full of feathers, remembered how
the one lapse of Noah, in that "aged surprisal of six
hundred years and unexpected inebriation from the unknown effects of wine," has been excused by religion
and the unanimous voice of posterity. She, and her
neighbours with her, however, had hastily misjudged the
geese, and, finding them dead drunk, had stripped them,
without remembering for a moment that if feathers are
easy to get off, they are very hard to put on. Here were
the geese before her, bald, penitent, and shaking with
the cold. There in the corner were their feathers, in a
bag. But how could they be brought together? Even
supposing each goose could recognize its own, how were
they to be re-clothed? Tarring and feathering was out
of the question, for that would be to add insult to injury,
and to try to stick all the feathers into their places again
one by one was a labour such as only folk in fairy tales
could ever hope to accomplish.

So she called in her neighbours again, but they proved
only sorry comforters, for they reminded her that after
all the fault was her own, that it was she and no one
else who had thrown the brandied cherries to the geese.
The poor fowls, brought up to confide in her, and repay-
ing her care of them by trustful reliance, could never

her neighbours said, have been 'expected to guess that, when she threw the vinous fruit in their path, she, their own familiar mistress, at whose hands they looked for all that was good, could have intended to betray them into the shocking excesses of intoxication, and deceive them to their ruin. Yet so it had been. Accepting the feast spread out before them, the geese had partaken gladly, gratefully, freely, of the insidious cherry, and the result was this, that the geese were in one place and their feathers were in another! At last, weary of the reproaches of her friends, the widow gathered all her bald poultry about her round the kitchen fire, and sat down to make them flannel jackets—registering a solemn vow, as she did so, never to jump hastily to conclusions about either bird or beast, lest she might again fall into the error of misconstruing their conduct.

The mischief, however, was done ; for the geese, who *Distrust of* had got drunk off brandied cherries, and been plucked *Mankind a result of* by mistake in consequence, had good reason for with- *this De-plorable* holding from human beings for ever afterwards that pleas- *Accident.* ing trustfulness which characterizes the domestic fowl. They would never again approach their food without suspicion, nor look upon a gathering of the neighbours except as a dark conspiracy against their feathers. The dame herself, whom hitherto they had been wont to greet with tumultuous acclaim, and whose footsteps to and fro they had been accustomed to follow so closely, would become to them an object of distrust. Instead of tumbling over each other in their glad hurry to meet her in the morning, or crowding round her full of gossip and small goose confidences when she came to pen them up for the night, they would eye her askance from a distance, approach her only strategically, and accept her gifts with reproachful hesitation. And how keenly the dame would feel such estrangement I leave my readers to judge for themselves.

*   *   *   *   *

This untoward inebriation of the geese points, however, another lesson ; for I cannot but see in it one more of those deplorable instances of moral deterioration of the animal world which from time to time obtrude themselves, unwelcome, upon the notice of lovers of nature.

Demoralization of animals. In Belgium and other places men try to make dogs believe they are donkeys or ponies, by harnessing them to carts, but the attempt can never succeed. For a dog thus employed will always be a very indifferent donkey, and never a good dog. In Paris, again, the other day a man demoralized all his bees by bringing their hives into the city and putting them down next a sugar warehouse. The bees, hitherto as pure-minded and upright insects as one could have wished to meet in a summer's day, developed at once an unnatural aversion to labour, and a not less unnatural tendency to larceny. Instead of winging their industrious way to the distant clover-fields, and there gathering the innocent honey, they swarmed in disorderly mobs upon the sugar casks next door, and crawled about with their ill-gotten burdens upon the surrounding pavement. The owner of the hives benefited immensely by the proximity of the saccharine deposits, but it was at the sacrifice of all moral tone in the bees which he had tempted and which had fallen.

I have often in the streets seen a cat trained to sit on the showman's stall, while linnets and canaries hopped on and off its head, examining its paws, looking into its mouth, and otherwise testing the discipline of the little beast of prey. And I confess that, as often as I see the exhibition, I wish that, in assertion of the dignity of the great instincts of nature, the cat would forget its fears and bite off an inquisitive canary's head. It is not good for cats that they should respect little birds, nor for little birds that they should hold cats in contempt. *Impropriety of Cats respecting Little Birds.*

We never tire of protesting against the unnatural relations of lion and lion-tamer, and of reminding the keepers of menageries that instinct is irrepressible, untameable, and immortal. And every now and then, a lion, tired of foolery, knocks a man into mummy. The last case was at Birmingham. A lion's keeper had gone into the beast's cage to clean it, and having, as he supposed, seen all the occupants safely out, set to work. As it happened, however, the sliding door which divided off the two compartments of the cage had not fallen securely into its place, and an old lion seeing his opportunity sprang at the opening. The door gave way, and the next instant the beast had seized his keeper. The man had a broom in his hand, but the lion cared little for that. A number of people, powerless of course to give assistance, were looking on, but fortunately there was also present a professional "lion-tamer," belonging to the establishment, and this man, with great courage, rushed straight into the cage and confronted the lion. He had in his hand a pistol loaded with blank cartridge, which he flashed in the brute's face without making any impression upon it, and then commenced beating it upon the head with the heavily loaded handle of the whip which he carried. At first the blows were received only with roars, but at last a smashing one between the eyes seemed partially to stun the lion, for it released its prey, and the unfortunate keeper was at once dragged out.

Now, it is easy enough, after such an incident as this, to talk of lions as "savage brutes," and then to moralize over the foolhardiness of men who have grown accustomed to lions, and think that lions have therefore grown accustomed to them. But surely it is much more just to the animals to remember that it is the most natural thing in the world for a flesh-eating animal to spring at meat when it sees it within its reach.

Suppose we were to catch a healthy street-boy, and, having shut him up in a small cage, were all day long to roll plum-puddings backwards and forwards in front of the bars. Would this be humane? It is true that every afternoon the captive would receive a slice of pudding, to keep him alive from day to day; but as he could take no exercise, he could never, for his own health's sake, be allowed to eat his fill. Every day, therefore, on a half-empty stomach, the wretched boy would have to sit in his cage and watch plum-puddings rolling about just beyond his reach. After a while, of course, he would give up all hopes of getting at them, and would blink at them from behind his bars as if he had quite forgotten that plum-puddings were eatable. But suppose one day that he suddenly looked up and saw under his very nose a whole round pudding—not a meagre slice such as he was accustomed to get of an afternoon, but a real genuine plum-pudding in all the comfortable perfection of its rotundity !

What should we expect the street-boy to do ? Would it be fair to ask him to point out the extraordinary occurrence to the keeper, and beg him to restore the pudding to its owner? Would he growl at it as a nuisance, and testily kick it out again through the bars? Would he turn his back upon it and pretend that he did not see it, or affect to misunderstand its character and play foot-ball with it? He would be a very extraordinary boy indeed if he did, a supernatural and unnatural boy, a monstrous freak of nature—no boy at all. What, then, *would* he do? Why pounce on the pudding at once, and proceed to eat it.

Considering, therefore, how extremely natural it is for a lion to help itself to a human being, and remembering *The propriety of lions eating keepers.*

also how continually for years and years the hungry animal had sat watching men, women, and little children, wandering about the front of his cage, without ever getting a chance of catching one, there is surely no reason whatever for blaming the particular lion in question, or calling him abusive names.

The marvel, indeed, in the narrative is the lion's forbearance. In the end that staggering blow right between the eyes was accepted by him as a very forcible argument, but before the gallant " lion-tamer " came to his friend's rescue at such a terrible risk to himself, he had had plenty of time to do what he liked with the keeper he had caught. When a lion is in a hurry, it does not as a rule take him long to make a meal; but in the present case it does not seem to have occurred to the beast that there was any necessity for haste. He had caught a man sure enough, for there the man was, and it was quite early in the morning. He had all the day before him, so he thought; and, though he remarked that there was a great deal of unusual excitement on the other side of his bars, and that the human beings who were generally so leisurely seemed strangely flurried about something on this particular occasion, he had the cage to himself, and there was no occasion that he saw for making a hurried meal. But he had misunderstood the facts of the case. He had no right to eat the keeper, for the man had only come in to clean his cage, and not to be eaten. The excitement outside was owing to the lion's own inconsiderate and greedy conduct, and, though the day was still young, the minutes of his pleasure were already numbered.

And suddenly he became aware that the din of voices had ceased. There was a moment of silent expectation, and then through the shuddering crowd stepped a stalwart man, calm-faced and with a voice of authority that the lion knew only too well.

What had he come for? To make him jump through those abominable hoops again, and leave his meat while he did it? There is that hateful pistol in his hand, so perhaps he will have to stand up on his hind legs and pretend to smoke a detestable pipe with a ridiculous hat on his head.

While he lies there wondering what is going to happen, with his eyes fixed on the calm face which always cows him, the door goes up with a rattle and falls to with a clang, and the one man in all the world whom he would rather have had stay away just then takes two steps up to him and stands over the bleeding body.

On the instant follows a double flash and then a storm of blows, and before the lion can master his bewilderment at the intrepid attack, there falls upon his forehead, exactly between the eyes, a crushing stroke. For a moment it is all dark ; then there is a sudden roar of voices, and the rattle of the door lifting and the clang of it falling—and the lion raises his bruised head.

Some one else coming to beat him? No, it is only

to let the brave fellow, the "lion-tamer," pass out with his rescued comrade. But the lion, for the life of him, cannot understand the rights and wrongs of the matter. If they did not want him to eat the keeper why did they put him into the cage?

* * * * *

Man's influence not always demoraliz-ing. Yet I grant with pleasure, and with pride too, that the world's history abounds with proofs of the immense services which man confers upon beasts and birds. It is wrong to say, as some have done, that we always demoralize. The Zoological Gardens themselves are a splendid refutation, for though many of its pensioners have no doubt declined from nobler conditions of life and been robbed of a glorious liberty, yet many more have gained by captivity, and confess it by every gesture of their lives. And what have the detractors of human influence to say about the effects of Christmas on the beasts of the field and the fowls of the farm-yard?

Will they deny that our Yule-tide dinners fulfil a great moral purpose, teaching the pig how to live and the turkey how to die?—that they bring an honourable ambi-tion within a measurable distance of every bullock, and point the fat goose to the skies? Be it fowl or beast, the reward in this life, if it does its duty and fattens well, is ease and peace, and after death there is honour of men and gratitude and immortality.

Moral lessons of Christmas. Fat poultry and prize oxen, look forward, no doubt, to the great holiday at the end of the year with very mixed emotions. It is a time of festivity, but to them of a somewhat solemn kind, for their share in the merry-making is only passive. The goose knows nothing of apple-sauce, nor does the ox set much store by the sprigs of holly that will adorn him on the table. The turkey, it may be, does not care an atom whether he is symmetrically stuffed or not ; and the boar never troubles himself as to the glazing of his head.

Yet why should they not pride themselves upon these December honours ? It is not every chick that pips its shell who lives so long as the ribanded victims of Christmas, or so well ; and the oxen and sheep which fill the markets at Yule-tide owe the comforts of months, and infinite ease, to the simple fact that they were destined for consumption on the 25th. Which is better for a goose—that it should have waddled out a brief and ignoble span upon the village common and then suddenly one day furnished forth the rude board of some strangely-feeding rustics, or that it should have its months of life prolonged, being carefully fed and tended all the while, and ultimately be cooked with appreciative skill, and consumed with honour ? Give the cattle their choice, and which would they prefer—the existence that leads only to some suburban meat-stall in the fly-blown months of summer, or that which, fattening on " patent foods," and enjoying the delights of careful grooming and ample repose, is crowned with winter dignities at Smithfield, and concludes in general homage ?

As yet, of course, these birds and animals have not learned how to reason in this fashion. Nevertheless, the Ancients believed that the beeves dedicated to the altar walked to the scene of their sacrifice with a nobler gait than was their wont in the pastures. The garlands about their necks and the fillets between their horns made them, no doubt, conscious of some exceptional dignity, and so they paced to honourable death with becoming stateliness. So it may easily be that the Ancients were right, and that turkeys are proud of being reserved for Christmas, preferring the sacrificial dignity of December to the undistinguished fate of other months.

The Christmas dinner a worthy end. At all events I hope it is so. For I cannot help thinking it must be better, morally, for bullocks and geese to believe that they are living for a day of final probation, and to have set before them the high standard of Christmas excellence, that they may try to live up to it.

The pig that lies in his pen, doing his duty with all his might, reading for Greats as it were, and conscientiously doing his best to get as fat as possible within the time allotted, is, in its way, an inspiriting spectacle. There is a nobility in the effort with which men and women ought to sympathize. It should brace them up to their own labours in life. A turkey, in the same way, cramming or being crammed for the Christmas examination, presents itself to the well-regulated mind as an admirable exemplar of hard work honestly undergone; and when eventually we see the same fowl with the blue riband of Smithfield round his neck, we are satisfied to know that solid worth has met with the recognition which was its due. Whether pigs and turkeys understand this, and exhibit such heartiness of co-operation with their owners from a high moral sense of duty and loyalty, is a question which they alone can answer; but in the meantime it is our privilege to extend to them the benefit of the doubt.

Yet even supposing that it is not so, and that the obese hog only eats so prodigiously because he likes it, and that the turkey fattens simply because it cannot help it, there still remains the argument in favour of Christmas consumption, that their lives are lengthened by the process of preparation, and that their enjoyments all the time are largely increased.

Had it not been for the festive 25th the pig might have been nipped in the bud months ago, and the turkey died a poult. The prize bullock is a noble animal, " splendid in his ashes and pompous in his grave." Yet once it had companions in the meadows every whit as good as itself; and where are they? For them, the playmates of the prize bullock's sportive infancy, no rosettes of coloured ribbon blossomed among sprigs of bright-leaved holly; no roses carved from carrots or camellias made from a turnip decorated their remains; no butcher turned on with lavish hand the superfluous gas to do honour by extra illumination to their display. They died unwept, unhonoured, and unsung. Such, however, is not the case with the heroes of the Christmas market, for after a life of luxury and attentions they find themselves the cynosure of admiring thousands, and even after death still live in the pious memory of those who had the good fortune to eat them.

De mortuis nil nisi bonum—"it may be said of the dead that they were nothing if not good."

CHAPTER II.

THE WORLD'S GREAT BEAST-GATHERINGS.

SHUT UP IN THE ARK——RELEASED ON ARARAT——ZOOLO-
GICAL MYSTERY OF NOAH'S ARK——CATTUS DEUCALION
AND CANIS ADAM-AND-EVE——IN THE ARENA——BARODA
A TRAVESTY OF ROME——OLD CRONIES REFUSING TO FIGHT
——RHINOCEROS-ETIQUETTE—— IN THE ZOO —— FORGET-
TING TO BE AFRAID——RECLAIMED JACKALS——THE HAIRY-
NOSED WOMBAT.

ADAM, it is evident—from his facility in nomen- *Adam a*
clature—was a naturalist of the highest order. *Naturalist;*
Indeed, nothing less could have been ex-
pected, considering his manner of life in Eden, his
rural surroundings, his constant companionship with
beasts and birds, and his large leisure. He saw all the
creatures daily in their most natural moods of life, and
enjoyed unprecedented opportunities for undisturbed
observation.

Noah, on the other hand, was no naturalist. His *Noah not.*
connexion with beasts and birds was fortuitous, unsought
and miraculous. Perhaps he never saw a bird's nest in
his life. He was beset with anxieties, domestic, social,
and religious. Not only was his lot cast in the midst of

human beings at a period when society was threatened with a crisis of unparalleled gravity, but he was himself essentially what is called a family man. Previous, therefore, to the Deluge it is improbable that he had concerned himself much with the animal world, and it is obvious that during the six months of his enforced seclusion in his ark of gopher wood, he had but few opportunities for prosecuting researches in natural history. It was with him Unnatural History. For the animals having by a special miracle abandoned their own natures for the time being, were not themselves at all. A monotony of character overtook the whole beast-world, and laying aside their differences of tastes, they all became, as it were, *sheep-lions*, for the nonce, and except in outward appearance there was nothing to choose between a vulture and a robin red-breast.

Under such circumstances, therefore, it is improbable that Noah or his family made much progress in Natural History ; while much of the good that might have resulted from their long fellowship with the beasts personally, must have been frustrated by Noah's haste to sacrifice them on emerging from the Ark.

The mystery of Diluvian Zoology.

What these beasts were it is now of course difficult to say. Some might maintain, with a specious reasonableness—seeing that the animals went into the ark *before* the Flood—that they were of the antediluvian species—megatheriums and dinornithes, and such ; that the Hebrews trying to specify them used the best names

they could, just as we nowadays speak approximately
of extinct "elephants," "rhinoceroses," "deer," "oxen,"
and so forth. Do we not call the terrific harpagornis a
"condor," and the earth-drilling glyptodon an "armadillo"? In the same way the old writer translated Noah's
"black thing" that he let loose a "raven," and the next
as "a dove," though, under the theory that I am now
supposing, the winged creatures that the patriarch released
may really have been pterodactyles or some other extinct species of bat-crocodiles. Under this aspect, then,
our children's toys should be revolutionized, and instead
of Noah's Arks containing the familiar creatures of our
own world, they should be furnished with megatheriums
and mammoths, mastodons and moas.

But for myself, I confess I prefer the orthodox Ark *Pleasing*
of the modern nursery, for even in such slurred versions *ambiguity as to species.*
of the great miracle as can be bought for eighteen-pence
there is a certain delightful acquiescence in the mystery of
Diluvian zoology which contents me. You shall observe, for instance, that there is in it no mean servility to
science, but rather a fine concession to human perplexity.
Without calling upon you to identify a particular variety,
it is not permitted that you should ignore a class, and
with complete specific confusion there is no margin left
for generic ambiguity. There may be no *felis leo*, but
there is a thing of the lion kind, while the eagle is not
aquila this, that, or the other, but only rather an eagleish
bird. This, I think, is exactly as it should be, for knowing

how rapidly varieties develope from an original stock, it is not difficult to believe that so long ago as Noah's time the modern genera of beasts and birds were represented by only one, the primitive, species. There was only "*the* cat" and "*the* dog."

What a fine liberal uncertainty, for instance, is there not about some of the animals! Edith says this one in my hand is "pussy," and she is right. It is true that its remaining ear suggests a lynx, that the stripes on one side lend it somewhat of a tigerish look, while the one *The Ark-* spot on the other side gives us a hint of the origin of all *dog and the* the leopard kind. But though thus distracted between *Ark-cat.* species, I have no hesitation as to genus, and "pussy" it is —the primeval grimalkin—father-and-mother of all pussies, the Deucalion cat. Lying in my inkstand is another animal which, though it has been out in the rain in the back garden all night, I have no doubt whatever is a dog. It has a longer nose than the other, and from the stump of its tail I gather that it was originally of a bushy shape. Edith says it is a "bow-wow," and though it is not either a black-and-tan terrier or a wolf, she is again right. It is emphatically a dog—the dog that had its day first of all dogs—the primitive bow-wow—the Ark-dog—Canis Adam-and-Eve. And so on through the whole menagerie. Inequalities of texture in the wood may here and there have led to obliquities of outline, or the tendency of the timber to split diagonally have caused alterations from the received importraitures of the beasts, but what does this matter in such a generous treatment of the subject? It is no time this for hair-splitting. Are we to sit here squabbling over colours when the artist has impartially dipped all the birds into two colours, some head first into the brown and tail first into the blue, the others head first into the blue and tail first into the brown? Why should not camels have had three humps, or the off hind leg of the jackal been shorter than the rest? When we know more about Noah's animals, let us, if you will, be contentious, but meanwhile, setting all fastidiousness on one side, let us enjoy those that we have. They have been provided for us in a liberal spirit, and it is ungenerous to be captious. Noah's Ark itself was a miracle, and to expect it to be imitated exactly now, is to expect another.

*   *   *   *   *

Released upon Ararat, the animals, we may easily *Wild beast* believe, lost no time in returning to their natural lives. *fights.* Indeed Noah in the alacrity of his preparations for sacrifice gave them but small leisure for looking about them. Since then they have shunned men, and not without reason, for the next time that we find the beasts assembled it is again for immolation. The arenas of Rome expect them, and a nation is waiting to see them killed. How suddenly the terrible passion for slaughter seized upon Rome, and how suddenly was it extinguished! In effigy, however, it still lingers, and I myself have seen in the East, at Baroda, the modern rendering of the terrible tragedies of the Cæsars. It was a farce, however, that was played, for the actors in it treated the performance as a pantomime, and all wanted to play clown at once.

In the Arena. As it very fortunately happens, the Gaekwar's fighting animals are, most of them, very old friends. They have known each other as neighbours intimately for a long time, and regard one another, therefore, with that matured esteem which results from an old-established and harmonious friendship. It is true they are periodically turned into an enclosure " to fight ;" but whatever may be their public professions, nothing is further from their private intention than mutual destruction ; and what with the crackers that have to be let off to drive the antagonists into proximity, and the squibs that have then to be exploded, lest they should get too near each other, the exhibition is more like a display of fireworks than a gladiatorial combat.

As a relic of the past, however, the scene is curious and full of interest. A wild-beast fight is not a common spectacle now, in any part of the world, and even where it still exists, as in Baroda, it has been shorn of all its old-world splendours, and become a travesty of the magnificence of Roman cruelty.[1]

The elephants lounged about the enclosure in the most indifferent manner, pretending to look for things in the dust, and begging for pieces of sugar-cane among the

---

[1] See De Quincey on *The Cæsars.*

spectators. Every now and then the attendant told off *Too friend-* for the purpose would attempt to irritate Behemoth with *ly to fight.* a squib or a sharp stick, and the great creature, thoroughly aware of what was expected of him, would give a vast roar, as if to announce to his adversary that he was going to begin. Sometimes he would turn upon his human tormentor, and try to catch him, just to show the other elephant that he might rely upon his friendship; and upon one occasion both the elephants, although told off to fight with each other, actually conspired to chase the man, and very nearly caught him. Now and then the squibs and sharp sticks result in bringing the opponents face to face, and at last, as if bothered into it, and anxious to get the sham fight over, they bang themselves together. One then turns tail and makes for his door, the other trotting after him in a lazy manner, and thumping him on the hind-quarters with his trunk as he goes. Both the creatures roar prodigiously all the time, thinking, no doubt, that if they are only sufficiently vociferous their otherwise amiable demeanour may escape public criticism. Why *should* they fight? They are too old, in the first place, for such gymnastic performances; and, in the next, they are very good friends in private life, so that perhaps they could not fight if they would, and certainly would not if they could. A century ago, it may be, these venerable tuskers, then in the heyday of sexagenarian youth, gambolled together on the Nepal Terai or on the mountain plateaux of Madras, and as neigh-

bours in captivity ever since, have been able to recall
many scenes and associations in common. They have
outlived some two dozen Gaekwars, and now, because a
child of a dozen summers or so, even though he is
Sivaji III., tells them to fight, are the huge antiquities to
make fools of themselves to please a gaping crowd ? Not
they; so they are ordered off to their stables again, and
the rhinoceroses are formally introduced to the public,
and then to each other.

Two old
cronies.

Rhinoceros etiquette appears to be very elaborate,
and the two monsters become so tedious, rubbing their
noses affably together, that the attendant ventures to
squib them. Both beasts promptly charge him, and the
native vanishes with great agility over the enclosure,
after which the rhinoceroses, having snorted a vague defiance at the public, and reconnoitred the still smoulder-
ing firework, proceed to root in the dust side by side like
a couple of gigantic swine, grunting good-humouredly
as they go ; and when they reach their door they saunter
out, one behind the other, and the arena is again
clear.

Plenty of other animals are in turn displayed, and now
and then, in spite of old associations and in spite of careful keepers, it happens that two wild things will try to
settle old forest scores or pay off an inherited grudge.
No life, however, and but little blood, is ever lost in these
engagements ; and, as a matter of fact, the only creatures
that are allowed to do as they like are the rams. But to

see fighting rams, residents in India need not go to a Prince's Court, for they may be found in every bazaar, —and duller entertainment there never was.

Such is the modern "wild-beast fight"—probably one *Baroda* of the last surviving examples of the ancient arena con- *and Rome.* flicts. But what a caricature is Baroda of Rome! "The civilization of a magnificent paganism" alone made possible that splendid development of gladiatorial shows with which the City of the Cæsars was familiar; and now another and a nobler civilization has made the same shows impossible. No princes nowadays ransack the earth for curious or terrible animals for their subjects to massacre. Thousands of forest things are never, as then, turned loose into a vast pen to be slaughtered "without reserve"—a crowd of terrified struggling animals collected at enormous cost from all the quarters of the world—some of them, like the great stag of Britain and the European ox, now extinct, and, in addition, nearly all those that still survive, from the reindeer of the eternal snows to the ostriches of Mid-Africa. Still less is it possible now for a prince to descend himself into the arena, and, like Commodus, play the butcher to please his subjects. Superb as had been the shows of his predecessors, the young emperor's far exceeded all both in the quantity and rarity of the victims provided and in the number of the spectators. The whole world, literally, was asked to attend by formal invitations sent out to each nation by name, and the fauna of every

country was amply represented in the arena; for, from
the Arctic regions to the Sahara, and from Siam to
Britain, every beast that was worth an arrow was captured and sent to the vast Aceldamas of Rome. The
Emperor himself was to kill them all, and there in the
great amphitheatre he stood up, bow in hand, in the
sight of a million of his subjects, and slew the wild
creatures as they huddled together before him, and when
he was tired the populace were allowed to burst the
barriers and finish the work of slaughter.

There is nothing like this to be seen in the world now,
and such travesties of Roman holidays as exist in Asia
are absurd rather than exciting. And in time no doubt
even our Indian Princes will abandon the spectacle, and
allow their antiquated rhinoceroses to live out their days
in peace, and their amiable old elephants to go down to
their graves in friendship.

In Regent's Yet once more, to serve the purposes of man, do we
Park. find all the wild creatures of the earth brought together
by force, and compelled to lay aside their old habits of
forest, mountain, or prairie, and to simulate the respectable appearance of semi-civilization. All their old jungle
differences have to be shelved, and the eater and the
eaten, forgetting their former relations, blink at each
other sleepily across the pathway.

Now and again, no doubt, there falls on the ear of the
carnivora a voice—the bleat of a goat or the bark of
a deer—that recalls the reedy brakes of the Indian Terai,

the forest depths of South America, or the rolling grass dunes of Africa; and then on a sudden there rush in on the caged brute's mind all the associations of that sound—brighter skies and tropical foliage, the stealthy ambush and mad chase, the struggle and its triumph and, at last, the leisurely meal by the forest pool, with the starlight overhead.

To the other side, again, there must often be carried in the still night, or the dull gloom of twilight and day-break, the roar of the beast of prey, startling the horned captives into momentary terror, and making them peer out, in their old wild-life instinct, with their feet all gathered together for the first frantic bound through the under-growth, to catch the first glimpse of their prowling enemy.

But to the one and the other alike, the hunter and the hunted, there probably comes the next instant the re-collection of the actual present. The bars before them remind them that they now share a common fate; and if the deer is glad to know that the tiger can no longer pounce upon him,—the tiger, too, is probably contented enough at not having to chase his dinner. Perhaps he was getting old when he was caught, and he found his meals growing too nimble for him; and so he prefers to lie still in his cage unharassed, and to have his food put into his mouth at regular hours.

This levelling of all distinctions of existence, by making *The Old Order changeth.* every beast, as it were, an inmate of the same great almshouse, is a very striking aspect of a zoological garden. The nobler species acquiesce in it with evident contentment; for, though there is no guessing at the drift of the reveries of a bear, or fathoming the thoughts of a lion in a "brown study," it seems as if they had consented to the change of life with considerable cheerfulness, and that, taking it all round, existence in a cage with regular meals and no fighting was not a bad substitute for the forest and the plain, with troublesome food and quarrelsome neighbours. The humbler species make no concealment of their satisfaction with Regent's Park, and thinking, no doubt, that what such personages as lions and tigers, jaguars, leopards, and pumas—the aristocracy of the wilderness—put up with, must be worth having, they pass a happy life enough. Nothing tries to eat them. That alone is a great fact, and, recognizing it, they seem to have put behind, without regret, the plains and valleys in which they once snatched a perilous freedom.

Each batch of new arrivals at the gardens shows a curious medley of climates and countries. Every continent sends its representatives, and all alike are received with consideration and attention. Nothing comes amiss to so catholic an asylum. The rarest things brought from the strangest corners of the earth find themselves at once "at home," in food, temperature, and companions. Wombats that perhaps grovelled together in the same subterranean tunnels in Van Diemen's Land meet again to share the same nest of straw in London; and mar-

mosets that knew each other "just to speak to" in Brazilian forests, find again in Regent's Park a branch on
which they can renew acquaintance. The new comers,
no doubt, find their friends much changed. A soberer *Growing*
habit has stolen over them, and they have ceased to *tame.*
quarrel at meals. The nervous restlessness of the eye,
and ear, and limb—so characteristic of wild things—has
nearly disappeared, and in spite of the babel of human
voices and strange sounds around them, which a few
years ago would have sent the whole menagerie panic-
stricken into covert, they sit indifferent and calm. Great
natures among them rise to positive grandeur in their
stately complacency, while the baser ones learn a composure which almost dignifies them.

Take, for instance, that habitual criminal the jackal. *The Jackal*
Here in London he grows a thick close fur, his limbs *an*
example.
fill out comfortably, and, as he sits in the front of his
cage, clean, fat, and careless, looks almost worthy of the
admiration the children give him. Yet what creature
in all Asia—that continent of pariahs—has been in its
time such an outcast as he? The hyæna even managed
to retain some of the dignity of mystery by keeping
itself secluded, and the very musk-rat found apologists and friends. But the jackal was an utter
vagabond. While other creatures made themselves
homes he made none, but trusted from day to day to
find a convenient refuge from universal aversion. The
rest of the wild beasts had regular feeding-places, and

the nature of their food was the same from day to day
or from night to night; but the jackal ate everything
that no one else would eat, and in Asia that is so
little that he always went hungry. A fat jackal was a
marvel, a contented one an impossibility.

All night he prowled from house to house, passed on
by dog to dog, and perpetually running the gauntlet of
watchmen and servants. Sniffing at the doors of hen-
houses and howling outside kitchens made, however,
but a poor meal, so the jackal often found himself in
the morning as empty-stomached as when he started
on his rounds. An old shoe under the culvert was
the miserable but only resource left to him; and,
having frugally broken his fast thereupon, he would
curl himself up in the drain, and lie there all day—
fortunate indeed if some inquisitive dog did not find
him out, and hunt him through the sun-lit streets.

To hear him by night as he ranged the town, dismally
howling out his destitute condition, or yelping in a chorus
of hunger-stricken acquaintances, the jackal seemed the
very incarnation of famishing despair. Nor, seen in
daylight, did he attempt to conceal his wretched plight;
and, as he slunk away along the ditch, with dishevelled,
bedraggled coat, and lank, starved limbs, a generous dog
would be half ashamed to go after such a pitiable object.

Yet he did not think lightly of himself, for, conscious perhaps of latent worth, he never hesitated to
thrust his presence upon notice, and to risk the dangers

of civilization. Though fully aware of the perils he ran, he never avoided human habitations, and, given an open door, the jackal would always come in without pressing or even invitation. His loudest yells and most frantic expressions of famine were reserved for the porches or verandahs of inhabited houses, and through all his clamour, eloquent of desolation and want, there ran an exasperating tone of ribaldry and mocking. All night, perhaps, he had found no better provender than some eggshells thrown out near the cook-house and an oil-steeped rag lying at the stable door. Yet he would make bold, on such an empty stomach, to indulge in clamourous mirth, shouting, "Dead Hindoo—yah—dead Hindoo!" under your bed-room window, or to taunt the house-dog chained to his kennel, with a yelp that seemed to ask, "What! aren't you fit to eat yet?"

In Regent's Park this independence rises almost to the dignity of self-respect, for, the constant fear of missiles being removed, the jackal, in common with other plebeians of the beast-world, has abandoned that scared, shifty look which used to distinguish him in the days of hungry freedom. To his own great astonishment, no doubt, crowds of men and women pass him daily, and not one of them attacks him. He has not seen a dog for months, and, though he still at times seems to be expecting something to come round the corner and hunt him, he has, to *Forgetting to be Afraid.* all appearance, got over his first suspicion that the comfortable present was only a hoax and a snare. Gradually therefore he tames down into confidence and composure, takes an interest in his own appearance and his surroundings, and adopts cleanly habits and quiet manners. The stages of his improvement are just the same as those of any wild tribe of human beings that comes under civilizing influences, for once the scared look can be coaxed away from his eyes, a new revelation of life seems to dawn upon him, and in the orderly company of which he finds himself a member he gradually becomes worthy of the care he receives, and ranges himself on the side of law and peace.

To the presidents of this Zoological Republic great credit is due, for it can only be under an administration that respects all prejudices alike, and maintains a lofty impartiality in its protection of interests, that harmonious loyalty and order could be expected from such widely-different classes of subjects.

The hairy-nosed Wombat. In such a government, firm but lenient, just yet tolerant, it seems hypercritical to find a fault. I must, however, ask the Directors if they think it fair, or even becoming, to make any of their pensioners ridiculous among their neighbours, by giving them preposterous names. Why, for instance, should the broad-browed phascholomys be called "the hairy-nosed wombat"? That its nose is hairy is the wombat's misfortune, and good taste would surely seem to suggest avoiding public reference to it. No wonder the creature conceals himself in his straw, for what quadruped could sit in the light of day, at his ease and dignified, when he knows that visitors come to see him only because he is advertised as "hairy-nosed"? Science has acknowledged that he is latifrons, and if only out of regard to the wombat's feelings and the creation of that self-respect without which progress is impossible, I would suggest the poor wombat should be called the "broad-browed" or "the Verulam."

Above all things let us avoid personalities—even towards wombats.

CHAPTER III.

IN THE ZOOLOGICAL GARDENS.

A WORK ON NATURAL HISTORY, ILLUSTRATED FROM THE
LIFE——A NOAH'S ARK FOR GROWN-UP CHILDREN——TWO
VISIONS OF FREEDOM——ROUND THE WORLD WITH THE
ANIMALS——ARE THE THINGS HAPPY?——BITTERNESS OF
CAGES TO TYRANTS——MORAL OF THE CAPE HUNTING-
DOG——THE SATISFACTION OF NOT BEING EATEN——THE
DIGNITY OF EXTINCTION, WITH PARTICULAR APPLICATION
TO THE BADGER——A PRACTICAL BEAST AND PICTURESQUE.

"The Zoo." O a great number of visitors the Zoological
Gardens in Regent's Park are interesting because they afford a constant succession of
surprises, and so they go round the great menagerie
exploding, "Oh ! here's an elephant," "Oh ! here's an
ostrich," "Oh ! here's a hippopotamus." With this class
riding on camels and elephants, bear-feeding and re-
freshments for themselves, constitute a legitimate portion
of the day's proceedings, and with one thing and another
they invariably manage to make the day's outing one of
very evident enjoyment.

To an equally large number, the Zoo is interesting because in a single morning it turns hundreds of old ideas into as many new facts, and binds up for them, as it were, into one volume, superbly illustrated from the life, all the books of Natural History and travel that they have ever read, and sets before them on one great panoramic canvas all the pictures of the animal world they have ever looked at.   Each beast and bird in turn is recognized by some association already in the mind. It stands there as an old symbol verified.   And so, with this class of visitors, the morning passes in a pleasant process of translating off into fact from the great book open before them chapter after chapter of the romances of wild life that they have been familiar with from childhood.   It is not with them as with the others, a constant succession of unexpected sights, but the gradual verification by a series of delightful realities of long-cherished ideas.   It is like revealing a palimpsest. *A Volume illustrated from the life.*

What a number of things, for instance, seem to come true all on the instant when the hippopotamus thrusts his broad snout up out of the water of his tank ! With the gradual revelation of his whole form, all the stories of African adventure, the Nile, and the great inland seas of the Dark Continent, grow up into absolute truths, and when at last the unshapely beast stands dripping by his pond, his bulk glittering in the sunlight, and the half-munched green stuff hanging from his jaws, the apocalypse of Behemoth is complete.   Beds of giant *A Vision of Freedom.*

reed, bright with the lavish green of the tropics, and queer, large-leaved plants seem to spring up to hide the railings of the captive's courtyard, and the comrades of the river-horse in his native haunts step in one by one. The pelicans range themselves in file along the oozy brink, preening their rose and white plumage, and quackering in idle, happy gossip, and the careful ibis and the conscious egret step daintily from leaf to leaf, picking up their meal as they go. Through the deeply-trodden mud the solemn giraffes pace down to drink, and the swaying of the reeds behind tells of the desert herds that are waiting to slake their thirst, the restless zebras, and the·quaggas, the gnus, and shapely antelope of a dozen kinds. The sicsac flits nervously past, and ever and again from among the concealing foliage a lizard-creature slips with a rustle from perch to perch. And upon this happy, peaceful scene in the wild things' paradise, the sun begins to set.

The visitor to Regent's Park having thus wandered away into Central Africa is suddenly recalled to the present by the voices of a party that have just arrived, and they at once apostrophize the great beast " A 'ippo-potamus, oh, my!" And he turns away, half-sorry for the big amphibians that they should have been torn away from their quiet reed-shaded pools in Africa, and their innocent bird-companions.

But before he goes, he turns to take one more look at the sleepy-eyed monster wallowing in his tank, and

on the instant the same peaceful picture grows up
again with its pelicans, zebras, and giraffes complete.
Yet in that very instant there sweeps down upon the
tranquil scene a sudden gust of terror. A panic has
seized the quiet group, and the very reeds seem tossing
about in affright ! The pelicans, with one great scream,
fling themselves terrified into the air, and the ibis folk
dive deep among the leaves. The hippopotamus sinks
suddenly and without a ripple, like a river ghost, under *Another*
the water, and the drinking herds bound back in a mad *Vision of*
Freedom.
stampede. A deep sullen roar solves the enigma of
this sudden terror even before it has taken shape, and
lo ! in the midst of the harmless things, a lioness !

She has struck down a victim, and all its comrades,
horned and feathered, have left it to its slow and cruel
death—all but one, which, hoping to escape more easily
by a rush through the reeds, finds its feet held fast in the
yielding mud and, thus fettered to the spot, sees with
instinctive horror a great gnarled tree-root, for such it
had seemed, deliberately awaken into life, and come
creeping towards it, a terrible reptile, across the slime !
And so the sun sets after all upon a scene of death, and
the crocodile and the lioness feeding. And the visitor,
turning again to go, remembers that after all if wild
nature has its pleasures it has its terrors also, and that
the creatures who have been brought together as
prisoners in Regent's Park have escaped the hazards of
a very dangerous liberty.

*   *   *   *   *

Much in the same way, if we choose, we can let
fancy loose along the track of any other beast or bird,
and ramble in imagination after it, from the Polar ice—
with its auroras and zodiacal lights, its blubber-hunting
people and blubber-yielding monsters, its frozen wrecks
of gallant vessels—to torrid Bengal, where the tiger
asserts a fierce supremacy among the jungle creatures,
and where every other living thing goes in danger of its
life, the tiger alone fearing none, but giving such law as
it pleases to each of its forest neighbours, and regu-
lating all their daily lives by its own hours of appetite
or fatigue. There is, too, a delightful amplitude for
pleasant idle thought in the gradual transition from
beast to beast and country to country. Leaving the
Polar bear and Greenland, it is only a step to the seals
and Baffin's Bay, and the wapiti takes us over the
frontier from No Man's Land into Canada at a
single bound. We have only to cross the path to
the grizzly bear to find ourselves in the United
States, and whether we follow the wild-fowl down the
Mississippi, or the bears along the Rocky Mountains,
we can traverse the great continent, passing bison herds
and nations of antelopes on our way to Mexico, and then
find ourselves wandering southward with the alpaca,
across peccary-haunted Honduras, and Guatemala with its
dreadful reptiles and queer saurian folk, and so into South
America, and the cayman-swamps of Guiana, and up

into the highlands again, where the llama leads us along the Andes, its wooded slopes made brilliant by wondrous birds, down into the shadows of Brazilian forests with their pumas and jaguars, and so to Paraguay and its monkey tribes, and down the Plata, with marmosets in the trees and wild horses on the plains, to Patagonia, where the cavy shows us the way to the ocean again, and we find ourselves back among the seals. But these are the Antarctic and not the Arctic seals—so that the morning ramble has actually conducted us from pole to pole !

We can, therefore, either look at the beasts and birds in Regent's Park each singly and for itself as the centre of a society of its own, grouping round it the comrades of its native haunts and calling up those scenes of freedom over which and behind which the shadows of cruel and sudden death are always hovering and lurking, or we can view them all together as links in a long animal chain that encircles the earth and measures it from end to end—and whichever we do we find in " the Zoo " a whole world of interest for our purpose.

It is, in fact, a live Noah's Ark, and grown-up children *A Noah's* can take out the four-legged things and the two-legged, *Ark for Men and* and set them up us they like, in groups or in proces- *Women.* sionary files, knock them all down again into confusion and rearrange them, until they are tired of playing at Nature.

Apart, however, from the actual beasts and birds

*Can
Captivity
be ex-
plained to
the
animals?*

before us, and sitting, if we like, with our backs to all
the cages, we can, in an idle way, wander along many
curious lines of thought, and wonder as we go whether
this is the case or that; whether, for instance, all the
beasts are unhappy in captivity, or whether if they had
the choice they would steal back into their cages after
being set at liberty; whether the little animals triumph
over the big ones at the community of fate that has
overtaken them all alike, and are of opinion that it
serves the big ones right, and make faces at them through
the bars; whether the bird-people are ever puzzled at
their own want of wings; whether the snakes remember an
outer world where there was more sunshine and no
blankets lying about. Do the beasts ever sit thinking
over the extraordinary constitution of modern society,
wondering when the bars will move away from the front
of them and they can go and rub noses with their
friends across the path, and how it is that all their old
ideas about the world were so wrong? In the days
that are past they saw thousands of birds and monkeys,
but only on one memorable occasion, when they themselves were captured, did they ever see a man, and now
they see thousands and thousands of human beings but
never a monkey or a bird. There must have been great
changes somewhere, they think, no doubt, but where-
abouts the change happened the poor wheezy old wolf
there cannot, for his life, make out. Do the beasts
understand the meaning of captivity, and when they hear

the carnivora roaring and the monkeys chattering, and
the well-known voices of the river and the grove answering each other from the paddocks in Regent's Park, are
they conscious that every one of them is in a cage
like itself? Or do they think all the rest are free, and
that it alone has got, by some accident, into a place
that has no outlet, no tree-tops to scamper off among, no
ground to burrow away in, no hole to creep through into
the outside sunlight?

It is a pity things cannot be explained satisfactorily to
the bears. There is an old one yonder who has fallen
into the profoundest melancholy owing to a misappre-
hension. For many months he tried to make the
keepers understand that there had been a mistake in the
construction of his cage, that the bars went continuously
round from wall to wall, and that, do what he would,
he could find no gap fit for a bear to go through. But
the keepers put a wrong construction upon all his suggestions, and so at last the bear has given up arguing
with the public, and sits in a heap, blinking pensively,
waiting for the side of his cage to fall out. It is a pity
the beast cannot be put in possession of all the facts, for
he might become more cheerful.

Among the little animals there is abundant gaiety, *The Satis-*
and not without reason. In their wild state they be- *faction*
of not being
longed to the great zoological division of edible mammals, *eaten.*
and all their lives were spent in dodging their consumers,
but now, when they are not frisking among themselves,

E

they squat with their tongues out, complacently listening to the hungry roarings of the other great zoological division, the eaters, and wondering whom they are eating. It is enough for them to know that they are not being devoured themselves and gratifying to reflect that they are not likely to be devoured. Indeed, they have almost forgotten that they are edible, and this hideous consciousness being removed from their minds, they assume a placidity of demeanour such as might ensue from the possession of much money laid out at compound interest.

The zebra pokes his nose through his stall and smells that a wild ass is next to him, and, looking through a chink, sees the giraffes all sauntering about, and is not quite sure that this may not be some out-of-the-way part of Africa, after all, for, unless he was much mistaken, that was a hippopotamus that plumped into a pond close by, and from a distance he hears the familiar cry of the cranes. Finding they are all together, the striped creature concludes, perhaps, that there has only been a temporary accident, or a few earthquakes, and that by-and-by he will go into the giraffes' enclosure and take them with him to see what the hartebeest and the gnu have been doing all this time. But on his way to the antelopes he would have to pass the lion-house, and the first sniff of the terror-laden breeze would make him heartily glad to be back in his stall again. Thus, taking only a few of the captives, and listlessly watching them, themes for surmise come crowding into the visitor's mind, till every cage seems to become in turn the focus of a continent's wonders.

To a large number of visitors, however, the Zoological Gardens present, as I have said, a succession of surprises full of interest—and of use too, for few things are so good for men and women as being surprised.

The size of the elephant and the whiteness of the Polar bear, the unexpected absence of feathers suitable for hats in the ostrich, the long neck of the giraffe, the bulk of the hippopotamus, the feeding of the lions, suffice to fill them with astonishment, and when they have given the bear a bun, and the monkeys a Brazil nut, stroked the cockatoos, and recognized some of the common poultry among the ducks, they are sated with Nature, and wander about *blasés* of wild beasts, overlook the tapir as a pig, and the wild ass as a donkey, think most of the birds are very much alike, especially eagles, and grumble at the secluded habits of tame snakes.

"Well, and what have you seen in the Zoo, Polly?"

"Oh," said the child, "lots of things—elephants and lions and birds—and—and a kitten just like ours at home!"

*   *   *   *   *

Have you ever seen in Regent's Park that "Wild *The Cape hunting-dog.* Hunter of the Forest," the foe of the lion, whom men call the Cape hunting-dog? It is a queer beast, with shifty ways that give it an appearance of irresolution and occasionally of crazy bewilderment, induced, no doubt, by the consciousness that its features justify its being looked upon as neither dog nor anything else, but something half-way towards the first hyæna, and about as far from the last wolf. In a wild state it is a creature of intense ferocity, and as active as it is fierce, sweeping in packs from province to province, ravaging the colonists' flocks, and hunting down the wild herds of the plains. Nothing is safe from it when at liberty, and in captivity it is said to be untameable.

Probably, therefore, no other occupant of the Society's Gardens will find its new life so miserably circumscribed, so flat and dull, as will this wild hyæna-hound of Africa. The wolves have long ago quieted down, and the hyæna, the zebra, and the wild ass, commonly supposed to be completely irreclaimable, have taken kindly enough to their keepers, and to civilized life in stalls. As a matter of fact, the discontented occupants of the Gardens are very few. Appearances, indeed, must go for little, or the humble tortoise folk might be thought to be unhappy.

They move about their den with such an infirmity of gait that it seems as if they were mourning over some lost Seychelles, with sunny coral reefs and white-sand beaches sloping up to the very feet of the palms, and while they lugubriously crop the grass within the small enclosure, they appear to repine for the green caves of ocean and the juicy meadows of the sea, among which they once wandered and browsed at will.

From these perhaps we may not expect grateful canti- *General Content- ment of the Captives.* cles for their imprisonment, but if the tortoises would only speak the honest truth they must confess it is better to be creeping about alive in Regent's Park than to be tinned down into soup and cut up into hair-combs. They have escaped many enemies by falling victims to one, and so have most of the other creatures of the Gardens, and they, unlike the tortoises, make no concealment of their satisfaction with their state.

The vast majority of the inmates are manifestly at their ease, and conscious of their security. It took some of them, it is true, many months to learn that they were really safe from all attack, that nothing was about to eat them, that they need not always keep their ears laid back, or be looking for ever first on this side and then on that. Their old wild life was one of constant fear and perpetual suspicion. But now the bright-plumaged birds flit about their aviaries as happy, seemingly, as if they were in the tropics, and, for the first time in their lives, without a thought of enemies ; and in their different paddocks the harmless orders of feathered things loiter about with minds at rest. No bird of prey need be looked for in the sky ; no sudden rush of a foe from the reeds. The beasts, too, have all learned the same wonderful lesson of order and peace, and, setting aside as things of the past their memories of mutual ambush and conflict, and the ever-present terror of the great carnivora, have settled down to an existence uneventful enough, but without alarms.

To a few, however, besides the Cape hunting-dog,
captivity must have come as a bitter experience, but only
to a few, and they are of a kind with whom, perhaps, less
sympathy goes than with the rest—that is, the tyrants of
the animal world, typified in each class by the serpents,
crocodiles, vultures, and tigers. The rattlesnakes, for
instance, would far rather be lying basking in the American sun on the ledges of the rocks in which they live, and
where the deep-scarred fissures afford them a secure
asylum from enemies of all kinds and a dry retreat when
the mountain streams come down in flood; and the
cerastes, if it had its way, and could do so, would probably glide back to the Egyptian desert, and exchange
its comfortable bed and glazed cage for the arid liberty
of the Sahara. The cobra, notwithstanding its nimble
adversary, the mongoose, would give both its spectacles
and its hood to be back in the aloe hedge in India, hunting the field-mice or appropriating the drowsy frog. The
python would not stay an hour in Regent's Park if he
saw a chance of getting back to Malaya, and he would
abjure for ever the tame pleasures of pink-eyed rabbits
if he could only once again lie folded among the tropical
foliage of his native forests, wait for the browsing deer
to pass nibbling underneath, and then plunge down
in a sudden splendour of gold and velvet among the
herd.

The boa constrictor, too, which in the Gardens occasionally exercises his digestion upon the bedding pro-

vided for him, would say good-bye without a tear or a
sigh to civilization and science, and as he drove headlong
through the undergrowth beneath the Brazilian trees
would wonder at himself for having lived so ignobly
under a single rug, and wonder still more, no doubt,
as he bolted the succulent monkeys and fruit-fed
squirrels of the leafy wilderness, that he should ever have
descended to swallowing the innutritious blanket.

From the serpents to the lizards is a short step, and *The Lizards.*
here also we find some of the pensioners of Regent's
Park, who, though standing "in the foremost files of
time," would gladly give up cycles of our Europe for a
single summer of their Cathay. "The tearful crocodile,"
it may be, is more sentimental than he looks; for probably he cares nothing for science, seeing that it has done
nothing for him but mischief, and, being somewhat slow of
movement himself, is no zealous advocate of bustling progress. Yet he may easily remember with maudlin regret,
the sleepy African high-noon, when he lay log-wise among
the squashy green stuff on the banks of the Nile, almost
too lazy to keep his jaws open while the little "sic-sac"
plover picked his teeth. His companion remembers no
less affectionately the pleasant evening-time when the
cattle were driven down to drink at the Ganges stream,
and the unsuspecting Hindoo loitered at the river's edge,
and when he rose up suddenly, like some water-fiend,
with a flounder and a splash, and sank again as sud-

denly, leaving the astonished kine to deplore the loss of
a comrade or of their master. What pleasures have captivity and personal notoriety given this gentle pair, in
exchange for their old delights?

The Birds. Yet surely neither snake nor lizard can feel the loss of
liberty as keenly as the feathered despots of the air. The
caged eagles hop from perch to perch as if they had
weights about their feet, and there is a world of sharp
complaining in their cry. The empire to which they
were born was nothing less than that of all the sky, and
when they went circling about each other high up in the
blue vault they thought of themselves, no doubt, as belonging to the firmament rather than to the earth,
satellites of the planets rather than creatures of the
ground. They know better now, but the lesson they
have been taught is hardly one they could have cared to
learn; for, though it is no doubt a fine thing to sit
all day on a pedestal and receive the admiring homage
of passing people, the Eagle would rather be up in the
sky again, wheeling round some solitary mountain top,
and watching the valleys beneath in which the flocks are
grazing. What right has the Osprey to sit moping behind bars so long as the spring breezes are ruffling the
waters of Huron and Erie, and the lake trout are leaping
in the sun; and why is the Lammergeyer here in a cage
while there are chamois on the Swiss hills and kids upon
the slopes? Has the Condor tired of the Andes, or the

King Vulture abdicated,·that they are here in captivity at
the breaking of summer?

Running thus over the great classes of the animate *Only the*
world, we find here and there in each some members *Tyrants*
unhappy.
that can easily be supposed to regret the loss of space
and freedom and power. For such as these the sad exchange of the sky, the forest and the river for cages, has
no compensating sense of security and ease, for neither
the python in the jungle, nor the cayman in the swamp,
nor the condor in the air had enemies to fear or famine
to dread. Nor, going on to the chief class of animals,
the quadrupeds, can we imagine the more fierce and
powerful among them grateful for captivity. The lion perhaps would rather be back in Central Africa and the tiger
in the Nepaulese Terai; but it is still, we find, only the
same grim minority of the tyrants that repine at the
change—the cowardly and malignant reptile that kills, as
it were, with lightning, and gives its victim no opportunity of combat; the armour-plated leviathan that
might laugh at weapons and yet meanly compasses its
meals by stealth; the great raptorial birds who, monarchs though they be, stoop to feed on carrion; and
the mighty beasts of prey whose presence desolates
the plain, and whose voices strike the forests dumb.
These alone, the self-elected oligarchy of the beast
world, resent their bars altogether, obstinately sulking
or hoarsely complaining, for it is either from the lion-
house or the eagles' piazza that the voices of caged

lamentation are most persistent and clamorous in their utterance.

For the rest of the creatures—the commoners of wild nature, that have escaped from hazardous freedom —there comes, it is true, a babel of voices, but taken individually they are found to be only the social chatterings of parrots, the congratulations of the storks, the common-places of ducks, or the badinage of the monkey folk. Whatever it may be that they are really saying to each other it does not occur to the human visitor that they are complaining, but, on the contrary, whenever the sun is bright and the " out-of-doors " looks pleasant, they seem to have happily forgotten both the joys and dangers of the old savage life.

*　　*　　*　　*　　*

A very few of them, the badger, otter, and pine-marten, for instance, are British, and for them captivity is hardly so sharp a stroke of fate as for the other creatures of a safer freedom, for they could hardly have hoped for any long continuance of wild security. It is probable, indeed, that their capture has rescued them from early death and perhaps, eventually, their species from extinction.

Badgers, so an authority on the subject has recently assured the public, are rapidly becoming rarer. Like the otter, their tastes happen, unfortunately for them, to coincide with those of human beings, and, when it becomes a question between man and beast, the beast has to give way. Where there is room for it to emigrate, it does so; but where there is not, it quietly submits to the inevitable, and "becomes extinct."

Not that becoming extinct is an active process. The animals do not, like the sensitive and high-minded Japanese, perform the happy despatch when they find themselves odious to the public. They do not meet in council, and, in accordance with a motion from the chair that "the present company do now extinguish themselves," formally wind up their mundane affairs and commit suicide. They are not as the heroic women of Carthage. On the contrary, although they know that the edict has gone forth, and the fatal table is hanging up in the Forum ; that the seal is affixed to the warrant; that the barn-door is waiting for their skeletons, and every thumb demanding their lives, they go about their daily business with a Ciceronian disregard of impending doom, and one by one succumb to gun and trap.

The otter must have fish to eat for itself and for its little ones ; and so, in spite of river-conserving societies and the ubiquitous angler, it sets out in quest of the tender trout and the dainty grayling. But it is soon marked down, and the end is always the same.

So too with the badger. It has inherited from its primitive ancestor a taste for the eggs of pheasant and partridge, and it surely is not for a humble badger to fly in the face of time-honoured precedent, disorganize its family traditions, and reverse history, by pretending not to like such luxuries. Can we, and ought we, to expect

the small creatures of the world to change their tastes ?
Natural history would soon fall into hopeless confusion
if they did. Yet either they or man must do so, and, as
I have said, if men persist in preserving fish and game,
the badger and the otter have only "three courses"
open to them. They must either change their ways of
living, which is undesirable, as tending to upset science
and to send naturalists mad ; or they must emigrate,
which, under the geographical conditions of the British
Isles, is impossible ; or they must become extinct.

The Dignity of Extinction. The servile rabbit may consent to be hutched, and the
plausible cat pretend to abhor pet birds, but the badger
and the otter are not of a pliant kind. They are creatures
of a wild life, and prefer the crust of freedom to the
pudding of domestication. So they cling to the woodland and the stream, in spite of all efforts to dislodge
them, hunt the plump perch and suck the nutritious
egg, and, unable to emigrate, accept the posthumous
honour of extinction.

For to become extinct adds dignity to a beast. An
extinct mouse, I take it, is somewhat greater than a live
hippopotamus. The process, moreover, has, in the
sound of it, something of a Buddhistic calm.

The dodo has now been translated, as it were, to the
nobler company of the roc and the sirmurg, the phœnix
and the allerion. It now knows Garuda, the vulture
king, and Jatayus; Kahgahgee, the monarch of the
ravens, and Keneu, the great war eagle, and all the

other famous birds of story and of song. In some
Paradise of Birds, where danger is a word unknown,
islanded by seas on which halcyons brood perennially
and the great auk basks upon the sunny rocks, and the
moa and the dinornis stalk contemplative across the
plains, the dodo is at rest at last. It is extinct, and so
no one comes to hunt it. Indeed it was always unsuited
for being hunted, for its legs would not let it do more
than waddle, and fly it could not ; but now, sublimated
by extinction, it is more unfitted for pursuit than ever.
Translated from this grosser sphere, and ranging with its
peers in lands to which the simple fact of existence as
a species debars admission, the etherealized bird need
fear, in its dignified Nirvana, no presumptuous ornitho-
logist. What man, indeed, would dare to lay rude hands
upon the ancient fowl with the mastodon and the mammoth looking on? and could ever a birdcatcher be
found to make prize of the dodo, with the megatherium's
eye upon him? We might as well try to think of a
human being, having intruded upon some synod of the
Elder Gods, stalking Saturn with a butterfly net, or
liming the twigs to catch Enceladus.

The extinct animals therefore are safe from annoyance *A practical*
and pursuit, and they advance also in personal dignity *Beast.*
by being removed from the earth. But it is doubtful whether such arguments would suffice to reconcile
the badger and the otter to translation. It must be confessed that they do not appeal sufficiently to the mate-

rial side of animal nature, and the badger and the otter are both of them very material. It might content the Last of the Mohicans to know that, becoming extinct, he would rejoin his tribe in happier hunting-grounds ; but the badger would much prefer being left in enjoyment of those he was born in and already possesses, and the otter would rather be let alone in one simple English stream than be made free throughout eternity of all the four rivers of Eden. What the badger wants is not posthu-mous fame but pheasants' eggs, and for a well-filled nest would go even beyond Esau's foolishness, and barter away all the dignified calm of extinction in prospect for one good moonlight night alone in a preserve.

It is not of an argumentative sort, nor when it has business on hand does it go "finicking" about it. Whatever it has to do it goes through with outright, in a thick-necked, short-legged, and tough-skinned way which is characteristic of the animal. It never gets up until late in the evening, and goes to bed very early in the morning, for it is a comfort-loving beast, and if it does not like the look of the weather, it stays in bed twenty-four hours at a stretch, or until things get pleasant. Though thoroughly aware of enemies being on the watch, it never goes abroad discreetly on tip-toe, but always in a flat-footed and assertive way that says a great deal for its courage; but when surprised in its rambles by the keeper or his terriers, the badger manages to vanish from sight with very creditable celerity. Cut off from its own burrow, it has an extraordinary knack of opportunely finding another convenient hole, and, if left undisturbed, rapidly tunnels a way for itself through the soil beyond the reach of danger, throwing up earthworks behind it as it goes, and thus baffling pursuit.

It is a picturesque animal, the badger, after all, and, in a country that has no other "wild beasts" but itself and the otter, the occasional pine-marten and still rarer "wild cat," it is an ornament to the woodland. Living as it does in such obstinate seclusion—each animal, indeed, lives as a rule by itself—it has earned all the harsh opinions that somehow attach to solitary creatures. Nevertheless, the badger is so sturdily respectable that if it were not for the temptation of birds' eggs he might live among us as an honoured guest. Building his burrows in the remotest corners of our coppices, he seeks no society but that of his own kind occasionally, and troubles no one. He does not make night hideous, as owls or cats do ; but, silent, methodical, and self-respecting, goes about his work with a reliant yet watchful demeanour that is admirable. He hears every twig snap in the trees above him, every berry fall rustling on to the leaves beneath, but plods along his accustomed path, apparently as unconcerned as if only the moon was watching him ; yet if danger threatens, if the soft night-wind brings to his nose or ear the least suspicion of peril, the creature suddenly vanishes where he stands like a phantom, and though all the kings of the earth should come there together to see it, the badger will not be seen again that night.

Its extinction to be lamented.

CHAPTER IV.

THE MONKEY-FOLK.

Monkeys are Metaphysics.

MONKEYS are metaphysics, and it is no idle work meditating among them.

In the first place, there is an objective difficulty, for the monkeys themselves seem possessed by a demon of unrest, and are perpetually in kaleidoscopic motion. The individual that was here when you began to take a note is nowhere when you have finished. In the interval it has probably turned a dozen somersaults on as many different perches, taken a swing on the trapeze, pulled all the

tails it found hanging about, and is now busy scratching
a small friend up in the roof. In the next place, there is
a subjective difficulty, for in thinking about monkeys the
mind cannot relax itself as it would in thinking about
cats or parrots, nor get into undress over it as it might
over a more trifling subject. A monkey suggests something more than matter. There is a suspicion of mind
about the creature that prevents one thinking idly, and all
its problems seem somehow or another to resolve themselves into human questions of psychology or ethics.
Many of their actions require a rational explanation, and,
though each one may be turned off with a laugh, the
gravity of the monkey will tell in the long-run, and the
looker-on will find himself at last speculating as to
"whether" and "if," and hesitating as to the neuter
gender of pronouns being proper to be used when speaking of monkeys. Fortunately for us the monkey is not
proud. He has no reserve whatever, and betrays by his
candour much that, if he were more reticent, would
puzzle human beings beyond endurance. But the monkey makes us free of the whole of him and conceals
nothing. Yet, in spite of all this, the monkey remains
a conundrum to human beings, and the more one thinks
about him the less one feels sure of understanding.

If pedigree and lofty traditions could make any
creatures proud, surely the monkeys should be proud,
for their history runs back without a fault to the heroic
times when their ancestors, living in the very hills which

F

the monkey-folk still haunt, were the allies of the gods, and their chiefs were actually gods themselves.

How Seeta was found. The story goes—it is one of the oldest stories ever told —that when Seeta, the lady of the lotus eyes, the wife of Rama, had been carried away to Ceylon by Ravana, the black Raja of the Demons, her husband went out from the jungles of Dandaka to ask help of the Vulture King. This was Jatayus, the son of that Garuda the quills of whose feathers were like palm-tree trunks, and the shadow of his flying overhead like the passing of a thundercloud in the month of the rains. But the Demons had already killed the princely bird because Jatayus had tried to stop them from carrying Seeta away; so Rama, having lit the funeral pyre for his friend, went on farther, to ask the help of one who was even more powerful than the Vulture King. This was Hanuman, the son of Vargu, the chief of all the monkey nations, who held his court upon the mountain peaks by the Pampas Lake. And the sentinel apes sitting on the topmost rocks saw Rama approaching and recognized him, and Hanuman himself came down towards him reverently, stepping from ridge to ridge, and led the hero up to the council-peaks, and called all the princes of the four-handed folk together, to give him their advice. Hanuman himself sate apart upon a peak alone, for there was not room enough on one mountain top for both him and the rest, for to the council had come all the greatest monkey warriors—Varana, the white ape, was there, resting at full length upon a ridge, and looking like a snow-drift that rests upon the Himalayas—and there too was Arundha of the portentous tail, with the strength of a whole herd of elephants in each of his hairy arms, and there too Darvindha, that matchless baboon. And after long council it was decided that the monkey nation should be divided into four armies, and that each army should search a quarter of the universe. The southern quarter fell to Hanuman, and he linked his warriors together in long lines and they searched the whole south before them, examining the ravines among the mountains and the creeks along the sea shores as narrowly as the ants search the crevices of the bark in the neem-trees ; but night came on and they had not found Seeta. " So she must be beyond the Black Water," the monkeys said, as they stood at the end of the land looking about them across the sea for other countries. And when the day broke they saw a cloud lying upon the sea, and told Hanuman, but as soon as he saw it the sagacious son of Vargu said "It is an island," and, stepping back a few paces, he ran and jumped, right away from India and across the straits into the Island of Ceylon. There he found Seeta shut up in a garden, and went back and told Rama. And then the old story goes on to say how Nala, the monkey-wizard, made stones float upon the sea for a bridge, and how Jambuvat, the king of the shaggy bears, led his people down from the hills to help the monkeys, and how the whole host crossed over to Ceylon and

F 2

fought for many days with the Demons, and were always beaten till Sushena, the wisest of all the apes, sent Hanuman back to the Himalayas for the mystical Herb of Life, and with it called back all the souls of the dead monkey warriors, and how even then they could not conquer Indrajit, the mighty son of Ravana. At last the Gods took part with Rama against the Demons. Vishnu lent him his chariot and Brahma gave him his quiver, and then, after a terrible fight, the steed of Indrajit went back riderless into the city, and Ravana, seeing his son was dead, came out himself to lead his hosts, bursting from the city gates as fire bursts from the peaks of the islands in the Eastern Sea, and slew one by one all the monkey chiefs, and last of them all slew Hanuman himself. Then Rama, the husband of Seeta, stood up in his chariot before Ravana, and would neither die nor move, and the Demon King at last grew faint with fighting, and turned towards the city, but the monkeys had set it on fire, and when he saw the smoke ascending, Ravana turned again in his despair, and sent his chariot forward with the crash of a thunderbolt against Rama. But Rama was immovable, and standing upright among the dead, he loosed a great bolt, and Ravana's soul fled to Yama, where it floats in the River of the Dead. Then the monkeys destroyed the city of the Demons, and escorted Rama back to India, and Sushena, the magician ape, made the stone bridge sink again, and Rama went back with his wife to Ayodhya, and the monkey people back to their merry hills by the Pampas Lake.

This is surely a splendid episode in the history of a people; and the monkeys of to-day are the lineal descendants of those very monkeys that fought for Rama. There is no gap in the long descent, and to-day the inheritors of Hanuman's fame inherit also his sanctity, sharing in the East the abodes and property of men, and possessing besides many temples of their own.

Yet the monkeys are not proud. They will condescend *Monkeys not proud.* quite cheerfully to eat the Hindoo's humble stores of grain and fruit put out for sale on the village stall, and when these fail, in consequence perhaps of the grain-dealer's miserly interference, they will fall to with an appetite upon the wild berries and green shoots of the jungle, or even pick a light luncheon off an ant-hill. No, there is no pride about them, but much gravity and sadness of face, induced, perhaps, by the recollection of their classical glories and a consciousness of the present decadence of their race.

The ape in Æsop wept copiously on passing through a cemetery. " What ails you, my friend?" asked the fox, affected by this display of grief. " Oh, nothing," was the reply of the sensitive creature, "but I always weep like this when I am reminded of my poor dead ancestors!"

Such susceptibility to grief is honourable, but in the *Their Sad-* monkeys, by constant indulgence, it has stereotyped a *facedness.* tearful expression of countenance, which even when at play is never altogether lost. In the corner of the cage there three monkeys have tied themselves into a knot, and are pretending in sport that they cannot undo themselves. But look at the faces that peep out of the bundle of tails and paws! They might belong to orphans of an hour's standing, so wistful and disconsolate are their eyes. Another one, peeling an orange, gazes on it with a look of such immeasurable grief as the Douglas's features might have showed when holding the Bruce's heart in his hand; and next to him sits an ape, sorrowfully cuffing a youngster; while overhead, surveying all the heedless throng, sits an old baboon, with a profound expression of melancholy pity on his reverend countenance, that recalls to my mind a Sunday picture-book of my early youth, and, as depicted therein, the aspect of Moses when, from a mountain top, he sadly overlooked the Hebrews dancing round the golden calves.

Hanuman himself, saddest of monkeys, is not here, for the last specimen—that it should ever have come to this!—was only "lent" to the gardens, and has been taken away again by its owner. But there are others present of high renown. Here, looking wofully among the straw *Decayed* for a fallen nut, sits the very god of "mad Egypt," the *Divinities.* green monkey of Ethiopia, which was held in such reverence in old Memphis as the type of the God of Letters, or as Thoth himself, the emblem of the moon, symbol of the Bacchus of the Nile, and dignifying the obelisks of Luxor and the central sanctity of a hundred shrines. Yonder, musing pensively over a paper-bag still redolent of the ginger-bread it once contained, sits Pthah, the pigmy baboon, the God of Learning, without whom Hermopolis would have been desolate, at once the genius of life and the holder of the dreadful scales after death, more potent than the ibis, and guardian of all the approaches to hundred-gated Thebes. A reverend pair, truly, and sadly come down in the world.

Do they know it? It is hard to say. They inherited their sad faces, no doubt, from some sad-faced progenitor; but how came he—the primitive ape—by so mournful a countenance? Did some tremendous catastrophe in the beginning of time overtake the four-handed folk, so terrible in its ruin, that the sorrow of the survivors was impressed for ever upon their features, and transmitted by them to their kind? Everything, we are told, is inherited. The farmyard goats in Wales, when doing nothing else, still perch themselves on the highest point of the bank they can find or on the wall, because their wild ancestors used once upon a time to stand on Alpine peaks as sentinels for the herd to watch for the hunter and the eagle and the lynx. The dog still turns himself round before going to sleep, because in the old wolf days his progenitors, before they lay down, cautiously took one last look all round them. Is there, then, any reason in the far past for the melancholy demeanour of the monkeys of the present?

Perhaps they still remember the Flood with personal regret.

Who is this that comes up to the wires with so bashful a demeanour to see what Thoth is doing? This is the grivet monkey, and the antiquity of his lineage might be almost inferred from the mossy appearance of his fur, which seems all green with age and mildew. It was at one time the most familiar of the simian kind to European eyes, for in ancient Greece and Rome the grivet used to be kept as a pet; while in Africa, its home, it was so common that the Libyans of Herodotus lived upon it. They ate in Nubia that which was worshipped in Egypt, and transferred to Æthiopian saucepans the sacred custodian of the graves of Dendyra. It is impossible to speak with disrespect of animals having such antecedents, and, besides, this little grivet here knows perhaps a secret that science cannot find out—the secret of the Sources of the Nile. As he passes by, a tail hanging down from the perch above him attracts his notice, and, pulling it, he brings down upon himself a little capuchin monkey, which had thought itself concealed, but had forgotten its dependent tail. The capuchin is to-day "the new boy" of the school, and, as yet, has found his comrades rude and unsympathetic.

" The new boy " of the Monkey-house.

They ask his sisters' names, and where he came from, how old he is, and what he can do; and whatever his answer may be, the rejoinder is much the same, either a pinch or a push, a tug at his tail, or a box on the ear. So, as the keeper says, " whenever he sees one coming towards him he just sits down and hollers; but he'll get used to it. They all hollers a bit at first."

But the grivet after all is only going to scratch the capuchin, in a sociable sort of way. They are most of them sociable and a pleasing community of fur obtains among them. Yet, by natural habits some seem solitary enough. That little baboon there, except when passers-by stop to bestow a perfunctory attention to its hair, appears to be always alone; and how hard it thinks! In Madras its relatives are called "the wise ones," and if contemplation induces wisdom, they should be very wise indeed. In the pleasant old days, when Pan was still king of the country-side, these pigmies waged, so it is said, an annual war with the cranes, and, mounted on goats, used to make raids on the big birds' nests. It might be worth while, just to verify the tradition, to fetch in a goat and turn the baboon mounted into the cranes' paddock. Hereditary instinct would perhaps come out, and in the shock of combat the little creature's features lose for a moment their expression of painful thought. But near him, puzzling over a cork, sits a "monk," with a look of distress upon its face that would befit a victim of the Inquisition. Its hair seems blanched with extreme old age, and on its crown rests a small black skull cap, to keep, one would suppose, the cold from its bald head. But the creature is a hoax altogether, a joke, in some idle moment of old Dame Nature, — for that wizened old greybeard is quite young, and the

aspect of weary thought was in its eyes, and the skull
cap was on its head when it was born. Yet in the Brazils,
if monkeys have joint-stock companies, he might have
been a Director by this time, for his countenance
invites confidence, while his reverend appearance almost
justifies it.

They must not be watched too long. But you must not watch it too long at a time, or it
will be certain to abuse your curiosity by flippant con-
duct, and the illusion of respectability will be at once
destroyed. Turn, for instance, for a moment to this
family of Mona monkeys, two young ones and a senior,
and for a time nothing can be more becoming than their
behaviour. The young ones romp, while the old one,
discountenancing such frivolity, sits severely on a perch,
turning every now and then to look out wistfully over the
spectators' heads at the bright sun shining out of doors.
But on a sudden a change comes over the scene. A
young one, grovelling under the straw, forgets that it has
left its tail protruding, and the temptation is greater than
the old one can resist. In a twinkling the challenge to
a romp is accepted ; and, lo ! while the senior makes a fool
of himself among the straw with one of the children, the
other child is on his perch looking just as grave as he did,
and gazing at intervals in the same wistful way out into the
open air. The old monkey, lately so solemn, so respectable, so careworn, has suddenly resolved itself into an irresponsible fool, committing itself to every possible absurdity, and subjected to the irreverent liberties of its juniors.

Those who do not respect themselves cannot, of course, look for respect from others ; but, from the elder monkey's attitude when we first approached it, such a complete abandonment to buffoonery was hardly to be expected.

Or, take again that austere-looking Diana monkey next door. She has apparently no temptations to romp, for she has no comrades, but here again the same deplorable disregard of appearances occurs. Her cage is lined with straw, and in the centre of the straw she sits, as composed as a mummy and with a face like an old Mussulman moulvie. Surely, the crack of doom itself could not disturb such serene equanimity. The thought, however, is hardly past before the monkey, with a velocity that suggests an explosion from below, springs to the roof, carrying with her as much of the bed as her four hands can hold, and in the next instant is down again and spinning round and round on the bare floor in pursuit of her own tail, while the straw comes straggling down upon her silly old head from the perch above. The creature has suddenly, to all appearance, become a hopeless idiot !

It is just the same in the next cage, and the next, and the next. Intervals of profound contemplation and admirable gravity alternate with fits of irrelevant frivolity.

Look at this silky marmozet here, standing up on its *Melancholy* hind legs and holding out its tiny paws in supplication, *only an Affectation* and crying continuously—a wee, shrill cry that is sur-*with some.* passing in its tone of utter desolation—while the long soft locks hang down on each side of the forlorn little face, and the poor mite looks as if entreating for sudden death as a relief from its present misery. Does it think we are Brazilian savages, armed with blow-pipes and poison-tipped arrows, that the creature bewails itself so bitterly, or does it mistake us for anacondas? Not a bit of it. The marmozet only wants a cherry, and if you give it one, all that piteous affectation of grief will be abandoned at once, and, with a merry little chirrup, the tiny creature will fall to at its meal. Its neighbour the squirrel-monkey—more like a lizard than a monkey in its deliberate movements and sudden activities—makes the same pretence of woe, but indulges itself even further in the luxury of an absurdly fictitious sorrow. For when the dinner is brought in, slices of orange and apple and cherries with fragments of carrots and other vegetables, the squirrel-monkey creeps down sadly, and, approaching the tempting heap round which the chattering marmozets are already sitting, selects, in the ludicrous humility of its affliction, a miserable shred of cabbage leaf, with which it mournfully retires to a distant corner. But this exquisite affectation of asceticism is only of brief duration, as the marmozets seem to know, for they are tasting everything in turn and gobbling up a little of each as fast as they can; and, sure enough, here comes the squirrel-monkey back again as desponding as ever, with the sorry cabbage leaf still carefully held in its hand. It replaces it pensively on the heap, and, while the marmozets shrink back deferentially from the viands, deliberately spreads out the whole of the meal for a leisurely inspection, and then, sorting out at least one half for itself, sits upon the remainder till it is satisfied.

It is these extraordinary alternations of conduct and demeanour that make monkeys metaphysics. There is no arguing from probabilities with them or concluding from premisses. It is always the unforeseen that occurs.

Here in one cage together are monkeys from all parts of the world—from China and India, America and Africa—and they are all alike in having no rules of conduct, no code of manners. Yet though their progenitors, through a myriad of generations, were never in each other's company, they seem to understand one another, for each *Perhaps they* finds out at once what the other would like best in the *understand* basketful of food thrown into the cage and takes it for *each other.* itself; and a number will sometimes combine for a concerted game. Perhaps, therefore, they may have a *lingua franca* among themselves, but against man they conspire together to be dumb, provoking him to speculation by imitating human manners and then frustrating all his conclusions by suddenly lapsing—into monkeys.

It is difficult enough to catch a monkey's eye, but to catch one of its ideas is impossible. Neither in look nor in mind will it positively confront man, but just as it lets its eye pass over his, yet never rest upon it full, so its "mind" glances to one side or the other of the human intelligence, but never coincides with it.[1] It may be that they were once all human, that the link still exists, and that in time all will be human again ; but meanwhile it is quite certain that race after race is becoming extinct and that as yet no single individual in all the " wilderness of monkeys " is quite a man.

*   *   *   *   *

The Africans discovering Stanley.

Stanley the traveller has told us that sometimes when he entered an African boma, intending to take notes of the strange beings who lived in it and their odd appearance and eccentric ways, he was greatly disconcerted to find that he himself, and not the natives, was considered singular in that part of the world. They, the savages, were ordinary, everyday folk ; but he, their discoverer, was a curious novelty, that deserved, in their opinion, to be better known than he was. So the majority turned the tables on the explorer, for while they were all of one orthodoxy, in looks, habits, and language, the stranger appeared to them a ridiculous exception. He had not a single precedent to cite, or example to appeal to, in justification of the preposterous colour of his skin, the ludicrous clothing he wore, or his queer ways. In the middle of Africa he found himself a natural solecism, a " sport," as botanists say, from the normal type, a *lusus naturæ*, an interesting monstrosity.

---

[1] For an admirably sympathetic sketch of monkey character—and much more besides—read Miss Frances Power Cobbe's delightful book " False Beasts and True."

The savages, therefore, would solemnly proceed to "discover" Stanley, and after deliberate examination pronounce him, in Brobdingnagian phrase, to be simply a "relplum salcath"—something, in fact, which they could not understand, but which they considered very absurd. Meanwhile, what with taking his clothes off and putting them on again to please his explorers, and beating up the various articles of property, socks and so forth, which different households had appropriated as curiosities, the traveller found his time so fully occupied that his notes of the other manners and customs of the natives were often of the briefest description, and he had to go on his way, considerably out of countenance at finding that, while he thought he was discovering Central Africa, the Central Africans were really discovering him.

Something of the same feeling grows upon the observer after a morning with monkeys. We, on the one hand, remark the pensive demeanour of the four-handed folk, and sympathize with the unknown causes of their melancholy; are amused by their irrational outbreaks of frivolity, and scandalized by their sudden relapses from an almost superhuman gravity and self-respect into monkey indecorum and candour. But while we are watching one of them it suddenly occurs to us that we ourselves are being watched by the rest, and that as we take notes of the monkeys so they take notes of us.

They, no doubt, remark that our faces are usually

*The lofty
Com-
passion of
Apes.*

characterized by a senseless smile and, full of lofty pity for us, wonder at creatures that can thus pass their days in causeless mirth, and differ so much in their fur and feathers that it is nothing short of a marvel that they ever distinguish each other's species. While we, the spectators, are moralizing over the divine honours of the ape in the Past and his fallen state, the ape of the Present sits puzzling over the man of the Future. Some of the types which he sees round his cage are so like his own that he seems to make an involuntary gesture of recognition, but his relative has gone by before he has been able to explain himself; so he retires again into contemplation, regretting his lost opportunity, but content to wait patiently till, as he says, " some more of my sort happen to come round."

*Monkeys
taking
notes.*

While we outside are noting the unformed heel, the leg without a calf, the lines of the skeleton that prevent an erect attitude, they within have observed that human beings cannot run up the wire netting, or swing by their tails on the railings; that they have no flea-hunting to relieve the tedium of life, and that when a child wishes to look over any obstacle its parents have to hold it aloft to do so, as the poor little thing cannot scamper up a pole. While we are commiserating the monkeys on their narrow escape from human intelligence, the monkeys are wondering how long it will be before men grow wise enough to use their tails instead of hiding them, and see the folly of keeping two of their hands in boots.

We surmise enough about their antecedents to feel misgivings as to relationship, but do you really suppose that
these creatures with the thoughtful eyes think nothing?
They look at you quite as keenly as you at them,
whenever you happen to turn your head aside, and if
you suddenly surprise them in their scrutiny they shift
their glance at once with affected indifference but extraordinary rapidity, and subside into a studied careless-
ness, the perfection of acting, it is true, but nevertheless
so palpably assumed that it fills you with "uncanny"
suspicions. Again and again the experiment may be
tried, and every time with the same result—the swift
withdrawal of that furtive searching gaze and the utter
collapse into vacuous but sinister complacency. By
perseverance you can pursue the monkey, so it seems,
through a regular series of human thoughts, stare it out
of countenance, make it ashamed of its stealthy scrutiny,
and feel uncomfortable and conscious; you can even
make it get up and go away, further and further and
further, drive it from one untenable subterfuge to another,
till at last it loses its temper at your relentless pursuit of
its inner thoughts, and, jumping on to a perch, tries to
shake the cage about your ears, chattering furiously and
showing all its teeth. Does such a creature as this never
retaliate in its meditations upon men and women, or find
amusement in our proceedings?

Look for one minute at these two monkeys here.
The grivet has just pulled a little capuchin off its perch.

It found a tail dangling down and gave it a tug, and down came the little "new boy" of the school, very deprecatory and very frightened. But the grivet is in a kindly mood, and, turning the little cowled creature over on its back, proceeds to examine its fur, regardless of the capuchin's loud expressions of terror, and with all the serious determination of a nurse who knows her duty and means to do it. In time the capuchin is soothed, and lies down so flat that it looks at last like a monkey skin stretched out on the straw, while the grivet, with an elaborate affectation of studious interest, searches each tuft of fur.

*No mon-
key's Fur
its own.*

This possession of each other is, by the way, a curious feature of monkey life, for they seem to hold their fur in common. No one individual may take himself off to the top of the cage, and say, "You shan't scratch me," for his skin belongs to all his neighbours alike, and if a larger monkey than himself expresses a wish to scratch him, the smaller must at once turn over on his back and submit to the process. Nor is it etiquette to refuse one-self to be scratched by another of equal size ; and indeed, without derogation of dignity, a larger may abandon the surface of his stomach to a smaller. At times, it is true, scratching degenerates into sycophancy, for several tiny monkeys may be seen tickling one large, lazy ape-person-age. They hold up his arms for him while they tickle his ribs, and watch obsequiously the motions of his head, as the luxurious magnate turns first one cheek and then

the other to be attended to. But this is a mere accident
in habits, and does not affect that singular commonwealth of fur which seems to obtain among the monkey-
folk, and which prevents any single member of it selfishly
retiring into solitude with his own fleas.

Now follow the direction of that other monkey's eyes.
It is watching a nursemaid with a fractious child, and is
just as interested as you were a minute ago in the procedure of the grivet and the little capuchin—and with
just as much reason. The nurse has thrown the squalling
infant down on its back, and is apparently about to murder
it with a bottle, but very soon a genial sense of balm steals
over the noisy scene, and the turbulent baby is soothed
into dreamy contentment. The monkey looks on much
gratified, and when the nursemaid gets up, carrying the
child, begins to soliloquize upon the amusing obstinacy
of human beings in carrying their young in such a labori-
ous fashion : "Why, my good woman, do you not put
the baby on your back, and let it curl its tail round your
waist, and put its arms round your neck? or, when it
goes to sleep, why in the name of conscience do you
not let it lie where it is? If the baby has half the sense
of a monkey of that age it will find its way home when
it wakes up ; and even if it should not, what does it
matter? There must be plenty of nuts and oranges
growing about outside, to judge from the quantity that
come in here, and the young one would do well enough
in the trees for a night."

*　　*　　*　　*　　*

Ape-men and Man-apes. Have the monkeys, again, nothing to say about the man-ape problems that have puzzled humanity from the first?

Beginning with the dog-faced men of Tartary and Libya, whom Herodotus and Pliny handed down to Marco Polo and to Mandeville, or "the men of the Hen Yeung kingdom,"—those Chinese pigmy-men who had short tails and always walked arm in arm, lest the birds should think they were insects—and ending, at present, with the Soko of the Uregga forests, and the Susumete of Honduras, the list of man-apes is both long and varied. For want of absolute contradiction or confirmation we human beings have to hold our decision in abeyance, but why should the monkeys have any doubt about the connecting link? Here, for instance, is an East African creature who has rambled along the palm-grown banks of the Gaboon, and seen, no doubt, the dreadful Eugeena in its home, while its little kinsman there knows well the jungle growths of Angola, in which, as the Portuguese colonists maintain, the rowdy Pongoes range in companies, armed with clubs, disturbing the peace of other quiet monkey-folk, and turning their common pleasure-grounds into scenes of riot and ruffianism. Need monkeys go so far as Africa to find Pongoes?

Again, Hanno tells us that, sailing down the African coast, he came to "the Horn of the South," where he found "the gorillas," a race of men more hairy than any he had seen before—an uncouth, big-limbed, and brutal-mannered sort, who met his approaches with such surly incivility that, finally, they had to be attacked for their behaviour, and Hanno took a skin or two back with him to Carthage to show what an unkempt and ape-like set of miscreants these natives were. Here in the cage before us is a visitor from that same "Horn of the South," an ape from Guinea, with neatly-combed hair, and the demeanour of a justice of the peace, walking "like one of those who take themselves to be very wise," and he could tell us probably of more gorillas than either Hanno or Du Chaillu met, and might even, here in London, affirm that the type survives. Sometimes, per- *Human Gorillas.* haps, on a half-price morning, when the monkeys find their cage surrounded by a loud-voiced, rough-mannered crowd—who think it fun to tease and hurt the small caged people that come up to the wires confiding in their offers of food—who prick with pins the tiny fingers thrust through the bars for the cherry that is never given —who spit in the wistful little faces that look out won-deringly at them—it is quite possible that the monkey mind, on such occasions, reverts in some vague way to those old African days when, as they were gambolling along the woodland, happily picking their meal of berries as they went, they would sometimes find themselves among a company of man-like apes that compelled them by ill-treatment to take refuge in the tree-tops. At any rate, the instinct to take flight upwards still remains, for when ape-like men beset them, the monkeys, recognizing the character of their visitors, clamber up one by one into the roof of their cage, and sit there huddled all together till the coast seems clear.

The Secrets of Monkeys. The monkeys, therefore, have probably no doubts whatever about the missing link; but what a pity it is that they cannot also settle ours! If that terrible phantom of the Eastern forests, the Fesse, is really a man, this little creature fresh from the Sumatran camphor-trees and groves of eagle-wood could tell us; and so could his congener here, that still remembers the clove and nutmeg growths of Borneo, and its pleasant shades of sandalwood and ebony. Ask that Indian rhesus to whisper to you the secret of the Mum—part bear, part ape, part man—or that Guiana saju may perhaps have heard from ape-friends, and tell you the truth, about the Susumete.

Men have said that it is more human in appearance than some of the other natives of Central America; and if the stories of its intelligence may be believed, it should rank among the best of savages. What again is the nature of that "hairy man with a club" that haunts the forest depths of Surinam, and, dying, seems to regret having so long defended the secret of its humanity, and tries to use, when it is too late, the speech which men have never heard, but which, broken by its death-sobs and failing breath, is then quite inarticulate? Above all, will none of these monkeys by bribe or entreaty or threat be persuaded to solve for us the fascinating mystery of the Soko ?

What a work might be written, both horrible and gro- *" False* tesque, about all the ape-men or man-apes that have been *Beasts and* *True."* introduced by travellers to the notice of the world ! Science, it is true, ignores them all, but Fancy, I think, gets along better without science. Classification and microscopic investigation are no doubt excellent things in their way, but they interfere very awkwardly with the hearty conception of a good all-round monster; and, as a matter of fact, if travellers had been mere hair-splitting, " finicking" professors, we should never have had that substantial Fauna of Mystery which we now possess. Fortunately, however, they have, as a rule, been courageous, open-handed fellows, who would as soon think of sticking at an extra horn or hoof, or shirking a mane or a tail, as of deserting a comrade in danger.

The result of their generous labours has been the collection of as wholesome a set of monsters as could have been wished, gravitating, moreover, as it is right they should, towards mankind, until, indeed, they actually merge in humanity. Professor Owen, who wages desperate war, and very properly, against the existence of all things of which he has not seen a bit, refuses, of course, to admit the last gradation altogether. But Professor Huxley, who, I believe, is really in his heart of hearts, pining secretly for a tailed man to be found, laughs to scorn the dry theory of the hippocampus minor, and if

he were only to travel to-morrow into an unknown land,
I am not at all sure that he would not ultimately emerge
from some primeval forest hand in hand with the "missing link." Every successive discovery has brought the
beasts nearer to man, and with a very little further improvement indeed there would be no reason for humanity
to be ashamed of its poor cousins. Thus Hanno's
gorillas were merely "ape-men," but the susumete of
Honduras is, according to a European [2] who saw one
killed, "as much a man as himself;" so that here, at any
rate, is an instance of one human being, a European of
the nineteenth century, one of "the heirs of all the ages
in the foremost files of time" not ashamed to welcome a
long-lost brother !

*Missing
links.*

Between these two, the earliest and the latest of his-
torically-recorded connecting links, a great number of
man-apes have been scattered up and down the world,
some, like the allies of Rama, or the gods of Egypt, very
advanced indeed in the arts and sciences ; others, again,
like the dreadful "fesse"—a cannibal ape that entices
its victims into its traps by mimicking the laughter of
girls—pure beasts of the forest. The "men with long
tails" who cruised along the western coasts of Africa and
bartered parrots for piece goods could not have been
very much worse than the modern Ashantee ; nor in the
"pongo" of a thousand years ago, that buried its dead
under leaves, built shelters against rain, and availed itself

[2] M. Auguste, of Cay.

eagerly of the embers left behind in the woods by human travellers, is there much to distinguish it from the present inhabitants of the Gold Coast. Linnæus himself had half a mind to include a " man of the woods," that conversed with his kind by whistling, among his animal kingdom, and if, therefore, the public chooses to accept the Susumete and the Soko as facts, and to imagine a forest race of monkey-men, it is only following the example of all preceding ages.

The Susumete of Central America is, if possible, an *The Soko.* improvement upon the Soko. But the Soko has already a literature of its own ; whereas the Susumete has only just been discovered. In time, of course, the latter may grow as well defined as the former, but meanwhile it is a name and no more. For the establishment of the Soko's individuality, however, there are teeth, skin, and skulls in existence, and the last have been declared by Professor Huxley to be human. They were brought from Africa by Mr. H. M. Stanley as being the fragments of a great ape which certain natives had eaten, and which they themselves called "meat of the forest." Nevertheless, the Professor declares that they are the remains of defunct humanity, male and female.

After this "the soko " must rank as one of the most interesting mysteries of Nature. Is it human or not ? Is it the chief of monkeys or the lowest of men ? Dr. Livingstone was not quite certain, and Mr. Stanley told

me he was himself only half convinced.[3] In reviewing
the work of the latter explorer for a London journal, I
drew special attention to the Soko, for though actually
known only by report, the repeated references to it make
this ape-man one of the features of the book. On one
occasion Mr. Stanley actually startled to its feet a great
monkey person that was asleep on the river-bank; but
his boat was shooting down the stream so swiftly that he
could not tell whether it was beast or man. Circum-
stantial evidence of the existence of a half-human creature,
however, thrust itself upon the explorer day after day. In
Manyema, in the Uregga Forests, at Wane Kirumbu,
at Mwana Ntaba the Soko was heard after nightfall
or during broad daylight roaring and chattering. At
more than one place its "nest" was seen in the
fork of a tall bombax, and both at Kampunzu and a
village on the Ariwimi, its teeth, skin, and skulls were
obtained from the people, who never differed in their
description of the creature they called "the Soko," and
insisted that it was only a monkey. The skulls at any
rate have been proved to be human, and the teeth are
some of them human too; but if the tough skin thickly
set with close grey hair came off the body of a man or

[3] When editing Mr. Stanley's "Through the Dark Continent,"
I heard from the explorer and read in his notes much that was not
published. His Soko lore was considerable; but in a few words
his man-ape problem is this. The natives gave Stanley skulls,
teeth, and skins of a creature *they* called an ape. Professor Huxley
says the skulls are human. The teeth and skin are not.

a woman, he or she must have been of a species hitherto unknown to science. For as yet no family of our race has confessed to a soft grey fur, nearly an inch long in parts, and inclining to white at the tips. Yet such is the skin of the soko, the creature whose skull Professor Huxley says is human.

Two fascinating theories at once suggest themselves to *Man or* help us out of the soko mystery, for, premising that Mr. *Monkey?* Stanley and Professor Huxley are both right—and it is very difficult to see how either can be wrong—it may happen that under either theory the thing described by the tribes along the Livingstone river as "a fruit-stealing ape, five feet in height, and walking erect with a staff in its left hand," may prove to be human. The first is that the tribes who eat the soko are really cannibals, and that they know it, but feeling that curious shame on this point which is common to nearly all cannibals, they will not confess to the horrid practice, and prefer, when on their company manners with uneatable strangers, to pass off their human victims as apes. The other is that there actually does exist in the centre of the Dark Continent a race of forest men so degraded and brute-like that even the cannibals living on the outskirts of their jungles really think them to be something less than human, and as such hunt them and eat them. Either theory suffices to supply "the missing link," for if it be true that the skulls of the soko are human skulls—and that the "soko-skin" belongs to the "soko-skulls"—then the tribes of the Livingstone have among them a furry-skinned race of men that feed by night and have no articulate speech. If, on the other hand, these furred creatures are so like monkeys that even savages cannot recognize their humanity, and yet so like men that even Professor Huxley cannot recognize any trace of monkey in their skulls, the person called the soko must be a very satisfactory "missing link" indeed, for it is essential in such a person that he should so nearly resemble both his next of kin as to be exactly assignable to neither.

Man himself would, I believe, be glad in his present advanced state of "sympathetic civilization" to admit the monkey's claim to alliance with himself, for it is a fact that our race finds a pleasure in referring loftily to the obscurity of its own origin, and feels a natural pride *Do the* in having raised itself above its fortunes. Yet are we *Monkeys value our* quite sure that the monkey would care for this igno- *Relation-* minious kinship, and that the ape disagrees with the *ship.* philosopher who said that its resemblance to us was its misfortune? Possibly the simians may not be pleased to rank as the dregs of human-kind while they have the alternative of remaining the cream of the beast-world, and it is just as possible, too, that the reason why "the missing link" is so difficult to find is that he, she, or it, takes the best possible care not to be found.

* * * * *

Why do they not help us? The monkeys, therefore, if they would only be serious for half an hour together, might do Science great ser-

vices in unravelling these man-ape puzzles. But then
we must not forget that if they were suddenly to eschew
all frivolity, and begin to speak, we should lose our
poor relations altogether, and have no "monkeys" left
to expend our lofty sympathies upon and to patronize.
It is only human after all to think better of ourselves
for having rubbed off our tails and learned the use of
speech; but it has taken us nineteen centuries to
become so enlightened as to acknowledge our pedigree.
A few hundred years ago the resemblance of the ape to
man only made our forefathers dislike the ape, and
ridicule him, and to this day we agree with Bacon that
" it adds a deformity to the ape to be so like a man."

Yet in India, where the monkeys live among men, and *Village*
are the playmates of their children, the Hindoos have *Communi-*
ties in
grown so fond of them, that the four-handed folk par- *India.*
ticipate in all their simple household rites.   In the early
morning, when the peasant goes out to yoke his plough,
and the crow wakes up, and the dog stretches himself
and shakes off the dust in which he has slept all night,
the old monkey creeps down from the peepul-tree, only
half awake, and yawns, and looks about him, puts a straw
in his mouth, and scratches himself contemplatively.

Then one by one the whole family come slipping down
the tree-trunk, and they all yawn and look about, and
scratch.   But they are sleepy and peevish, and the
youngsters get cuffed for nothing, and begin to think
life dull.   Yet the toilette has to be performed; and,

whether they like it or not, the young ones are sternly pulled up, one by one, to their mother to undergo the process. The scene, though regularly repeated every morning, loses nothing of its delightful comicality, and the monkey-brats never tire of the joke of "taking in mamma." But mamma was young herself not so very long ago, and treats each ludicrous affectation of suffering with profoundest unconcern, and, as she dismisses one "cleaned" youngster with a cuff, stretches out her hand for the next one's tail or leg in the most business-like and serious manner possible. The youngsters know their turns quite well, and as each one sees the moment arriving it throws itself on its stomach, as if overwhelmed with apprehension, the others meanwhile stifling their laughter at the capital way " so-and-so is doing it," and the instant the maternal paw is extended to grasp its tail the subject of the next experiment utters a dolorous wail, and, throwing its arms forward in the dust, allows itself to be dragged along, a limp and helpless carcass, winking all the time, no doubt, at its brothers and sisters, at the way it is imposing on the old lady. But the old lady will stand no nonsense, and turning the child right side up proceeds to put it to rights ; takes the kinks out of its tail, and the knots out of its fur ; pokes its fingers into its ears, and looks at each of its toes, the inexpressible brat all the time wearing on its face an absurd expression of hopeless and incurable grief. Those who have been already cleaned look on with delight at the

screaming farce, while those who are waiting wear a
becoming aspect of enormous gravity. The old lady,
however, has her joke, too, which is to cuff every
youngster before she lets it go ; and, nimble as her
offspring are, she generally, to her credit be it said,
manages to give each of them a box on the ears before
it is out of reach. The father, meanwhile, sits gravely
with his back to all these domestic matters, waiting for
breakfast.

Presently the mats before the hut-doors are pushed
down, and women with brass vessels in their hands come
out ; and, while they scour the pots and pans with dust,
exchange between yawns the compliments of the morning.

The monkeys by this time have come closer to the preparations for food, and sit solemnly household by household watching every movement. Hindoos do not hurry
themselves in anything they do, but the monkey has lots
of time to spare and plenty of patience, and in the end
after the crow has stolen a little, and the dog has had
its morsel, and the children are all satisfied, the poor
fragments of the meal are thrown out on the ground for
the " bhunder-logue," the monkey-people, and it is soon
discussed—the mother feeding the baby before she eats
herself. When every house has thus, in turn, been
visited, and no chance of further " out-door relief "
remains, the monkeys go off to the well. The women
are all here again, drawing the water for the day, and
the monkeys sit and wait, the old ones in the front, sen-

tentious and serious, and the youngsters rolling about
in the dust behind them, till at last some girl sees the
creatures waiting, and "in the name of Ram" spills a
lotah full of water in a hollow of the ground, and the
monkeys come round it in a circle, and stoop down and
drink, with their tails all curled up over their backs like
notes of interrogation. There is no contention or jostling.
A forward child gets a box on the ear, perhaps, but each
one, as it has satisfied its thirst, steps quietly out of
the circle and wipes its mouth. The day thus fairly
commenced, they go off to see what luck may bring
them.

The grain-dealer's shop tempts them to loiter, but the
experience of previous attempts makes theft hopeless ; for
the bunnya, with all his years, is very nimble on his legs,
and an astonishing good shot with a pipkin. So the
monkeys merely make their salaams to him and pass on
to the fields. If the corn is ripe they can soon eat
enough for the day; but, if not, they go wandering about
picking up morsels, here an insect and there a berry,
till the sun gets too hot, and then they creep up into the
dark shade of the mango tope and snooze through the
afternoon. In the evening they are back in the village
again to share in its comforts and entertainments.

They assist at the convocation of the elders and the
romps of the children, looking on when the faquir comes
up to collect his little dues of salt and corn and oil, and
from him in their turn exacting a pious toll. They listen

gravely to the village musician till they get sleepy, and then, one by one, they clamber up into the peepul.

And the men sitting round the fire with their pipes can see, if they look up, the whole colony of the bhunder-logue asleep in rows in the tree above them.

* * * * *

Here in Europe the monkey has never become a *In Europe.* friend, even though we have adopted him as a relative. Our literature has nothing to his credit and our art ignores him. In olden times they never took augury from a monkey, and nowadays no one even takes it for armorial bearings.

Yet the tailed ones are already considerably advanced towards civilization. As Darwin tells us, they catch colds and die of consumption, suffer from apoplexy and from cholera, inflammation, cataracts, and so forth, can pass on a contagious affection to men, or take the sickness from them, eat and drink all that human beings do, and suffer from surfeits precisely as men and women do; for if drunk overnight they have headaches next morning, scorn solid food, and are exasperated by the mere smell of strong liquors, but turn with relish to the juice of lemons and effervescing draughts.

Those who know them say that every monkey has its own individual character, its own peculiarities of disposition and temper, its special likes and dislikes; and it has been established beyond the reach of doubt that by education these differences can be exaggerated or diminished,

H

and communicated by example from one individual to another.   How, by the way, did the monkeys find out that hard-shelled nuts could be broken open with stones, and by what process of publication did all the species acquire this knowledge?   Or, to take an instance in another class of reasoning, how can the monkey plot so rationally to take revenge?   An officer at the Cape had offended a baboon, and one day, as he was approaching, the creature deliberately poured water into a hole, hastily made up a mud pie, and flung it at his tormentor as he passed : nay, what is even more noteworthy, "rejoiced and triumphed for long afterwards, whenever he saw his victim."

They can be taught, when attentive, to be such respectable members of society, that a magistrate might reasonably permit them to make a "solemn affirmation" in a court of justice ; but, unfortunately, attention is a rare gift, and the scholar, as a rule, prefers watching the flies on the wall or playing with straws to learning his lessons, while punishment only makes him sulky.   Yet in India, and simply by the process of being humoured, the monkey has become something very different from a wild beast, and it is a puzzle to guess what would happen if the School Board were to extend its jurisdiction to the monkey-house at the Zoo, and to educate the baboons.

A Mutiny of the Baboons.   But monkeys sometimes rise in India from village obscurity to political prominence, as for instance in 1878, when a monkey campaign threatened to complicate

the affairs of our Eastern Empire. A vagabond detachment of baboons had taken forcible possession of the
village of Augurpara, on the high road to the military
station of Barrackpore, and, having ejected by violence
and intimidation all the more human inhabitants, had
billeted themselves on the orchards and gardens of the
hamlet, whence they directed various offensive strategic
movements, night attacks, and predatory raids upon the
neighbourhood.

This was, of course, an exceptional incident, but over
and over again we find the Indian monkeys a puzzle to
local administrations, in consequence of their characteristic tendency to mischief conflicting with the sentimental veneration in which they are held by the people.

But the Hindu, even though he may deplore the monkey's shortcomings, is shackled by his religious scruples
in his conduct towards them, and, in spite of his rifled
grain stores, dares not openly affront the creatures.

In many cities of India the monkeys inhabit recognized *Conflicting*
quarters, and are allowed every morning to descend from *prejudices.*
temple-top and tree into the market-place, and there to
eat their fill of whatever may be exposed for sale. The
owner sits by, pretending to grant the meal without grudg-
ing, but when no one else is looking he often takes the
opportunity of giving the intruder a hearty cuff to send it
on to the next stall for the rest of its breakfast. This
semi-sacred character complicates official interference
with them, for if one street complains that the monkeys

have mischievously picked half the tiles off the houses and begs to have them deported, the next street petitions that their religious prejudices may not be outraged by any curtailment of the creatures' liberty.

Sometimes, however, a whole town agrees that the monkey nuisance has become intolerable, and, gods or not, votes for their wholesale deportation. But Hanuman is as astute as his neighbours, and, though submitting to be coaxed across the river, or carted off to a neighbouring jungle, utilizes both ferry and high-road for a speedy and comfortable return. Thus, between Benares and Ramnagar a constant transportation of monkeys was at one time carried on; but since as many came back by boat of their own accord as went—the ferryman not daring to refuse them—the local officials abandoned the enterprise, and to this day the animals share both sides of the river with the human inhabitants. In the hill districts whole fields of corn are ravaged in a morning by the long-tailed troops; but the superstitious villager will not do more than shout at them his respectful request to go away.

Now an English vestry called upon suddenly to catch and turn out of the parish any section of a menagerie that might have got loose, without offering personal insult to any of the animals, would be intolerably puzzled; yet in India the constant antagonism of popular sentiment and public advantage sometimes places the authorities in ludicrous positions. When, for instance, in a village

notorious for its liability to small-pox, a peasant refuses
to have his family vaccinated lest "the evil eye" of
the operator should harm his offspring; or when, in a
crowded corner of a city, a householder refuses to pull
up a peepul-tree that has struck roots into his walls
and thereby threatens the safety of the inmates and
neighbours, because he believes the peepul embodies the
collective attributes of the Hindu Trinity—there is a
direct conflict between two obvious duties, respect for
life and respect for popular prejudice.

An illustration of this absurd conflict is the well-known *The Rats*
episode of the palm-rats in the Laccadives. In those *of the*
Laccadives.
islands the palm-trees, which (with fish) form the chief
food supply of the people, became infested by a species
of rat, which, living in the crowns of the trees, nibbled off
the young nuts, and thus threatened to ruin the colony.
The Government was appealed to for help, and the European magistrate, in response, sent over cats. But the cats,
we are told, finding plenty of good fish to eat below, did
not recognize the necessity for going up seventy feet of
tree trunk in search of possible rats; so the magistrate
sent over some tree snakes. But the people preferred
rats to snakes, and killed all the new-comers at the first
opportunity, still, however, pleading for protection. The
magistrate next tried mongooses, but nothing would persuade these creatures to climb palm-trees. On the
contrary, they ate up the islanders' fowls. So yet once
more the great rat question came before the magistrate.

With cats and mongooses on the ground refusing to ascend to the rats, that official very sapiently decided that all that was required was to make the rats descend to the cats and mongooses, so he sent the islanders over some owls. But he had overlooked the popular prejudice against these birds, and the people in committee assembled decided that even rats up the trees were better than "devil-birds."

"What ails the Government?" said the elders. "Is it not enough that they sent snakes amongst us, so that we went in terror of our lives ; that they turned loose on our hencoops bushy-tailed vermin that sucked the eggs and choked the chickens ; that now they want to afflict us with these devil-birds, which frighten our children into fits, and set all the old women foretelling death and ruin ?"

But they accepted the birds in all apparent gratitude. As soon, however, as the coast was clear, the owls, cats, and mongooses, were all conveyed in procession to a boat, and solemnly deported to an uninhabited reef!

*　　*　　*　　*　　*

Elsewhere also than in India the ape-folk are held in respect, for in Borneo and the Malaccas the natives speak of them with deference, and treat them with consideration. "Ourang" is an honourable Malay title, though we who only see our captives sulking behind cage-bars are hardly able perhaps to do them justice. Not that we have often had the opportunity in England of passing judgment upon ourang-outangs, for it was only very recently that an adult specimen was added to the Zoological Gardens.   He stands five feet without his *The Man* stockings, and, being a little bald and well-whiskered, *of the* *Woods.* is a very respectable-looking specimen of the man-ape. The baby ourangs who have hitherto been exhibited have been guileless urchins of no decided character, solemn of countenance like other babies, and easily put out of sorts. Visitors called them "poor little things," and, though they were coddled with blankets and feeding-bottles and sop, women thought it, on the whole, rather a shame that they were not also *Baby* allowed perambulators and rattles.   The human help- *Ourang-* *outangs.* lessness of the very young ourangs certainly justified this maternal solicitude on their behalf, and the re- peated failure to rear them to maturity told a pitiful tale of lungs too delicate to bear our climate.   Their ways and habits, as Wallace, who kept them as pets, has told us, are exactly those of human babies.   They refuse to sleep alone, and even if left by themselves when awake will cry fretfully for a nurse.   They like being rocked in a cradle, and hate being washed.   When anything is offered them not to their taste, they kick violently, just as human beings of the same age do, but when satisfied with the bottle or plaything given them they croon in a contented way over it until placidity merges in sleep.   Toys have to be provided for them, and they break them all punctually, after, of course,

having tried firmly but ineffectually to choke themselves with them. When happiest, they lie in a helpless
fashion on their backs, turning their heads occasionally
from one side to the other, with all four hands in the
air, hoping apparently to find something to take hold
of, but unable to guide their fingers to any particular
object. As time passes and they grow adventurous, they
try to tumble out of their cradles, and often succeed, to
their own immense discomfiture, for their legs being
too weak to hold them up, they have to lie on the ground
on their stomachs until friendly hands place them right
side up. All these baby traits of conduct and character
commended the very juvenile ourangs to the tender
sympathy of their visitors, and their wistful child-eyes
always made them the pets of the public. But who, I
should like to know, is going to pet the elderly ape that
has now arrived; or how can we lavish any gentle sentiment over a creature that stands five feet high and has
a bald head and big whiskers?

The adult Ourang. The great strength of the ourang-outang now among
us necessitated at first extraordinary precautions in his
confinement. The cage in which he travelled was so small
that he could not have fair play for his tremendous arms,
and the bars so thick that he could not make any impression upon them with his enormous teeth. Impotent,
therefore, for mischief, the hairy prisoner sate huddled
up and roaring. Any interference with him, however
kindly meant, was at once resented by language which

might easily be translated into human equivalents, and the vigour with which he shook his cage proved the sincerity of his ill-feeling. One long arm was being perpetually thrust out between the bars, in the hope apparently of finding some one or something to lay hold of, and it only needs a glance at the curving fingers of the foot-hand to understand how desperate would be their grasp, or at the muscular forearm and shoulder to imagine how difficult it would be, if once clutched, to get released from the monster's power. It is not likely, therefore, that much sympathy will be extended to this poor wild man of the woods. He is not of the interesting age *Not easily coddled.* that excites the soft-hearted compassion of the gentler sex, for it is impossible to connect this great hairy ape with any idea so tenderly suggestive as feeding-bottles and perambulators. If given blankets he will probably eat them, and as for coddling him, the keepers might as well think of coddling a steam-engine. There is no pretty baby helplessness about this five-foot person.

He would indeed be a rash man who tried to put it into a cradle, or when it was asleep attempted to tuck it up. When it wants anything it will not sprawl pathetically on its back with its legs up in the air, but will go for what it wants and take it, or else throw the furniture about. Instead of whimpering when being washed it will brain its attendant with the basin, or strangle him with the towel, and if any one would like to administer a soothing powder to it when it is fretful—he is at liberty to try. But his experiences would probably be remarkable, for adult ourangs—more especially when they have stomach-aches—are not to be trifled with.

In their native haunts they are never trifled with. For the only neighbours capable of molesting them are the infrequent crocodile and the still rarer python; while even these, so the natives say, the ourang does not fear to meet in single combat. The huge ape, it is said, will leap upon the back of an alligator and tear its jaws asunder. Literally translated "ourang-outang" means "the man of the woods," and the first half of the name is a title implying an especial measure of wisdom, for the chiefs of the Malays are styled "ourang," and so also, in compliment to its intelligent sagacity, is the elephant.

Arguments for its Humanity. Nor is it at all surprising that this great monkey should have received so dignified a name, for not only native legends, but authentic European accounts, agree in describing "the man of the woods" as singularly un-ape-like. Thus, when attacked with guns, it retreats to the top of the highest tree it can find, and deliberately constructs a barricade of branches between itself and its assailants. At night it makes up a sleeping platform for itself, and in rainy weather it covers its body over with large leaves or ferns. The ourang lies in bed of a morning until the sun is well up and the dew gone off the foliage, and dines with his family in the middle of the day. These are certainly suggestive facts, and make us hesitate in deciding whether purchasing such creatures

for the Zoological Gardens might not reasonably be
objected to by opponents of the slave-trade. In their
natural state they are not only inoffensive, but when
suddenly intruded upon betray no symptoms of alarm,
behaving from first to last with the greatest presence of
mind, and always dying with pathetic dignity. Naturalists tell us that these apes watched them when trespass-
ing on their haunts with curiosity, but without fear, and
would remain quietly where first seen, in spite of preparations for attack being in progress. If escape seemed
desperate, they made no effort to run from the enemy,
but, utilizing the best cover that was available, avoided
the missiles, spears or bullets, as long as they could, and
when badly wounded moved away leisurely into the thickest foliage they could reach, and expired without a cry.

Irritated by captivity, the ourang who has now
visited us against his will, is the reverse of amiable, and
certainly not an object for much tender feeling. Yet a
sincere pathos nevertheless gathers round the poor beast
in its cage, when we think of the wonderfully-happy life
of freedom and security which it led in some beautiful
island of the East. In Malacca, Sumatra, and Borneo,
where these great apes are found, Nature has excelled
herself in the variety and profusion of her vegetable
wonders, clothing the banks of the streams and the hill-
sides alike with masses of densely-foliaged fruit-bearing
trees. Among these—with no wild things to dispute
possession, except birds and the smaller species of the

monkey-folk—the ourangs loiter through life idle and
secure, quietly retiring from the clearings that men make
and living harmlessly secluded in the remotest coverts.

So completely are their wants provided for, that the
absence of progress among them is no reproach.   Invention after all is the brat of detestable necessity.
And, indeed, it is hardly a libel upon the nobility of
our own species to suspect that if, without effort, we too
could support life in the same luxury and the same utter
freedom from care, many of us would be content to
surrender some of our aspirations, and forego the harass
ing ambitions of humanity.

*His
opinion of
England
dis-
paraging.*

But it is a pity that the ourang cannot tell us what he
thinks of England and of civilization.   If he could, he
would probably regret in his first sentence the vast wild
orchards of dorian fruit and mangosteen among which
he made perpetual feast, and the wilderness of berry-
bearing trees that provided him with such endless variety
of pleasant food, and would ask us what we can offer
him in exchange for such profusion of luscious eatables?
Our sunlight, he would go on to say, is a wretched substitute for the glorious days he remembers, and solitude,
he would tell us, adds bitterness to his captivity.   He
will find us, we fear, very full of prejudices, as compared
with the easy-going society which he has hitherto enjoyed
in the pandanus jungles of his native island, and will
draw invidious comparisons between Regent's Park and
Malacca, in the matter of wild pumpkins.   If, however,

he is as intelligent as his fellow-countrymen would have us believe, he may come to understand before long that everything is kindly meant and " for the best," and now that his travels are over, his life will be as peaceful as walking-sticks and umbrellas will permit.

CHAPTER V.

THE ELEPHANTS.

Popular depreciation of the Elephant. LEPHANTS are square animals with a leg at each corner—and a tail at both ends. This may be said to be the "popular" description of the Titan among mammals.

Nor is its moral character more accurately summed up by the crowd. It has, indeed, come to be a time-honoured custom when looking at the elephant in the Zoo, to applaud, first its sagacity—as evidenced, they say, in that old story of the tailor who pricked an elephant's trunk with his imprudent needle—next its docility as shown (so the crowd would have us believe) by its carrying children about on its back ; in the third place, the great sensitiveness of its trunk, inasmuch as it can pick up a pin with it; and, finally, its great size. After this, nothing apparently remains but to congratulate ourselves, in a lofty way, upon having thus comprehensively traversed all the elephant's claims to respect, and to pass on to the next beast in the show.

But, as a matter of fact, nothing could well be more offensive, more unsympathetic, more unworthy of the elephant, than this stereotyped formula of admiration. That an elephant did once so unbecomingly demean himself as to squirt the contents of a puddle over a tailor and his shop is infinitely discreditable to the gigantic pachyderm, and every compliment of "sagacity" paid to it on account of that dirty street-boy trick is an affront to the lordly beast which ranks to-day, in the Belgian expedition to Africa, as one of the noblest pioneers of modern commerce and the greatest of living missionaries; and in the Afghan war as one of the most devoted and valued of her Majesty's servants in the East.

His "docility," again, is an easy cry, for is not the elephant in the Zoological Gardens to be seen, every day of the week, carrying children up and down a path, and round and round a clump of bushes, backwards and forwards, forwards and backwards, without doing the children any harm, or even needing the keeper's voice to tell him when a fair pennyworth of ride has been enjoyed ?   But upon such docility as this it is

an insult to found respect, for surprise at such results
argues a prior suspicion that the elephant would eat
the children or run amuck among the visitors to the
Gardens.   Of its splendid docility there are abundant
anecdotes, and among them are some which are really
worthy of the sole living representative of the family of
the mastodon and the mammoth.

*The
Peishwa's
Elephant.*   Such a one is the old Mahratta story of the standard-
bearing elephant that by its docility won a great victory for its master the Peishwa.   The huge embattled
beast was carrying on its back the Royal ensign, the
rallying-point of the Poona host, and at the very commencement of the engagement the elephant's mahout,
just as he had ordered it to halt, received his death
wound and fell off its back.   The elephant, in obedience
to his order, stood its ground.   The shock of battle
closed round it and the standard it carried, and the
uproar of contending armies filled the scene with
unusual terrors.   But the elephant never moved a yard,
refusing to advance or to retire the standard entrusted to
it by so much as a step, and the Mahrattas, seeing the
flag still flying in its place, would not believe that the
day was going against them, and rallied again and again
round their immovable standard-bearer.   Meanwhile, the
elephant stood there in the very heart of the conflict,
straining its ears all the while to catch above the din of
battle the sound of the voice which would never speak
again.

And soon the wave of war passed on, leaving the field deserted, and though the Mahrattas swept by in victorious pursuit of the now routed foe, still as a rock standing out from the ebbing flood was the elephant in its place, with the slain heaped round it, and the standard still floating above its castled back! For three days and nights it remained where it had been told to remain, and neither bribe nor threat would move it, till they sent to the village on the Nerbudda, a hundred miles away, and fetched the mahout's little son, a round-eyed, lisping child—and then at last the hero of that victorious day, remembering how its dead master had often in brief absence delegated authority to the child, confessed its allegiance, and with the shattered battle harness clanging at each stately stride, swung slowly along the road behind the boy.

Such splendid docility as this—the docility which in our human veterans we call discipline—is worthy of our recollection when we look at the great captives in Regent's Park. But why should we offend against the majesty of the elephant by applauding him for carrying children to and fro unhurt? A bullock could not do less.

Then, again, the marvel that the elephant should *That it* pick up a pin! It can do so, of course, but it is a pity *picks up* *pins.* that it should; for elephants that go about picking up pins derogate something from their dignity, just as much as those others who, to amuse the guests of Germanicus, carried a comrade on a litter along tight ropes, and

I

executed thereafter a Pyrrhic dance. It is surely preferable, recalling the elephants of history, to forget these
unseemly saltations and the mocking records of Ælian
and of Pliny, and to remember, rather, that one single
elephant alone sufficed to frighten the whole nation of
Britons into fits; that as the leaders of armies they
played a splendid part in nearly every old world invasion from that of Bacchus to that of Hannibal; and
that their classic glories and the traditions of their intelligent co-operation with men have invested them with
special sanctity for millions of men and women in the
East. How magnificently they loom out from the military records of Pyrrhus and Mithridates, Semiramis and
Alexander and Cæsar, and what a world of tender
reverence gathers round their name when we think of
them to-day as the objects of gentle worship in India.
"My lord, the elephant!" It is permissible perhaps to
the botanist to think of the Alps only as the home of
a particular flower, or the entomologist to make the
smallest and duskiest of our British butterflies cover
with its name one of the largest of our counties. But
to look at an elephant in the same way through the
wrong end of a telescope is to put an affront upon the
animal to whom Asia and Africa now appeal for an assistance, otherwise impossible, in war and in commerce.

It was they who dragged to Candahar and Cabul the
guns that shook Shere Ali from his Afghan throne and
avenged our Envoy's murder, and now they are swinging

across Africa from the East to meet the steamers coming up the Livingstone from the West, and thus clasp the girdle of commerce round the Dark Continent.

But the narrative of this Expedition is so full, as it seems to me, of picturesque interest, that I think it may find a place in these discursive pages.

The animals, then, were supplied by the Poona stud —at the expense of the King of the Belgians—and in marching them along the high road to Bombay, elephants being "common objects of the country" in that Presidency, no exceptional difficulties presented themselves. *The King of the Belgians' Elephants.*

Arrived, however, at the sea-shore, where elephants do not abound, it was discovered that no one knew what to do with the bulky pachyderms, or how to get them off the wharf into the ship. A crowd collected round the strangers, and, while everybody was offering advice, the elephants took fright and charged the council, who precipitately fled. To a practical person, who, it would appear, had remained out of the way while the charging was going on, it then suggested itself that, as elephants had been slung on board ship during the Abyssinian War, they might be slung again, provided the gear was of elephantine calibre. The weight of an elephant, however, was an unknown quantity, but a general average of twenty tons being mooted was accepted by the company as a safe estimate—an elephant as a rule being something less than three tons. The gear was therefore adapted to a weight of twenty tons, and the mammoths, being got into position, were safely slung on board, and the steamer sailed.

During the voyage the elephants would persist in standing up all day and night, and the swaying of their huge bodies with the motion of the ship, nearly dislocated even their columnar legs—nearly fractured, also, the timbers of the deck. But at last they were urged into kneeling down, while a judicious addition of props kept the deck in its place; and thus the elephants got safely across the seas to Zanzibar. Then came another difficulty; how were the creatures to be landed? The ship could not go nearer to the shore than two miles, and there was neither raft, nor lighter, nor any other appliance for transporting them to land. Could they swim? No one knew.

There was nothing for it but to try. So one of the monsters—its name was "The Budding Lily" and it stood ten feet high—was gravely dropped overboard, with a man on its back. The elephant solemnly sank until the man was under water, and then as solemnly reappeared. One look round sufficed to explain the position to the poor beast, which, hopeless of ever reaching the distant shore, turned round and made frantic efforts to get on board again! In vain the mahout belaboured it. The elephant kept its head against the ship's side. In vain they tried to tow it behind a boat, for though, when exhausted with struggling, the huge bulk was dragged a short distance, returning strength soon enabled it to drag the boat back to the ship.

And so for an hour, rain pelting hard all the time, the wretched monster floundered about in the sea, and scrambled against the ship's timbers, now floating alongside without any sign of life, now plunging madly round with the ridiculous boat in tow. That it would have drowned ultimately seemed beyond doubt, but on a sudden the great thing's intelligence supplemented that of the human beings who were with it, and making up its mind that life was worth another effort, and that the ship was unscaleable, the elephant began to swim. Again and again, before it reached the first sandbank, its strength or pluck failed; but the boat was always at hand to encourage or irritate it to renewed exertions, and so at last, after nearly four hours' immersion, the first Behemoth got on shore. Away in the distance those watching from the ship could make out the great black bulk creeping up the sward. Under a tree close by stood its attendant, and in the enjoyment of the monstrous cakes of sugar, rum, flour, and spices which had been prepared for it, and the luxury of a careful rubbing down with warm blankets, the Captain Webb of the elephant world recovered its equanimity and spirits.

Her companions "The Flower Garland," "Beauty," and "The Wonder-Inspirer," emboldened by Budding Lily's performance, soon joined her on African soil.

The object of their deportation was twofold, for they

had in the first place to prove, in their own persons, the adaptability of their kind to be the carriers of merchandise across the Central African solitudes, and in the next to tame and civilize to the service of man the great herds of their wild congeners, the African elephants, roaming in the forests through which the highways of Arab trade now pass.

Gigantic relics of the Past. There is very little difference between the two species, the Indian and the African. The latter has much larger ears and finer tusks, and its forehead is convex, while the Asiatic animal prefers to have it concave. The African elephant, however, is as amenable to discipline as the other. For there can be no doubt that it was the African elephant which charged with the armies of Hannibal and Pyrrhus, and danced before Nero and Galba.

He is, indeed, a truly splendid mammal, a remnant worthy of the great diluvian period when giant pachyderms divided among them the empire of a world of mud. He remains, like the one colossal ruin of the old Egyptian city, to remind us what the old Africa was like.

But the world of trade stands in need to-day of the African elephant; and out of his stately solitude, therefore, he must come to carry from the forest to the coast the produce which our markets demand. And for his capture the Arab and Zanzibari can have no more skilful assistants, or it may be teachers, than the veterans of the Indian khedda that have now gone out. Many a wild tusker, no doubt, has "Beauty" pommelled into servility, and many a one has "Budding Lily" coaxed by her treacherous blandishments into the toils of the Philistines. The tame females, it is well known, seem to take a positive delight in betraying the Samsons of the jungle into slavery; for, after lavishing their caresses upon them till they have tempted them within the fatal circle, they leave them, with a spiteful thump at parting, to the mercy of their captors.

When the Prince of Wales was in India, an elephant-hunt was among the amusements provided for his Royal Highness by that most royal of entertainers, and of murderers, Jung Bahadur, of Nepal, and in the contemporary records of the expedition, full justice has been done to that thrilling episode of the Prince's visit. The heroes of the capture were "Jung Pershad" and "Bijli Pershad." The former, in height, weight, and courage, was superior to all the 800 elephants of the Nepalese stud, while Bijli, "The Lightning," had no match for speed and pluck combined. The first wild tusker sighted was a magnificent fellow, sulking and fuming in a clump of tall jungle grass, and whenever he charged out of it the ordinary fighting elephants brought up at first against him fled before him. Then, with all the leisurely solemnity befitting his renown, old Jung Pershad came swinging up. But, no sooner had the huge bruiser hove in sight than the wild giant, measuring him at a glance, confessed his master, and fled before the overpowering presence. The

A triumph of Science over Nature.

grand old gladiator did not attempt pursuit. His bulk forbade it, and so did the etiquette of his profession.

To his friend and colleague in many a previous fight, Bijli the swift-footed, pertained the privilege of pursuit, and from the moment when the quarry perceived the strangely rapid advance of his new antagonist, he recognized the gravity of his peril. Flight from Bijli was as vain as contest with Jung. So he swung round in his stride, and for full two minutes the pursuer and pursued stood absolutely motionless and silent, face to face. And then, on a sudden, and with one accord, " with their trunks upraised and their great ears spread, and with a crash like two rocks falling together, the giants rushed upon each other. There was no reservation about that charge : they came together with all their weight, and all their speed, and all their heart." But the skill that comes of practice, gave the professional just the one point he needed to beat so splendid an amateur—and he beat him—"by sometimes ramming him against a tree, sometimes poking him in the side so as almost to knock him over, sometimes raising his trunk above his head, and bringing it down on the poor tusker's neck. At last the wild elephant fairly gave up, surrendered, and made no further pretence of either fighting or flying."

Henceforth in far other scenes other Jung Pershads and other Bijlis, mighty in battle, will win renown, and, winning it, will do for Central Africa what the camel has done for Central Asia, and what ships have done for all the world's coasts. They will be the pioneers of trade, true missionaries, Asia's contingent in the little army that has set out to conquer, but without bloodshed, the desperate savagery of the Dark Continent.

At any rate it was a finely picturesque conception this of compelling the Behemoths of the Indian jungles to serve in the subjection of the Titans of the African forests, and to have brought thus face to face, in the centre of a continent, the two sole survivors of a once mighty Order; and I can never look at the great beast lounging along the path in Regent's Park without thinking also of his noble kinsmen working their way in the cause of civilization and of man across the Dark Continent.

*   *   *   *   *

Sagacity and docility are, no doubt, therefore, virtues which the elephant shares with man, but it is hardly fair to it to illustrate its intelligence by quoting the deplorable incident of the tailor, unless we are also prepared to illustrate the sagacity of men and women by referring to the performances of the Artful Dodger. Let us rather generously forget that elephantine lapse, just as we remember that, after all, Noah—in that "aged surprisal of six hundred years"—only got drunk once.

Nor, when we speak loftily of the elephant's "docility," *Elephantine Potentialities.* should we forget that the measure of this virtue may be gauged by the individual's capacities for the reverse. A white mouse is one of the most docile of animals, but what would it matter if it were not? A pinch of the tail would always suffice to frighten it into abject sub-mission. But when the sagacious elephant decides for itself, as it often does, that docility is not worth the candle, that occasional turbulence, good all-round rebel-lion, is wholesome for its temper and constitution, who is going to pinch its tail? With one swing of its trunk it lays all the attendants flat, butts its head through an inconvenient wall, and is free! They are brave men who capture the wild elephants, but no one, however brave, tries to capture " a mad one." It has to be shot in its tracks, dropped standing, for it is then something more than a mere wild animal. It has developed into a creature of deliberate will, and having in its own mind weighed the pros and cons, has come to the fixed con-clusion that captivity is a mistake, and proceeds there-fore on a definite line of intelligent and malignant action.

A mad Elephant. Indeed, among the episodes of Indian rural life there are few more appalling than such a one as that of the Mad Elephant of Mundla. It had been for many years a docile inmate of a Government stud, but one day made up its mind to be infamous. Wise men have before now told the world that it is well to be drunk once a month, and others that we should not always abstain from that which is hurtful, so the elephant, determining upon a bout of wrong-doing, had some precedent to excuse him. The elephantine proportions of his misdemeanours, how-ever, made his lapse from docility appalling to mere men and women whose individual wicked acts are naturally on so diminutive a scale; but comparatively speaking, the gigantic mammal was simply " on the spree." Nevertheless, it desolated villages with nearly every horrible circumstance of cruelty lately practised by the Christians of Bulgaria, and laid its plans with such consummate cunning that skilled police, well mounted and patrolling the country, were baffled for many days in their pursuit of the midnight terror. It came and went with extraordinary secrecy and speed from point to point, eaving none alive upon the high roads to tell the pursuers which way it had gone, and only a smashed village and trampled corpses to show where it had last appeared. It confused its own tracks by doubling upon its pursuers and crossing the spoor of the elephants that accompanied them.

It was not merely wild. It was also "*mad*"—and as cunning and as cruel as a mad man.

But insanity itself may be accepted, if you like, as a tribute to the animal's intelligence, for sudden downright madness presumes strong brain power. Owls never go mad. They may go "silly," or they may be born idiots; but, as Oliver Wendell Holmes says, a weak mind does not accumulate force enough to hurt itself. Stupidity often saves a man from insanity.

It is also curious to notice how the size of the elephant strikes so many as being somehow very creditable to Behemoth. But praise of such a kind is hardly worth the

acceptance of even the hippopotamus.   "The wisdom
of God," says Sir Thomas Browne, "receives small honour
from those vulgar heads that rudely stare about, and
with a gross rusticity admire His works," and it is
certainly "gross rusticity" to attribute credit to the elephant for being big.   After all, he is not so big as other
creatures living, nor as he himself might have been a few
centuries ago.   Moreover, though giants seem always
popular, there is little virtue in mere size.   The whale,
driving along through vast ocean spaces, displaces, it is
true, prodigious quantities of water, but the only admirable points about him, nevertheless, are his whalebone
and his blubber.   He is simply a wild oil barrel, and the
more cheaply he can be caught and bottled off the better.

But speaking of personal bulk as a feature to be com-
plimented on, there is an illustration to my hand here
in the next enclosure—for who could honestly congratulate the hippopotamus upon its proportions?

Men ought to have a grudge against this inflated
monster, for it is one of the happiest and most useless of living things.   Its happiness in a natural state
is simply abominable when taken in connexion with its
worthlessness ; and the rhinoceros, next door there, is
no better.   Providence, to quote the well-known judge,
has given them health and strength—"*instead of which,*"
they go about munching vegetables and wallowing in
warm pools.   They do absolutely nothing for their liveli-
hood, except now and then affront the elephant.   Even

for this the hippopotamus is too sensual and too indolent, but the rhinoceros often presumes to hold the path against the King of the Forests. Their bulk, therefore, is either abused by them or wasted, so that their monstrous size and strength really become a reproach.

With the elephant it is very different. Every ounce of his weight goes to the help of man, and every inch of his stature to his service.

* * * * *

I have said above that "giants are always popular," *A digression on the meekness of giants.* and as perhaps the observation may be contested in the nursery, I would here, in the chapter on gigantic animals, interpolate my defence. To begin with a recent case. Two bulky Irishmen were walking the other day in *Giants a benevolent kind.* San Francisco, when they met "a foreigner" sauntering along the street. Now, they both hated foreigners, so they proceeded to assault him, whereupon the stranger took his hands out of his pockets, and, catching hold of the two Irishmen, banged their bodies together until they were half dead. The foreigner's performance drew the attention of passers-by to him, for even in San Francisco such a sight was not ordinary, and they noticed, what the Irishmen had not discovered until too late, that the stranger was a man of gigantic physical strength. They also remarked that but for the feat he had performed this Hercules might have gone to and fro unsuspected, for not only was his demeanour modest and unassuming, but his face wore "*a gentle and benevolent expression.*" He was, in fact, of the true giant breed, reduced in proportions to suit modern times, but having about him, nevertheless, all the thews and the inoffensive disposition of the original Blunderbore.

To explain my meaning further I need only refer to the history of that overgrown but otherwise estimable person whose lodgings were burglariously entered by a young person named Jack, who for no apparent reason—such was the laxity of the public morals in those days— climbed up, so we are asked to believe, the stalk of a leguminous vegetable of the bean kind, and, having effected a forcible entry into the giant's premises, robbed the amiable, but stertorous, Blunderbore of the most valuable of his effects. Here, then, is a case in point of a person of retiring habits being assaulted simply because he was of gigantic size and strength, and of the public condoning the assault on that account alone. It is contended, I know, that Jack was incited to his crimes by a cock-and-bull story about the giant's castle having belonged to Jack's father, told to the boy by an old woman whom he chanced to find loitering about his mother's cottage—with one eye, depend upon it, all the time on the linen spread out on the hedge. But it was just like the vagabond's impudence to foist her nonsense on a mere child. For after all how could Jack's father have had a castle in the clouds, unless he had been a magician?— in which case Jack himself was little better, and his mother, by presumption, a witch; in which case they ought all to have been ducked in the horse-pond together.

Whether this Jack was the same person who, in after-life, settled down to industrious habits, and, presumably unassisted, built a House for himself, chiefly remarkable for the zoological experiences in which it resulted, I am unable to determine. But looking to the antecedents of the Giant-killer, his laziness at home, and his unthrifty bargain in that matter of his mother's cow, I should hesitate, even with the memory of Alcibiades' conversion to Spartan austerity in my mind, to believe in such a reformation as this, of a young burglar · turning into a middle-aged and respectable householder. In the mean-time it is noteworthy that the Jack "of the Beanstalk" was a boy of forward and larcenous habits, that he committed an unprovoked series of outrages upon a giant in whose house he had been well treated, and that the giant was an affable personage of great sim-plicity of mind and easily amused, kind to poultry and fond of string music.

Indeed, had he not been so excessively large it is pro-bable he would have been a very ordinary person in-deed. This, at any rate, seems certain, that if he had been any smaller he would not have been either so simple or so shabbily treated. It has always been the misfortune of huge stature to be taken advantage of, and so many "men of strength" have been betrayed and brought to grief by Jacks and Aladdins, Omphales and Delilahs, that

Mis-fortunes pursue bulk.

it has come to be understood that when a man is preternaturally strong he should be also extremely unassuming in demeanour, and liable, therefore, to unprovoked aggression.

It has, I know, been gravely endeavoured by a certain class to shake the world's belief in the existence of giants, but the attempt has been fortunately unsuccessful. No argument, however ingenious, erudite, or forcible, can knock out of sight such an extremely obvious fact as a giant; and I consider, therefore, that Maclaurin, who attempted to demonstrate, by "the destructive method" and mathematics, the impossibility of giants, might have saved himself the labour of such profane calculations.

That Giants are weak in the Knees. The destructive argument, however, I confess, has this much in its favour, that it explains why many of the Anakim are weak in the knees, for, inasmuch as the forces tending to destroy cohesion in masses of matter arising from their own gravity only increase in the quadruplicate ratio of their lengths, the opposite forces tending to preserve that cohesion increase only in the triplicate ratio. It follows, therefore, that if we only make the giant long enough he must, by mathematics, go at the knee joints.

Indeed, in our own English literature will be found much excellent matter with regard to weak-kneed giants, from which it appears that the show-frequenting public take no delight whatever in infirm Goliaths; and those who may have any to exhibit will do better to put the feeble-legged Gogs and Magogs to useful tasks about the house or back-garden than display them in public for gain. In one of these stories the giants, when they became decrepid, waited upon the dwarfs attached to the show. The tendency to mock at a giant becomes, among the lower orders, uncontrollable when Blunderbore is shaky in the lower limbs, and, under these circumstances, as it is not legal to make away with giants when used up, he should be either kept in entire obscurity, or only have the uppermost half of him exhibited.

This inclination to make fun of men of exceptionally large stature or extraordinary strength may be due to a half-recognized impression on the mind that such persons are out of our own sphere, superhuman, and preposterous. They are out of date, too, being, as it were, relics of fables and the representatives of a past world, in which they kept the company of gnomes and dwarfs, ogres, hob-goblins, and other absurd gentry of the kind, living irregular lives, perpetually subject from their great size to dangerous accidents, and, as a rule, coming to sud-den and ridiculous ends. It was very seldom, indeed, that a giant maintained his dignity to the last, and there hangs, therefore, a vapour of the ludicrous about the memory of the race, so that nowadays men speak of them all as laughable and rather foolish folk.

In the stories which are so precious to childhood, *Giants* giants, when they have not got ogresses as wives, are never *favourites in* objects of complete aversion. On the contrary, the *Nurseries.*

K

young reader rejoices over the downfall of the bulky one, not on the score of his vices, or because he deserved his fate, but because the child's sympathies naturally incline towards the undersized personages of the story, and if the poor blundering old giant could be only brought up smiling over a hasty pudding on the last page, the story would not be thought, in the nursery, to be any the worse for that—so long, of course, as there was no doubt left in anybody's mind as to Jack being able to kill Blunderbore again, should Blunderbore's conduct again justify his destruction. To older minds it may also, in the same way, occur that Jupiter and his colleagues behaved with unbecoming malignity to the conquered Titans, and that they declined somewhat from the true Olympian level when they heaped indignity upon them. Did old Saturn and Tellus, Cottus and Iapetus and the rest deserve the contemptuous treatment they received, and was grinding Juno's scissors a fit occupation for the Cyclops? Enceladus was smothered under a mountain, but allowed, as a joke, to puff and blow through a hole in the top, (whence our volcano of Etna); Atlas stands ridiculous for ever, shifting the twirling globe from shoulder to shoulder; and Tithonus was turned into a grasshopper. Other heroes of story, too, stand out from the past as subject for mirth : the credulous monster Cadmus dragging herds of cattle backwards by the tails, *in order to show that they had not gone to his cave;* Hercules at the spinning-wheel ; Samson, a joker himself, captured in laughter; old Polyphemus, groping, profane and sore, about his cave, trying to catch · "Nobody;" Vulcan, the dupe of a pretty wife; the "very strong man, Kwasind," pelted to death with fir-cones; and so on, through an ever-lengthening list. In each of these there was something absurd; but then men never hate what they laugh at, and so it happens that a touch of sympathy goes with each simple-minded giant. In mythology there is nothing more touching than the story of Jubal, and in chivalry no Knight so lovable as the rough Sir Bors. Sympathy always goes with Kambukharna in the story of the "Ramayana," and in modern history whom have we more popular than Gog and Magog? There must be, therefore, in great strength something that engages affection; for though the giants of romance— Timorant and Aliofernes, Radamante and Tremalion, and all the others—fell, as was proper, under the swords of Christian knights, the reader cannot help remarking that it was very seldom the giant that provoked the combat, but nearly always the knight, and that, if the knight would only have been civil, the giant would not even have looked at him. Sometimes, I regret to remember, the giants went about collecting children for pies, and from such as these all right-minded men should withhold their esteem; but, for the rest, the ordinary muscular and inoffensive giant, it is impossible to deny a certain liking, nor, *Digression* when he is provoked to display his strength, a great *concluded.* admiration.

K 2

* * * * *

*Domestic
felicity of
Elephants.*
To return to my elephants, no animals are more
conspicuous than they in natural affection, and indeed
in one respect, mutual rejoicing among friends upon the
birth of a baby elephant, they have no imitators except
among men and women. In human society no domestic
event probably gives rise to more lively exhibitions of
feeling than a birth in the house. In all classes of
the community the occurrence causes a spontaneous
display of sympathetic interest within a certain circle,
while in some a birth in a family is regarded by the
neighbours—especially the female neighbours—as a
public, and not a private, affair, and the baby is, for a
time, looked upon as common property, with the rever-
sion, however, in favour of the original parents. This
trait in human character is, no doubt, very admirable.
When, however, we find the same simplicity of tenderness extended to elephants, it becomes doubly pleasing.
That a mother should rejoice, and her friends with her,
seeing that she " has brought a man into the world," is
rational, human, and delightful ; but that elephants
should thus abandon themselves to the sweet raptures of
a sympathetic joy is a fact replete with quite novel interest.

Not long ago a young elephant was born (so it is said)
in a menagerie in the United States, and no sooner was
the fact recognized by the stable companions of the
mother than the whole company gave themselves up to

prodigious rejoicings. Waving their trunks aloft they saluted the little stranger with a perfect tempest of elephantine applause, and at last, surrendering themselves entirely to a paroxysm of glee, they all with one accord got up on their hind legs and danced before the infant.

The mother, "in whose gentle bosom joy was lord," was carried away by the enthusiasm of her comrades, and, alike regardless of consequences and appearances, snapped the chain that had fastened her to a pillar, and, lifting up her offspring in her trunk, executed a pas-seul of great originality and merit, and then, dropping the little one into the manger, proceeded to gyrate on her hind legs. It is not, however, to be supposed that such monstrous saltations could be carried on in a confined space without damage to the surroundings, and the elephants, therefore, ponderously revolving on their axes, very soon wrecked the apartment. Being unaccustomed to motion on two legs, they could not keep their balance in their unwieldy gambols, and whenever they lurched against the woodwork of their stable ruin spread itself around. The keeper, meanwhile, had ventured upon the scene of revelry; but, finding his position among the dancing pachyderms one of no small danger, made his escape, and having obtained help, returned, and, after a while, succeeded in calming down the transports of his demonstrative charges.

That the elephant should share in the maternal instinct common to the rest of the world is not surprising, but

it is certainly unusual for the friends and neighbours of
an animal to combine for such a tremendous exhibition
of kindly interest. When that intelligent person the
dog fills a box with puppies we do not find all the kennels
of the neighbourhood emptied for a party in celebration
of the event ; nor, as far as we know, do the cats of a
parish foregather to dance round kittens' cradles. The
birds of the air show no sympathetic curiosity in each
other's nursery affairs, for it is not on record that crows
have ever been seen collected at a christening, or that
the ducks meet in council to discuss the customary pin-
cushion. Nor are any reptiles known to rejoice in concert over the birth of one of their kind, for works on
natural history say nothing of convivial assemblies of
rattlesnakes on such occasions, and travellers have not
yet observed pythons making merry over a domestic
occurrence of this sort. The lizards, again, are unde-
monstrative, and there is no general uplifting of souls
among the crocodiles when a young leviathan is hatched.
The fishes, poor things, can hardly be expected to concentrate their delight upon the addition of a unit to their
number. The cod-fish, for instance, bringing its millions
into the world annually, has to dissipate its affections
over so large an area that rejoicing in welcome over each
new arrival would be impossible. Descending still lower
in the scale of nature, to the insects, are we to look for
domestic festivities from the frivolous butterfly, or think
harshly of the earwig for its lack of lively interest in the

nativities of its neighbours? We need not speak of the lowest class of creatures in the wonderful multitude that stretches through the corals, from the protozoa to the sea-anemones; for they, so far from holding revel over a birth, hardly know when they are born themselves or how they are born.

The elephants, therefore, have this advantage over the star-fishes, that the advent of a stranger among them is unmistakable and self-evident. It is impossible to be blind to the existence of even a baby elephant; for, delicate and interesting though it may be, the infant soon weighs the better part of a ton, and has a strength in proportion to its weight. Over many of the beasts, birds, reptiles, and fishes the elephant has also this other superiority, that it is strictly a vegetable feeder, and never at any time regards the baby as a possible article of food. It is not so with some of the carnivora, who eat each other's young, or with some birds, who suck each other's eggs; so that to them the affectionate process of rearing their offspring is always associated in their minds, more or less, with the pleasures of the table. The lively interest which the crow shows in a neighbour's nest does not arise from any genial regard for its welfare, but from a natural taste for fresh eggs and fledgelings; while the nurseries of some kinds of fish are the regular feeding grounds of other species. The jackal, hungrily watching a friend's cubs at play, is no doubt influenced by emotions; but they are not of a tender sort, although the

Carnivorous interest in neighbours' nurseries.

cubs may be; and the frogs, croaking in chorus round a tadpole swarm are probably not congratulating the small fry on coming into the world, as might be supposed, but merely saying grace before meat. The elephant, however, has no temptation to eat its young, while, as regards its size, it has no excuse for being unmindful of it.

The sight of a child elephant among them can, indeed, be easily imagined to have strongly affected these creatures of long memories. For years and years they had seen nothing but full-grown relatives and all, like themselves, trained to one dull round of circus performances. Under such circumstances, they must have come in time to look upon each other and themselves as degenerated and unnatural specimens of their kind, enslaved for ever for the amusement of the human public, and compelled to make fools of themselves in return for their board and lodging. To such as these the sudden appearance of an unsophisticated baby elephant, unconventional and light-hearted, can be easily supposed to have been a welcome relief from the dreary monotony of their own company, and to have recalled also old associations of jungles in India and forests in Africa.

Old Associations. The youngster's first cry reminded the great captives, it may be, of a childhood of freedom, and its gambols cheated them for a time into the belief that they, too, were at liberty to frolic. The crashing timbers of their stables sounded to them in the first delirium of their rejoicings as if the branches and undergrowth of their native forest-depths were snapping before them as they ranged the woods, and their trumpeting in concert recalled the past when they swept like a hurricane from the hunter's sight, trampling a broad track through the jungle wastes, and sending back to the baffled decoys a blast of scornful triumph.

But the crack of the whip rang sharply through the building, and there fell upon the great brutes the knowledge of the actual present, and the old bonds of discipline settled about them as close as ever, as they swung back to their stalls. Still the outburst, no doubt, did them good, and the presence of " the baby "—for such it will always be to its comrades of the menagerie—may be expected to enliven their dull existence, and to give them a centre of common sympathy, and one plaything, at any rate, for which they owe no thanks to their captors.

To the Secretary of the Zoological Gardens, Regent's Park.

SIR,—Among the furniture of the Zoological Gardens none, perhaps, is more freely criticized by a candid public than the elephant. Some of this criticism is naturally flippant and irrelevant, for, where so many speak, a proportion of nonsense must be expected. But, putting all captious remark-making on one side, I would myself venture to suggest that the old African elephant which carries children about requires re-stuffing. He has become shabby by long use, and, after all, even leather requires renewing. An upholsterer would be able, no doubt, to make a very good job of him, and the estimate need not be excessive. In the first place, the elephant ought to be re-covered from end to end, and the old tail might with great advantage be renewed. The shoulder-blades and the articulations of the spine should be padded (for the greater comfort of the animal's riders), and a generous coat of paint and varnish be given to the whole beast, especially at the knees, which are so seedy in appearance as to discredit an institution otherwise so well appointed as your Zoological Gardens. The lesser elephant is not so shabby as his monstrous companion, but even he would be improved if his present skin were removed, and he were neatly covered in some appropriate cretonne. Or, since black and gold is so fashionable in furniture, he might be agreeably ebonised and gilded. It is a pity, I think, that these useful animals should be allowed to fall into disrepair.

> Yours,
> PHIL ROBINSON.

CHAPTER VI.

THE ELEPHANTS' FELLOW-COUNTRYMEN.

ELEPHANTS, there is no doubt, are favourites *The Rhino-ceros.* with the public, and they merit their popularity. It is difficult, perhaps, to say as much for their cousins, the rhinoceroses. For some reason or another, the public resent the personal appearance of these animals, and no one compliments them. Straightforward opprobrium is bad enough, no doubt, but depreciatory innuendo is still harder to bear, just as the old writer in the matter of the patient patriarch, that "the expostulations of his friends were a deeper injury than the downright blows of the Devil."

The rhinoceros, therefore, when he stands at the bars with his mouth open in expectation of the donation which is seldom thrown in, hears much that must embitter his hours of solitary reflection. The remarks of visitors are never relieved by any reference to his "sagacity" or "docility," as in the case of the elephant; nor does any appreciation of usefulness to man temper the severity of their judgments upon him. That he is very ugly and looks very wicked is the burden of all *Public* criticism, and it is a wonder that under such perpetual *Disfavour* *towards it.* provocation to do so, he does not grow uglier and look wickeder than he is. No ordinary man could go on being called "a hideous brute" for any great number of years without assuming a truculent and unlovable aspect; and it would not, therefore, be much matter for surprise if the rhinoceros, although such conduct were altogether foreign to his character and even distasteful to his feelings, should develope a taste for human flesh.

As it is he munches hay—not with any enthusiasm, it is true, but with a subdued satisfaction that bespeaks a philosophic and contented mind.

In the wild state, whether he be the African species or the Asiatic, the rhinoceros is a lazy, quiet-loving beast, passing his days in slumber in some secluded swamp of reed-bed, and coming out at night to browse along the wild pastures that offer themselves on forest edges or the water-side. In his caged condition his life is simply reversed, for his days are spent under the public eye, in wakefulness and mental irritation, while his nights are given unnaturally to repose and solitude. There are no succulent expanses of grass and river herbage to tempt him abroad with his fellows as in the nights of liberty in Nubia or Assam; and let the moonlight be ever so bright he cannot now, as once, saunter away for miles along the lush banks of some Javan stream, or loiter feeding among the squashy brakes of the Nile. But captivity, if it robs him of freedom, injures the rhinoceros less than most of *On the* the beasts of the field, for he was never given to much *Banks of the Nile.* exercise, and his life was an indolent one. Now and again, it is true, the hunters found him out, and awakened him to an unusual vivacity, and on such occasions he developed a nimbleness of limb and ferocity of temper that might hardly have been expected of so bulky and retiring an individual. Sometimes also he crossed the elephant on his jungle path, and in a sudden rush upon his noble kinsman vindicated his right of way, and expended all the stored-up energy of many months of luxurious idleness. But such sensations were few and far between. As a rule, his company were diminutive and deferential—wading birds of cautious habits and the deliberative pelicans, wild pigs and creatures of the ichneumon kind. The great carnivora never troubled their heads about such a preposterous victim, and the nations of the deer kind, couching by day in the forest depths and feeding by night in the open plain, saw nothing of the bulky rhinoceros. He lived, therefore in virtual solitude—for water-fowl and weasels were hardly worth calling companions—and was indeed so vigilant in guarding his concealment that he remained a secret for ages.

Obsolete Rhino- ceroses. Once upon a time, before Great Britain was an island, rhinoceroses browsed in herds along the Thames valley and rollicked where the waters of the German Ocean are now spread. Time passed—"it is a way it has." Oceans usurped the place of continents, and then our rhinoceroses found themselves obsolete, and decently became extinct. In the South, however, they held their own, and, lurking among the vegetable wildernesses of Asia and Africa, lived unsuspected until the luxurious Roman, ransacking the earth for rare animals to kill in the amphitheatre, chanced upon the bulky mammal hiding in the Nubian fens.

Great was the delight in Rome over the shield-protected stranger, and greater still the enthusiasm when it was found how willingly he charged the elephants confronted with him in the arena, and how long it took to kill him. The populace had been debauched by the easy slaughter of bears and leopards, and were almost surfeited with tigers and lions, when the hide-bound rhinoceros appeared upon the scene and rewarded sightseers with the novel spectacle of a beast that was not only formidable in offence but panoplied for defence. In time, however, this also grew stale and then the rhinoceros relapsed into its old oblivion, not being thought good enough even to kill, so that except for some nomad tribe that met it in the African wastes, or the Assam villagers who waged war against the crop-destroyer, it was unknown to men.

The rhinoceros, therefore, figures nowhere in folk-lore, and neither fairy tale nor fable have anything to tell us of it. Art owes little to it, and commerce nothing. It points no moral and adorns no tale. Unassisted by associations, and possessing neither a literature nor a place in the fauna of fancy, the monstrous thing relies for sympathy and regard simply upon its merits, and how sadly these have failed to ingratiate it with the British public any visitor to the Zoological Gardens can easily assure himself.

*   *   *   *   *

With the hippopotamus the case is somewhat different. *The Hippopotamus.* One of them was born in the Gardens, and is a citizen of London, while all of them share alike in the traditionary honours that attach to "Behemoth" and the reverend object of ancient Egypt's worship.

It happens also that the apparently defenceless nature of the river-horse enlists public sympathy on his behalf, while the very absurdity of his appearance disarms ill-natured criticism. The horn of the rhinoceros is its ruin, for the popular esteem will never be extended to a creature that carries about on the tip of his nose such formidable implements of offence. The hippopotamus, fortunately for itself, is unarmed, so that a certain compassionate regard is not considered out of place. Its skin, though

ludicrous, looks smooth and tight, suggesting vulnera-
bility, or even a tendency to burst on any occasion of
violent impact with a foreign body, while the rhinoceros
wears an ill-fitting suit of inpenetrab!e leather, which
hangs so easily upon its limbs as to lead the spectator
to suppose the brute had deliberately put it on as a kind
of overcoat for defence against any possible assailants.
Thus prepared for emergencies, it carries its bulk about
with a self-reliant demeanour that, taken in conjunction
with the aggressive tone in which it grunts, alienates all
tenderness of feeling, and makes sentiment impossible.

Popular Sympathy with it.   The hippopotamus, on the other hand, seems to have
had all its arrangements made for it without being con-
sulted beforehand, and to submit to the personal incon-
veniences that result with a mild and deprecatory manner
that commends it to sympathetic consideration. Had
proofs of its own future appearance been sent in to the
hippopotamus to revise, it might have suggested several
useful alterations—a greater length of leg in order to
keep its stomach off the ground, and a head on such a
reasonably reduced scale that it could hold it up.

As matters stand, Behemoth lives under considerable
disadvantages. It is true that he is amphibious, and
that when tired of dragging his bulky person about on
the land he can roll into the water and float there. But
this dual existence hardly makes amends for the discomforts of such a bladder-like body. The world, however, owes both the hippopotamus and the rhinoceros a

grudge, inasmuch as neither contributes to human welfare. That their hides make good leather is no adequate justification for such huge entities, and the fact of their teeth and horns being useful for paper-knives and walking-sticks hardly authorizes two prodigious creatures occupying so much terrestrial space. It is centuries ago since the elephant made good its claim to be considered a friend and benefactor of the human race, but neither of its great companions has ever bestirred itself in the service of men. Their day, perhaps, is coming.

Immense tracts of country are being now opened up in Africa to the world's industries, and the high-ways of future commerce lie right through the homes of the rhinoceros and hippopotamus. How startling will be the effect upon the wild creatures of the forest and the rivers! Long-established nations of monkeys and baboons will be driven by the busy axe from the shades they have haunted for generations, and as, league after league, the creepers and undergrowth are cleared away, multitudes of animal life will have notice to quit. Progress will order them to move on, and so by their families and parishes they will have to go—the sulky leopard-folk and solemn lemurs, troops of squirrel and wild-cat, and the weasels by their tribes. Diligent men will mow down the cane-beds that have housed centuries of crocodiles, and the exquisite islands will be cleared of jungle that human beings may take possession of the ancestral domains of the lizard kinds. Wilder-

Disturbance without compensation.

L

nesses of snakes will have to go, and out of the giant
reeds flocks of great water-fowl will rush startled from
their hiding-places. Advancing to where the older
timber grows and the nobler plains are spread, the
colonist will disturb the bulky rhinoceros and the lordly
elephant, and in the creeks of river and lake that will
come under man's dominion the hippopotamus will find
its right of place challenged. The time, therefore, it
may be, is not far distant when the present waste of
traction power will cease, and the two monsters, hitherto
useless, be trained to drag our caravans across the plains
and our barges down the rivers of the Dark Continent.

Hippopota- A yoke of rhinoceroses would do as much work as a
muses "as
a mode of score of oxen, while a team of hippopotamuses harnessed
motion." to a barge would leave steam far behind as a means of
river navigation. In deep water, they would swim, in
shallow they would walk, and when the wharf was reached
they would drag the boat and all its cargo high and dry.
· It is true that sometimes in mid-stream the team might ·
conspire to dive, or, simultaneously closing their nostrils,
to sink solemnly to the bottom of the river, and, as they
are able to stay several minutes at a time beneath the
water, such conduct might prove serious to the passengers
in the saloon of "the hippopotamus boat," but man is
nothing if not inventive, and means might easily be
devised for keeping the creatures on the surface.

They would then, at any rate, deserve their name of
"river-horses."

From my speaking of the elephant as "a mammoth," of the rhinoceros as a Titan, and the hippopotamus as Behemoth, you might fairly charge me, reader, with having forgotten that these animals, big as we think them, are really after all only the pigmies of their species. But I had not really forgotten it, for before me lies a paragraph announcing the discovery, in Siberia, of one of those colossal animals, which nature is very fond of dropping in, in a st*o*ccato way, just to keep our pride down *a* and to remind us, the creatures of a degenerate growth, what "winter" meant in the years gone by, and what kind of person an inhabitant of the earth then was.

He had to be very big indeed, very strong, and very *"There* warmly clad, to be called "the fittest," in the Glacial *were Giants in* Period, and to survive the fierce assaults of the Palæo- *those* lithic cold. This rhinoceros, therefore, exceeds by some *days."* cubits the stature of the modern beast, and is also by some tons heavier.

It appears that an affluent of the Tana River was making alterations in its course, and in so doing cut away its banks, revealing the embedded presence of a truly Titanic pachyderm, which, for want of a fitter name, has been temporarily called "a rhinoceros." But it is such a creature that if it were to show itself now in the swamps of Assam or on the plains of Central Africa, it would terrify off its path all the species of the present day, whether one-horned or two-horned, and make no more of an obstinate elephant than an avalanche does of a goatherd's hut that happens to stand in the line of its advance. At one time, the whole skeleton of the great dead thing stood revealed to human eyes, such an apocalypse of mummy as should have had some evangelist like Professor Owen close at hand to translate it to the world : a vision of dry bones fit for the Prophet of South Kensington himself. Unfortunately, however, there is no large choice of professors in Siberia. They are wise beyond measure in Arctic suffering and graduates in the miseries of cold, but they know very little about fossils. So the stream that was cutting away its banks took the old rhinoceros in its day's work, and cut the monster of the past away, too. Its head was eventually rescued, and so was one foot said to be at Irkutsk. *Ex pede Herculem.* This foot if set down upon one of the rhinoceroses of modern times would have flattened it as smooth as the pilosopher's tub rolled out those naughty boys of Corinth, who had ventured to tickle the cynic through the bunghole with a straw. Besides its size, the huge monster in question asserts its superiority over existing species by being clothed in long hair, a fleece to guard it against the climate in which it lived, and from which even the tremendous panoply of the nineteenth-century rhinoceros could not sufficiently protect the wearer. Thus, clad in a woolly hide and colossal in physique, the Siberian mammal not only lived, but lived happily, amid snowy glaciers that would have frozen the polar bear and made icicles of Arctic foxes.

They were, indeed, a fine race, those giants of prehistoric times, whether beast, or bird, or reptile. We in England have had three elephants of our own, fleece-clothed monsters, that roamed over our country in the days when there were no seas round it. The mammoth itself lived and died in Essex, and its splendid effigy stands to-day in that "Temple to Nature" which has been built for Professor Owen in South Kensington, and besides it, the "primo-genius" of science, there was the "elephas antiquus" and the "priscus"—a trinity of proboscidians such as no other continent but Europe can boast.

Many centuries ago these great creatures, now herding together in the Ilford pits, roamed at will amongst the prodigious vegetation of a Pleistocene "Britain"—and in those days there was no such thing as a German Ocean. Their bones are to be found to-day, within sound of London bells, lying, so to speak, side by side—the fleece-covered mammoth and the woolly rhinoceros, the hippopotamus and the wild horse, the elk and the bison, the huge urus, father of all oxen, and the wolf and bear and lion. There is thus a large choice of sport in these Essex hunting-grounds. If his luck be good, the hunter may range, not only through the great mammal world of the glacial period, but may bring to bag, within sight of London chimneys, the mighty beasts that still have dominion over their fellows in American prairies, African rivers, and Asiatic jungles. There is no need to cross

Mammoth hunting in Essex.

the Atlantic to bring home the bison's head, or to tempt
the savages of the Nile in quest of hippopotamus ivory,
for these giant folk are lying together here at our doors,
waiting to surrender themselves to the patient and skilful pursuit of their old enemy, Man.

*Our
Ancestors'
difficulties
with
mastodons.*
Perhaps even man himself did not exist then; at any
rate, if he did, he had the decency to secrete himself in
holes and burrows, and when the mammoths came along
the road to get out of their way.   He was a feeble creature at first, and his best accomplishments were those
that taught him how to escape his many foes, for our
ancestors had but little time for the cultivation of other
arts and sciences when the best part of their days and
nights had to be spent in scrambling up trees out of the
reach of prowling carnivora and running away from ill-
tempered things of the rhinoceros and elephant kind.
Gradually, however, he began to defend himself, and from
defence he rose at last to the dignity of offence.   Armed
only with flint stones, he had the audacity, this progenitor of ours, to attack the bulky pachyderms; and,
if the testimony of the crags and clay may be believed,
he actually overcame the Goliaths of the forest with
his pebbles.   Were it not, indeed, for these relics of
the age of flint weapons, it might be doubted whether
man was ever contemporary in Britain with the mammoth;
but, as matters stand, there is every reason for supposing
that he was.   Whether this juxtaposition of human implements and animal skeletons means that our ancestors

slew the beast or that the beast ate our ancestors, it is impossible to say. Probably they both gave and took.

It was an age of silence and twilight and snow; an epoch of monstres.

In Australia a huge marsupial, with the head of an ox, *An Epoch of Monsters.* and compared to which our kangaroo is only a great rat, straddled and hopped about as it pleased, in the company of wombats as big as bears; and in America the megatherian sloth crept browsing among the forests of the primæval continent, like some bulky thing of Dreamland, voiceless, solitary, and slow-footed; while the glyptodon —the wondrous armadillo of the past, that could have driven its way through a street of houses as easily as the mole tunnels through the furrows of a field—wandered with the same strange loitering pace along the river banks. In those days there was no need for the beasts to hurry, for life was long and there was nothing to harm them; so they crawled about on land and waded in the water as lazily as they pleased. It is true that the extinct kangaroo, as big as a hippopotamus in the body, had an enemy in the "pouched lion;" but there were twenty kinds of lesser kangaroos which the carnivorous beast could attack first; so the largest lived on in peace and flourished, growing more and more huge, until at last Man appeared upon the scene and annihilated the genus. For reptiles, our own colonies in Africa supply individuals worthy in every way to have been the contemporaries of these giants. Huge herbivorous dragons—two-tusked reptiles with the skulls of crocodiles—grazed along the rich pastures of the antediluvian "Cape;" while in England, in the Weald, there lived the iguanadons, prodigious creatures of the lizard kind, with large, flattened, crushing teeth, covering the palate above like a pavement, and working upon a corresponding breadth of surface in the lower jaw.

For birds, again, we need go no farther—for we should certainly fare no better—than our own colony of New Zealand, which monopolizes the wonders of the bird paradise, where a score of gigantic feathered things, as big as camels, had the islands all to themselves, feeding to their heart's content on the nutritious fern roots. The nurseries of the dinornis and the moa had, however, their "bogey" in the terrible Harpagornis, a bird of prey far larger than the condor or the lammergeyer, and sufficient in itself to justify the old-world traditions of the roc, the sirmurg, and the other gigantic fowls of story. But the adult birds had no cause for fear even from such an eagle as this; and so the geese grew so big that they could not fly, and gradually dispensed with wings, and the coots became so prodigious that they, too, gave up flying as a troublesome and unnecessary method of locomotion, and everything at last came to waddling about together, too fat to go fast, and so secure from harm that they had no cause for haste.

The Idle Age. It was a grand world in one sense, but a stupid, useless world in other respects. The leviathans and the behemoths of the time—creatures of unlimited space and time and food—prowled about, without any horizon to their migrations, cropping the herbage as they went and dying where they happened to be standing last. They would not even take the trouble to settle for posterity the question as to the exact limits of their habitation, but dropped their preposterous bones into snowdrifts, which melted and swept them off to distant sea-beds, or into rivers which tumbled their venerable remains along from the centres of continents to their shores, or left them stranded with all sorts of incongruous anachronisms to puzzle the ages to come.

In a small way, it is true, we take our revenge of them by using their old frozen-up tusks and bones for knife-handles, but the triumph is a poor one. It is far more to the purpose that in spite of their obstinate attempts to make their history a puzzle, and the conspiracy of streams and glaciers to obscure their antecedents and surroundings, we have nowadays men of science who can extort her secrets from Nature, and squeeze all mystery out of the rocks and the fossils they hold. Fifty years, it is true, may elapse between the fitting of one bone on to another, as has happened with some of those "extinct animals" which Professor Owen has created afresh for us, but in the end human patience and brains triumph, and, bit by bit, we see the prodigies of a glacial Britain or Siberia restored to shape and assigned to their several places in time and nature.

Ours is a world of smaller beings, but it is a world of life and mind and work, and there is no room in it for the old idle things that lounged about the earth's surface in the days when the woolly rhinoceros made our Britain its home. •

* * * * *

The Giraffe; its Neck. For ever so many centuries nobody with any pretensions to intelligence would believe that such a creature as the giraffe existed. It was its neck that did it, and a man who persisted in believing in that part of its body might have been sent to the stake for it. It was in vain that travellers tried to convince Europe that they had seen such an animal with their own eyes, for as soon as they came to the neck part of their description they were put out of court at once. Yet it was a case of "neck or nothing," and, as our forefathers would not have the neck at any price, they had nothing.

Zebras gone to seed. The idea of a zebra was difficult enough for them to entertain, but of a zebra *gone to seed* in such a way as these travellers described the giraffe, appeared preposterous and impossible—so they said. Yet in earlier days the giraffe was known to Europe, for Imperial wild-beast-killing Rome had not only known the "camel-leopard," but had been much amused by it, for the giraffe has a method of fighting which is entirely original and is a very pleasing illustration of the instinct which teaches wild animals to make the most of nature's gifts. The giraffe has neither claws nor tusks nor beak nor sting nor poison fangs nor

sharp teeth nor yet hobnailed boots; so when it is out of temper with one of its own kind it does not fly in the face of
Providence by trying to scratch its antagonist's bowels out
as a tiger might, or toss it like a rhinoceros, or peck its eyes
out like a vulture, or sting it like a scorpion, or strike it
like a cobra, or fly at its throat like a wolf, or jump on it as
the costermonger does. The sagacious animal is conscious how foolish and futile such conduct on its part
would be. On the contrary, the giraffe, remarking that
it has been provided by nature with a long and pliable *Its in-*
neck, terminating in a very solid head, uses the upper *telligent*
method of
half of itself like a flail, and, swinging its neck round *Fighting.*
and round in a way that does immense credit to its
organization, brings its head down at each swing with a
thump on its adversary. The other combatant is equally
sagacious, and adopts precisely the same tactics ; and
the two animals, planting themselves as firmly as possible
by stretching out all four legs to the utmost, stand
opposite each other hammering with their heads, till one
or the other either splits its skull or bolts.

Their heads are furnished with two stumpy horn-
like processes, so that the giraffes, when busy at this
hammer and tongs, remind the spectators somewhat
of two ancient warriors thumping each other with the
spiked balls they used to carry for that purpose at the end
of a chain. It is possible that the knowledge of this fact
about giraffes would have gone far towards convincing
our obstinate forefathers and foremothers of the creature's

actual existence, and it is impossible, therefore, to deplore
too sincerely the lamentable ignorance of natural history
which deprived preceding generations of the enjoyment
of this animal. To the Romans so eccentric a procedure
in combat greatly endeared the giraffe, and it is within
the limits of reasonable expectation to believe that our
ancestors of the Dark Ages would similarly have appre-
ciated it had they allowed themselves to be so far convinced of its entity as to get one caught.

For the giraffe is distinctly an enjoyment. It is a pity,
perhaps, that it has not got wings; but we must accept
things as we find them, and, taken all round, there is
no doubt that the "camelopard" is a comfort and a
pleasure. It gives us hopes of further eccentricities,
and contracts the limits of the marvellous. It is about
the best instalment of the impossible that has been
vouchsafed us.

The high living of the Giraffe.

The hippopotamus is a great prodigy in its way, and
the kangaroo is out of the common. But they are
neither of them of the same class as this sky-raking
animal, that passes all its life, so to speak, looking out
of a fourth-story window. Think of the places it could
live in! A steeple would be as comfortable as possible
for it, or its body might be put into a back kitchen and
its head up the chimney. The cowl at the top outside
would keep the rain off its head, and, as the wind blew
it round and round, the giraffe, from its sweep's
eminence, would be gratified by a gyroscopic view of the
surrounding country. It is the only animal that lives

on the earth and never thinks about the ground it walks on.

It takes terra firma as a matter of course, and does not even trouble itself to find out where the trees grow from. It browses on the tops of them without troubling itself to wonder how leaves got so high up in the air; and while other animals are snuffing about on the earth, and blowing up the dust to their own inconvenience, the giraffe reconnoitres the ceilings, and knows all about the beams. The hippopotamus in the next house would never even surmise that there was such a thing as a roof over him unless it were to fall on his head, but he thoroughly understands the bricks and flagstones with which his apartments are paved; but with the giraffe it is just the reverse. Spiders, as a rule, build their cobwebs in the cornices, in order to be out of harm's way; but in the giraffes' house, if they do not wish to be perpetually molested by sniffing, they have to build in the angles of the floor; and, in the countries where giraffes are common, we may similarly presume that little birds never sit and sing on the tops of bushes, but always about the roots—or else the giraffes might accidentally nibble them off the twigs. Sometimes, it is true, the giraffe stoops to mammalian levels; but there is something so lofty even in its condescension that the very act of bending enhances the haughtiness of its erect posture, and suggests that it does it from policy. To be always keeping state, and for ever in the clouds, might make shorter animals accuse it of acting superciliously; so, remembering Bacon's maxim, that "amongst a man's inferiors one shall be sure of reverence, and therefore it is good a little to be familiar," it affably condescends at intervals. Its usual gestures are all cast in Alexandrines, and so, like the poets, it breaks a line every now and then to relieve the over-stateliness of the measure.

Is it a dull animal? It is difficult to believe that the giraffe finds much fun in life—for, after all, most of the fun of the animal world goes on upon the ground. Of course, if the giraffe thinks itself a bird, it may be contented enough all by itself in the air, but its aspect is one of subdued melancholy, such as appertains to all anomalous positions, whether those of queen-dowagers or dodos. The dodo, for instance, left all by itself as the last of its race (like Kingsley's poor old gairfowl on the All Alone Stone), must have had many sad moments. It was prevented, on the one hand, by the demise of all its kindred, from enjoying the society of its own species, and, on the other, by the dignity of being-about-to-become-extinct, from mingling in the social life of more modern fowls. The giraffe, in the same way, moves about with a high-bred languid grace that has more than a suspicion of weariness about it.

Seven feet of Sore Throat. Yet, taken all for all, it has not been hardly treated by nature. If its neck had been telescopic like a turtle's, it would, indeed, have been unduly favoured, but as it is it comes off impartially. Its long neck must necessarily betray it to its enemies, for no lion worth its salt could help seeing a giraffe as it lounged about browsing in the middle of the sky, with its upper-t'gallant-stunsails set ; but then again the giraffe, from such an elevated look-out, should be able to descry the prowling beast of prey at a greater distance. Its length of neck, again, so medical science assures us, secures it from all danger of apoplexy; but, on the other hand, it is terrible to think what a giraffe's "sore throat" would be like. *Imagine seven feet of sore throat!* Again, the camelopard carries no water-butts inside it, as the camels do, although it lives in the plains of Africa, where water often fails ; but in recompense it has a tongue about two feet long—no small comfort to it when thirsty—and eyes that project after the manner of a shrimp, so that, if it likes, it can look behind it and in front at the same time. Thus, counter-balancing defect and advantage, we find the giraffe very fairly off, while in the conditions of its wild life there is much to rank it among the happier of the beasts.

*   *   *   *   *

Next door to the giraffes are the zebras, and, passing from one to the other, the thought occurs how plea-santly art might be made to supplement nature in the colouring of animals, or how agreeable it would have been if in the first instance Nature herself had painted a few more of the larger animals as she has decorated these two comrades of the African wilderness.

The Zebras.

In the bird-world colour has been lavished prodigally, and among insects we find hues of every tone and bril-liance. The wicked caterpillar, for instance, is defended from those who would take away his ill-spent life by shades of green and brown that harmonize with the vegetables he ravages, and why was the same considerate anxiety for its welfare not extended to the gentle hippopotamus ?

Some sug-
gestions for
Painting
more
animals.

A pea-green river-horse browsing among the reed-beds of Old Nile would have added a charm to the scene, and Stanley would hardly have been so angry with the Behemoths of Victoria Nyanza if he had found them floating among the lotus-pads painted in imitation of water-lilies. The rhinoceros, again, is a hideous object from its vast expanse of mud-coloured skin; yet what a surface he presents for a noble study in browns !

What fine effects of shade might not be obtained among those corrugated folds of hide, or let us for a moment consider what he would look like *burnished!* Nature has not stinted metallic tints in bird, or insect, or fish, or reptile ; and yet in the mammals, where such magnificent results might have been attained, she withheld her hand. It is difficult, indeed, in these degenerate days to imagine such a superb spectacle as a herd of brazen elephants crashing their way through a primeval forest, or rhino-ceroses, glittering like Prince Albert in his Memorial statue, wandering among the ruins of old Memphis, or hippopotamuses, mother-o'-pearl, sporting on the bosom of Old Nile with electro-plated crocodiles ! The splendour of such objects would materially enhance the charms of African landscape, and rescue many dumb but deserving animals from the ill-natured criticism their present aspect provokes. How much might thus be done to relieve the sensitive feelings of the creatures we have caught and caged, is shown by the deference paid to tigers and lions, leopards and jaguars on account of their personal beauty. Commodus was so beautiful that Rome forgave him all his atrocities again and again.

The carnivora in the same way advantage by the accident of their painted skins, but the zebra and the giraffe need no excusings for crime, for they commit none. They are innocent and beautiful at one and the same time. The hippopotamus, poor monster! is only innocent, and the rhinoceros is neither, and each, therefore, receives from the public its proportion of depreciative comment, the former being patronized for its helplessness, and bantered on its personal appearance; the latter being rudely spoken of, not only for the ugliness of its looks, but the wickedness of them, the malicious twinkle in its little eyes, and that offensive horn at the tip of its nose, which Pliny tells us he always sharpens upon an agate before attacking the elephant.

Now, if all were impartially adorned in colours, all would share more largely in public sympathy; for, just as no one now would think of shooting the gold and silver pheasants, no one then would think of prodding a golden rhinoceros with umbrellas and walking-sticks, or betraying the confidence of a silver hippopotamus with empty paper bags or the ungrateful pebble.

Yet, in spite of good looks, and in spite, too, of the singular aptness with which they lend themselves to the poetical metaphors and hieroglyphic significances of heraldry, neither the zebra nor the giraffe has arrived at the dignity of being a crest. The ungainly rhinoceros *has*—but it was out of spite—for during the Imperial war against Rome the King of Portugal sent an elephant to the Pope, to be used in battle, whereupon the Dukes of Medici took the rhinoceros for their badge, as being the natural enemy of the elephant. Yet as symbols of indomitable freedom and unrelaxing caution, these two painted creatures are incomparable, for the zebra scorns capture by its amazing swiftness, its courage, and its resource, while the giraffe, an object of envy to pickpockets and of admiration to diplomats, always looks both ways at once.

CHAPTER VII.

CATS.[1]

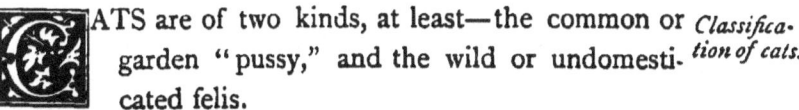 ATS are of two kinds, at least—the common or *Classifica-*
garden "pussy," and the wild or undomesti- *tion of cats.*
cated felis.

[1] The late Mr. Doubleday had an English kangaroo. It is true
it was only a cat. But then it was the best kangaroo the British

M 2

The former is of various colours and qualities, the grey specimens being called tabbies and the larger ones "toms." Both are equally fond of fish, and their young (which are born blind) are called "kittens," and are generally drowned.

The latter, or undomesticated kind, is exactly like the former, but it is usually much larger, and when offered milk it does not purr. One of these cats is called " the lion." The lion, to be precise, is also of two sorts— the natural and the artificial—and on the whole the latter animal is the better of the two. It is generous and brave, the King of Beasts, and one of the supporters of the British Arms.

Artificial Lions. Landseer has done a great deal for this lion, and in Trafalgar Square has left on record four specimens, which all other lions, "vel Africanus vel Asiaticus," should try and live up to. Other artists, also, notably Doré on canvas, and Thorwaldsen in stone, have advantaged the artificial lion very considerably, and both poets and " lion-slayers " have done their best to elevate its moral and physical virtues in the public estimation— the former from a mistaken estimate of this animal's

Isles have ever accomplished out of their own unaided resources. The cat in question had no fore paws—at least none worth mentioning—mere trifles of fur—so it at once abandoned the idea of being a cat altogether and decided to try being a kangaroo. It sate upright, as orthodox kangaroos do, practised leaping on two legs, and imitated the kangaroo's trick of thumping its tail on the ground every time it jumped. The cat is a very versatile animal.

character derived from Antiquity, the latter from a natural desire to represent themselves as being men of an extraordinary courage. These powerful agencies between them have succeeded in rehabilitating the artificial lion, who was at one time becoming rapidly absurd by the liberties taken with it in heraldry and on sign-boards.

A' lion rampant with his tongue lolling out, and two knobs at the end of his tail, is only one of a hundred heraldic aberrations from the normal type which lovers of nature must agree in deploring; and the Green, Blue, and Red lions of our wayside hostelries were all such "fearful wild-fowl" as might make cats weep. There have even been *spotted* lions ! It was high time therefore for the artistic champions of the great cat to come to the front, or we might soon have had "Tabby" and "Tortoiseshell" lions and "Tom" lions on our sign-boards.

What dignity after this would have attached to that haughty speech of the lioness who, being rallied by a grasshopper upon having only one cub, loftily replied, "Yes, true, I have only one—*but that one is a lion.*"

The story has long been popular, and often been applauded, but, as it seems to me, without sufficient judgment. What else could the lioness have expected to produce but a lion? Such was only to be anticipated.

Now, if her cub had been a camel or a rhinoceros, her pride would have been justified by the exceptional character of her performance, or if her offspring had been a hippopotamus or a giraffe, we might have accepted such complacency as not unnatural under the circumstances. But what are the facts of the case? Or if again it had been even a lion rampant with its tongue out, or a green lion, or a spotted one, we might have understood the tawny mother's exultation. As it was her *hauteur* was surely misplaced. A lioness gives birth to a cub and it turns out a lion—*voilà tout!* Yet she was pleased on this account to snub the prolific insect who addressed her, as if she herself had done something out of the common, rare and worth talking about. As a matter of fact, after all, it was only an ordinary, every-day lion. Moreover, it would have been quite within the grasshopper's right to retort, "A lion? Nonsense. It is only a cat—a kitten. I can hear it mewing." For the baby lion is faintly brindled, like the most ordinary of pussies, and mews precisely like the kitten in the nursery.

The Lion unsuitable as a Domestic Animal.

Nevertheless, the artificial (or supernatural) lion differs in many valuable respects from the natural animal. It is magnanimous, as witness that story of the mouse that released the lion from a net and was dismissed by the lion with thanks. Now, in a wild state the lion would have eaten the mouse, for it has the usual cat's taste for mice and rats, and though, if the truth must be told, only an indifferent mouser, might no doubt be made useful in a kitchen. Besides clearing the domestic precincts of the cheese-nibbling folk, it would not be above catching the crickets on the hearth or the humble cockroach—and eating them. The lion in a wild state never disdains such small deer as insects. But whether our modern cooks and kitchen maids would care to have a promiscuous lion downstairs is another matter, and the doubt on this point suggests a very painful contrast between the manners of the larger and the lesser cats.

The lesser cat, it is only too true, is often so carried away by her feelings as to indulge in the surreptitious canary, and she has been known to forget herself so far during the night-watches, as to skirmish on the window-sill in the company of the " cat from next door " with such vivacity and want of judgment as to upset flower-pots into the area. The gravity of these misdemeanours cannot be slurred over, but, after all, to what do they amount compared to the havoc that would result from the domestication of some of the larger cats—such as lions?

Confessing his sins in a parliament of the beasts, the lion in the fable says: " J'ai dévoré force moutons ; même il m'est arrivé quelquefois de manger le Berger ! " and from a shepherd to a cook is only a brief step. But between a canary and a cook there is a distance of many parasangs, and the enormity of the one offence is barely comparable to that of the other. Again, the light-hearted cat, when foregathering for frivolous converse with her kind, does damage, as has been said, to occasional flower-pots, and has even in her gaiety been known to fall ruinously through the scullery window. But supposing we tried to keep lions about the place, and " our lion " were to get on to the roof of the summer-house or on the garden wall with "the lion from next door," what would be the result ? The roaring of the lion when at liberty is said by those who have heard it to be something terrific. It lays its head, we are told, close to the earth, and in this position emits a tremendous utterance, which rolls growling along the ground like the first mutterings of a volcano. It could be heard all over the Square, and we should never get a wink of sleep ! But if the lions got frolicsome the consequences would be even more dreadful. The gardens, with their uprooted shrubs, twisted railings, and dilapidated walls, would look next morning as if some earthquakes had been on the premises overnight and got drunk before leaving.

All this, without prejudice or ill-feeling, tells against the lion ; for if cats are to get worse the bigger they grow—why, the smaller we keep them the better. The diminutive felidæ who give their best energies to domestic vermin, and in whom the females of the household have confidence, are obviously preferable to the overgrown species which could never be admitted to the nursery, and which, if hilariously inclined, would do such serious damage in our enclosures and thoroughfares—letting alone the fact that a lion catching mice in the kitchen would be likely to cause considerable injuries to the crockery and fittings generally.

This, however, is somewhat of a digression. To re-

turn to the artificial lion and the points in which it differs
from the natural animal, we find, besides its magnanimity,
that this species possesses an unusual sense of honour.
It is said, for instance, by those who wish to magnify it,
that it roars before entering a jungle—in order to give
all the little creatures in it a chance of running away.
The lion is too no ble a beast, they say, to take a mean
advantage of its neighbours, or to surprise any of them,
even the humblest, so it gives warning to the bystanders,
like Mr. Snodgrass, that it is "going to begin." But
what are the facts? The lion when on the look-out for *The natural Lion.*
a meal is as stealthy as a cat when compassing the ruin
of the garden sparrow. It crawls along on its stomach,
taking advantage of every tuft of cover and inequality of
the ground, and maintaining a perfect silence. More
often still it lies in ambush for its victim, and those who
have watched a lion under a tamarisk waiting for the
antelope to come browsing by, say there is no difference
whatever between its tactics and those of Grimalkin
when she lurks under a gooseberry bush for the casual
robin. Another fact is that the lion is only bold in the
dark. It becomes savage, of course, at all hours, if
passers-by take the liberty of wounding it; but during
the daytime and on moonlight nights it is, as a rule, so
timid that travellers in the Lion-veldt of Africa never
even trouble themselves to tether their waggon cattle.
Yet this is the King of Beasts.

In what, then, is it kingly? Certainly not in generosity, nor yet in its habits. Kings do not go about catching rats, and frogs, and insects, nor in their own dominions do they skulk among the undergrowth when in search of a meal. Is it its size? Certainly not, for the elephant is its companion, and the lion never dares to cross the mammoth's path, confessing by its deference a sense of superiority which other beasts, the lion's " subjects," refuse to entertain—notably the tiger, the wild boar, and the rhinoceros. These three do not hesitate to affront the elephant in broad daylight, and certainly would not turn tail for their " king " if they met him. Is it then in its appearance that this animal claims to be royal among the quadrupeds? It is true that in repose—notably in the splendid bronzes of Trafalgar Square—there is a surpassing majesty in the lions' heads. They have the countenances of gods. Their manes sweep down upon their shoulders like the terrible hair of the Olympian Zeus, and there is that in their eyes that speaks of a foreknowledge of things and of days, grand as fallen Saturn and implacable as the Sphinx.

But then this is in bronze. In Nature, only one-half of the world's lions have any manes at all, and even of these, the African species, there are but few, so travellers assure us, that reflect in any considerable degree the dignity of Landseer's effigies, while one writer speaks of "the blandness of his (the lion's) Harold Skimpole-like countenance !"

Yet, after all, if we dethrone the lion, which of the

Beasts shall wear the crown? The elephant is infinitely superior, both morally and physically; but the ermine would hardly sit well upon the unwieldy pachyderm. The tiger is more courageous and as strong, but there is too much blood on its claws for a royal sceptre. Shall we give the beasts a Dictator in the violent rhinoceros, or raise them an Emir from the people by crowning the wild boar? But why have a Monarchy at all? Let the quadrupeds be a Republic. They have their communists already in the wolves, and the dasyures are *intransigeants*. Revolution, moreover, never comes amiss to bears and hyenas, foxes, tiger-cats, gluttons, baboons, wild asses—and a number more.

But the suggestion is quite worthy of consideration whether the modern ideal of "the lion" is not really due to a misconception of the object of our predecessors in making this animal so prominent. Originally, there is no doubt, the people fixed upon the lion as "the king" *not* because he had any of the kingly virtues, but because he had all the kingly vices. They satirized monarchy under this symbol. By endowing him with royalty they intended, therefore, to mark him out for public odium, and not for public reverence, just as in more modern days "the wolf" has stood in Ireland for "the landlord." With this explanation as a key, all the fables and stories told of the lion which hitherto have misled the popular mind as to the regal qualifications of the lion fall to pieces at once, and are seen to illustrate the failings and iniquities of the purple, and not its virtues or its grandeur.

Take Æsop alone, and translate his fables by this light. The lion and the boar fight, and the match is an equal one—king against the people—but seeing the vultures, a foreign enemy, on the look-out for the corpse of the vanquished, whichever it might happen to be, they make up their quarrel. * * * A lion (the king) saw three bulls (his turbulent barons) pasturing together, and he made them quarrel and separate, when he ate them up one after the other. * * * A lion (the king's army) made an alliance with a dolphin (the king's navy) in order to have everything their own way, and then the lion tried to oppress a wild bull—his people—and got the worst of it, and the navy could not help him a bit. * * * Two kings, a lion and a bear, fall to fighting over a kid, and are at length so exhausted with the combat that a passing fox carries off the kid. * * * A lion, an ass, and a fox went a-hunting, and on their return the king ordered the ass to apportion the spoil. The ass divided it carefully into three equal portions, which so enraged the lion that he devoured him on the spot, and ordered the fox to make a fresh partition. The fox put everything into one great heap as the king's "half," and kept only an accidental fragment of offal for himself, upon which the lion commended his art in division, and asked him where he had learnt it. "From the ass," replied the sycophant. * * * A great king, a lion asked a humble neighbour for a favour, which was granted on condition that the lion would dismiss his armed followers—have his teeth drawn in fact; and as soon as he had consented, the humble neighbour whipped the king off his premises. * * * The lion is represented as afraid of the crowing of the cock—the awaking of the people; as putting himself to great trouble to catch a mouse that had annoyed him ; as the dupe of councillors, and as being constantly overmatched by his subjects.

These fables, therefore, and a hundred others, are not written to dignify the royalty of the lion among the beasts, but to depreciate royalty among men under the symbol of a lion—an animal that has a majestic aspect and noble antecedents, but is both tyrannical and mean, mutton-headed and stealthy. His friends are always the cunning, and his natural enemies the courageous. The poets, however (of course), entirely misunderstand these parables of antiquity, and having often heard and read of "the King of Beasts," they invest the lion with all the insignia of monarchy. But the poets, until the nineteenth century, were as a class curiously and ludicrously ignorant of natural history, and more completely at discord with Nature generally, more unsympathetic, more imitative, and more incorrect, than could be supposed possible. So their championship of the lion goes for nothing, unless we are content to accept all their fictions in a lump together, and to think of bears ravaging sheepfolds, baboons swinging by their tails, and vultures chasing turtle-doves.

Not feared when wild. The travellers who seek a "lion-slayer's" fame are no less at fault, for they also misuse their facts. Other travellers on the same hunting-grounds have described the great cat to us too often to make the Bombastes Furioso of spurious adventures a reality. Instead of the huge beast standing erect on the plain in mid-day, and advancing with terrific roaring upon the hunter, every hair of the magnificent mane erect and the eyes flashing fire, we are introduced to a sulky cat that trots away round the corner on the first warning of man's approach, and which, so far from provoking conflict, takes advantage of every feature of the country that offers it concealment, or affords it a way of escape from its dreaded persecutor. The Dutchmen in Africa have named the districts in which this animal ranges, the Lion-veldt, and this is a splendid compliment. But they regard "the king of beasts" as a pest, and do not fear it as a danger, *A Voice.* while the natives reverence it as *a voice*, and a terrible one, but *præterea nihil*. It was for this same majesty of voice, that Ali the Caliph was named the Lion of Allah. In the "Pilgrim's Progress" it was the *sound* of the lions that first terrified Faithful and his party, for we are told it had "a hollow voice of roaring;" and it was the same roaring that frightened poor Thisbe to her death. Perhaps, then, after all, it is with beasts as it is often with men, that he who roars loudest and oftenest is counted the best in the crowd, and that the lion's only claim to kingship is in the power of his lungs. If this be so, we can only say, with the Duke in the play, " Well roared, lion."

*   *   *   *   *

Another large cat is called " the tiger." It is not a *The Tiger.* suitable kind to make a nursery pet of, for its tastes are unreliable.

This reminds me to make a digression, and to say that I think it almost a pity that the beasts in the Zoological Gardens cannot be admitted to a share of Christmas *Christmas* festivity. *in the Zoo.*

During the holidays, of course, there are larger crowds than usual to feed the bears and the elephant, and it may be that something of a Christmas flavour, arising from extra currants, may be imparted to the broken cates with which the animals are regaled by visitors. But one currant does not make a Christmas, and the creatures in the Zoo must be less intelligent than men and women think them if they do not remark the fortuitous and inadequate character of these preparations for their delectation at this season of general merrymaking. You shall observe, too, that though the fragmentary bun may have an unusually festive flavour, the number of umbrellas also is unusually great ; and if there is anything in the world calculated to sour a wild beast's Christmas, it is perpetual prodding with umbrellas.

A certain air of gaiety, no doubt, is imparted to a hyæna

by making it jump suddenly and variously with thrusts of an umbrella, but the hyæna, nevertheless, is not really gay. It is saddest when it jumps.

Nor can the observant bear have failed to note that on these public holidays the edible morsels which he receives bear no proportion to the indigestible, that empty match-boxes predominate over sponge-cakes, and that corks come to the surface more readily than biscuits. On the whole, therefore, they do not care for public holidays. They think them deleterious to the popular *morale.* But this need not be always thus. We have forcibly invited all these birds and beasts and snakes to come together as our guests, and it is hardly fair, when subjecting them to the cramping exigencies of civilization, not to expand their simple minds with its generous influences also. We inflict upon them many details of daily life which are quite foreign to their characters and tastes, forbidding them to fight each other, to roam abroad or to sleep when they are inclined, and it would only be just if, on the other hand, we allowed them to participate in the more pleasurable features of civilized society. The monkeys, for instance, would be delighted with a Christmas tree, and provided there were no lighted tapers the amusement might be as innocent as gratifying. Imagine the tailed folk gamboling among the branches of the festive shrub, or sitting secluded to pull the complimentary cracker! A generous distribution of mince-pies would help to impress the memory of the highday very pleasantly upon nearly all the smaller mammals. The bears would be at home with a plum pudding, and when snapdragons came on, the salamanders would be "all there." Indeed, a Christmas dinner for the animals at the Zoo, is quite a legitimate direction for kind-hearted efforts, and though the majority of them might not care for puddings and pies, there are few who would not appreciate the beef.

Among the cats, for instance, it would be quite useless to offer to take the jaguars to the pantomime or to send Christmas cards to the leopards. The panther does not care much for holly and mistletoe; and, unless he might eat a few of them, the tiger sees no merit in the "waits."

* * * * *

The Tiger not of a Festive Kind.

The tiger, indeed, would be a very difficult animal to make festive, for he is not of a merry-making kind. Sometimes, it is true, he diverts himself, but it is in a grim way. Artemus Ward had a tiger, and he tells us of an attempt made by the Southerners to confiscate this animal, which was only very partially successful.

It may be remembered that he was travelling with his show, "actuated," as he tells us, "by one of the most loftiest desires that can swell the human bosom"— to give the people their money's worth by showing them "Sagashus Beests and Wax Statoos," and had arrived in the State of Alabama just before the outbreak of the war. The Northern flag flying over "that waterproof

N

pavilion wherein instruction and amusement had been so muchly combined at fifteen cents per head" exasperated the "Seseshers," and they went for the erection, crying, "Hang the bald-headed aberlitionist and bust up his immoral exhibition." They "confisticated" the statues by smashing them, and then "confisticated" the loose change in the money-box. "They then," says Artemus, "went and bust in my cages, lettin' all the animals loose, a small but helthy tiger among the rest. This tiger always had a excentric way of tearin' dogs to peaces, and I always 'sposed from his gineral conduct that he'd have no hesitashun in serving human bein's in the same way if he could git at them. Excuse me if it was crooil, but I larfed boysterrussly when I see that tiger spring among the crowd. . . . I can't say for certain that the tiger serisly injured any of them, but as he was seen a few days after, sum miles distant, with a large and well-selected assortment of seats of trousers in his mouth, and as he looked as tho' he had bin having sum vilent exercise, I rayther guess he did. You will therefore perceive that they didn't confisticate him much."

No non-sense about Tigers. There is no nonsense about the tiger as there is about the lion. He is not an impostor. Wolves may go about, pretending that they are only dogs that have had the misfortune of a bad bringing up, and the lion may swagger round, trying to look as if he were something else than a cat; but the tiger never descends to such prevarication setting himself up for better than he is, or claiming respect for qualities which he does not possess. There is no ambiguity about anything he does. All his character is on the surface. " I am," he says, " a thoroughgoing, downright wild beast, and, if you don't like me, you may lump me ; but, in the meanwhile, you had better get out of my way." There is no pompous affectation of superior " intelligence " about the tiger, no straining after a false reputation for " magnanimity." If he is met with in a jungle, he does not make-believe for the purpose of impressing the traveller with his uncommon sagacity, or waste time like the lion in superfluous roaring, shaking of manes, and " looking kingly." On the contrary, he behaves honestly and candidly, like the beast he is. He either retires precipitately with every confession of alarm, or, in his own fine outspoken fashion, " goes for " the stranger. Nor, when he makes off, does he do it as if he liked it, wasting his time in pretentious attitudes, or in trying to save appearances. He has no idea of showing off. If he has to go he goes, like lightning, and does not think for a moment of the figure he is cutting. But if, on the other hand, he means fighting, he gives the stranger very little leisure for misunderstanding his intentions. The tiger, therefore, deserves to be considered a model wild beast, and to be held in respect accordingly. He knows his station and keeps it, doing the work that Nature has given him to do with all his might.

The result of this honesty is that no one misrepresents the tiger. Exaggerated praise and slander are alike impossible of an animal that refuses to be misjudged. There is no opening for dishonest description, for he is always in the same character; no scope for romancing about a beast that is so consistently practical, or for fable when he does nothing in parables. Moreover, most of the other beasts play a second part in the world, and have a moral significance, like the creatures grouped about Solomon's throne, or the standard-emblazonments of the tribes of Israel, or the armorial bearings of families and nations, or the badges of the Apostles. But no one uses the tiger in this way as a metaphor. There is not sufficient subtlety in the emblem. It is too coarse, too downright. A tiger is a tiger, and nothing more or less. Once only it was made a Royal emblem—by Tippoo, the Sultan of Mysore—but then professedly out of mere brutal ferocity. In the same vein that amiable prince constructed a mechanical toy, now in the South Kensington collection, which represented a tiger, life-size, mumbling the body of an English soldier; and when the machinery was in proper order, the tiger growled and the soldier groaned with considerable power. But Mr. John Bright, so they say, finding time heavy on his hands during the Sultan's ball, amused himself with Tippoo's toy, and, by overwinding the machine, broke it. At any rate, the tiger goes through his growling performances now in a very perfunctory and feeble manner.

For the same reason, namely, that the tiger affords no room for the play of fancy, the poets prefer "leopards" to tigers. There is more left to the imagination in the sound of the smaller animal's name, and as it is not so well known as the tiger, they have wider margin for poetical licence. The moralist, for a similar reason, avoids the tiger, for no amount of ingenuity will extract a moral out of its conduct.

In short, then, the tiger may be taken as the supreme *A supreme type.* type of the pure wild beast. Life has only one end for him—enjoyment; and to this he gives all his magnificent energies. Endowed with superb capabilities, he exercises them to the utmost in this one direction, without ever forgetting for an instant that he is only a huge cat, or flying in the face of Nature by pretending to be anything else.

Speed, strength, and cunning are his in a degree to which in the same combination no other animal can lay claim; in daring none exceed him, while for physical beauty he has absolutely no rival. A tiger has been known to spring over a wall five feet high into a cattle enclosure, and to jump back again with a full-grown animal in its jaws, and has been seen to leap, holding a bullock, across a wide ditch. As regards its speed, the first bounds of a tiger are so rapid as to bring it alongside the antelope; while for strength, a single blow of its paw will stun a charging bull. Its stealth may be illustrated by the anecdote of the tiger carrying away the bait while the sportsmen were actually busy putting up the shelters from which they intended to shoot it " when it came ;" and its daring, by the fact that numbers do not appal it, that it will single out and carry off a man out of the middle of a party, and that it regularly helps itself to cattle in broad daylight, in full sight of the herdsmen or the whole village. I have not gone for my illustrations to any traveller's tale, but to records of Indian shikar that are absolutely beyond suspicion. To enable it to achieve such feats as these Nature has created in the tiger the very ideal of brute symmetry and power. The paws, moreover, are fitted with large soft pads which enable this bulky animal to move without a rustle over ground where the lizard can hardly stir without being heard, while its colouring, though it seems conspicuous enough when seen in Regent's Park behind bars and against a background of whitewash, assimilates with astonishing exactness to its surroundings when the tiger lies in ambush under the overhanging roots or crouches amongst the cane-grass.

The Tiger not Quixotic. For the tiger makes no pretence to invincible courage. On the contrary, he prefers, as a rule, to enjoy life rather than die heroically. When death is inevitable he is always heroic, or even when danger presses him too closely. But, if he can, he avoids the unequal contest between brute courage and explosive shells, and makes off at once for more sequestered woodlands, where he can reign supreme and be at ease. It is indeed a splendid life that this autocrat of the jungle leads. The day commences for him as the sun begins to set, and he then stalks from his lair to drink at the neighbouring pool, after which, his thirst slaked, he creeps out towards the glade where the deer are feeding. The vigilant, restless herd has need now for all its acuteness of ear and nostril, but it will certainly be unavailing, for the tiger is hungry, and, his prey once sighted, there is no gainsaying him. Using all the craft of his kind, the great cat steals upon his victims with consummate patience, *Its Plea-* and in such silence that even the deer have no suspicion *sures.* how swiftly that stealthy death is approaching. It is like being killed by a shadow or a ghost, for not a sound of moving leaf or breaking twig, has given them warning ; and yet, all on a sudden, right in their midst it may be, there is an instant's swaying of the grass, and, lo ! the tiger.

The next instant he is flying through the air in a terrific bound, and as the herd sweeps away down the glade, one of their number is left behind, and is already dead.

The tyrant eats what he wants, and then strolls back into the jungle, indolently, and, so to speak, in good humour with all the world. We can then imagine him stalking a company of sambhur " in fun," and afterwards see him standing up alone in the open space, laughing grimly, shaking his sides at the joke, as the antlered creatures fly terrified before his form revealed ; or we may watch him insolently stretching himself in the full moonlight upon the ground near the favourite drinking pool, and daring all the beasts of the jungle to slake their thirst there so long as he remains. What strange wild scenes he must witness in the grey morning, as the world begins to wake up to life and the night-feeding things go back to their lairs—with the bears shuffling along in good-humoured company, the slinking wolves, and the careless trotting boars; and the multitude of smaller creatures, furred and feathered, going out for the work of the day, or coming home tired with the work of the night.

Its Perils. Nor is his life without brilliant episodes of excitement, for apart from the keen triumphs that he enjoys whenever he seeks his food, there are thrilling intervals in each recurring summer when the hunt is equipped for his destruction, with all the pomp of marshalled elephants and an army of beaters.

The heat of May has scorched up the covert and the water, except in a few pools where a fringe of vegetation still lingers and the tiger can still find a midday lair. Here the hunters seek him, and, whether we look at the quarry they pursue or the picturesque surroundings of the day's excitement, it must be confessed that tiger-shooting has no rival in all the range of sport. Even if no tiger is seen, if the elephant grass is beaten in vain, and the coverts of cane-clump and rustling reed are drawn without a glimpse of the great striped beast, there is such a multitude of incidents in the day's adventure that it is never a blank. As the drive comes on towards the ambushed rifles, the park-like glades that stretch away to right and left are never wanting in animal life. The pea-fowl and the wild pig, the partridges and grouse of several kinds, are all afoot, hurrying along before the advancing line. The jackals sneak from brake to brake, and, pacing out of the jungle that marks the watercourse, come the swamp deer and the noble sambhur. Here a wolf breaks cover sullenly, looking back over his shoulder as he goes, in the direction of the shouting beaters. There a bear goes by complaining of his rest disturbed. The monkey-folk come swinging along in a tumult of the foliage overhead, and small creatures of the civet kind with an occasional hare or wild cat, slip by, all wondering at the uproar—but all unmolested alike. For the honour of death is reserved to-day for the tiger only, and he, as a rule, is the last of all the denizens of the jungle to allow his repose to be broken, or to confess that he is alarmed. But even he has eventually to admit that this advancing line of noisy men means danger, and so he retires before them, creeping from clump to clump with consummate skill. Yet the swaying tassels of the tall plumed grass betray his moving, and on a sudden he finds himself in the ambush laid for him, and from the tree above him or from some overhanging rock the sharp cracks of the rifle proclaim that the tyrant of the jungle is dead.

When the tiger is followed up with elephants, fresh elements of adventure and picturesqueness are added to the day's sport—but the theme is an old one. The fact, however, remains that whatever the method employed for encompassing his death, or wherever he may be found, the tiger proves himself a splendid beast. If he can, he will avoid the unfair contest with bullet and shell ; but let him only have his chance and he shows both man and elephant how royally he can defend his jungle realm against them.

Its terrible Cry. His voice, it has been contended, is not regal. To dispute this one has only to go to Regent's Park, where though the lion's roar may be the loudest, the tiger's is not less terrific. Nor when he is heard roaming abroad in the jungles in the night can anything be imagined more terribly weird or unnatural than his utterances.

He has found, perhaps, that a pack of wild dogs—voiceless hunters of the forest—are crossing his path ; and his angry protest delivered in rapid, startling coughs is certainly among the most terrifying sounds of Nature, while nothing can surpass the utter desolation that seems to possess the night when the tiger passes along the jungle to his lair with his long-drawn, whining yawn. The lion's roar is, of course, unapproachable in its grandeur, but the tiger compresses into a cough and a yawn such an infinity of cruelty and rage, such unfathomable depths of fierce wild-beast nature as cannot be matched in forest languages.

Man-eating tigers, and, even more, man-eating tigresses have always commanded among human beings a certain awful respect. Nor is this to be wondered at in

India, when each year's returns tell us that about a thousand persons perish annually by these brutes. When, there- *The poor old Man-eater.* fore, to the word " tiger "—itself a synonym in every lan- guage, civilized or savage, for stealthy, cruel, strong-limbed ferocity—is prefixed the aggravating epithet of "man-eating," the imagination prepares itself for the worst, and the great carnivore stalks past, in the mind's eyes, a very compendium of horrors, bearing about with it on its striped hide a Newgate calendar of its many iniquities. But is it not just possible that the sensitiveness of huma- nity with regard to itself and all that pertains to its own security and dignity may have exaggerated the terrors of "the man-eater"? A lion-eating tiger would in reality be quite as fearful a thing as one that, with toothless jaws and unnerved limbs, falls upon miserable men and women; but a lion-eating tiger would not be considered an abominable monster. We should speak of it as a wise dispensation of Nature for keeping the equilibrium among the carnivora, as a respectable and commendable beast that apologized for and justified its own existence by killing something else as noxious as itself—just as the cockroach has retained some shreds of reputation by eating mosquitoes. But alas for the tiger! the day *Exiled from its own Jungles.* comes when the wretched animal is so ill-conditioned that its kith and kin will not admit its relationship, and drive it forth; so feeble that the wild pig turns upon it and mocks it; so slow of foot that everything escapes from it; so old that its teeth fall out and its claws splinter ; and, in this pitiful state, it has to go far a-field for food.   It has to leave the jungles it has lorded it over for so many years ; the pleasant pools to which, in the evening, the doomed stag used to lead his hinds to water; the great beds of reed and grass in which, lazily basking, it heard the thoughtless buffaloes come grazing to their fate, crushing down the tall herbage as they sauntered on : the deep coverts of bamboo and under-growth where the nylghai reposed his unwieldy bulk ; the grand rock-strewn lair, whither he and his tigress used to drag the carcases that were to feed their cubs.

But where is he to go in his old age ? He must eat to live, but what hope is there for such as he to earn an honest meal ? With the best intentions possible, no one would believe him.   His mere appearance in a vil-lage suffices to empty it of all but the bedridden.   What is he to do ? If the headmen of the village would only stay and hear what he had to say, the tiger, it may be, would explain his conduct satisfactorily, and thencefor-ward might go decently, like any other hungry wretch, from hamlet to hamlet, with a begging-dish in his mouth.

Here, again, society is against him. In India the peo-ple do not eat meat—not enough of it, at any rate, to satisfy a tiger on their leavings—and to offer an empty tiger parched grain and vegetable marrows wherewith to fill itself is to mock the animal and to trifle with its ten-derest feelings.   So the tiger, despairing of assistance or even sympathy, looks about him in the deserted village, and, finding an old bedridden female in a hut, helps himself to her and goes away, annoyed, no doubt, at her toughness, but all the same, poor easy beast, glad of the meal.

Perhaps it is such a one as this that was caught not long ago by a Baboo, one Rameshwar Prasad, in a pit, and is now comfortably lodged and boarded at the expense of the Zoological Gardens in Regent's Park. A man-eating tiger that would fall into a pit could hardly have been in the enjoyment of the full complement of its senses ; and when, having tumbled like a sack of potatoes into the hole, we hear that it did not jump out again, but permitted itself to be tied up and carted away, we must confess that something of the awesome terrors attaching by tradition to the anthropophagous cat fall away from it. An average sheep would have behaved with more spirit.

Meanwhile, it does not detract from the gallantry of the capture, or the originality of the conception, that the tiger should have behaved so tamely. For the Baboo there can be only one feeling of respectful admiration. It would not occur to every one to dig a hole for a tiger, and sit by with a rope. Pits have, of course, often been used to compass the deaths of wild beasts ; but then they were generally furnished with spikes to receive the falling body, and rifles were ready to despatch the captured brute. The Baboo, however, did not want to hurt his tiger ; he wished merely to catch the specimen and send it to England—and he did it. That the successful sports-

How a Bengalee Baboo caught a Tiger.

man should have been a Bengalee is a healthy sign, for the Bengalees do not often affect such stirring scenes. Indeed, when Sir George Campbell, then Lieutenant-Governor of Bengal, insisted on all native candidates for the Civil Service qualifying in " equitation," the Bengalee Baboos petitioned against the addition of such a danger-ous pastime as riding on horses being added to the col-legiate course, and gravely adduced, in support of their plea, that no one ever expected Bengalees to be brave. As a matter of fact, very few in India ever do, be they European or native, and every instance, therefore, like the present helps to remove from a nation of some thirty millions the absurd, because general, charge of cowar-dice. For his exploit, so creditable to himself, so dis-creditable to the tiger, the Baboo had some precedents, for the terror of the jungles has often, from pure rashness, stumbled into ridiculous positions with fatal consequences. Whether it is true that two British sailors once caught a tiger by tempting him into a barrel, and then, having pulled his tail through the bung-hole, tying a knot in it, I do not undertake to decide. But that a tiger has been taken prisoner in a blanket is beyond dispute, as also that a tiger, having thrust its head through a wicker crate which was filled with ducks, could not withdraw it, and in this ignominious plight, with the ducks making a prodigious noise all the while, blundered about the camp until, getting among the horses, it was kicked to death. Tigers have choked themselves by trying to swallow frogs, and in single combat with smaller animals been shamefully defeated.

Thus, a man-eating tiger of immense proportions, *How a* at one time the pride of the Calcutta collection, was *Sheep killed* killed under circumstances that covered it with ridicule. *a Tiger.* It happened that a fighting ram belonging to a soldier in one of the regiments cantoned in the neighbourhood, became so extremely troublesome that the colonel ordered it to be sent to " the Zoological Gardens." Yet there it was as troublesome as ever, and being no curiosity, though excellent mutton, it was decided to give it to the great tiger. So ferocious was this creature supposed to be that it had a specially constructed cage, and its food was let down through a sliding grating in the roof. Down this, accordingly, the ram was lowered. The tiger was dozing in the corner, but when it saw the mutton descend, it rose and, after a long sleepy yawn, began to stretch itself. Meanwhile, the ram, who had no notion that he had been put there to be eaten, was watching the monster's lazy preparations for his meal with the eye of an old gladiator, and seeing the tiger stretch himself, supposed the fight was commencing. Accordingly he stepped nimbly back to the farthest corner of the cage —just as the tiger, of course, all along expected he would do—and then—*which the tiger had not in the least expected* – put down his head and went straight at the striped beast. The old tiger had not a chance from the first, and, as there was no way of getting the ram out again, the agonized owners had to look on while the sheep killed the tiger !

Nor are such instances at all uncommon. Old cows have gored them, village dogs have worried them, horses have kicked their ribs to fragments, and even man himself, the proper lawful food of the man-eating tiger, has turned upon his consumer, and beaten him off with a stick. When a tiger can thus be set at naught by his supper, he hardly deserves all the reverent admiration with which tradition and story-books have invested him, and which an untravelled public has superstitiously entertained towards him.

"Generally speaking," says Dr. Jerdon, a great authority on Indian zoology, " the Bengal tiger is a harmless, timid animal "—very much like a rabbit, in fact. "When once it takes to killing man it almost always perseveres in its endeavours to procure the same food, and, in general, it has been found that very old tigers, whose teeth are blunted or gone, and whose strength has failed, are those that relish human food, finding an easy prey.

Toothless old Tigers. Now, I would contend, there is no malignity here. The picture, indeed, is a pathetic one. Content, so long as it had good eyesight and sound teeth, to hunt wild beasts, the tiger, at an age when comfort and idleness should have been its lot, is compelled, poor wretch, to quit its natural haunts for the highways of men and their habitations. Its life becomes now a terror to itself, and the very quest for food is no longer the supreme pleasure it was in the days when it flashed like a streak of flame from its ambush upon the stately sambhur, or stalked with consummate skill the wary bison, and then, plunging upon the great beast, bore it to the ground by the terrific impetus of its spring, and stunned it into beef with one tremendous blow. In those strong, fierce days, its roar silenced the many-voiced jungle; but now, as it creeps among the growing crops, or lurks in the shadow of the village wall, it has to hold its breath, lest a sound should betray it into danger. For everything is now a peril to it, even a company of unarmed men, or a pack of village curs, or a herd of kine. So it lays its helpless old body close along the ditch, where some weeds suffice to hide its terror-striking appearance, once its pride but now its ruin, and waits by the pathway for some returning villager, man, woman, or child, some belated goat or wandering calf. To be sure of its dinner it must be certain there will be no resistance, and every meal is, therefore, snatched with anxiety and fear. To such a life of degradation and shame does the splendid quadruped descend, and, if only because it puts a period to the sufferings of toothless old age, the destruction of man-eating tigers is commendable. But to the highly sympathetic mind more admirable still is it when a humane Baboo digs a hole for the beast, and, having tied it up with ropes, ships it to England.

Here, in the bosom of the Society, the degraded animal

o

finds an asylum and easy feeding; and, under Dr. Schlater's careful keeping, its declining years glide by, exempted from all harsh influences, in the comfortable almshouses for decrepid, but deserving, carnivora in Regent's Park. Here fallen majesty need fear no insult from contemptuous wild pig, and no longer need resort to shameful artifices to catch old women and little boys. Blinking behind his bars, the man-eater seems even to have forgotten that his human captors are edible : and not to be behind him in generosity let us also forget that he has ever eaten any of our species. Forgive and Forget.

"The lesser carnivora, as they are called, play a very important part in the political system of the beasts. They are the great feudatory princes and independent barons of the wild world.

*Cat-
princes.* Claiming kinship with royalty, they possess within their respective earldoms all the privileges of independent sovereigns and the powers of life and death. At the head of fierce clans they defy the central authority, and retiring within their own demesnes maintain there almost regal state. Such are the puma, jaguar, leopard, and panther.

The puma, indeed, calls itself "the lion" in South America; the leopard "the tiger" among the Zulus and throughout South Africa; and the panther is "the tiger" of Ceylon. But of these four furred princes, the jaguar rises most nearly to the standard of royalty, and it is certainly, both in appearance and the circumstances of its life, a splendid cat.

Unaccustomed to being annoyed, travellers see him *The Jaguar.* in broad daylight lying stretched out at full length on the soft turf, under the shade of some Amazonian tree, thoroughly careless of danger, because so completely unused to being attacked. The explorer's boat passing along the river does not make him do more than raise his head, for the river is not in his own domain. It belongs to the cayman and the manatee, and it is their business, not his, to see to the boat. Wherever he goes, animal life is so abundant that he finds no trouble in securing food, and, like the negroes of the Seychelles, he grows, from pure laziness and full feeding, sleek, large-limbed, and heavy. His coat becomes strangely glossy, soft, and close; the colours on it deepen and grow rich in sumptuous shades of velvety chestnut, brown and black; his limbs thicken, his body plumps out, and his jaws assume the full sensual contour characteristic of tropical man. He moves along with a lounging gait, often resting as he goes, and his eyes, as he turns his head incuriously to this side or to that, are large and soft and lustrous, while his voice, when he takes the trouble to warn away an incautious peccary or indiscreet capybara, is rich and low in tone. In every aspect, in fact, the jaguar presents himself to the mind as a pampered child of Nature, the representative in the beast world of the creole and negro of the Seychelles. In those wondrous islands the black man spends his day in utter idleness, lying on the white sea-beach or under the breadfruit trees, smoking the cigars his wife makes, watching the big fish chasing the little ones in the lagoon, or his fowls scratching among the wild melon beds. When he is hungry his wife goes down to the sea and catches a fish, one of his children plucks a pile of plantains and shakes down the green cocoanuts, and thus, indolent and full fed, he grows, like the jaguar, sleek and strong with glossy skin and huge limbs.

The Puma. The puma is a companion of the jaguar, but they seldom meet, for mutual respect defines for them their respective domains, and neither cares to trespass on the other. Nature has been equally kind to both, but the puma is of a restless temperament, and neither the abundance of food nor the temptations of the Brazils to idleness are enough to damp its energy. There is something of the immigrant and colonist about it. It is perpetually in quest of adventure or work to do, climbing about among the interwoven foliage, or prowling among the brushwood of more open country. Its one great object in life seems to be the chase, for the sport's sake, for it kills far more than it can ever eat, and often indeed does not attempt to consume its prey. This has given the puma a character for ferocity in works of natural history which its appearance in a cage would hardly justify, for its comfortable fur and sleek limbs might be thought to belong to a gentler creature.

The leopard and panther are to the east what the *Leopards and Panthers.* jaguar and puma are to the west; and their lives, whether we consider the kindliness of Nature to them or their strange immunity from harm, are equally to be envied. They live, it is true, within the empire of the tiger, but only as in the days of the Heptarchy the Mercian or the Northumbrian prince would have called himself "within the realm" of the Bretwalda; or as, in the early days of France, the Dukes of Soissons or of Burgundy were "subject" to Paris; or earlier still only as Acarnania or Locris confessed the hegemony of Sparta. There is respect on both sides, and therefore a large measure of peace within the earldoms and duchies of the big cats.

The domesticated cat is an animal that can be best *The Common or Garden Cat.* approached sideways. Direct description, that is to say, does not bring out its peculiarities quite so well as the oblique form, which throws slanting lights upon the subject. To illustrate my meaning, let us take that frivolous proposition of our neighbours across the Channel to impose a tax upon cats; and following it out, note how the character of the animal developes itself by incidence.

How the tax is to be collected no senator dares to *Absurd proposal to tax Cats.* explain, and when the project comes to the touchstone of practice we may confidently expect it to fall through. For the difficulties in the way of the collection of such a tax are immense. It is true they are not all on the surface, and so the impost may at the first glance pass as plausible ; but, in reality, it would be hardly less easy to assess the householder on the mice that might infest his kitchen, or the sparrows that hop about on his window-sill, than upon the vagabond grimalkins that may choose to "squat" upon his premises. Putting on one side, however, the fact that both the social and the domestic systems would be shaken to their foundations by the exaction of such a duty—that every cook would be set in opposition to her master by being called upon to pay the tax or dismiss her cat—there remains this one great difficulty to a successful collection of a tax on cats, that no one would pay it. Some few eccentric persons—those, for instance, who pay "conscience money"—would, no doubt, come forward to be mulcted, but the vast majority of ratepayers would simply disclaim possession of cats, and throw the onus of proof upon the rate-collectors. "*My* cat !" the landlady would say to him, feigning astonishment, "Bless you, that's not *my* cat ! It came in quite promiscuous one night, and I have been trying ever since to drive it away. If you don't believe me, sir, you can take it away with you now."

Under the circumstances, what could a collector, with ordinary human feelings, say or do? Is he to throw discredit upon a respectable person's statement, supported, moreover, by her unmistakable sincerity in offering the cat there and then to the representative of Government, by assessing her in spite of her protests ?

Moreover, if the landlady, before his very eyes, should

proceed to hunt the cat out of her parlour, should, farther, chase it downstairs into the kitchen with a duster,
thence through the scullery into the back garden, and,
not content with that, pursue it even to the uttermost
angle of the garden wall, so that it should be entirely off
her premises, the collector's position would be greatly
aggravated—for what more could a person do than this to
prove that their was no conspiracy in the matter, no
attempt at fraudulent evasion of a legal demand? It is
true that, if she were of a nimble kind, the landlady might
prosecute her chase even farther, and not desist until
she had seen pussy fairly out of the parish ; but it
surely has not come to this, in a free England, too,
that elderly ladies must satisfy tax-collectors by such
violent exercise, to the detriment of their domestic and
other duties, or, because a minion of the law insists upon
it that wherever a cat is to be found there it is to be
taxed, that females of all ages, delicately nurtured it may
be, or otherwise incapacitated from rapid pursuit of animals, are to be set running about the streets and climbing trees, in order to rid themselves of importunate cats !
The idea is preposterous.

Here, indeed, I have touched the very heart of the *Cats Vaga-*
difficulty, for a cat does not of necessity belong to the *bond rather*
place where she is found. Cats, in fact, belong to no- *Domestic.*
where in particular. They are called "domestic," I know,
but they are really not so at all. They come inside houses
for warmth, and because saucers with milk in them are

more often found in houses than on garden walls, or in the
roads, or up in trees ; because street boys do not go about
throwing stones in houses, and because there are no idle
dogs there, looking round corners for something to hunt.

Besides, when it rains it is dry inside a house, as compared with out of doors, and sleep can be more comfortably arrived at in the daytime under a kitchen dresser
than in such exposed and draughty spots as the roofs of
outhouses or under the bushes in the garden of the
square. The cat, therefore, comes into our midst from
motives of pure self-interest alone, joins the domestic
circle simply for the sake of the comforts it affords her,
and seats herself upon our particular hearth and home
only because she finds herself warm there and safe.

But at heart she is a vagabond, a tramp, and a gipsy.
She is always " on the patter." Our dwelling-places are
really only so many casual wards to her, and she looks
upon the basement floor of our houses as a fortuitous but
convenient combination of a municipal soup-kitchen and
a charitable lying-in hospital. When homeless she does
not drown herself in despair, or go and buy poison from
a chemist, and kill herself. On the contrary, she avoids
water with all the precaution possible, even so much as a
puddle on the pavement, and carefully sniffs everything
she sees lying about before she thinks of trying to eat it.

Nor does she, in desperation, go and steal something off
a stall, in order to get locked up in shelter for the night,
for she has instincts that teach her to avoid the coarse

expedients with which homeless and starving humanity has so often to make such pathetic shift. The cat's plan is the simplest possible. She merely walks along the street as far as the first area gate, and, to guard against passing dogs, puts herself at once on the right side of the railings. Here she sits until the back-door opens, and as soon as she sees a domestic coming out she mews plaintively. If the domestic says "Shoo" to her, she *Cat's* shoos at once, for she understands that there is one *Artifices.* cat already in the house. But she only goes next door, and there repeats her manœuvre. The odds are that the next kitchen-maid does not say "shoo" to her, but only calls out to somebody else inside, "Here's a cat on the airy steps, a-mewing like anything." The adventurer, meanwhile, has got up and, still mewing, rubs herself suggestively on the gatepost, arching up her back and leaning very much on one side—to show, no doubt, that she has no other visible means of support. The kitchen-maid duly reports the cat's proceedings, and some original-minded domestic at once hazards the suggestion that "the poor thing has lost hisself." This bold hypothesis is at once accepted as satisfying all the conditions of the problem, and ultimately, from one guileful gesture to another, the cat is found at last rubbing herself—still very much out of the perpendicular and still mewing—against the cook's skirts in front of the kitchen fire.

A cat has as keen an instinct for a cook as a policeman *Its Instinct* has, and makes straight for her. A strange dog, they say, *for Cooks.*

will find out the master of a house at once, and immediately attach itself to him. The cat, however, does not trouble herself about such superficial differences of position as these, but goes without hesitation to the great dispenser of creature comforts—*the cook.* Masters, she says, are untrustworthy; they come and go, and in some houses do not even exist at all; but the kitchen fire is a fixed star, and the cook a satellite that may always be depended upon to be found revolving in her proper orbit. She attaches herself, therefore, to this important domestic at once, and forthwith becomes "our cat."

Yet she is only "our cat" as distinguished from "the cat next door." In no other sense is she ours at all. The chances are that the master of the house does not even know that there is such an animal on the establishment. Upon one occasion, certainly, he remembers rudely expelling a cat, more in anger than in sorrow, which he found in the library; but he had no idea, probably, that it was a pensioner of his household, and a recognized retainer. Now, how can such a man be called upon to pay a tax on a cat? The animal, by every one's confession, quartered itself by guile upon the premises, and belongs to nobody. The cook says it can "go" (for she knows very well that it will immediately come back again), and even the tax-collector could hardly, under the circumstances of a general disclaimer, persist in assessing the little animal. As I have already pointed out, therefore, the presence of a cat in a house does not imply ownership in the householder, for it would be just as fair to infer from the presence of a tea-party of cats in a back garden that they all "belonged" to the contiguous house. A cat is "at home" nowhere, for she makes herself at home everywhere. All workhouses are much the same to paupers. It is very difficult, therefore, to see how the collector will collect his tax. His alternatives will be equally disagreeable, for he must either refuse to believe what he is told on oath by every person he calls upon, or else he must remove the cats. For this purpose he would have to go about accompanied by some conveyance not smaller in size than a Pickford van or an omnibus, for any ordinary square would supply enough cats to fill a large vehicle. And, when he has got them, what will he do with them ? Cats cannot be impounded—except in a well, and even then it would be necessary to keep the lid down. Nor would it be permissible in these days of advanced humanity to destroy them by cremation in the "Queen's Pipe," as if they were so much contraband tobacco, nor could they be served out to the parochial authorities for the sustenance of the aged poor. No decent person would consent to be a pauper and to live in a workhouse under conditions that involved cat soup. The question, in fact, is beset with immense difficulties ; for one of two things must happen wherever the tax-collector calls—either injustice must be perpetrated upon the householder, or the law be brought into contempt. Now, if some plan could be devised for ascertaining precisely whose cats they are that always pass the nights in such melancholy hilarity in their neighbours' gardens, and if these particular cats could be either heavily taxed or carted off—say, to the Welsh mountains—Government, I feel sure, and I speak for myself at all events, might depend upon the hearty co-operation of the public. As the project stands at present, however, a universal cat-tax appears to me impossible.

Looking for Lost Cats. As another sidelong illustration of cat character, let us take the case of the gentleman found "looking for a lost cat" at one in the morning in a neighbour's till—a proceeding which may be called, at any rate, curious. Whether he was really doing so or not, the magistrate before whom the case came had to decide for himself. The narrative itself is sufficient for my present purpose. Mr. James Cartwright, aged twenty-one, was charged at a metropolitan Police-court, with breaking into a house at midnight, and stealing a gold mourning ring and twenty-six shillings, for after an exciting chase over the roofs of several outbuildings he had been caught, and the stolen property above referred to was found upon him. Mr. Cartwright, in explanation of his position, said that he was looking for a cat which he had lost. The simplicity of the defence is charming, and the readiness with which it was offered no less admirable, for it is one of the virtues of thought that it should be rapid, and one of the essentials in a hypothesis that it should be simple. Mr. Cartwright's mind must have flashed to its decision on the instant, and the only hypothesis that could possibly have covered all the suspicious circumstances—the hour of his capture, the position on the roof of an outbuilding, the headlong scramble over adjoining premises—was at once off his tongue. *He was looking for a cat.*

What more natural, he would ask, than that puss should have gone out at night, should have been on the roof of an outbuilding, and should have tried to elude capture by hasty flight over other roofs? Mr. Cartwright, no doubt, was much attached to his little friend—I can hardly call a cat a "dumb" companion—and, having missed it from the hearth, braved the discomforts of the night air, by going forth to seek it in its favourite haunts, which with cats are always a neighbour's premises. Failing to see it at the first cursory glance, he determined to go farther, but, apprehending resistance from the cat, he armed himself with an iron bar which a neighbouring rag-dealer used for securing a side door, and, the door happening to open, Mr. Cartwright, naturally enough, went into the house to look for his pet. In his pathetic anxiety he searched every place, whether probable or improbable—and eventually the till.

The sight of the money in it probably suggested to him the feasibility of bribing the cat to return, and he took sufficient for the purpose—twenty-six shillings—and in his then forlorn and disconsolate condition the mourning ring naturally occurred to him as an appropriate and becoming possession. Had he found the cat he would, no doubt, have restored the ring and the money too, and mended the door as well : but, unfortunately, before his object was accomplished, and at the moment of hottest pursuit after the vagabond animal, he was himself captured, and, the circumstances looking suspicious, (which it must be candidly admitted they did,) he was taken up and committed for trial.

Of an Evasive Kind. Looking for a cat at night requires good eyes, and might have been safely given to Hercules as an additional labour. For the cat is of an evasive kind. Its person is so inconsiderable that small holes suffice for its entrances and its exits, while a very trifling patch of shadow is enough to conceal a whole *soirée* of cats. Its feet, again, are so admirably padded that it makes no noise as it goes, and, having been born to habits of sudden and silent escape, it vanishes from the vision like a whiff of mist. Terrier dogs think the cat a mean animal, and they have some reason on their side, for the cat never scruples to profit by every possible advantage which nature or accident may offer. Not content with having actually escaped, it perches itself comfortably upon a branch or roof just out of the pursuer's reach, and while the latter, frantic with tantalizing hopes, is dancing on its hind legs beneath it, the cat pretends to go to sleep, and blinks blandly upon the gradually desponding acrobat. Grimalkin has always this nice consciousness of safety, and does only just sufficient to secure it, enjoying for the rest the pleasure of watching its baffled adversary. Instead of disappearing altogether from sight through the scullery window, the cat is content with squeezing through the area railings, and sitting on the window-sill in full view of the demented terrier, who can only thrust half his head through the bars, and stands there whimpering—"for the touch of a vanished cat and the sound of a puss that is still."

There is one more charge against the cat, that, though *Saddest* well cared for and well fed, she affects a homeless con- *when they* dition and, going out on the pantiles, foregathers with *trespass.* other vagabonds of her kind, and in their company indulges in the music of the future, expressive of many mixed emotions, but irregular and depressing.

Cats seem saddest when they trespass. At home they are silent, but entering a neighbour's premises they at once commence to confide their sorrows to the whole parish in melancholy dialogue, which in the morning are found to have been accompanied by violent saltations upon the flower-beds. Altogether, therefore, the cat out at night is one who deserves to be caught, and Mr. James Cartwright certainly had my sympathies in the object of his search. But for the means he employed to catch the cat it is impossible to entertain more than a very indifferent degree of respect. In the first place, he might have looked for his cat before one in the morning, which is an unconscionable hour to go running over the roofs of neighbours' outhouses. Nor in his search need he have wrenched off the iron bar which closed the rag-dealer's door, for it is not in evidence that his cat was of any extraordinary ferocity or proportions requiring so formidable a weapon of capture ; nor, again, need he have looked in the till for his cat. Landladies' cats, it is notorious, go into remarkable places, and sometimes demean themselves in a manner quite surprising in such small animals ; for they will play on the lodger's piano with dirty fingers, try on the lodger's bonnets, and eat prodigious quantities of the lodger's dessert, after taking the key of the chiffonnière out of the pocket of the dress that was hanging in the wardrobe in the bedroom. Mr. Cartwright's cat, however, does not appear to have been of this kind, and, unless its master meant to bribe the cat to return to him, all other methods failing, I do not see why he should have taken the twenty-six shillings. The mourning ring is more comprehensible, perhaps ; but, on the whole, there was a doubtful complexion about that cat-hunt which certainly justified the severe view which the magistrate took.

The Jungles of the Common Cat. The particular jungle which the domesticated cat frequents is called " the back garden." [2] There are large tracts of these still unreclaimed in London, for even in the midst of cities the human instinct turns to the soil and digs in it.

Spring, it is true, has lost much of its traditional

---

[2] This must not be confounded with "the Terai," in which tigers and other large cats are found.

honours in this age of business, and we keep no
Floralia. It is not that men have changed, but the
times—for who would not rather any day of July be taking
part in some great Feast of Flowers in the sunny country
side than doing his dull round of duty in the City?

In the spring time a vision of posied primroses dis-
tracts the mind from the honourable but unromantic
ledger, and over and above the rolling thunders of the
street traffic is heard the whisper of the young-leaved
trees and the nursery nonsense of the birds. But for the
splendid privilege of living in London the price must be
paid. And, after all, when the lagging holiday does come
round, and we find ourselves on river bank or sea cliff,
under rustling woods or out on the sweet-scented heather,
it is another pleasure added to our enjoyment that we
have had to wait so long for it.

Meanwhile, though we speak of ourselves as living "pent *Spring in*
up" in a labyrinth of masonry, there is country enough *London.*
scattered up and down it to satisfy for the time people of
moderate wishes, and to keep alive by art the remem-
brance of the pleasures of green places and bright flowers
which by-and-by we may enjoy in nature. It is not
only in our well-kept public parks, and in the gardens,
often very beautiful, of our squares and mansions, that
the memory and hope of Spring's delights are perpetuated
for us. The flower-markets and flower-shops, the little
gardens before suburban houses, with their lilacs just
coming into bloom, and almond-trees in full bridal glory,

P

the window-boxes filled with the painted darlings of the spring, and the trellised creepers lighting up all over with taper points of green, testify that the great city is not a mere "wilderness of bricks and mortar." The air, even though it be London air, is instinct with associations of the coming summer, and the children are clamouring to be off into the country; for, let cynics say what they will of the "usual severity" of May, the "blue-eyed banditti" of the household know that next month the hedges and meadows, the riverside and copse, will be filled with the delights and treasures which childhood holds from Nature in perpetual fief. But the adults cannot go away, for there is all the world's daily work to be done; yet in spring-time man is impelled by some irresistible force to confess himself in sympathy with the season, to do something, however little, to help on the year; and many thousands give expression to this feeling by "doing up the back garden."

"*My Summer in a Garden.*" (I have been reading one of the most delightful books ever written,[3] and if any fun has escaped into this chapter, I put forward no claim to it.)

Back gardens are sometimes given over to vegetables, and are then called "kitchen gardens." But a kitchen garden, I find, is chiefly valuable to a man because it teaches him patience and philosophy and the higher

[3] Have you read "My Summer in a Garden," by Charles Dudley Warner, and published in this country by Messrs. Sampson Low, Marston, and Co. ? If not, read it—and thank me.

virtues, leading directly to resignation. As a rule, it is not valuable to him on account of the produce it yields; for, in the majority of cases, vegetables and fruit can be bought cheaper and better than they can be grown. Yet, such is the strength of conviction that most people undertake a kitchen garden simply and solely for the purpose of raising edible vegetables, and not in the least for discipline. They sow *Back-gardening.* cabbages and carrots under the impression that, having done this, they will forthwith commence to eat those things more cheaply and of a better quality than hitherto, quite regardless of the fact that vegetables are falling in price every day, and that by the time their own plants have come up, been pricked out, and been daily weeded, watered, snailed, and caterpillared for a number of weeks, their value will have dropped to exactly its minimum, as the season for them will be then just at its height, and all the markets glutted with the same articles.

When they sowed lettuces, those admirable salads were expensive—fourpence apiece, perhaps, being asked for about as much green surface as would victual a healthy caterpillar for a day; yet when they come to pick their plants they are no longer costing fourpence a piece, but, on the contrary, are being sold at two a penny, and this, too, for very respectable specimens. If prices had only kept up, the private gardener's triumph would, of course, have been complete, but, as matters stand, it gloomily occurs to him that it is hardly worth while to pay a boy half-a-crown a week for half the year to look after a sovereign's worth of vegetables.

Moral Discipline of Gardening. Yet this despondent reflection is combated as often as it occurs to him, by the noble thought that what he eats he has grown himself, and that even an indifferent cauliflower from his own garden is preferable to a superior vegetable from a shop. Though a poor thing, it is his own. He feels that he has joined the great army of the world's benefactors, the producers, and has demonstrated that independence which is the birthright of man.

His cabbages, it is true, are somewhat perforated by worm creatures, but what of that? The residue he knows to be wholesome, for he has grown it himself. His lettuces, again, have a generous, full-blown appearance about them, in which the market-gardener's tied-up plants are wanting. It is true, they lack the close white kernel of tight-packed, tender, crinkled leaves, of which the tradesman seems to make such a point, but then there is an open-hearted diffuseness about them which appeals to the eye, and after all, if somewhat bitter, they are undeniably fresh. Peas, if privately grown, have a way of ripening only two at a time, and the carrots when they do not concentrate *Home-grown Vegetables.* into nodular processes of great hardness, dissipate their juices through an attenuated root about as long and quite as tough as a whip-lash, abundantly fringed throughout its length with hairy filaments. Neither variety cooks well, but then they are eaten leniently. Their defects are charitably slurred over and winked at, while their virtues

of home-growth and "freshness" are conspicuously
dilated on and made much of. No experiences, therefore, however saddening, are sufficient to dissuade men
from becoming their own kitchen gardeners, for though
the reason which they give for their conduct—that they
will thereby raise an economical and superior crop of
vegetables for the table—is ostensibly that which leads
them into melancholy experiments, the real reason lies
much deeper and far below the reach of discouraging
influences. It is rooted in human nature.

Everybody shares the desire of possessing a piece of
ground which he may call his own, and everybody is
anxious, more or less, to have it in accord with the
season ; for who, when summer, for instance, is coming
on, can be content to see his garden contributing nothing
to the general fund of vegetable beauty and utility?
But before any plunge into the great moral discipline of
a kitchen garden is made, the experiences of the author
of "My Summer in a Garden" should be laid to heart.
In the first place, it should be remembered that no advice
offered by friends should be adopted, for if counsel is
taken the year will pass without anything but weeds.
One will suggest what another will most gravely warn
against, and each vegetable in turn will have to be
avoided lest the feelings of well-meaning neighbours
should be hurt. In the next place, nature must be
anticipated, for she is an enthusiastic gardener, and
wherever she finds a surface of soil she will plant, not

asparagus, celery, or cucumbers, but dandelions, chick-
weed, and grass. The conflict must, therefore, be
entered upon with a clear determination as to the ends
in view and regardless of friends' opposing counsels. A
bold challenge must be given to Nature and all her works.
Compel her, and she is a slave; humour her, and she
becomes a tyrant.

Nature in a Garden. "Nature," says Mr. Charles Dudley Warner, "is
prompt, decided, and inexhaustible, thrusting up her
plants with an admirable vigour and freedom, and the
more worthless the plant the more rapid and splendid
its growth. She is at it early and late, and all night."
He who undertakes a garden is relentlessly pursued, and
weeds are as hard to fight as original sin. Their roots
go deeper than conscience, and ramify like vice. There
is no season for folding the hands in placid consideration of work achieved, for he who puts a seed into the
ground "has done that which will keep him awake of
nights, and drive rest from his bones by day." But weeds
are not all. "I awake in the morning," says that delightful humourist of the American garden, "and think
of the tomato plants, the leaves like fine lace-work owing
to black bugs that skip around and can't be caught.
Somebody ought to get up before the dew is off—why
does not the dew stay on till after a reasonable breakfast?—and sprinkle soot on the leaves. I wonder if it
is I. Soot is so much blacker than the bugs that they
are disgusted and go away. You cannot get up too

early, if you have a garden, to get ahead of the bugs. I think, on the whole, it would be best to sit up all night and sleep day-times. Things appear to go on in the night in the garden uncommonly. It would be less trouble to stay up than it is to get up so early."

He found bugs to be of several varieties. "The striped *Of Garden* bug," as he calls it, "is the saddest of the year. He *Bugs.* is a moral double-ender, and is unpleasant in two ways. He burrows in the ground so that you cannot find him, and he flies away so that you cannot catch him. The best way to deal with the striped bug is to sit down and watch for him. If you are spry, you can annoy him. This, however, takes time. It takes all day and part of the night. For he flieth in darkness and wasteth at noonday. But the best thing to do is to set a toad to catch the bugs. The toad at once establishes the most intimate relations with the bug. It is a pleasure to see such unity among the lower animals, but the difficulty is to make the toad stay and watch the bugs. If you know your toad it is all right." The yellow squash bug is another, and he can only be disheartened by covering plants so thickly with soot and wood-ashes that he cannot find them. These creatures, fortunately, are not English pests, but we have their representatives in the innumerable small things—caterpillars and beetles, slugs and snails—that are so invaluable in a kitchen garden as teaching man that vegetable culture is a moral discipline.

Yet in spite of weed invasions and insect plagues, in

*Digging
moderately
a Pleasure.* spite of all the time given and the anxiety bestowed, in
spite, too, of the indifferent results obtained, men persist
in kitchen gardening. The conflict with wild nature
does them good, just as the missionary feels braced up
and pulled together by a good set-to with moral depra-
vity. But more things than weeds and insects go to
make the pursuit of indigenous cabbages a serious and
responsible undertaking. Digging is undoubtedly a
pleasure, digging moderately; but when the sun is hot
upon the back, and the back is found to have no hinge
in it, the reflection arises whether it is not better to pay
another to dig, or, at any rate, to devise some method
of working in the shade. Even hoeing would be a
greater delight under a canopy held over the toiler's
head as he worked, "and with a servant standing at each
end of the rows of vegetables with some cool and re-
freshing drink." Every one, therefore, undertaking a
kitchen garden should be prepared to carry on the
struggle manfully to the end, or not enter upon it at
all, and, besides a trial of his powers of physical endur-
·ance, must be prepared to have his moral patience put
to the test. It is not pleasant, as Mr. Warner says, to
find neighbour's hens in your garden, for, apart from
their depredations, "they go straddling about the beds in
a jerky, high-stepping, speculative manner, picking in-
quisitively here and there," which is very disagreeable to
the possessor of the soil.

Nor are children less out of place. We all appreciate

the value of children, and each of us feels, with the *Neigh-* *bours' Chil-* humourist, that "it would not be right, aside from the law, *dren.* to take the life even of the smallest child for the sake of a little fruit more or less in a garden," and at the year's end it will, undoubtedly, be a satisfaction to every one of us who can do so, to reflect that he has "never, in the way of gardening, disposed of the humblest child unne- cessarily." Nevertheless, they are out of place, and tend to exasperation, which again tends to violent crime, and unless, therefore, the intending gardener is conscious of his own powers of resisting every temptation to infanti- cide, he should hesitate before commencing the culture of vegetables. Kitchen gardening is indisputably, there- fore, a moral discipline, and as such deserves to com- mand all the enthusiasm possible; but as a method of providing the table with green food it is often open to some objection as being both costly in performance and indifferent in results. Of this, however, no kitchen gar- dener will ever be convinced, and it may therefore be looked upon as a beneficent scheme of nature that man shall be persuaded to labour for the good of his health, and the strengthening of his moral fibre, by making him believe that he is working all the time for his pecuniary profit.

The back garden, however, is sometimes a place for *Geology* *of Back* experiments with flowers and not for vegetables. It is *Gardens.* then as often the despair as the pride of the owner Each tenant of the house, in succession, has had his own ideas on the subject of horticulture, and has inflicted them upon the same patch of ground, so that, at last, with ruin upon ruin, the back garden presents a strati- fied chronology of occupancies. As in a section of a cliff, the discerning eye can trace here the vestiges of each succeeding age—the dust-heap and rubbish age, the gooseberry bush and rhubarb age, the gravelled drying- ground age, the lawn and shell-grotto age, the swing and parallel-bars-playground age—and so on through a long series of waves of whims, until the little obscure oblong of ground is as full of relics of the past as an old trilobite bed, and with its alternated history written just as plainly upon it. It is upon this desperate space—a garden if it were not so much of a dust-heap, a courtyard if it were not for a suspicion of box edging—the Londoner expends his horticultural enthusiasm, and one more stratum is added to the soil. The mould has to be imported, for that already existing is too largely composed of crockery and cinders to be healthy for plants. Paths have to be aligned and gravelled, and " the lawn " has to be turfed. The last is in itself a suffi- ciently serious responsibility. It is not exactly a " lawn," but rather a grass-plot ; nor yet that either, for the word plot suggests a continuity of the grassy surface, which does not really exist. In the first instance the sods used for its construction were not of an encouraging kind.

Back-Gar- They were ragged and dissipated-looking specimens of
den Lawns. verdure, with much foreign matter flourishing among the grass. The man who sold it called these miscellaneous

vegetables "clover," and he said that clover was good for grass, and strengthened it. In a back garden, however, clover cannot be as it is elsewhere, or how is that it generally comes up with the blossoms of dandelions and sends down the roots of buttercups, and that when these are pulled out of the sod nothing remains but some indifferent soil, only held together, it seems, by a particularly large and healthy-looking lob-worm? The weeds have to be pulled out nevertheless, and the result is that the lawn looks as if it had been unskilfully plucked, while the bald spots are so numerous that the little grass that remains looks out of place and ridiculous. Yet what is easier than to "renew" a lawn by sowing grass seed? It is only necessary to buy the very best, and then, having with a light hand loosened the surface of the soil, to enrich it with a compost of bones and guano, after which the seed is scattered with judicious liberality over the prepared area and top-dressed—that is all. Could anything be simpler? It is true that the amateur finds a rake the most exasperating of implements when trying to loosen the surface of turf, and that the preparation of manures is somewhat of a mystery to him. Even when the whole is done the general appearance of the lawn is depressing, looking as if a leaky dust-cart had been wandering about on it, or as if a wilderness of dogs and cats had been supping on it and had left the bony fragments of their repast behind.

Meanwhile, the ingenuous sparrow has been surveying,

pleased, the liberal feast prepared, and, having informed
his friends, who accept his general invitation cordially, he
comes down, and gathers up the seed. Soon convinced
that it is of the best quality, he does full justice to the
meal. The diligence of the sparrow in eating what does
not belong to him is very remarkable, and nowhere more
conspicuous than in the back garden. Sitting on the
spouts or chimney-pots of the houses round, he remarks
all that goes on beneath, makes a note of the cat that has
just gone under the currant bush at No. 25, and ponders
at the top of his voice, on the proceedings of the inhabitants of the row generally. Satisfied that grass-sowing
is in progress in one of the gardens, he descends, and
having collected his friends, remains with them upon the
scene of operations, industrious to the last grain of
seed.

With one little black eye applied close to the surface
of the soil, and the other doing general duty by keeping
a watch upon the overlooking windows, whence sudden
missiles might issue, he continues his patient but cheerful
scrutiny until certain that nothing remains. It is of no
use trying to tempt him from the larcenous repast by the
exhibition of honest viands upon the adjoining path, for
he knows, perhaps, that the bread will wait for him, but
that if he does not eat the seed at once it will be
grown beyond his powers of digestion. When he has
nothing else to do, he will make fun of the crumbled
loaf; will provoke his acquaintances to chase him by fly-

ing off with the largest lump; will play at prisoner's base with it, or drop it down gratings; will carry it up to the roof of a house and lose it down a spout; will do anything with it, in fact, but eat it in a proper and thankful manner.

The back-garden sparrow, indeed, is a fowl of very *Town Cats* loose morality, but his habits of life have so sharpened *and Town Sparrows.* his intelligence that the cats find it as difficult to catch him as the policemen do the urchins of the streets. Rustic sparrows, country-bumpkin birds, fall clumsily into the snares of the village tabby, but in the back gardens of London the cat very seldom indeed brings the birds to bag. It is not that the quadruped has lost her taste for sparrows, or that she has forgotten all her cunning, for now that the shrubs are in leaf and afford her convenient ambuscade, she may be seen on any sunny morning practising her old wild-life arts in order to circumvent the wily sparrow. But domestication blunts the ferine intelligence, and after a long residence in kitchens and daily familiarities with milkmen and cat's-meat-men, the spell of civilization and its hum-drum ways of life falls upon her, and, though she may hunt for sport, the comfortable assurance of a saucer daily replenished dulls her enthusiasm for strange meats, and, without forgetting that the sparrow is toothsome, she remembers more than she used to do that the sparrow is also nimble.

I have observed that the controversy as to whether sparrows are blessings or otherwise to the farmer, and whether in these days of bad harvests, when almost every

grain of corn is precious, the little birds should be encou-
raged or exterminated, is one that is regularly revived.

*It is the
Street boy
among
Birds.*

All the poets have formally denounced the sparrow—
" the meanest of the feathered race "—and how shall any
one be found to speak well of him ? The best that can
be said in the defence of the familiar little fowl is very
bad indeed, for no criminal code that yet exists would
suffice to exhaust the calendar of his crimes and convict
him for all his offences. Not only does the sparrow despise
police regulations and make sport of bye-laws, but he
affronts all our standards of ethics, public morality, and
religion.   In a church he behaves with no more decorum
than in a magistrate's court, and whether in the pulpit or
the dock betrays an unseemly levity that will require the
utmost extension of the Arminian doctrines of universal
grace to compass his salvation. He is the street boy
among birds, and his affronts are gratuitous and unprovoked.   It is of no use to retort upon him, or threaten
him with the law.   The water-pipe suffices as an answer
to every repartee, be it a gibe or a menace, and when a
sparrow has hopped up a long spout who would care to
bandy arguments with him ? Impervious to the battery
of exhortation, he perches on the window-sill invulnerable
to the most formidable assaults of reason or the most
ferocious onsets of sarcasm, and thoroughly comprehends
upon which side of the glass he sits. Pelt him with hard
names, and he only chirps monotonously ; but if you
throw a stone at him you must pay for the damages.

The sparrow carries no purse, for he steals all he wants ; and his name is in no directory, for he lives everywhere. His address is the world, and when changing his residence he apprises no one. There is no city whose freedom he has not conferred upon himself, and no corporation whose privileges he does not habitually usurp. Collectors of rates might well despair if directed to get their dues from him, and school boards need not hope for his reclamation. A long immunity from reprisals have so emboldened this feathered gamin that he seems now to fear nothing, riding on omnibuses free of charge, occupying tenements without paying rent, and feeding everywhere at no cost to himself. It is but damning with faint praise to call him a public scavenger, for, even presuming a scavenger to be respectable, the sparrow does little towards clearing up the litter of the streets. He builds his nests out of the fresh hay and clean straw provided for horses' food, and eats comfortably in stables, at shop-doors, or off the floors of warehouses, going only into the public streets for recreation and mischief.

Such, summarized, would stand the indictment against the sparrow, a contemner of all law, and a rebel against all order, a criminal egotist of a very serious type. But what can be said for the defence ? That he is consistently the friend of the farmer is still disputed, and that he fills any important place in the economy of nature, a close observation of his habits must make every one doubt. *As an Article of* Imported into foreign countries as " the friend of man," *Export*

the sparrow, both in Australia and New York, has multiplied into a public nuisance, and in return for the gift of
new worlds to colonize, the graceless birds have
developed into a multitudinous evil.   They have also been
called "the nightingales of our roofs," and if they
remained upon the roofs only they might be permitted to
retain the flattering title of nightingales.   Since, however,
they come down off the slates into our houses and
swagger about in our pleasure-grounds and business
premises alike, giving us in return no pleasant song, their
claims to the honour of "the queen of the feathered choir"
cannot be gravely entertained.   Upon the house-tops, if
they always stopped there, we might extend to them a
generous admiration; but when they contest with us the
habitations which we have built for ourselves, and repay
us for our protection with impudence only, such sympathy
is difficult.

How then can he be defended, this chief vagabond of
the air ?   On his merits he stands categorically convicted,
and for his shortcomings it is difficult to find excuse or
palliation.   Did he ever suffer from winter as the wild
things of copse and hedge do, or from drought, or from
the encroachments of civilization, his small presumptions
might pass unchallenged, as do those of the robins and
the finches.   But for him there is no frost so severe that
it checks the supply of food in the stables, no snow so
thick that it blocks up the sparrow's entrance to goods
sheds and storehouses.   His year has no Ramazan for

him, and from January to December he is assured of his daily food. For drought or flood he cares as little. His nurseries do not suffer by rising rivers, nor are his meals curtailed by any severity of the seasons. Nor yet when man, advancing, pushes back the domains of wild things in waste land and wood, does the sparrow share in the troubles which fall to the lot of the songsters of the country side. Wherever man goes he follows him, a parasite of his grain bags, and no city in which our countrymen have settled is without him.

I remember myself noticing, during the late campaigns *As a* in Afghanistan and Zululand, how the sparrows went *Symbol of* wherever the commissariat waggons went and established *Conquest.* a colony at every depôt. They crossed the Cabul River and the Buffalo with our armies, claiming at once privileges of conquest which our generals hesitated to assert. They levied instant toll on the grain fields, and billeted themselves upon the natives.

The area of their prevalence coincides with the empire of Europeans, for wherever, and as soon as, the flag goes up, in sign of the white man's rule, the sparrow perches on the top of it. Ships of all nations carry him as a stowaway from port to port, and, thus defrauding every Company alike, these birds range the world, settling where they will. And everywhere the sparrow is safe alike.

At home, who cares to catch him? Youth, it is true, lays preposterous snares of bricks to entrap him, and sparrow clubs conspire against him; but no sportsman goes out to make a prey of him. Who indeed, would expend time and patience in fetching a compass about a sparrow, or sit a summer's day with net and line, decoy bird and call, with a sparrow before his mind as his reward?

Vos non vobis. Abroad, also, the sparrow's arrival is hailed with patriotic glee, and municipalities incontinently go to and legislate for his protection. The sparrow soon discovers that he is favoured, and no sooner makes the discovery than he presumes upon it. Selecting prominent corners of public buildings, he stuffs rubbish into the crevices of the friezes, and advertises by long rags which he leaves fluttering and flapping outside that he has built a nest. Secure from cats and assured of man's patronage, he thrives and multiplies his kind, each generation adding to the general stock of effrontery and presumptuously acquired privileges, until nations turn in wrath upon their oppressors. Officious vergers rake out the sparrows' nurseries from under the eaves of the churches, and beadles purge the town hall. But the sparrow cares little for such clumsy retaliation. One house is as good as another, and as for a nest being destroyed, he is glad of an excuse for beginning the honeymoon all over again.

And this reminds me that it is not only in his public character that this vagabond fowl calls for animadversion. In private life his conduct is disreputable. As a frivolous parent, given to rolling eggs out of the nest, and even also his infant progeny ; as an unworthy spouse, transferring his affections lightly, and often assaulting the partner of his joys and sorrows; as a bad neighbour, scuffling with his kind wherever he meets with them—in each aspect he presents himself to the moral mind as undeserving of respect. Yet, with something of that eccentricity of judgment which commends the infamous Punch of the street-show to the public regard, we persist in looking upon the sparrow, with all his notorious faults, as a popular favourite, and resent any exposure of his obliquities.

The explanation of this may be found in the very *Why popular.* traits of character and habits I have above hinted at. The sparrow is our national emblem, the outward and visible sign of the Englishman's supremacy in foreign lands. He goes out to conquer with us, and follows faithfully the vicissitudes of our arms. Content, too, with the security of the British flag, he tempts the sea, keeping our regiments company from continent to continent, and finding a new home wherever Englishmen will stay. In his character, too, the robust independence that is impatient of trammels and frets under the vexatious provisions of parochial legislation, the stubborn retention of his own opinion, the obstinate assertion of rights, the preference for communities and for the comforts and conveniences of civilization, the dogged refusal to become, in spite of all temptation, other than nature made him, are all traits that should appeal to a thorough Briton's sympathy.

The tyranny of the sparrow, in fact, is the price of civilization. Only savages are exempt.

CHAPTER VIII.

BEARS—WOLVES—DOGS—RATS.

BEARS ARE OF THREE KINDS, BIG BEARS, MIDDLE-SIZED BEARS, AND LITTLE WEE BEARS——EASILY PROVOKED——A PROTEST OF ROUTINE AGAINST REFORM——BUT UNRELIABLE——UNFAIRLY TREATED IN LITERATURE——HOW ROBBERS WENT TO STEAL THE WIDOW'S PIG, BUT FOUND THE BEAR IN THE STY——THE DELIGHTFUL TRIUMPH OF CONVICTIONS IN THE NURSERY——THE WILD HUNTER OF THE WOODS ——ITS SPLENDID HEROISM——A PALIMPSEST——WOLF-MEN ——WOLF-DOGS——THE RAT EPIDEMIC IN INDIA——ENDEMIC IN ENGLAND——WESTERN PREJUDICE AND EASTERN TENDERNESS——EMBLEMS OF SUCCESSFUL INVASION—— THEIR ABUSE OF INTELLIGENCE——EDAX RERUM.

Classification of Bears.

BEARS are of three kinds—as every child knows. There is the Great Big Bear, the Middle-sized Bear, and the Little Wee Bear. They are all of a domestic kind, and generally go out for a walk in the forest before breakfast, in order to give their porridge time to cool. When met with in a wild state they can be easily distinguished by their size, and by their subsequent conduct, for the bigger the bear is the more of

you it will eat. If there is not much of you left when it
has done, you may decide without hesitation that it was
the Big bear you met: while if you are only moderately
consumed, you may safely conclude it was the Middle-
sized bear. The Little Wee bear, or bear-kin, will only
trifle with you, take a mere snack, as it were—make a
trifling collation or luncheon, so to speak, off you.

But if still in doubt as to the species encountered, the
Hindoo student's description of the Bheel may assist the
stranger in arriving at a correct conclusion, for the Big
bear is black, "only much more hairy," and when it has
killed you it leaves your body in a ditch. By this you
may know the Big bear.

But, unless provoked to attack you, these creatures *Easily*
will not do so—so naturalists assure us. A bear's *Provoked.*
notions of provocation, however, are so peculiar that
perhaps the safest rule for strangers to observe is not to
let the animal see you. The bear never attacks any
person whom it cannot see. This is a golden rule for
persons who are in the habit of meeting bears to observe.

Otherwise there seem to be no limits to a bear's provo-
cations. If it comes up behind you, and finds you
not looking that way, it knocks off the back part of your
head with one blow of its curved claws; and if it meets
you face to face it knocks off the front part of your head.
But there is nothing agreeable in this variety. Again, if
it discovers you sitting below it on the same hill-side as
itself, it rolls itself up, and comes trundling down the

slope upon top of you like an ill-tempered portmanteau ;
or if it is down below you, and becomes "provoked,"
it comes scrambling up the hill with a speed that in a
creature of such a shape is described by those who have
been charged, as "quite incredible." Sometimes, on the
other hand, bears receive very solid provocation without
showing any resentment, for, as Captain Kinloch, a
noted Indian Shikarry, has told us, the amount of lead
which an old black bear will carry away in his quarters
is amazing. But, as a rule, bears will not stand nonsense. It is well known how they behaved in the matter
of Goldylocks, who, after all, had only eaten up the
Little Wee Bear's porridge, and broken the seat of the
Little Wee Bear's chair, and gone to sleep in Little Wee
Bear's bed. Yet, if the family had caught her, poor
Goldylocks would probably never have got home to her
mother to tell the tale.

Unfairly   This characteristic animosity to man has given many
reated in   writers on the bear a handle for great unfairness to-
Literature. wards it.

I far prefer myself to see in the bear only some
dull-witted, obstinate Mars, pathetic Jubal, or rough, but
staunch Sir Bors ; some slumberous man of might, a lazy
Kwasind, or sluggard Kambu Kharna ; an easily-befooled
Giant Dumbledore or Calabadran ; some loyal Earl
Arthgal of the Table Round, or moody margrave of
Brandenberg — both of whom did not despise the fighting
sobriquet of "the Bear." For myself, I think no worse

of the bear than Toussenel does,[1] indeed, hardly so badly,
for I hesitate to agree with him that it symbolizes only
the spirit of persistent savagery, the incorrigible protest
of Routine against Reform ; that it is the feral incarnation of hostility to progress, and the champion-in-arms
of the pretended rights of the Beast against the authority
of Man. Men of science assure us that it is one of the
senior quadrupeds of the earth, and it was certainly the first
among them that arrived at any idea of using fore paws
as hands. But unfortunately for itself it has never raised
itself any further in the scale; and now that it has been
driven into the forest and wilderness, it seems to consider
itself unfairly displaced, and sulkily maintains in the
solitudes of the hills the character of a misanthrope, the
laudator temporis acti, the Legitimist " in retreat." He *It protests*
ranges himself among the " fauteurs d'obscurantisme *against*
systématique et de superstition," who speak of the Dark *Revolu-*
Ages as " the good old times," and who treat the apostles *tion.*
of new ideas and progress as heretics and pagans.

Gloomily retiring before the footsteps of men wherever
Europe can boast itself progressive and free, the bear
has now made Russia its asylum, content to know that
there, at any rate, it will not be disturbed by anything
more active in reform than Nihilism. As a matter of
fact, the bear is not at liberty to recognize the claims
of man without abdicating his own pretensions to supre-

---

[1] Read " L'Esprit des Bêtes," by A. Toussenel. (Published by
J. Hetzel, Rue Jacob, Paris.)

macy, or, to use the orthodox style of pretenders to crowns and representatives of hopeless dynasties, without "dishonouring the hereditary traditions of his House." Following further the example of Pretenders, the bear, instead of allowing its claims to die out, prefers to become extinct itself. The bear, therefore, is rapidly disappearing, and already "la barbare Moscovie, espoir des prétendants, refuge du droit divin et de l'autocratie, est dans la vieille Europe, sa patrie d'adoption." A Czar is the only ruler a bear can tolerate. All the rest, it says, are unbearable.

But, unfortunately for it, even in Russia, where the animal is held in semi-reverential awe, its flesh is considered a dainty by the hard-living races among whom it has raised its gloomy standard of protest, and its skin is valued everywhere ; while its pomatum—the " pomade de lion " of Paris, the " bear's grease " of London—is alone sufficient for its utter ruin. Pretenders should be poor if they wish to be unmolested. Yet the bear obstinately maintains the unequal struggle, appealing to its semi-erect posture, its hand-like paws, its almost-absent tail, *Said to be a Generous Beast.* and its innocent tastes, for the clemency and consideration of man. It would, too, recall the facts of history, and remind us how, in the olden days of Roman beast fights, the bear was hissed from the arena because it refused to fight with the Christians and other captives provided for it, and, pointing to the East, would remind us that there it is called a generous brute, because it will not molest the dead. If a man pursued by a bear feigns death, the bear passes on after a most cursory examination, generously preferring to be thus easily deceived rather than push examination beyond the limits of good taste. You shall also see in this way a truly benevolent man giving alms to a beggar sooner than scrutinize too narrowly the necessity for giving relief.

But I fear that none of these pleas avail the bear, for it is impossible to forget how lamentable are the exceptions to that innocent appetite for leaves, and berries, and roots which it displays in Europe, and how abominably carnivorous are the grizzly bear of America, and the Polar Bruin of the Arctic snows. These are facts beyond dispute—but I would not be unjust. I would not throw in their teeth, as some have done, the conduct of those she-bears of Judea, who avenged the touchy prophet by desolating the nurseries of all the country side, for that was a miracle over which the she-bears had no control. Nor would I give credence to Daniel, when he takes the bear as an emblem of faithlessness; nor to the libellous narratives of Gesner, who tells us how bears make a practice of stealing young women; nor yet would I admit in evidence the mocking eulogies of Ælian. Pliny and Aristotle are of course to be discredited, and we must therefore come to modern times to find the bear justly judged. The delightful La Fontaine speaks of it as "a blundering friend," and points the moral by the story of the bear who, wishing to brush away the fly that disturbed its master's slumbers, accidentally knocked off the top of its master's skull, and Artemus Ward tells us how it can be taught to do " many interestin' things—but is onreliable."

The immortal showman once had a bear himself "who could dance and larf and lay down and bow his head in grief, and give a mournful wale," but it often annoyed Artemus. Thus on one occasion, when told to exhibit its grief at the national disgrace of Bull's Run, it commenced, in spite of the slow music, to exhibit every symptom of uncontrollable mirth, and the show was nearly wrecked in consequence by an indignant but patriotic public. On another occasion, when supposed to be exhibiting "the affekshun of the bear for its master," the unreliable animal, instead of reposing sweetly on the showman's bosom, seized him round the waist, and began waltzing with him, up and down the platform, "in a friteful manner." On the evidence, therefore, of both La Fontaine and Artemus Ward, the bear is shown to be unreliable. But, after all, this is no excessive disparagement, and within the moderate limits of justice.

In Heraldry and History.
It is significant of the large space this species has filled in the world's eye that every peculiarity in the bear's natural history which distinguishes it from other quadrupeds has been made use of at one time or another by illustrious families or societies to symbolize

their own fortunes or estate. One academy has taken
for its arms the hybernating bear, since rest invigorates
to activity; and another the bear robbing a beehive,
with the motto "Stings sharpen his appetite." A
princely family wears on its crest the bear sucking its
paws, as an emblem of self-resource; another the same
animal licking its young into shape, a third the creature
climbing ambitiously, and a fourth the bear out in the
rain, as auguring fine weather to follow. Among other
houses, noble, though not royal, a hundred claim the
bear as their cognizance and badge, while more cities
than Berne, "the City of Bears," take Bruin for their
tutelary device. Oursine has been the name of more
than one great lady, and Orsini is a patronymic that the
world knows well. The order of the Bear is an Imperial
decoration; St. Ursus, no mean saint; and the firmament,
in the sons of Calisto, holds the bear twice over in its
constellations. Individual bears of fame are numerous
—the bear of Gundramnus, that helped to build a
church, and Restaurco, the musical·bear, whom the
Grand Seignior bought for many strings of pearls—and
was glad to give as many more to get rid of him—the
bear-king of the Ramayana, and the bear-gnomes of the
pine forests of Dardistan; the mysterious "Mum" of
Sind; the bear which Tony Lumpkin knew, that "only
danced to the genteelest of tunes;" and Sackerston, the
Bruin on which Master Slender vaunted his prowess;
Martin, the popular favourite of the Jardin des Plantes;

and Marco, the good bear of Lorraine; the bear that
made St. Medard's fortune as a saint, by assisting at a
miracle—and many others that memory might easily recall. But these suffice to show that though—as Slender
says in the "Merry Wives of Windsor"—"Woman
cannot abide them, they are very ill-favoured rough
things," bears have often, not only as a species, but as individuals, commended themselves to the esteem of man.

*   *   *   *   *

The Bear and the Widow's Pig.

Among the stories which have delighted children of
all countries, and probably from all time, is one that tells
how certain evil-minded men went to steal a widow's
pig, but how they found a bear in the sty instead, and
how thereupon disaster, sudden and complete, overtook
the robbers.

No child ever doubted the truth of that story; indeed,
how could it be doubted? It is well known that widows
do as a fact frequently keep a pig, and where should they
keep it but in a sty? Again, thieves are notoriously given
to stealing, and what could be more advantageously
purloined than a pig—above all a pig belonging to a
lone and unprotected widow? It is not with swine as
with poultry or cattle, for the pig can be eaten up from
end to end; even his skin makes crackling, and nothing
need be left behind. There are no accusing feathers to
lie about the scene of larcenous revel, as is the case
when hens have been devoured by stealth, and no bulky
hide and horns to get rid of on the sly, as happens

whenever robbers irregularly consume a neighbour's cow or calf. Again, a widow is, as a rule, a person who lives alone—I confidently appeal to all story-books to support this statement—and, except for such assistance as her cat can give her, is virtually defenceless at midnight against a number of armed and determined men. A widow's pig is, therefore, and beyond all doubt, just the very thing to get itself stolen, and indeed we would venture to say that, as a matter of fact, it always *is* stolen.

Is it not natural, then, in children to believe implicitly the story we refer to? As for the other incidents of it —those in which the bear takes a prominent part—they, too, are exactly such as might be expected to occur frequently under similar circumstances.

A poor bear-leader on his way to the neighbouring town is benighted, on a stormy evening, in a solitary place—just such a place as widows live in—and, knowing from a large and varied experience of men and cities that widows are kind of heart, he intercedes for a night's lodging for himself and his beast. It is no sooner asked than granted. The widow turns the cat off the hearth to make room for the man, and the pig out of his sty to make room for the bear. The cat and the pig grumble, of course, at having to make their own arrangements for the night; but, at any rate, the sacred duties of hospitality have been faithfully discharged, and, in the sequel, the widow is rewarded. The stormy night has suggested itself to certain good-for-nothing vagabonds—who, in their tramps along the road, have marked down the widow's pig for their prey—as an excellent opportunity of coming at some home-fed bacon cheaply; and, unconscious of the change of occupant, stealthily approach the sty, hoping, under cover of the night, high wind, and pelting rain, to carry off the porker in a sack which they have provided for the purpose. How differently the case falls out is quickly told. The bear, instead of allowing itself to be put into the sack like a lamb, gets up on its hind legs, and nearly kills the robbers.

From first to last the story has always been completely credible, for, given a widow with a pig, a man with a bear, and robbers with a sack, the incident is one that might happen at any time.

Delightful triumph of child's convictions. Such being the story, so consistent in its circumstances and so complete in its action, it is very pleasing to find that the implicit faith of children in it has, after all, been rewarded by its actual occurrence. Everything is true that really happens, and it does not matter whether the story or the event comes first. Where the incidents have already actually transpired, and a writer sits down to describe them, the narrative is, no doubt, often excellent, vivid, picturesque, faithful, and so forth. Nevertheless, it is rather a commonplace performance after all, and depends for its virtues either upon the state of the narrator's eyesight and his propinquity to the scene of the event, or else to his judicial capacity for appraising the value of the evidence of others. But where the writer describes occurrences which have not yet occurred, the merits of his work are infinitely enhanced, and the wisdom of the Prophets is nowhere more conspicuous than in their selection of this method of narration.

They made it a rule to speak before the event, instead of after it, and it is owing almost entirely to this that their utterances have been so highly spoken of.

Truth, it is said, is stranger than fiction, and so it is in a certain sense: because it is in the nature of fiction to be strange but truth is a prosaic, every-day sort of thing, and when it is romantic it strikes the mind as being peculiarly wonderful. We do not as a rule expect facts to surprise us, so when they do, they startle us much more than any narrative ever created by novelist or poet. In that case they are more like fiction than fiction itself, and are therefore all the more charming. Thus, "'The Bear in the Pig-sty" story may be considered admirable, while a pleasure is superadded by the reflection that the faith of childhood, which is at once the most solemn and the most fascinating attribute of that reverend and delightful age, has not been trifled with and betrayed. That the story was true the children have known all along, but now everybody knows it too, and acknowledges that the children were right.

At the village of Massegros (in France), only the other day, a bear-man came along the road with a bear, and asked for a night's lodging, and the bear was put into the pig-sty. At night three men came to steal the pig ; but, on the contrary, one of the men died, the second very nearly, and the third went mad with fright. The bear did it—just as it was written in the story-book years upon years ago—and the pig is back in his sty again.

No wonder one man went mad from fright, for the difference between pigs and bears is very considerable; and the thief putting out his arm to take hold, as he thought, of the sleek and inoffensive porker, might well be startled out of his senses to find himself handling the shaggy hide of a bear. The horror of the discovery, the utter impossibility of guessing what had happened, the first bewildering instant when Bruin rose with a roar from the litter, the next of horrid and inexplicable pain as the great brute closed with its assailant, combined to make such an experience as might well terrify the reason out of a man. Suddenness and darkness are the most awful allies of the dreadful, and when to these are added a consciousness of guilt and superstitious fear, the wits might easily take to flight, and a cunning thief go out a gibbering idiot.

For those who were hurt, fatally, so the report says, the horrors of the incident were in one sense even aggravated, as the bear is monstrously cruel in its attack. Thus natives of India look upon the wounds which it inflicts with even greater dread than they regard those from a tiger, for the latter are either clear gashes or bone-shattering blows; but, as a rule, the bear, standing erect before it closes with a man, strikes at the head, and its

huge blunt claws tear the skin down off the scalp, and
over the face, or lay the throat bare, in either case
blinding and stunning the unhappy wretch. The pain
of even such an attack as that, however, could hardly
increase for the unfortunate men the terrors of their position, when there rose up out of the pig's straw the giant
apparition of a growling beast, a great black monster all
hair and fury, that was upon them in an instant, roaring
like an earthquake, and striking with the arms of a giant.
No wonder that two of the three are dead, and the other
one is mad !

But the triumph of virtue was delightfully complete,
and the pig came by his own again. The widow who
hospitably entertained the homeless bear-man, and the
cat that surrendered her corner by the fire to the stranger
were rewarded ; the wicked men who went about stealing
pigs were punished, and the story of the old fairy-tale
book came true.

The moral of this evidently is that no one should refuse charity even to bears, and no one should steal pigs ;
for, though bear ham is good, it is not the same as pork
ham, and it is better to save your own bacon than to
steal your neighbour's. There is a second moral also,
and that is that children are wiser than grown-up people,
inasmuch as they believe that there is nothing so wonderful but it may really come to pass, and that everything
which will happen has already happened before. Children
never give over expecting and hoping, and this is why

The Moral of this story.

R

they alone are never disappointed, and why they deserve
so thoroughly to enjoy the triumph of their convictions.

*   *   *   *   *

*Wolves
criminal
by inheri-
tance.*

The wolf is a creature of very bad character, and
deserves most of it. Born of poor but dishonest parents,
he inherits the family instinct for crime, and industriously
commits it. No jury would recommend him to mercy,
even on the score of youth, nor any chaplain pretend
after execution that the deceased had died repentant.

Contrition, it is true, is a mandrake. It springs up
under the gallows.

But the wolf, even in the very shadow of death
remains a wolf still, and, according to the condition
of his stomach, shows either one abominable phase of
his character or the other. If hungry he is abject, and
curls himself up meekly to receive the fatal blow, dying
without half the protest that even a healthy lamb would
make. But if he has just dined he snarls and snaps to
the last. Yet even the wolf has found his apologists.

We have been told that he is only a dog gone wrong,
that evil communications have corrupted his original
manners, and that under more wholesome home influences he might have developed into a " good
dog Tray," instead of the bandit and assassin that
he is.

*The
splendid
Heroism of
Wolves.*

The poetry of crime, however, is a dangerous theme,
and when sentiment indulges itself upon the picturesqueness of a criminal's career, it is liable to degenerate into

a whimsical justification of wrong-doing and its doer.
I can appreciate the solemnity of the wolf's murders,
supreme tragedies as they often are—or the splendour of
its ravages when, Attila-like, it descends upon the fat
plains to scourge the lowland folk—or the nobility of its
recklessness as, from age to age, it challenges man to
the unequal conflict—or the heroism which sends it out
alone into the haunts of men to carry away a child, so
that its own whelps may not starve. Nor in all the records of human violence is there to be found anything
more tremendous than the deadly patience with which
the trooped wolves pursue their victims, or the fierce
élan with which they launch themselves from the forest
depths upon the passing prey. A party of eighty
Russian soldiers, fully armed, were moving in mid-winter
from one post to another, when, just as the shades of
evening were closing round them, an immense pack of
wolves—scouring the black country-side for food—came
suddenly across their line of march. Rather than swerve
from their course, the intrepid brutes flung themselves
upon the soldiers, and tore every man of the detachment
to pieces.

This is literally an instance of that " Berserker rage ,"
that fearless unarmed rage, of which the Scandinavian
chroniclers tell us in terms of awesome admiration, so
long as the heroes were the fair-bearded men who followed
their Erics and Olafs to the sea. Now, for myself, I do
not grudge the same admiration to the wolf when it acts

as bravely as those old heroes of the Sagas, especially since the Norsemen themselves, to express the intensity of their valour and the surpassing ferocity of their attack, had to go to the wolf for a simile. But, after all, no pleading can avail the wolf, for the whole history of man—black or white, brown, red, or yellow—convicts these animals of persistent and ineradicable wickedness—rising, often, it is true, to a considerable dignity in the proportions and manner of their crime, but as a rule taking rank only as misdemeanants of the lowest type. Some few have proved themselves Hernanis, Laras, and Robin Hoods, and been distinguished in the chronicles of their times as intrepid leaders of jungle brigands and captains of hill-side Vehmgerichts. But the majority of them—the rank and file of these wolf-societies—are ordinary sheep-stealers, killing simply to satisfy hunger, and confessing by their submissiveness when captured the justice of their fate.

The Wolf not a Dog. Children looking at the wolves in the Zoological Gardens greet them as " bow-wows," and in their pretty sympathy offer the Wild Hunter of the Forest morsels of bun. Such cates, however, are not to the wolf's taste ; he would far rather have the children themselves. But he knows that that is out of the question, so he blinks his eyes wearily, and with a sharp expression of discontent at his lot resumes his restless motion up and down the cage.

Only very young children, however, mistake the wolf

for a dog, for there is that in its ugly eyes, set so close together and so sinister in their expression, that tells the elder ones that the creature before them is no dog, or, at any rate, not an honest specimen. Besides, nursery stories, fairy tales, and fables have taught them long ago the likeness of the wolf and its character, and the first look at the sharp snout set in grey fur reminds them of that face that little Red Riding Hood found looking out at her, one fine May morning, from under her dear old grandmother's nightcap. If the literature of the nursery has thus familiarized the wolf to the younger generation, their elders also, of whatever nation they may be, and whatever language they may speak, have continued to learn from a hundred sources of the implacable brute that makes the great highways of forest and plain in Northern and Eastern Europe and the mountain paths of the Pyrenees and Apennines so perilous to belated travellers—that robs the Indian mothers of their children, or pulls down the solitary wood-gatherer as he goes trudging home at nightfall, along the pathway that skirts the .jungle. Tales of horror crowd into their memory as they look at the unkempt and restless creatures, condemned to-day to civilization and mono-tony, but once, perhaps, actors themselves in the very scenes that make the narratives of wolf adventure so appalling. In a bare cage, with iron bars before it, it is difficult to realize the full meaning of the thing before you.

*A hiero-
glyphic.* The wolf is the hieroglyphic which Nature uses to
symbolize the mortal hatred of races, and to typify piti-
less cruelty; it is the emblem of perpetual strife between
law and the lawless, the formula for implacable rebellion.
All this is not to be read on the instant, for the cypher
in which Nature writes is as secret as the inscriptions
upon an Egyptian obelisk, or the " key " characters of
a Chinese scroll. Who would guess, for instance, without telling, that a bee stands upon Pharaoh's pillars for
the symbol of a contented and obedient people, or that
a bundle of reeds on a Chinese manuscript represents
the blessings of education, or that in both antiquities a
drop of falling dew symbolizes science? So in Nature
it is easy to find characters and symbols that represent,
in cryptograph, all the different circumstances and conditions of human life and character. Some of these can
be read off at once, and we find no difficulty in deci-
phering, for instance, the signs of the dog, or mole, or
serpent. But the wolf is, perhaps, a more occult metaphor, a kind of palimpsest, and it needs both memory
and imagination to clothe the wild beast before you
with all the picturesque terrors that naturally belong
to this thing of a terrible and pathetic isolation.

*Its Appear-
ance mis-
leading.* There is nothing in its appearance, except that sinister
proximity of its eyes, to betoken a creature so eminently
dangerous when wild; no significance of cruel fury in
its voice, no profession of murderous strength in its
limbs. It looks like a shabby dog, and howls like an

unhappy one. There is no fierce tiger-eloquence of eye, no ravening hyæna-clamour in its voice, no lion-majesty of form. It seems a poor thing for any one, even a child, to be afraid of, for it appears half-fed and weak-limbed. As it trots backwards and forwards it is hard to believe that these pattering feet are really the same as those that can swing along the country-side in an un-tiring gallop, defy the horse and laugh the greyhound to scorn, or that the thin neck craning out of the kennel there could ever bear a dead child's weight. Yet this is indeed the very creature that has made countries ring with its dreadful deeds of blood, that has held mountain passes and lonesome wood-ways against all comers, has desolated villages and aroused the resentment of kings. There must, then, be something more, after all, in the thin-bodied thing than the eye catches at first sight, or why should we, in this very England of ours, have had two monarchs that waged Imperial war against it, or have had a month named after it—the modern January, the old "wolf-monath," so called because the depreda-tions of the beast were then especially terrible; or why should the wolf have been included in our Litanies as one of the chief perils of life? "From caterans and all other kinds of robbers; from wolves and all other kinds of evil beasts, deliver us, O, Lord?"

In other countries it has been at times a veritable scourge, and wherever this has happened local legend and folk-lore have invested the animal with strange, gaunt terrors. In the hungry North, where Arctic snows forbid the multiplication of small animal life, and the wolf would often be starved but for man and his domestic beasts, the wolf·is the popular symbol of all that is tragic or to be dreaded, and signifies, in their superstition, the *Wolf* supreme superlative of ruin—for they say that when the *legends.* last tremendous Night overshadows the earth, and our planet sinks out of the darkened firmament into eternal gloom, the Fenris-wolf and the Sköll-wolf will appear and devour the gods and the firmament! Further to the South, we find Scandinavian tradition replete with weird wolf-lore; and it is the same in Finland and all over Russia, Germany, and France, where the horrible fiction of the loup-garou—partly ghoul and partly wolf-man— still holds its own. Indeed, so terribly associated are the crimes of wolves and the sufferings of men that all over Europe, from the snows of Lapland to sunny Spain, the gruesome legend is a household story, and the wehr-wolf and wolf-children carry on the old Greek and Latin superstitions of the Lycanthropes.

That there is any real sympathy of natures is incredible; yet how comes it that from the days of antiquity, when the citizens of Rome boasted of their descent from the wolf-suckled twins, and exalted Lúpa, that fiercest of foster-mothers, in every place of honour in the city, to the present day—when in the East children are actually living who have been found in wolves' dens,[2] and

---

[2] Indian officials might give some very curious information about these "wolf-children."

possess the habits of carnivorous quadrupeds, and in the
West men go positively " wolf-mad," think themselves
wolves, and under that horrible insanity attack their own
kind and try to tear them to pieces with. their teeth—
how is it that through all the intervening years the same
uncanny suspicion of some affinity with wolves has been
kept alive by the human race?

In England, thanks to Master Peter Corbett, to whom
was entrusted the duty of extirpating wolves, they
have ceased to be indigenous for many centuries ; but
two hundred years ago they were to be found both in
Scotland and Ireland.   On the Continent they are still
a serious existing fact, and in parts even of Italy and
France, to say nothing of Russia and Finland, are dangerous to human life.

It is, however, in the East—in India—that the wolf at- *Wolves in*
tains the complete measure of its obliquities, for just as the *India.*
korait snake kills a greater number of human beings than
the far more deadly cobra, so the wolf takes infinitely more
lives than the tiger.   Thousands of adults fall victims
annually to this animal's daring and ferocity, and the
destruction of child-life by it is prodigious.   It is not
only in the remoter districts, where jungles and rocky
wildernesses are found, that the wolves thus prey upon
man, but in the very midst of busy towns.

They will creep, so the natives say, into houses, and lick
the babies from the sleeping mother's arms.   The soft
warm touch of the wild beast's tongue melts the guardian
fingers open.   One by one they loosen their hold, and, as

the wrists sink apart, the baby slides gradually out of the protecting arms against the soft coat of the wolf. It does not wake, and then the brute bends down its head to find the child's throat. There is a sudden snap of closing teeth, a little strangling cry, and the mother starts to her feet to hear the rustle of the grass screen before the door as it is pushed ajar, and to feel her own feet slip in the blood at her side.

No wonder all men dread them, and from East to West—whether as the Won-tola of Madras or the loup-garou, the graveyard phantom of Brittany—represent the wolf as the unrelenting enemy of our kind. Kings of Hungary have taken this animal for their badge, and in the old world of Rome it had great honour; but it would be difficult to find in all the range of literature, sacred or profane, anything on record to make us feel tenderly towards the wolf. There are those who would gloss over its crimes by declaring it to be the brother of the dog, and it may be true enough that wolves learn to bark when fostered by canine mothers, that the "dogs" of the Arctic regions are in reality only wolves, and that till the white man came the Red Indian had no quadruped companion but the wolf. But, after all, such facts only amount to this—that though wolves are never fit to be called dogs, there are some undeveloped specimens of dogs only fit to be called wolves.

* * * * *

Dogs we have all met.

I am very fond of dogs, and have indeed, in India

had as many as seven upon my establishment at one time.
Some I knew intimately, others were mere acquaintances,
but speaking dispassionately of them, and taking one with
another, I should hesitate to say that they were superior
to ordinary men and women. It is, I know, the fashion
to cite the dog as a better species of human and to depreciate men as if they were dogs gone wrong. I am not
at all sure that this is just to ourselves, for, speaking of
the dogs I have met—the same dogs in fact that we
have all met—I must say that on the whole, I look upon
the dog as only a kind of beast after all. At any rate I am
prepared to produce from amongst my acquaintances
as many sensible men as sensible dogs, and if necessary,
a large number of human beings who if taken by accident
or design out of their road will set themselves right again, *Are Men*
who if separated for years from friends, will readily recog- *only second-*
nize them and welcome them, who on meeting those who *rate Dogs?*
have done them previous injuries will show at once by
their demeanour that they remember the old grudge, who
will detect false notes in a player's performance, catch
thieves, carry baskets to the butchers, defend their masters,
and never worry sheep. On the other hand I will produce
in equal number dogs who get themselves lost regularly
and " for good," until a reward is offered, who never recognize old acquaintances, but will fawn upon those who
have injured them, who will sleep complacently through
the performances of organ-grinders and never wake up
when thieves are on the premises, who cannot be trusted

with meat, and who will run away from their masters if
danger threatens. Being quite certain of this, I think
I am justified in maintaining that dogs are no better
than men, and indeed I should not quarrel with him if
any one were to say that but for man the dog would have
been much worse than he is—probably, only a wolf still.

As a matter of fact, most of the dogs of my acquaintance have been positively stupid. One that I remember
well was, however, considered by my friends of remarkable intelligence; but this story often told of him, to
illustrate his intelligence, did not give me, when I heard
it, any high opinion of his intellect. But I may be
wrong. He was accustomed, it appears, to go with the
family to church. But one day the old church roof
began to leak, so workmen were set at the job and the
building was closed. But when Sunday came this intelligent dog trotted off as he was wont to do, to the
church, and, composing himself in the porch as usual,
remained there the customary time and trotted complacently home again. Now, where does the intelligence
come in, in this anecdote?

Anger. In a similar way stories are told in illustration of other
feelings and passions, but most of them, so it seems to me,
cut both ways. There are, indeed, many human feelings
which the dog evinces in a marked way, and often upon
very little provocation. The dog, for instance, expresses
anger precisely as we do, and in accordance with the
human precept, " When the boy hits you, kick the

post," will bite his friend to show his displeasure at a stranger. I had a little bull-terrier which went frantic if a pedlar or beggar came to the door, and being restrained from flying at the innocent itinerant, would rush out as soon as released into the shrubbery and go for the gardener. The gardener knew the dog's ways, for he had had a sharp nip vicariously before, and when he saw Nellie on her way towards him, used to charge her with the lawn mower. Now at other times, the gardener and Nellie were inseparable friends, and, weather permitting, the gardener's coat and waistcoat were Nellie's favourite bed. In human nature it is much the same, when the husband, because the news in the paper is disagreeable, grumbles at his wife's cap.

Hatred also the dog feels keenly — in the matter of cats *Hatred.* notably. I have seen one of the exceptionally intelligent dogs referred to above, stop and jump under a tree for an hour, and go back every day for a month afterwards to jump about ridiculously under the same tree, all because a cat which he had once been after, and wanted to catch, had got up that tree out of his way. There is no doubt in my mind whatever from that dog's behaviour that he *hated* the cat.

Jealousy again is a common trait, and in Thornley's *Jealousy.* book there is an instance given of a dog that was so jealous of another pet that when the latter died, and had been stuffed, he always snarled if attention was drawn to the glass case from which his rival gazed with

Envy. glassy eye upon the scene. The *envy* of the dog has given rise to the well-known fable of the dog in the manger, and the storry told in "False Beasts and True" (in illustration of canine sagacity) exemplifies this trait in a striking way. Leo was a large and lawless dog, belonging to an establishment where lived also a mild Maltese terrier. The latter, however, fed daintily, and was clad in fine linen, whereas Leo got as many rough words as bones, and was not allowed into the pretty rooms of which the terrier was a favoured inmate. From the reports furnished of the judicial inquiry which followed the crime, it seems that the lesser (very much lesser) dog had been missed for several days, and his absence bewailed, while something in the demeanour of the big dog suggested to all beholders that some terrible tragedy had occurred and that Leo was darkly privy thereto. At length a servant going to the coal-hole heard a feeble moaning proceeding from the farthest corner, and on investigating with a candle, the Maltese terrier was found buried under lumps of coal. The supposition was that Leo had carried his diminutive rival to the coal-hole, and there scratched down an avalanche of coals upon him, and the manners of the two dogs when confronted bore striking evidence to the truth of the theory. Of Leo's *envy* there can hardly therefore be a suspicion.

Gluttony. *Gluttony* is common to all dogs, but their general aversion to *drunkenness* is supposed, by their partial eulogists, to be demonstrated by the fact attested by the Rev. F. Jackson of a dog who, having been once made so drunk with malt liquor that he could not get upstairs without help, always growled and snarled *at the sight of a pewter pot!* To establish in a feeble way this individual's dislike of malt liquor, the eulogist, it seems to me, has trifled away the dog's intelligence altogether. Nor, as illustrating sagacity, is the following anecdote so very forcible as it might be. Begum was a small red cocker who, with a very strange perception of her own importance, engaged as her attendant a mild Pomeranian of her own sex, who *Ingrati-tude.* having only three available legs, displayed the gentler manners of a confirmed invalid. Begum, several times in her long and respected career, became the joyful mother of puppies, and on all these interesting occasions her friend Rip (or Mrs. Gamp, as she came to be called) presided over her nursery, kept beside the mother in her temporary seclusion, exhibited the " little strangers " to visitors with all the mother's pride during her absences, and in short, behaved herself like a devoted friend. "Strange to say," says the author, "when the poor nurse herself was dying, and Begum was brought to her bedside to cheer her, the ' sagacious ' cocker snuffed her friend, and then leaping gaily over her prostrate, gasping form, left the stable for a frolic—and never looked in again on her faithful attendant." This narrative, however, hardly illustrates the remarkable *gratitude* "which may be almost said to be a dog's leading principle."

Regret and Grief. — *Regret* and *grief* dogs no doubt share also with men, for my own terrier when he stands with sadly oscillating tail and his head stuck through the area railings, whimpering for "the touch of a vanished cat" and "the sound of a puss that is still," bears ample testimony to the former, nor when, out ferreting, the rabbit has mysteriously disappeared into an impassable earth, is there any room for hesitation as to Tim's *grief*. His regret at the rabbit's evasive habits is unmistakable. Mrs. Sumner Gibson, to illustrate *joy*, tells us of her pet, which on seeing her unexpectedly return after a long absence *was violently sick*. I remember when at school seeing a violent physical shock, accompanied by the same symptoms, affect a boy when suddenly approached by a master while in the act of eating gooseberries in class. But none of us attributed the result to any excess of delight.

Laziness. — *Laziness* is a trait well exemplified in dogs. Thus Cole's dog of ancient fame was so lazy that he always leaned his head against a wall to bark. So did Ludlam's.

Courage. — *Courage* is not more common among dogs than among men. I had once three dogs who accompanied me on a certain occasion to a museum. The hall at the entrance was devoted to the larger mammalia, and the dogs on passing the folding doors found themselves suddenly confronted by the whole Order of the Carnivora all drawn up according to their families and genera, ready to fall upon and devour them. With a howl of the most dismal horror, all three flung themselves against the door, and if I had not rushed to open it, would certainly have died or gone mad then and there from sheer terror. As it was, they flew through the open door with every individual hair on their bodies standing out like a wire, and arrived at home, some three miles off, in such a state of alarm that my servants were seriously alarmed for my safety. One of the three always slept in my room at night, but on the night after the fright howled so lamentably, and had such bad dreams, that I had to expel him. Miss Cobbe in her delightful book illustrates this whimsical cowardice by a bull terrior, who ready apparently to fight anything, went into "paroxysms of hysterical screaming" if an India-rubber cushion was filled or emptied with air in her presence, and the garden-hose filled her with such terror that on the day when it was in use "Trip" was never to be found on the premises, nor would any coaxing or commands persuade her to go into the room where the tube was kept all the rest of the week.

Pride affects the dog mind, for who has not heard *Pride.* of Dawson's dog that was too proud to take the wall . of a dung-cart, and so got flattened under the wheels? *Vanity* was admirably displayed by an old setter, who *Vanity.* often caused us great inconvenience by insisting on following members of the family whenever they went out, usually most inopportunely. But one day the

s

children, playing with it, tied a bow of ribbon on to the tip of its tail, and on everybody laughing at the dog's appearance, the animal retired under the sofa and sulked for an hour. Next day therefore, when Nelson showed every symptom of being irrepressibly intent on accompanying the family to a croquet party to which he had not been invited, it occurred to one of the party to try the effect of a bow. The ribbon was accordingly brought, and Nelson being held quiet by two of the girls, the third decorated his tail. No sooner was he released, and discovered the adornment, than the self-conscious dog rushed into the house and hid under the sofa ! An hour after the party were gone, he came out as far as the doorstep, and when the family returned there was Nelson sitting on his haunches with the most comic air of having something mortifying to conceal and refraining from even wagging his tail, lest the hateful bow should be seen. Chivalry, magnanimity, treachery, meanness, a sense of propriety or utter absence of shame, humour, &c., may all in turn be similarly proved to be shared by the dog world ; but it is a singular fact that so many of the anecdotes put forward to illustrate the virtues of this animal should, if read with a little irreverence towards the dogs, lend themselves to conflicting if not opposite conclusions.

The woolly white Dog a Criminal. Indeed, I look upon the woolly little white dog we have all met so often as absolutely criminal. You can see what a timid creature it is by the way it jumps when any cabman shouts, and yet its foolishness and greedi-

ness have got as many men into gaol as a street riot
would have done.   You have only to look at it to see
what an easy dog it is to steal.   In fact, it was made to
be stolen, and it faithfully fufils its destiny.   One man—
the father of a young family, too—has been in prison
twice for stealing that same dog.   It is true that, on the
other hand, he has sold it at a splendid profit on five
other occasions, and has pocketed a handsome reward
for " finding " it several times besides, but he nevertheless
owes several weeks' incarceration to that same little dog's
infamously criminal habit of looking so stealable.   He
can no more keep his hands off the animal than needles
can help going to the nearest loadstone.   It is of no
use his trying to look the other way, or repeating the
Lord's Prayer, or thrusting his hands right down to the
bottom of his breeches' pockets, for as surely as ever that
little dog comes by, "Jerry" will have to steal it.   It is
chiefly the dog's fault.   It never follows its master or
mistress for the time being like a steady dog of business,
but trots flickeringly about the pavement, as if it was
going nowhere in particular with nobody.   It makes ex-
cursions up alleys on its own account, and comes running back in such a hurry that it forgets whether it ought
to turn to the right or the left; or it goes half across a *The Art of getting lost.*
road and then takes fright at a hansom, and runs speed-
ing down the highway in front of it under the impression
that the cab is in pursuit.   Or it loiters at a kerbstone to
talk canine common-places to another dog, and then, like

S 2

an idle errand boy, accompanies its new acquaintance a short way round several corners. Or it mixes itself up with an old gentleman's legs, and gets eventually trodden upon, and precipitately makes off squeaking down the middle of a crowded thoroughfare into which its owner cannot follow it. Of all these weaknesses Jerry and his comrades are perfectly well aware ; and if you will only follow the dog for a quarter of an hour you will see the little wretch get "lost," as it calls itself—or as Jerry calls it, when the policeman inquires about the dog. There are some people who go through life leaving watches on dressing-tables and money on mantelpieces, and then prosecute the servants who steal them; others who lend strangers sovereigns in order to show their "confidence" in them, and then call in the police to get the stranger punished ; others who post money in open envelopes, and are bitterly indignant with the authorities because it is never received by the addressee ; many again who walk about with their purses in pockets placed where morality never meant pockets to be ; who, in fact, are perpetually putting temptation into the way of their weak brethren, and then putting their weak brethren in gaol. And the foolish little white dog that is always getting itself stolen is exactly their representative in the canine society which, we are assured, reflects our own.

For myself, I think the dignified position which the dog fills in human society can be far more worthily treated, than by anecdotes of his various virtues and vices, for after all he is one of man's chiefest triumphs, and one of his noblest servants. "In the beginning *The eyes and ears of Man.* Allah created Man, and seeing what a helpless creature he was He gave him the Dog. And He charged the Dog that he should be the eyes and the ears, the understanding and the legs of the Man."

The writer, Toussenel, then goes on to show how the dog was fitted for his important duties by being inspired with an overwhelming sense of the privileges of friendship and loyal devotion, and a corresponding disregard of the time-wasting joys of family and fireside pleasures, thinking, no doubt, with Bacon, that those without families—the discipline of humanity—make always the best public servants. " He that hath wife and children hath given hostages to fortune ; for they are impediments to great enterprises, either of virtue or mischief." And again, "Charity will hardly water the ground where it must first fill a pool." The dog, therefore, was relieved of paternal affections in order that he might be able to give an undivided mind to the high task set before him, and thus afford primitive man, in the flock-tending days, the leisure necessary for discovering the arts and evolving the sciences.

If Tubal Cain, for instance, had had to run after his *Music due to Dogs.* own herds he could never have got on with his panpipes ; so the dog attended to the sheep and the goats, the kine and the camels, while his master sat in the shade by the river, testing the properties of reeds. Music was the result—thanks to the dog. In the same way, perhaps, we might trace all other great discoveries to the same canine source, and, really, seeing even nowadays, when man has become such a self-helping creature, how many dogs keep men and how many of them support old ladies, the philosopher would seem to have some basis for his fanciful theory that, but for dogs, men would still have been shepherds and human society still in its patriarchal stage. The Red Indians keep no dogs; and what is the result? All their time is given up to dog's work, and they lead a dog's life doing it—chasing wild things about and holloaing after them. Other peoples, however, who started with them in the race of nations, and who utilized the dog, are now enjoying all the comforts of nineteenth-century civilization, hunting only for amusement and shepherding only on valentines. Professor Huxley might, to the public advantage, follow out the great line of reasoning here so hastily hinted at, for perhaps he could prove that the origin of society has lain unsuspected all these many centuries, in the great fact that the dog after all is the germ, the protoplasm of civilization. And if the learned Professor wishes to fortify his own opinion on this point, he has only to go to the dogs and ask theirs. But he must be prepared for humiliating disclosures.

Dogs having their day. If, indeed, the dogs were ever to have their day all together, instead of as now frittering away their strength by every dog having his day by himself, provincial humanity would have a painful experience of its helpless condition, and many a single villager would go suddenly to his grave. At present old men and tiny children suffice to "tend" sheep and cattle; for their four-legged lieutenants are neither blear-eyed nor deaf, senseless nor decrepid, and they do all the work, remembering the original charge given to them on prediluvian plains that they should be "the eyes and the ears, the understanding and the legs of man." If, however, these useful animals were to combine for concerted action, and simultaneously take holiday all together, the terrible memory of those Dog Days would never perish from the country-side. The plough and the loom would be deserted, for all the able-bodied in every parish would be occupied with hounding their own cattle off neighbours' lands, and, so to speak, dogging their restless sheep from gap to gap. Every available public building would be turned for the time into a pound, and Bumble would clear out the unremunerative tenants of the parochial workhouse to make room for stray cattle. A far more serious result would be this : that the Metropolitan Meat Markets could not be supplied, for our beef and mutton, remarking the absence of the usual dog, would nimbly scatter themselves over the shires, instead of following the high roads to town. Starvation would ensue, and gaunt Famine, stalking forth—but such a prospect is too dreadful to pursue, even in fancy ; for, though in this dire strait the uselessness of the dog might certainly point it out for consumption, we could not, even for the sake of cheapened "mutton-pies," advise so suicidal a cuisine, for every one will surely agree with me on this point— that the dog, though not quite good enough to eat, is far too good to be eaten.

Dogs of Fame. Who, indeed, has not at his fingers' ends any number of stories of the intelligence, the fidelity, and other virtues of the dog? And who at a moment's notice could not conjure up all the great dogs of fame— Ulysses' dog and Punch's dog, Alcibiades' dog and Cerberus, Barry of St. Bernard's and "the member of the Humane Society," Gelert and Lance's dog "Crab," the dogs of Mtesa, the emperor of Uganda, and that other animal who, "to serve some private ends, went mad, and bit the man;" the dog of Montargis and Mother Hubbard's dog, and the Greater and the Lesser Dogs of the constellations; the spaniel of Mary Queen of Scots and Anubis of Egypt; the pack of the Spectre Huntsman and the Red Dog of the Savana-durga; Ketmir that went with the Seven Sleepers into their cave, and the poodle that saved the Prince of Orange; the barometer dog of the Ptamphaoniens, and the dog "that worried the cat" in the notable history of the "House that Jack Built;" Tobit's dog and the dog in the Moon, Bill Sikes's mongrel and the dogs of Jezreel—with probably as many more that might be recollected with little effort. Each and all of them have done duty again and again to point a moral or adorn a tale, and what an avalanche of reminiscences and associations falls upon the mind when we summon before us, in all their miscellaneous array, the ban-dogs and bloodhounds of story, the war-hounds of savage tribes, the turnspits and truffle dogs and lapdogs of a past day, the Newfoundlands and Scotch shepherd dogs of the present, the dogs used for sport in England, for work as in the snows of Greenland, and in battle as in the plains of Equatorial Africa ! What a multitude they become, these dogs of a hundred varieties, and yet they say the original of them all was a wretched thing of the wolf kind; and that the jackal, a poor dog gone wrong, shows what the type might degenerate into if the alliance between man and dog were ruptured !

Problems enough even to satisfy modern inquirers abound, therefore, in the subject of the Dog. The origin of its varieties traverses all the field of natural science, and the question of its "consciousness" involves all metaphysics—a Pelion of enigmas piled on an Ossa of puzzles. Writers on the dog claim for it the noblest attributes of humanity, and share with it our meanest failings ; and, although the vast majority of instances of canine "mind" may be classified under the phenomena of self-interest and imitation, it is humiliating to feel that, if the dogs were to give their opinions of men, the same classification would hold good, and that for each of their own weaknesses they could cite a parallel among men. Were, then, the Egyptians right in thinking these animals mysteries beyond human comprehension ; and is all the East wrong when it declares that dogs have every

one of the gifts of humanity, and one more besides, the
gift of seeing the air and the spirits of the air, of per-
ceiving that which man is mercifully prevented from
seeing—Asrael, the Angel of Death, as he moves about
among the living? Some day, perhaps, some one will be
able to tell us where dog consciousness begins and ends,
and how far dog intellect coincides with our own. An
authoritative decision would be welcome, for, as the
matter stands, man seems in some danger of being
reckoned only the second-best of animals.

In a dispassionate view of the subject, however, the
foibles of the dog should not be, as they so often are,
overlooked.

*Man not
inferior to
Dogs in
many ways.*
Indeed, it might be well if some one would compile a
"counter-blast" of remarkable instances of the intelligence and docility of man—the human Trustys and
good Dog Trays that abound in the world; the men who
have been known to lose their friends in the streets and
to find them again; who have been carried to immense
distances by wrong trains, and turned up at home after
all; who recognize acquaintances with every demonstration of delight after a long separation; who carry
baskets from the baker's, and do not eat the contents
by the way; who worry cats; who rescue men from
drowning and from other forms of death; who howl
when they hear street organs; who know a thief when
he comes creeping up the back stairs at midnight, and
hold him until help arrives; who fetch, and carry, and

beg; who, in fact, do everything that a dog can do, and have died for all the world like Christians.

Such instances of intelligence in men, and even women, abound, and are amply authenticated by eye-witnesses.

Nor are any of the passions which move dogs unknown to human kind, for anecdotes illustrative of anger, fear, envy, courage, and so forth, are plentifully scattered up and down the pages of history and biography. In short, looking at the matter from both sides, I really think myself that there is no reason for supposing that man is in any way inferior to the dog.

Yet I cannot help thinking that a dog-show is some- *Inhuman-ity of Dog-shows.* what of an anachronism, and a relic of the darker ages, for, unless a great deal that has been written on the subject is nonsense, the exhibition of these animals is both inhuman in the exhibitors and degrading to the animals. The dog, we have been told again and again, is something better than a mere beast, and instances have been heaped together of specimens that were even something better than human beings. They have been held up to us as examples to be imitated not only in fidelity, courage, and other moral virtues, but in intelligence also; and, if this be the case, if dogs think and feel like men and women, what right have we to " show" them as if they were mere horses, or cattle, or cats? It is true that babies are sometimes exhibited, but then infants at the exhibition age are not sensitive in matters affecting the display of their bodies, and are barely human after all. It is also true that barmaids have been " shown," but this was with their own consent, and because they liked it. Now, neither case is analogous to that of the dog-show, for " the friend of man " is especially sensitive on many points in which at a public exhibition his feelings are keenly wounded, but through which a baby sleeps or bottles without the slightest symptom of affliction ; while, again, the dog's permission to be shown is never asked, as the barmaid's is.

A really corresponding case would be that presented if some limited liability company were to collect as many specimens of " inferior humanity " as they could, and cage them all up for the amusement of the public. But what would be thought of such a show of South Sea Islanders and Zulus, Red Indians, Esquimaux, Maoris, and Bushmen, Australians and Bheels, Hottentots, Aztecs and Patagonians, dreadful nameless savages from Central Africa, and queer nomad folk from Central Asia, Tchik-Tchiks from Tchuk-Tchuk, cannibals and Cuban slaves, idiots, atheists, and habitual drunkards, half breeds of all kinds, dwarfs and giants, Albinos, and " the hairy families of Burmah," troglodytes, lake and tree dwellers, two-headed nightingales and Macrobians, Arimasps, anthropophagi, and all the other eccentricities and diversities of mankind, which as yet are only by courtesy admitted as men ? Everybody would of course go to see them, but many would come away shocked. Imagine, for

example, the feelings of the cannibal in the centre of such
an exhibition, and the mental torture to which the poor
creature would be subjected ; or think for a moment of
the sufferings of the Choctaw at seeing all day and hear-
ing all through the night the voice of a hereditary foe of
the Sioux tribe in the next cage. Have dwarfs no feelings, or giants no susceptibilities? Yet we have been
repeatedly told that the dog is a link between man and
beast, sometimes even that man is only a second-rate
dog; and, notwithstanding this, we deliberately take
advantage of our superior cunning and appliances for
transport, to carry off to a " Show " all the kinds of dogs
we can find, the little ones in hampers, the big ones in
four-wheeled cabs, and, having arranged our fellow-beings
according to classes, solemnly proceed to award them
prizes for excellence ! Either, then, the dog-show is an
anachronism, or the superior theory of dogs is untenable,
and, at any rate, the two are not compatible in reason.

Whether the dogs will ever be able to turn the tables on
us and organize a man-show it is, of course, impossible
to say : but there is no doubt that if they did, and if
they would admit the general public on payment to the
exhibition, the spectacle would be immensely diverting
and also very remunerative. A foxhunter in a cage
would be an infinitely more interesting object than a
foxhound, and a monk of St. Bernard's certainly not less
attractive than his mastiff. At present we go to look at
lapdogs grouped together in pens, but who would not

prefer going to see their pretty owners, all dressed up for the day, with blue ribbons round their necks, and little silver bells that tinkled? In another class of pet dogs, the wheezy poodles, the display of elderly females would be full of instruction, and it would also be an admirable discipline to go round the various types of sportsmen, shepherds, carriage folk, blind men, drovers, rat-catchers, Humane Society's men, and other human correlates of the dogs, that would be exhibited if the dogs only had their day. Or the dog-show of the future might be an equitable fusion of the two species, men and dogs together. At present men and women have everything in their own hands, and for some reason, pretend one day that the dog is half-human, and on the next "show" him in public as if he were only a cat. In the future it may be the dogs will have the best of it, and put men up for prizes in the same objectionable way, awarding medals for the length of their legs or the blackness of the roofs of their mouths. Meanwhile, we may anticipate matters by acting honestly up to our theories, and exhibiting side by side the poacher and his cur, the hunting-man and his hound. This would be both generous and becoming, and we should escape the charge which may now be fairly levelled at us of sporting with the feelings of creatures which we declare to be as susceptible as ourselves.

Moral Dog-shows instructive. But if such a scheme should prove in advance of the times, we would suggest the compromise of showing only such dogs as are remarkable for moral and intellectual points rather than physical qualities. Thus, instead of degrading the creatures into classes of rat-hunting, long-haired, snub-nosed, or curly-tailed animals, we might exhibit them according to their degrees of virtue, in grades of fidelity, chivalry, humour, magnanimity, courage, modesty, patience, intelligence, gratitude, affection, and so forth—with a special department, it might be, for uncleanly, gluttonous, proud, covetous, and ill-tempered specimens, and for dogs that worry cats. No dog could object to such a show as this, for he would be at once placed on a par with ourselves, with Sunday-school children and the Victoria-cross heroes, men who save lives at the risk of their own, and prizemen at our Universities —with, in fact, every class of men who have to parade in public for the reception of honours worthily won. The dog that repeatedly carried a basket from a baker's, and never touched the contents would then feel no humiliation in being admired; and, in a community of admiration, the dogs that love their masters and know them when they meet them again need suffer from no wounded susceptibilities at such public exhibitions. A bandy-legged bull-dog is considered at present a prize medalist, and the more bandy the greater its merit; but what sensible dog could take credit to itself for such a shape? A glance at it, or at the turnspit, a mere cylinder on castors, suffices to show, if the expression on the face goes for anything, that each considers it is being made a fool of; while in the pathetic endurance of the larger breeds there is evident a very dignified protest against the process of exhibition, the monotony and the discomforts of it, the vulgar clamour of neighbours, the tedious length of the show, the triviality of the spectators' sympathy and the irrelevance of their observations. But in the kind of collection we suggest there need be no outrage to individual feelings, for Punch dogs would be there as representing the popular British drama, and not as mongrels; and the mangy old colley, that had saved its master a handsome fortune in sheep, would take precedence of the oiled and curled darlings of the drawing-room hearthrug.

As an improvement, therefore, upon the ordinary exhibition, I would suggest one either of men and dogs together, or else "a moral dog-show." A great number of people are tired of preposterous poodles and impossible cockers, and would like to see a more generous attention directed to the development of virtues. Legs and tails and other things of the kind are no doubt all excellent in their way, but now that we have proved by demonstration how much tail a dog can carry and how little leg he can do with, it would be interesting to know how often, for instance, a dog can be stolen and get home again, or how far he can go wrong and set himself right. It is beyond a doubt, now, that a dog's lower teeth can be made to project until he can nearly scratch his forehead with them; but would that dog, if his own master came creeping up the back stairs in listed slippers in the middle of the night, distinguish him from a housebreaker? Experiments have long ago satisfied us that the number of rats a terrier can kill in a given time is something prodigious; but where shall we look for the chivalrous dog who, being set after a rat, refused to catch it, because he saw it had a broken leg? Such specimens as these, the moral and intellectual animals—or perhaps we ought to call them persons—of whom we have read so much would constitute a dog-show of great interest; and if to them could only be added a few of the more celebrated dogs of the day, such as the Derby dog, Bismarck's dog, or the dog in the moon, the attractions of the collection would be much enhanced.

It is too late of course to think of any of the Crusaders' dogs, or the hound that followed the Indian prince so faithfully to heaven; the black brute in Faust, or the fifty animals of Acteon's pack; the dog that Socrates always swore by, or King Lear's ungrateful pets; Mœra, the dog of Icarios, whom we call Procyon, or the hounds of Ate; King Arthur's favourite mastiff Cavall, or Aubrey's champion; Fingal's dog Bran, or Boatswain, Lord Byron's retriever, or angry Zoilus the great dog of Thrace; Geryon's brutes, or "Glutton" and "the Bear-killer" that Orion owned. These and many another dog famous in the past are gone beyond recall. But the descendants of some of them survive, of the dogs that went into the Ark with Noah for instance, while the posterity of Anubis are still to be met prowling about the bazaars of the Nile villages, and

T

in Greece may be found the lineal posterity of the dogs
that tore Euripides to pieces, or even those to which the
wily Ulysses nearly fell a victim.　Agrippa's dog, that had
a devil chained to his collar—so contemporary history
gravely assures us—would be out of place, as he is certainly out of date, at the Crystal Palace; but there are
still to be had for the collecting, many dogs of great historical association.　The true breed of Sirius is a vexed
question to this day, but should be settled; and it will
need a great deal of special training to get little dogs to
laugh at the pranks of cats and fiddles, or greater ones,
like that of Alexander, to revenge themselves on enemies
only by silent contempt.　The problems of the dog
world, and the many phases of dog life which still remain
to be exhibited, are, therefore, it will be seen, both
numerous and varied, and if it were possible to combine
them by illustration in a single Exhibition, the moral dog-
show of the future would be both a pleasing and an
instructive novelty.

*　　*　　*　　*　　*

*Rats in
mythology.*

In science the dogs go after the rats.　So they do in
nature.　But in this book I was obliged to put the rats
behind the dogs, as dogs grow so naturally out of wolves
that I had it not in my heart to spoil the connexion
merely for the sake of being "scientific."　But the
connexion between rats and dogs, whichever way they
come in a book, is none the less very intimate indeed,
more so sometimes than the rats like.

But rats have a large history of their own, outside rat-pits. In Egypt and Chaldæa they were the symbol of utter destruction, while in India they are to-day the emblem of prosperous wisdom. The Romans took augury from rats—happy indeed the man who saw a white one; and Apollo, the most artistic of the Greek divinities, did not scorn the title of the " rat-killer." In this very England of ours, " the hardy Norseman" rats bore their share in the Conquest nobly, and on the continent they have ruined a city and a river. Rats, they say, have scuttled ships, and it is certain they once ate up a Bishop.

Not long ago, rat-catching engrossed much of the attention of the Government of India. The emergency was as serious as it was preposterous, for among the great vermin plagues that have afflicted the world the rat-invasion that devastated the Deccan must take high rank. Indeed, since the "croaking nuisance" took possession of the halls of Pharaoh, there have been very few visitations that have so directly insulted "the majesty of man's high birth," and so absurdly perplexed him.

Up and down the world at different times there have *Rat* been many plagues—plagues of locusts and cockchafers, *plagues.* of mice and caterpillars, plagues that have ravaged the vineyards and the corn-fields, the pine-forests and the orchards, plagues that have afflicted the farmer and the merchant, the prince and the peasant, the tradesman and the manufacturer, plagues of beasts, and birds, and insects. Armies have actually marched against little things with wings, and Senates have gravely sat in council over creeping creatures. The British force at Waterloo was not so numerous as that which the Moor sent against the advancing locusts, nor did the fathers of the city, fluttered by the news of Lars Porsena's approach, meet in more serious concern than did the French Assembly to concert measures, "the State being in danger," to resist the "sauterelle vorace." But in all these, quite apart from the gravity of the evil, there was a matter-of-fact sobriety about the circumstances of the impending danger, which separates them from the rodent visitation of the Deccan. Locusts are the avowed enemies of mankind, and their destruction has always been cheerfully assented to as a pleasing act of justice. No one when the vastatrix was at work among the vines held back the arm of retributive chemistry, nor when the cynips was vandalizing among our turnips was a kindly word spoken for the tiny foe. In India, however, everything, whether with fur or feathers, whether winged or wingless, finds a friend. Beautiful legends, orchid-like, have overgrown the old country, and so not only everything that moves, but every leaf that stirs, has a poem or a quaint conceit attached to it.

Western prejudice. We, in the West, have flung our prejudices at even inoffensive creatures. Thus, the cormorant is abused by every poet who has mentioned the bird. The owl has no more friends than the toad, and the buzzard and the raven are as unpopular and as heartily maligned by our imaginative writers and in our proverbs and ballads as the badger and the newt. Many others meet only with acidulated compliments, and some—like the glutton among beasts, the crow among birds—are ungenerously denied the possession of the most ordinary beast and fowl virtues. It is true that, on the other hand, we flatter unworthily the creatures of our own affection, embarrassing the pelican with our undeserved regard, and in the robin canonizing what in the sparrow we anathematise. But misplaced esteem does not compensate for wanton depreciation; nor does it affect our action when our prejudices are called into lively expression. Spiders fare ill with most of us, and no earwig of discernment comes for a holiday amongst us.

In India, however, everything alike is welcome at the *Eastern tenderness.* fountain of superstitious tenderness, and where European influences have not penetrated all creation seems to live in amity. The teaching of the compassionate Buddha, "the speechless world's interpreter," has elsewhere won for living things the same forbearance at the hands of other millions, and Asia thus stands apart from Europe as the refuge and asylum of the smaller worlds of creatures, harmful and harmless alike.

This pitifulness works often to strange results. A man-eating tiger establishes his shambles near a village, but the villagers, knowing him to be an old and esteemed acquaintance, lately deceased, steal away from their hamlet and deprecate any violent dislodgment of the human soul from its present tiger body. Monkeys rob the shops

in the bazaar, but who could think of reprisals against
such holy thieves? Snakes take human life, but pay
none in penalty. Elephants and cuckoos, bulls and
tortoises, quadruped and bird, fish and reptile, all come
in for their special honours and special privileges, and,
when danger threatens, for special immunity.

The rats in the Deccan in the same way enjoyed the full
benefit of this delightful catholicity of benevolence, not
from any virtues inherent in that forward rodent, or any
tradition of good done to man in a former state, but
simply from the Hindoo's tolerance of small life, and
the contemporary growth of superstition.

The famines that laid waste some of the fairest provinces
of India had stolen from every hearth one or more of the
family circle, and the peasant mind, loyal to its teachings,
refused to believe that the loved ones had been lost for
ever. Cruel drought bound the ground as with iron, and
so the seed sown never gave its increase. Starvation
crept round the hamlet, and one by one the weakest died.

Yet the wheels of time rolled on, and another har-
vest-time came round. The seasons were kindly, rain
was abundant, and the ground returned to the sower's
hand its hundred-fold. And back to the earth, glad with
full harvests, crept the poor defunct. What more natural?

Not, of course, in the likeness of their old selves, for
it is not given to man to live twice as man, nor yet in
nobler form, for what had the pitiful starved dead given
in alms to the Brahmins? So they came back to the

world that had treated them so badly—as rats. Killed by the want of grain, they returned as grain devourers, and the round completeness of this retaliation sufficed to satisfy the Hindoo mind as to the iniquity of injuring the still hungry victims of the great famine. That they suffered from their depredations their own memorials to the authorities attested amply. "We had promise of a good crop. But in came a multitude of rats, which have carried to their holes our ears of corn. Thus the morsel was taken from between our teeth, and the corn-stalks stand headless in the fields." The government in reply, assured them of its sympathy, assured them also of its knowledge of rat habits, and begged them to kill the rats. But there came the rub. Could a Hindu who was about to be starved kill another Hindu already once starved to death? Was it not just possible that when he himself had been starved he might return as a rat? To set such a precedent might be to commit suicide while committing murder—so they declined to kill the rats.

Government therefore had to appeal to the regular district staff. A rat committee was formally gazetted, and names eminent in various departments of official routine appeared upon it. "A special officer with a certain number of skilled men under him" was delegated to execute the sentences pronounced by the rat-destroying Sanhedrim, and by the time the harvest had been eaten up, and all the rats of the district were very fat, a campaign was undertaken.

An excellent minute from Sir Richard Temple's practised pen appeared, and without doubt had its proper
moral effect upon the rats. The priests paraded the fields
with bell, book, and candle, calling down rain to drown
them out of their holes; and the chemists of Bombay sate
busy in the concoction of fulminating powders, abominable in odour and copious in smoke. All "vermin-
destroying animals," as Sir Richard Temple put it, "that
were at the villagers' command," were brigaded against
the foe, and the administrative staff of each district
was specially and solemnly enjoined to proceed at once to
"hunt down and kill the rats, in real earnest." There
was to be no shilly-shallying. The rats were to be killed
as dead as possible—to be excessively put to death.

To offer suggestions, at this distance of time and in ignorance of the exact kind of rat that afflicted the people
of India and threatened its finances, is to challenge ill-
natured criticism. Still I cannot refrain from suggesting
nevertheless. The rat, I take it, is of a nimble kind,
and in the appointment of the committee I should, therefore, have been inclined to advise the selection of young
men—as young as possible. Agility goes a long way, I
am credibly informed, in the capture of a rat. In the
next place, "the skilled men" who had to operate under
the orders of the Rat Committee might very properly
have been rat-catchers. These gentlemen make the
catching of rats their special study, and it is not improbable that their technical training would have been

found useful when the actual operation of tail collecting had to be performed.

For Sir Richard decided that payment for work done should go by tails produced, and the headmen of the different villages were to be held responsible that no spurious imitations of the genuine article found their way into the market. It is not given to all to know a rat's tail when they find one, or when they ask for it to see that they get it ; and in India precedents abound of natural products being artificially counterfeited. It is notorious that rewards are paid away annually for wolves' heads and snakes which were never either one or the other, and when, "under the babul in the dale, each makadum tells his tale," it is just possible the bunches made up for official inspection may not be so honest in the centre as they are on the outside.

In England the rat plague is endemic among us. Only the other day the populousness of our subterranean adversaries was indicated by the disclosures connected with a case in the Woolwich police court ; for, in the evidence taken against some men charged with damaging the river bank while digging for rats, it was alleged that these creatures swarmed " by tens of thousands " at the mouths of the sewers. Here they work to admirable purpose, in so far as they clear refuse from the Thames' surface, but, in comparison with the mis- *Rats' abuse* chief done in accomplishing it, their good offices are *of Intelligence.* seriously depreciated. Few creatures have attained to such universal abuse as the rat, and few, perhaps, have deserved so much. It is true that its sagacity is prodigious, and every one knows that in the East it symbolizes Ganesha, the god of wisdom ; but its sagacity is so often displayed under compromising circumstances that the rat gains little respect for the possession of this valuable quality. It is very sagacious, no doubt, in an animal to dip its tail in a bottle of oil, and then carry its tail home to suck at leisure, but such larcenous refreshment will not commend itself to any but the disreputable. Nor is there much that is admirable in the wisdom which prompts the rat to make a wheelbarrow or truck of itself, for the greater convenience of removing stolen goods. It appears that, when a gang have come upon a larger plunder than they can carry away from the premises inside them, one of the number lies down on his back while the others load him up with the booty ; that he balances the pile with four legs, and, to make matters extra safe, folds his tail over the goods and holds the tip in his mouth, and that his " pals " then drag him off along the ground by the ears and fur ! This is excellent as far as the idea and its execution are concerned ; but, after all, the end to which such means are adapted —the nefarious removal of another's property—is immoral, and unworthy of imitation. It is impossible to extend sincere admiration to so deplorable a misapplication of genius.

Nor can the other virtues attributed to rats, such as

considerate treatment of the blind among them, their *Their doubtful* docility under domestication, and their industry, be re- *Virtues.* garded as unalloyed. Their industry, for instance, is shown by perpetual voracity, for the rat never ceases gnawing. It does not matter to the small beast what the substance may be, so long as its consumption does not immediately endanger its own person, for it takes a house just as it comes, and, beginning at the floor of the cellar, goes straight through to the slates. Yet this is not industry, although it may look like it, for the rat must either nibble or die. If it were to stop nibbling, and thus allow its teeth to grow unchecked, they would soon overlap each other, and cause lock-jaw, or, as from accident has sometimes occurred, would continue to grow in a curve until they pierced the eye or the brain.

On the rat's consideration for its kind, again, one might put a very sinister construction, for the knowledge of rat ways might prompt the belief that the infirm were only being cared for until they became fit to eat, and that the jealous solicitude apparently being displayed for the welfare of the afflicted relative was really only a series of selfish precautions to prevent others from surreptitiously making away with the object of their care before he was properly fattened for their own eating. The cannibal propensity is, indeed, grossly developed among rats. The parents eat their young, deciding for their offspring that death in infancy is better than a life of troubles, and the young who survive, seeing around them so much aged misery, and deploring such a future for their parents, piously consume their progenitors.

Thus too, among the earlier barbarians of the Oxus, did the Massagetæ who, if history has not traduced them, ate their infirm relatives, not from ill-will towards them, but as a public duty. Every man was expected to devour his own parents, and the interference of a stranger in the solemn rite might have been rudely resented. For a conscientious family, though they would not probably at other times have grudged him a seat at their board, might on such an occasion have misunderstood the stranger's offers of assistance, as reflecting upon their capacity to do their duty without outside help.

Ethnology of Rats. In its origin also the race of rats resembles exactly those successive waves of savage humanity that have swept westward over Europe, coming from the same Central Asian cradles, and tallying with them in the chronology of their invasions. Yet their great nation has also thrown out from time to time colonies of a far higher stamp of emigrant. Thus, though troops of rats followed and accompanied the Goth and the Hun and the Tartar, similar migrations marked also the Norman invasion and the Hanoverian accession. The rats, in fact, are the " doppelgängers " of invaders generally, following the provision chests of every human exodus, barbarian or otherwise ; and are the emblem not only of determined incursion, but permanent occupation. They are the type of the successful invader, sagacious in forecast, fierce in attack, and tenacious in possession. Wherever their colonies are planted, they take deep root at once and for ever, and the aborigines must either be absorbed into the conquering element, or disappear before it. Their motto is " Rats or nothing." Rat society, though thus maintaining with persistent ferocity the ground it has gained, and gradually extending its area, will be found, in its latest developments, to be everywhere representative of the most degraded classes of humanity.

" They are symbols," says an analyst of beast character, " of the miserable and prolific communities which now disgrace some parts of the earth, and whom hunger and hatred of honest labour compel to perpetual conflict and cannibalism. One fine day, no doubt, they will disappear —with war and pestilence and famine." Another writer deduces from them political reflections, advises the " Norman " and the " Russian " rats to coalesce instead of fighting, and to divide the East between them, and points out as remarkable that the two most aggressive species of rat known to the world, and which " have weighed most heavily upon Europe," are those of England and of Muscovy, "the two countries which were the last to shake off barbarism." Such, then, is the importance of this small creature in the system of the human economy that our neighbours judge us by our rats !

The inference drawn might be considered unfair, as it undoubtedly is ; but the coincidences of genealogy, origin, and chronology must be confessed to be remarkable.

Wherever it goes the rat retains its chief characteristics
of determination, pugnacity, and destructiveness.   It is
enough for it that its teeth require to be filed, so it
does not loiter to consider the nature or value of the
substance on which it has to file them.   Lead does as
well as wood, and whether it meets the former in the
shape of a gas-pipe, or the latter as a beer-cask, it matters
little, for it punctually performs its duties to itself by
gnawing a hole through the object.   That an escape of
gas or a rush of beer should follow the perforation strikes
the rat, perhaps, as a fact worth noting down, but only
in a degree as it finds its nose annoyed or its feet wet.
There is, then, little sympathy in rat nature.   It is true that,
in the sewers of great cities, where they reign supreme, no
other creature caring or daring to contest the occupancy
of such noisome haunts, these rodents live in vast communities, but their sole tie is that of necessity, and the
idea of Society suggests itself to its members only as an
aggregate of edible individuals, broadly divided into two
classes—those able to eat and those fit to be eaten.
Nor with other things than rats, such as men and their
belongings, have they any other code of ethics or any
wider range of sympathies, for everything, whether created
or made, falls in their philosophy into one or other of
the two great divisions, the eaters and the eaten.   Every
achievement of science is in turn submitted to the same
test, be it the rolling stock of the underground railway,
the concrete of the pneumatic tubes, or the pipes of the

City drainage, water-works, or telegraph, and each in turn is found to be edible. Every foundation that is dug up or laid down gives the rats in the same way a subject of brief interest ; but no sooner has the building taken shape than they drive a tunnel through it, and annex it to their previous possessions, and it soon becomes as commonplace as the rest, for, be it palace or prison, market, cathedral, or museum, the rat stamps his broad arrow upon it before it has even been formally " inaugurated."

It follows, therefore, that all our lives through we are being watched from underground by thousands of vigilant eyes, and whether in our gardens or our houses, at business or at pleasure, in the streets or on the river, a multitude of little creatures are waiting for us to finish and depart, that they may step in to occupy our places. Overwhelmed by this very consideration, the citizens of Montfaucon, not many years ago, met in council to consider the question of rats, and profoundly decided that the best way to get at the end of them was—to exterminate them.

But to this day there are far more rats in Paris than human beings.

CHAPTER IX.

THE SEA-FOLK.

ERMAIDS, though still reasonably abundant at country fairs in Europe, appear to have become extinct in England.

The latest authenticated appearance is that of the supposed mermaid which was discovered sporting in the sea off the Caithness shore, but which—by his own confession—turned out to be Sir Humphrey Davy bathing.

Since then, there have been several claimants to the title, but all have collapsed under the disintegrating touch of scientific inquiry, which, resolving the several compositions into their primal elements, classified them in detail as being part monkey, part salmon, and part leather.

Some, no doubt—and I for one—regret the extinction *Exter-* of "the mermaid," but the less superstitious majority *mination of Mer-* will congratulate Science on having at last reduced to *maids.* one or two facts all the miscellaneous congregation of syrens, mermaids, mermen, tritons, sea-cows, sea-swine, sea-horses, mer-devils, sea-lions, water-satyrs, and un-dines ;—all the wilderness of aquatic prodigies deli-neated in Aldrovandus his " History of Monsters," or spoken of from eye-witness by Maundeville ; that monk-cowled thing which Rondeletius knew all about, and the storm-ruling creatures, half-man, half-fish, which the curious reader will find so carefully recorded by Olaus Magnus and many another. The sub-order of the Sirenia now includes all the herbivorous cetacea, those wonderful animals that have given the silly world so much pleasant fable, and wise men so much trouble.

Science, revenging itself, has swept away these strange sea people, beautiful and bad together, and has given us in their place a family of inform things, the Rhytinidæ *The lost* and the Manatidæ. The first are now extinct. Like *Rhytina.* the dodos—which were so common in the Mauritius when that island was first discovered that the sailors chased them about by hundreds, knocking them on the head with stones, but of which now there are only two heads, one foot, and a few feathers to bear witness that this great bird ever existed—the Rhytina Stellerii, or Northern Manatee, was found swarming in 1741 upon the shores of an island in Behring's Straits. For ten months the shipwrecked sailors entirely supported life upon its flesh and oil, and so it happened that when, just twenty-seven years later, an expedition went out to inquire if a Manatee fishery would be profitable, it was found that not a single specimen remained. The family of Rhytina had been actually extinguished from the world's list of living things in twenty-seven years, and the only remains of this astonishing animal at present known to exist are one skull and a few other fragments in European museums. Of the other sub-family, the Manatidæ proper, many species are known to naturalists, and of the commonest of these, the Manatee of the American coast, a living specimen was lately exhibited in London as the " West India mermaid."

A Modern Mermaid. Those who went to visit it, however, had to dismiss from their minds all the fancies with which literature, poetry and prose alike, had invested them, of rosy mermaids golden-haired, and jolly mermen with Bacchus faces, crowned with coral. Some, no doubt, expected a shapely Triton with flowing beard and his conch-shell slung by his side, or dainty lady of those syren islands

> " Whence fairy-like music steals over the sea,
> Entrancing the senses with charm'd melody."

Others, on the other hand, visited it with preconceived ideas of some narwhal or whale creation, expecting a grampus-like thing, or anticipating a porpoise. But it was necessary to approach the "mermaid" with an imagination absolutely blank, for, whatever you tried to imagine, you were utterly discomfited by the reality.

Who, indeed, could soberly put before his mind the actual features of this sea monster, so absurd in its shapelessness that if it were to be exhibited dead the most credulous rustic would sneer at it as a clumsy hoax? Even alive, the thing looked a make-up, and a discreditable one; for where the tail and paddling-paws —they are not fins nor yet legs—had been injured, the " stuffing" appeared to be coming out. The ragged edges of the skin, if such an integument is to be called skin, had frayed away into threads, and, if it were not that the manatee winked occasionally, the spectator might be justified in asserting his own ability to make a better monster. But it is this very simplicity of its composition that renders the preposterous creature so astonishing and so absurd. Gustave Doré found out the secret, or learned it perhaps from the old German school, that, to depict the perfection of a monster, only one element of incongruous monstrosity should be utilized at a time, and the result of his knowledge has been his incomparable creatures of fancy. On the other hand, from igno- *Receipt for* rance of this rule the prodigious beings of Hindoo fable *Monsters.* are habitually stupid and foolish, for the artist overlays his subject with such a multitude of deformities that the complete composition is silly and senseless. The Hindoos, therefore, should go to the manatee, and take a lesson in the wonderful effects to be produced by avoiding elaborateness of detail, for nothing in the animal world can be imagined less diversified in feature than this "mermaid" of the West Indies. In the lower world of creatures the slug alone presents us with an equally sober monotony of outline, and, if a seven-foot slug were sown up in an old tarpaulin, the result would be a tolerable reproduction of the manatee. One end would have to be flattened out into a gigantic beaver's tail, and the other be shaped snoutwise. The details of mouth, nose, eyes, and ears might be left to the creature's own fancy or to accident. And the arrangements for its senses with which the manatee is content are delightfully simple.

For eyes it has circular apertures which can neither remain wide open nor shut up tight, but are constantly contracting and expanding, perhaps at the will of the manatee, though apparently of their own motion. For nose it has two holes with lids, and when it rises to the surface of the water for breath the lids open and when it sinks again they shut. The ear-holes are too small to be seen without keen searching, and are simply such holes as might be made anywhere with a gimlet. For mouth it has an opening with a flap over it, convenient as preventing things from going down its throat when the owner is not hungry, but sufficiently ugly to make the manatee the most humble of creatures—and humble, indeed, it looks. Having no legs, it stands on its tail, and to keep its balance has to bend the head forward and bow the body. In this attitude of helpless humility *The Solem-* the strange thing stands motionless many minutes to- *nity of Shapeless-* gether, and then, with a ghost-like, dreadful solemnity, *ness.* it begins slowly to stiffen and straighten its tail, and thus, gradually rising into an erect posture, thrusts its nostrils above the surface. But only for an instant, for ere it seems to have had time to take a breath, the great body begins to sink back into its despondent position, and the small paddling-paws drop motionless and helpless as before. The deliberate sloth with which the manœuvre is executed has something of dignity in it, but otherwise the manatee is as ridiculous as it is helpless. The clumsy snout is constantly twitching like a rabbit's, but the gesture that seems so appropriate in the nervous, vigilant little rodent is immeasurably ludicrous in this huge monstrosity. The eyes, again, now contracted to a pin's point, now expanded full to gaze at you with expressionless pupils, seem to move by a mechanism beyond the creature's control. Voiceless and limbless, the bulky cetacean sways to and fro, the very embodiment of stupid, feeble helplessness, a thing for shrimps to mock at and limpets to grow upon.

A carcase of such proportions, such an appalling contour, should, to satisfy æsthetic requirements, possess some *The Kine of Proteus.* stupendous villainy of character, should conceal under such an inert mass of flesh some hideous criminal instinct. Yet this great shapeless being, this numskull of the deep sea, is the most innocent of created things. *It lives on lettuce.* In its wild state it browses along the meadows of the ocean bed, cropping the seaweeds just as kine graze upon the pastures of earth, inoffensive and sociable, rallying as cattle do for mutual defence against a common danger, placing the calves in the middle, while the bulls range themselves on the threatened quarter. These are the herds which the poets make Proteus and the sea-gods tend, the harmless beeves with whom the sad Parthenope shared her sorrows! These are the actual realities that have given rise to so many a pretty fiction, the dull chrysalids from which have swarmed so many butterflies.

It is disappointing to those who cherish old-world fancies; but to Science the lazy uncouth manatee is a precious thing. Science, indeed, has seldom had a more pleasing labour than the examination and identification of this animal, for, though so ludicrously simple in appearance, it is a veritable casket of physiological wonders.

It is the only creature known that has three eyelids to each eye, and two hearts. In most of its points it bears a close affinity to the elephant, but in others of equal importance it is unmistakably a whale! Its "teeth," bones, and skin, are all delightful studies to the naturalist, and he is thankful, therefore, that the manatee is what it is, and not the veritable mermaid that less prosaic minds would have it. Even these, how-ever, may find some consolation for the loss of their ocean folk in learning of the strange ways of this strange beast, and its tranquil life below the sea, nibbling about in great meadows of painted seaweed. Some travellers have given it a voice. Captain Colnett has left it on record that one remained by his ship for three hours, "uttering sounds of lamentation like those produced by the female human voice when expressing the deepest distress;" and another mariner tells us how, when sailing in an open boat, they surprised a manatee asleep, and, thinking it to be a merman, they hesitated to harpoon it; and how on a sudden the creature awoke, and with an angry shout plunged into the depths! Anger, neverthe-less, appears to be utterly foreign to its character, for among the Malays the name of the Eastern species is a synonym for gentle affection, and every writer, from Buffon to our time, bears evidence to its sociability and remarkable absence of fear of men. But, alas for the manatee! Its virtues are its bane, for whether among the West India islands or the creeks of the Guiana and the Brazilian coast, in the estuaries of the Oronoko and the Amazon, in the river mouths of Western Africa, or in the archipelago of the Eastern seas, the same fearless confidence in man is rapidly hastening its extinction. The flesh is excellent food, the blubber yields a fine oil, the skin is of valuable toughness, and so before long the manatee of the warm seas may be expected to be as

"extinct" as its congener of the cold North—the lost
rhytina of Behring's Straits.

*   *   *   *   *

*Terrors
of the Deep
Sea.*

Victor Hugo, in his Guernsey romance, "The Toilers
of the Sea," presented the world with a monster, a terror
of the deep waters, something like the gruesome spider-
crab of Erckmann-Chatrian, but even more horrible.   It
was the "pieuvre," a colossal cuttle-fish, which had its
den far down in the sea among the roots of the rocks; a
terrible long-armed thing that lurked in the caverns of
the deep, grappling from its retreat with any passing
creature, paralyzing it by fastening one by one a thousand suckers upon it, and slowing dragging its victim,
numbed with pain, towards the awful iron beak that lay

*Hugo's
pieuvre.*

in the centre of the soft, cruel arms.   The novelist's
pieuvre was hideous enough, and his description surpassing in its horrors, but in Schiller's poem of "The
Diver," a *thing* of similar character, but rendered
even more awful by not being described at all, compasses
the death of the hero.   He did not, like Victor Hugo's
sailor, have a protracted struggle with the mysterious
creature and then come back to his friends with details
of its personal appearance, but he dived out of sight—and
never returned.   Schiller does not attempt, therefore, to
describe the indescribable thing, but, simply calling it
"*das*," throws the reader back in imagination upon all the
horrible legends of the Mediterranean coasts and islands,
to guess for himself the sort of monster it must have

been that had seized the hapless diver and devoured him at its leisure in the twilight depths of the sea.

Such monsters as these, it has been drily thought, *Schiller's* belong only to legend and fable and poem, but this is *"das."* not the case. Pieuvres of the Victor Hugo type, and "things" such as Schiller hints at, are, it is true, exaggerated specimens of the species, but their congeners —and dreadful ones, too—do actually exist, for they have been seen and fought with, and described, and scientific conditions are all amply satisfied by those descriptions. Not long ago, a Government diver at Belfast, Victoria, had a narrow escape from losing his life in the clutch of a huge octopus. It had seized his left arm, causing dreadful agony by the fastening of its suckers upon the limb; but the diver had an iron bar in his right hand, and, after a struggle that seemed to him to last twenty minutes, during which the monster tried hard to drag him down, he battered his assailant into a shapeless mass, and freed himself from its horrid grasp. Schiller's "Taucher" had no iron bar, and his bones, therefore, went to increase the heap which "pieuvres," so Victor Hugo says, accumulate at the mouths of their deep-sea dens.

It is all-important, for the existence of these monstrous *Unlimited* "poulpes," cuttle-fish, octopuses, or sepias, that Science *poulpes.* should countenance them; for, so long as professors array their calmly sceptical opinions on the one side, no number of sworn affidavits from the public as to personal encounters with the pieuvre will suffice to establish the creature as a verity. In the case of that other terror of the ocean, the Sea-Serpent, science goes dead against its existence, and Professor Owen speaks far too weightily for even sober official accounts of the great snake to be accepted as convincing evidence in its behalf. Thus Captain M'Quhae, of her Majesty's ship *Dædalus*, declared, in a report to the Admiralty thirty years ago, that he and his officers had seen sixty feet of a marine monster, with the head of a snake, under conditions which, taken with the trustworthiness and sobriety of his evidence, places the record of his encounter with "the great sea-serpent" above all others that either preceded or followed it. Yet even this account, so cautious in its language, and given by men so eminently capable of judging of objects seen at sea, was completely met at every point by the scientific verdict of "impossible."

That sixty-foot monsters besides whales may exist Professor Owen does not deny, for have we not already seals of thirty feet and sharks of forty, besides congers of unknown lengths? But he says this: if sea-serpents have been in the seas from the first, and are still there in such numbers as reports would have us believe, how is it that no single fragment of one, fossilized or not, has ever yet been washed ashore or dug up? The negative evidence from the utter absence of any remains weighs, therefore, with the scientific mind, and ought also with public opinion, against even such positive evidence as that of

the commander of the *Dædalus;* for, after all, just as
positive evidence from just as trustworthy witnesses
abounds for the proof of ghosts. So the grand old
Kraken, the great sea-worm, remains still without identity; and though, from a patriotic and conservative
point of view, I trust the British public will never
abandon any of its "glorious old traditions," especially
such a fascinating one as the sea-serpent, I would caution it in the matter of any kraken professing to be
more than a hundred yards long, lest it should be
said of them that they prefer "the excitement of the
imagination to the satisfaction of the judgment."

For monster cuttle-fishes, however, the British public
has the permission of science to believe anything it
likes; and, in fact, the more the better. It may swell
out the bag-like bodies of the poulpe to any dimensions
consistent with the containing capacities of an ocean, and
pull out their arms until, like Denys de Montford's octopus, they are able to twist one tentacle round each of
the masts of a line-of-battle ship, and, holding on with
the rest to the bottom of the sea, to engulf the gallant
vessel with all sail set. Science is helpless to oppose the
belief in such monsters, for they are scientifically possible, *Delightful possibilities*
and, from the sizes already recorded, there is no limit *in Cuttle-fish.*
reasonably assignable to their further extension, so that
everybody is at liberty to revel "by authority" in cuttle-
fishes as big as possible. The Victorian octopus referred
to above measured only eight feet, but this proved almost

sufficient to kill a strong man, while the body belonging to a specimen of such dimensions would have been quite heavy enough, had the arms once fairly grappled the victim, to sink him to the bottom of the sea, where, anchoring itself by its suckers to a rock in the sea-bed, the monster could have eaten its prey at leisure. The octopus, moreover, is very active, as the nature of its usual food—fishes and crustaceans—requires it should be, and the danger, therefore, to man, from the huge specimens which travellers have recorded—that of M. Sander Rang, for instance, the body of which was as large as "a large cask"—would be very terrible indeed; but fortunately gigantic specimens, though indisputably existing, are not common on populous coasts.

In a paper once read to the British Association by Colonel Smith, the writer adduced many instances of "colossal sepias," among them an enormity of forty feet, and another hardly less, of which fragments are preserved in the Haarlem Museum. General Eden records one of over twenty feet in length, and another creature of the same order, taken up on to a ship at sea, which had arms that measured no less than thirty-six feet. In this way, increasing foot by foot, each enlarging specimen becomes a possibility, until at last there would be no reason for disbelieving even that wonderful story of Captain Blaney, who mistook a dead cuttle-fish for a bank, and landed on it with sixty men! But this was of course

very long ago indeed, and may now be relegated to the
limbo of Pontoppidan's fabulous monsters—the krakens
with lions' manes, that got up on end and roared, and
pieuvres that hunted ships at sea.   Meanwhile, because
suspicions of exaggeration attach to particular individuals
that were measured by the fathom and weighed by the
ton, that sank barques by the simple process of pulling
them under water, and that crunched up boats as easily
as parrots crack nuts, there is no ground for disputing
the existence of monsters sufficiently formidable to
satisfy even exacting fancy, and to make life under the
sea very perilous to such poor things as men.   Though
a first cousin of the nautilus, one of the frailest and most
beautiful of marine creatures, and though it is itself eaten
in large quantities in the South of Europe, where it
forms a regular article of food, the poulpe or octopus,
calamary, squid, cuttle-fish, sepia, picœuvre, or "*das*"—
or whatever the different species of this order may be
called in science or romance—retains its repulsive appearance and its ferocious character.   Swift, voracious,
and unrelenting, it ranks, even when diminutive, among
the chief enemies of small deep-sea life, and, when it
attains the moderate dimensions of the Victorian octopus
referred to above, it becomes a formidable antagonist,
even for armed men.   When, however, it reaches its
fullest length and greatest bulk, the sea-serpent itself
would have but a poor chance with it, so that we have,
after all, the satisfaction of knowing that, though science

forbids us to possess a kraken, we do possess in actual fact another monster which, if the kraken did exist, could probably catch it and eat it up.

*   *   *   *   *

But the Kraken has reappeared—bless him. It has been distinctly seen by Captain Cox of the good ship *Privateer.* Henceforth they are an article of my creed.

The sea-worm.

Sea-serpents, in spite of repeated efforts to obtain respectable recognition, have been hitherto regarded as mythical. For one thing they showed no judgment in the selection of individuals to whom to exhibit themselves; and the testimony of their existence afforded by the master of ships unknown on Lloyd's registers, and by American captains "of undoubted veracity" served only to plunge the monsters of the deep seas more profoundly into the obscurity of fable. Their opportunities for declaring themselves have been many, but they have preferred to come to the surface only when unscientific and untrustworthy witnesses happened to be passing overhead. A

Immorality of ancient Sea-serpents.

score of "appearances" of the sea-serpent have been recorded in as many years, but not one has gained credence, because, in the first place, of this defect in the credibility of the narrators, and in the next, because each man described such a different monster.

The whole marine fauna, from the narwhal to the octopus, was drawn upon for contributions to the hybrid thing which we were asked to believe was the veritable Kraken; but when all the tusks and tails, legs and manes, fiery eyes and scales, horses' heads and wings came to be fitted on to a serpentine form of prodigious bulk and length, the miscellaneous result was so outrageous that credulity was staggered, and men, in despair, refused to believe even in a decent sea-serpent, or any sea-serpent at all.

A moderate animal of about fifty or a hundred feet in length, with the girth of an average barrel or two, and, say, half-a-dozen plausible propellers or even a twin screw; with a respectable snake's head at one end and coming to a proper point at the other—such a creature would have been admitted into every household as an article of belief, and have largely assisted in developing the young idea as to " Behemoth " and " Leviathan " and the other wonders of the sea, which, in default of a definite beast, have so long loomed hazily in the child-mind as mere figures of speech. When, however, we were gravely asked to introduce to the notice of our school children a heterogeneous patchwork monstrosity that stood up from its middle to rest its chin on the topgallant-stunsail-boom of a three-masted ship; that spouted and roared at one end and lashed up the sea into little bubbles at the other; that reared horned heads out of water, glaring the while with eyes of flame upon the trembling mariners, shaking aloft a more than leonine mane of hair, and paddling in the air with great uplifted paws—parents, I think, did well to warn off so disreputable an apparition from the sacred ground of infant schools and nurseries, and the scientific world showed judgment in withdrawing its approbation from such a disorganizing beast.

Nature insists upon her proprieties being observed, and so long as man remembers this, his zoological beliefs will remain fit to lie upon every breakfast table.

Credulity as to Monsters disastrous. But if once we fall from the strict paths of possibility, our facts become improbable, and there will be an inrush of creatures trampling across, flying over, and swimming through every rule of natural history, every law of creation. Basilisks will caper light-hearted, but exceedingly venomous, from the bird-world into the private precincts of the snakes; immoral dragons will make sport of all generic distinctions between the carnivorous and graminivorous; wyverns will cleave the sea with their tails and the air with their wings; and (supreme audacity) mermaids will assert man himself to be properly amphibious. If once the key is turned to let in these disturbing dualities, a mob of indeterminate things—gryphons and sphinxes, wolfmen and vampires, unicorns and cockatrices—will crowd into the orderly courts of knowledge, and, breaking down all the bulwarks of our rational beliefs, will seat themselves triumphantly among the ruins of science!

No such dismal prospect of scientific chaos need, however, be entertained from the latest appearance of the sea-serpent, an animal which, from its description, would seem one that may be confidently admitted into the best conducted families as an article of household faith. Captain Cox, master of the British ship *Privateer*, states that a hundred miles west of Brest, at five o'clock on *A well-regulated Kraken.* the afternoon of a fine, clear day, he saw, some three hundred yards off, about twenty feet of a black snake-like body, three feet in diameter, moving through the water towards his ship. As it approached, he distinctly perceived its eel-like head and its eyes; but the sea-serpent, when it got so close as this, took fright and plunged with a great splash under the water, and then, turning itself round with a mighty disturbance of the sea, made off, raising its head frequently as it went. Now, here there is no extraordinary demand made upon credulity, for the merest infant can comfortably entertain the idea, in twenty-foot lengths at any rate, of a snake as thick as an eighteen-gallon cask. The colour, too, is simple black, and the head has no features more surprising than eyes.

The great sea-serpent, therefore, is, after all, found to come within the compass of the ordinary human understanding, and we are not asked to believe in more than a somewhat magnified conger-eel. In behaviour, also, the present animal differs agreeably and rationally from all preceding " avatars " of the great sea-worm, as the Danes call it ; for except that it splashed extravagantly when it turned round in the water, it did not demean itself otherwise than might respectably be permitted to a snake of such dimensions. At the same time, however, such is the weakness of human nature, there will be vestiges of regret for the turbulent, ill-behaved, monstrosity that has hitherto done duty as the sea-serpent. The present worm is perhaps just a little too tame. If it had only shown a scale or two, or sparkled slightly at the nostrils, or betrayed some tendency towards horns or claws, shaken just a little mane—not too much, of course—or snorted, or brayed, or even squeaked moderately, we should have been better satisfied. We should have felt that we had got something. As it is, we have got only a huge eel—no crest of hair, no flames, no ravening jaws —a dull eel, too, that behaved with disappointing respectability, not even rising to a spout or a roar. It kept itself horizontal on the water, instead of standing on one end, and when it wished to go in the opposite direction, did so by the ordinary process of moving round, instead of leaping dolphin-wise or turning a prodigious somersault. All this is discouraging, but it is an ill-conditioned mind that cannot accept the inevitable with composure, and, after all, half a sea-serpent is better than none.

Disappointing but respectable. For until his latest revelation, we had really no sea-serpent to speak of; and now that we have at least twenty feet well authenticated, we may rest for the time contented. The only consolation is that the rest of the Soe Ormen may one day more completely fulfil our aspirations for something to wonder at and disbelieve in; for who can tell what singularities of contour remained hidden in the sea when the commonplace head and shoulders were exposed, or who even can guess at the length of the whole ? Delightful possibilities, therefore, still remain to us ; and, while we can safely add one end of the new monster to our marine zoology, we can cling with the other to all the fauna of old-world fancy. Twenty feet of an eel need not prevent us hoping for another hundred of something else ; nor are we compelled from so commonplace a commencement to argue a commonplace termination. Meanwhile, we have a solid instalment of three fathoms of a sea-serpent to work upon, and it will be discreditable to our national enterprise if something more—and a great deal more, too—does not come of it before long.

Favourable to such discovery is the habitat now assigned to the great conger, for it lies on the highway of our commerce. Hitherto, fiords on the Scandinavian coast, the headlands of Greenland, and other unfrequented waterways have been selected by krakens and "aale-tusts" for their exhibitions ; and though Danes, Swedes, and Norsemen generally, have long believed in the existence of these monsters of the deep, their haunts were so much out of the way of regular sea traffic, that only fishermen, the most superstitious and credulous of mankind, could say they had actually seen them. Now and again a glimpse was said to have been caught in more accessible waters of some bulky thing answering in length of body to the description of a serpent, but flaws in the evidence always marred the value of the great vision. Six hundred feet of one, was, for instance, recorded off

the English coast, but here the length alone sufficed to
quench belief; while the other, with eyes "large and blue,
like a couple of pewter plates," found basking off the
shore of Norway, was discredited by its possessing legs.
Exactly a hundred years ago a whole ship's crew vouched
for the following awful apocalypse of the terrors of the
sea: "A hundred fathoms long, with the head of a
horse; the mouth large and black, and a white mane
hanging from the neck. It raised itself so high that it
reached above the top of the mast, and it spouted water
like a whale;" and, what is more, the skipper shot it!

Captain Cox, then, will have to work hard before he
can bring his worm abreast of so thrilling a creature;
but, meanwhile, he has commenced well. To him we
owe the latest confirmation of one of the oldest of the
world's superstitions, and though, in confirming it, he
has divested the thing of our fancy of all that made it
precious, he has given us in place of the rampageous sea-
serpent of our ancestors, tinkered out of scraps from half
the beasts in nature, a plausible and well-conducted eel.
As a first attempt at a sea-serpent fit to be figured in a
standard book it is commendable, but what I should
like to see now is—the other end of it.

*   *   *   *   *

The Apostle of a new Snake cult. It is one of the disappointments of my life that I
have never heard Mr. Ruskin lecture on "Snakes."
Both the subject and the lecturer present to the imagination such boundless possibilities that no one could

guess where the snakes would take Mr. Ruskin before
he had done with them, or where Mr. Ruskin would
take the snakes. Without a horizon on any side of him,
the speaker could hold high revel among a multitude of
delightful phantasies, and make holiday with all the
beasts of fable. Ranging from Greek to Saxon and from
Latin to Norman, Mr. Ruskin could traverse all the cloud-
lands of myth and the solid fields of history, lighting the
way as he went with felicitous glimpses of a wise fancy,
and bringing up in quaint disorder, and yet in order too,
all the grotesque things that heraldry owns and the old
world in days past knew so much of—the wyvern, with its
vicious aspect but inadequate stomach ; the spiny and
always rampant dragon-kind ; the hydra, that unhappy
beast which must have suffered from so many headaches
at once, and been racked at times, no doubt, with a multi- *Incredible*
tudinous toothache ; the crowned basilisk, king of the *Vermin.*
reptiles and chiefest of vermin ; the gorgon, with snakes
for hair, and the terrible echidna ; the cockatrice, fell
worm, whose first glance was petrifaction, and whose
second death ; the salamander, of such subtle sort that
he digested flames ; the chimæra, shapeless yet deadly ;
the dread cerastes ; the aspic, " pretty worm of Nilus "
but fatal as lightning and as swift ; and the dypsas,
whose portentous aspect sufficed to hold the path against
an army of Rome's choicest legions. All these, and
many more, are at the lecturer's service as he travels
from age to age of serpent adoration, and turns

with skilful hand the different facets of his diamond subject to the listener's ear. From astronomy, where Serpentarius, baleful constellation, glitters, and refulgent Draco rears his impossible but delightful ·head, the speaker could run through all the forms of dragon idealism, recalling to his audience as he went on his way, beset with " unspeakable " monsters, the poems of Greek and of older mythologies, and touching on our own fictions of asp and adder, and other strange reptile things, defining, however, all the while, with the bold outlines of a master-hand, the vast scheme of creation, wherein the chain of resemblance is never snapped and like slides into like, until the whole stands revealed complete, a puzzle for the grown-up children of men to put together in a thousand different ways, but one which will never fit in properly, piece to piece, unless the ultimate design be a perfect circle, a serpent with its tail in its mouth, a coil without a break. Fresh, racy morals, too, are to be drawn from the reptile kind ; so that, though on an excursion into strange lands, and seeing only the strangest creatures in them, an audience might understand, even in such fantastic company, that the whole of them—the flowers that were snakes, and the birds that were beasts, and many things that were neither one nor the other—fitted in somehow or another, by hook or by crook, by tooth or by nail, into a comprehensive scheme of unity.

What a subject, indeed, for such a lecturer to choose ! Professor Huxley once selected the snake theme for his opening address of the season, in the Institute, and, bringing to bear on it all the vast resources of his scientific mind, had made the topic instinct with interest. There yet remained, however, for Mr. Ruskin's magic, ample space and verge for holiday-making, for just as it was with the chimæra in Coleridge's problem, that went "bombonating," booming like a bumble-bee, "in space," so there is such a prodigious quantity of room to spare in the realms of snake fancy that no lecturer need fear to come into collision with any solids, let him dissipate as he will. Again, it happens that nearly all *Charming* the world of myths converges upon, or radiates from, the *with Snakes.* great serpent fact; so that Mr. Ruskin, sitting in the very centre of the fairy web, could shake as he liked all the strands to its utmost circumference. Seated "by the shores of old romance," he could at any time have thrown his pebbles where he would, certain of raising ripples everywhere, and of disturbing from each haunted reed-bed flocks of fabled things. But how much greater was his power of raising these spirits of past story when he circled over the same regions of imagination bestriding a winged snake—churning up the old waters with a Shesh of his own, and summoning into sight at the sound of his pipe all the mystery-loving reptiles of mythology, like one of the old Psylli or the Marmarids, or one of the Magi, sons of Chus, "tame, at whose voice, spellbound, the dread cerastes lay."

Eastern charmers, with their bags of battered snakes,

not a tooth among them all, become very poor impostors
indeed, compared with our modern master of reptile
manipulation. The Hindoo's snakes are feeble, jaded
vermin, sick of the whole exhibition as mere ill-timed
foolery, tired of the everlasting old pipe that they have
to get up to dance to, and weary of longing for just one
hour of vigorous youth, when their poison fangs were
still in their jaws, that they might send the old man
who "charms" them to his forefathers in exactly twenty
minutes by the clock. But Mr. Ruskin works only
with fresh-caught subjects, or, at any rate, with old subjects so revivified that they leap from under his hand,
each of them a surprise. The wise snakes of Colchis,
and of Thebes, and of Delphi—I need not identify
them more exactly—fall briskly into their places in the
ring of the creative system, and every flower furnishes
forth a Pythonissa to tell our new Apollo the secrets of
a new cult. Does genius feed .on snakes, that it never
grows old? The Ancients said that the flesh of the
ophidians, though the deadliest of created things, gave
eternal youth, and even cured death itself; and, though
fatal as the shears of Atropos, the poison of asps was
the supreme drug in the cabinet of the God of Doctors.

Even to our own day the legend comes down,
tamed of course to suit the feeble representatives of the
serpent kind that are found in this country; for in our
English folk-lore it is an article of belief that the flesh of
vipers is an antidote to their poison, and that, though

"the beauteous adder hath a sting, it bears a balsam too." All dangerous swellings also, such as erysipelas and goîtres, may be cured, it is satisfactory to know on rustic authority, by eating a viper from the tail upwards, like a carrot; or, simpler still, by rubbing the affected part with a harmless grass snake, and then burying the worm alive in a bottle. But the justice here appears to me very defective, and will no doubt recall that duel the other day, where two women went out to fight "for all the world like men." They exchanged shots, and one bullet taking effect on a neighbour's boy, as he was scrambling through the hedge, and the other having hit a cow that was looking over the gate, the seconds declared that honour was satisfied. I recommend, therefore, that when the snake has effected the cure, it should not be bottled and buried, but should be put back into some bank or hedgerow to carry on its useful war against snails and slugs and worms.

There are few things a snake has not been found at *Ancient* one time or another to resemble, and there is nothing *Snakes and* *modern.* apparently that a snake is not able to do—except swallow a porcupine. One species, a native of Assam, is in itself an epitome of all the vices, for in its vindictive ferocity it not only stalks its prey and pounces upon it, but chases it swiftly, and tracks it like a bloodhound, relentlessly; drives it up trees, and climbs after it like a squirrel; hunts it into rivers, and dives after it like a seal; gets up on one end to pick it off a perch, or grovels like a mole after it if it tries to escape by tunnelling in the earth. So, at any rate, the Assamese say, and their word is as good as that of the Greeks in the matter of snakes. What awful parallels in the past, again, can be found in Nature adequate to the tales of terror that travellers have had to tell of the python, which arrests in full career the wind-footed bison ; of the boa-constrictor, that hurls itself from overhanging rocks and trees in coils of dreadful splendour upon even the jaguar and the puma ; of the anaconda, the superb dictator of the Brazilian forests ! Do the hydras, dragons, or chimæras of antiquity surpass these three in terrors ? Nor among the lesser evils of the serpent folk of old, the cockatrices, basilisks, and asps, do we find any to surpass our own life-shattering worms, the cobra or the rattlesnake.

The snakes of antiquity, it is true, have come down to us dignified and made terrible by the honours and fears of past ages, when the Egyptians and the Greeks bound the aspic round the heads of their idols as the most regal of tiaras, and crowned in fancy the adder and the cerastes ; when nations tenanted their sacred groves with even more sacred serpents ; entrusted to their care all that kings held most precious, and the gems that were still undug ; confided the diamond mines to one, and—more valued then than diamonds— the carbuncle to another ; deifying some of their worms, and giving the names of others to their gods. But the actual facts known to science of modern snakes, the deadlier sorts of the ophidians, invest them with terrors equal to any creatures of fable, and with the superstitious might entitle them to equal honours with the past objects of Ammonian worship and still the reverence of all Asia, the central figures in the rites of Ops or Thermuthis, or whatever we may call the old gods now.

Science has now driven out Superstition, planting a more beautiful growth of beliefs in its place, and of these beliefs Mr. Ruskin is the trustee, the python and the oracle, the artistic Apollo.

*   *   *   *   *

It is one of the penalties of extended empire that frontiers shall be constantly vexed, just as the sea along its margin is for ever astir. But it is seldom that our duties as a Great Power bring us into reluctant collision with such a strange, half-mythical folk as the Nagas of the North-Eastern frontiers of India. The Afghan hills *The Snake-men.* were picturesque enough, and the rolling grass lands of Zululand were instinct with romance; yet neither Afghan nor Zulu can claim a tithe of the superstitious obscurity of the dwellers on the Naga hills, or affect pretensions to half their traditions. Indeed, what people on earth would dare to measure pedigrees with the "snake-folk," or count ancestors against a race who claim to have a lineal descent from before the creation of man?

There are gaps, it is true, in the chain that would suffice to break even a herald's heart; but what else could be expected in the family trees of tribes that were old when the children of the Sun and the Moon, in the first generation, found them possessing the earth? Their progenitors flourished even before Time and Space had established their empire, and they count among the events of their national history the birth of the Creator. Deluges are mere stepping-stones in their chronicles, and the passing away of chaos from the country side and the convention of the gods to churn the sea are events in no way more out of the ordinary than with us the extinction of link-boys or coaches.

What, however, has time the reformer done for these Nagas of the Assam hills? Literally nothing. It has given them an antiquity as old as the mountains they live among, but little more. Centuries roll over them, leaving their plaintain-leafed huts exactly where they were and as they were, their bodies as naked, and their habits as wild as ever. Even the hills alter in contour and the streams change in their course, but the Naga tribes remain in all their pristine savagery, their corners unrounded off, their thoughts and habits flowing in the same old current. Where the aggressive civilization of British India has impinged upon their frontiers the people have been, it is true, surprised into novel modes of life and tastes; but even then there were many in each community who shrank from the disturbing impact of reform, and retired to the sullen barbarism of their wooded hills rather than share the soil with an improving

race. Utterly innocent of any higher standards of ethics
or morality than the tiger-cats or monkeys about them
possess, they lost no opportunities of asserting their
right to be savage if they chose, and punitive expeditions
have more than once been despatched against them to
extort a compulsory deference to peace and law. There
is to my mind something very wretched in this constant
necessity for punishing our frontier fellow-subjects. They
are savages, it is true, and like wolves or bears understand best the argument of pain. But does it make
them less savage than before to beat them? to excite
them to fight and to shoot them down? Wolves and
bears, treated so, only retire before civilization. They
do not become civilized.

Before our own history commences, and when gods *Antiquity*
were half men, and men were demi-gods, the Nagas *of Nagas.*
inhabited India. They were contemporaries of the pigmies who fought with the partridge-folk for possession of
the Ganges' banks ; contemporaries of the monkey races
that furnished long-tailed contingents to the conquering
army of Rama, and gave deities to India ; contemporaries of Garud, king of the bird-gods, and of Indra and
Krishna, and all the merry-making pantheon of Vedic
Hindostan. But there came from over the hill passes on
the north-west, which nowadays men call the Khyber
and the Kurram, nation after nation of Aryans, who, as
moon-children and sun-children, fell upon the aborigines,
and drove them from every spot worth possessing.

They hunted them to the tops of the mountains, and
into the very hearts of the forests, and, adding insult to injury, nicknamed the dispossessed people " snakes," "monkeys," and " devils," representing them in their history
as only half human, and thus hoped, no doubt, to justify
their ill-treatment of them.   Here and there these aboriginal tribes are still to be found in fragments, as primitive to-day as they were when first the Aryan invaders
pretended to mistake them for wild beasts and vermin.
Thus, in the north-eastern corner of India are the Nagas,
the " Snakes," a medley of small tribes without cohesion,
or even the power of cohesion, professing allegiance, in
this nineteenth century of ours, some of them to poten-
tates long ago extinct, others to the Empire of Burmah.
The authority of British India is, of course, gradually
becoming familiar to them and, very gradually also, being admitted; but it is probable that when the Afghan
hills have become as settled as the Punjab, and Zululand
as commonplace as Natal, the Nagas will still be found
cherishing those wild notions of aboriginal independence that have made their reclamation seem so hopeless.

Shesh the   How can they ever consent to the dry formalities of
snake-God.   civilization and the reign of law so long as they believe
that " Shesh," the great serpent, lies coiled under their
hills?—governing the upper earth through his snake-limbed
lieutenants, and recording his impressions of terrestrial
affairs by the lustre of the great gem, the Kanthi-stone,

which he erected in insolent revenge to light up his subterranean kingdom when he was driven from the sunlight by the more powerful gods of the Aryans.

This Shesh is a reptile worthy of homage, and may be
accepted without hesitation and in defiance of all sea-
serpents, past and future, as the greatest snake on record.
When Vishnu and the gods met to extort from the sea
the ichor of immortality, they plucked up from the Himalayan range the biggest mountain in it, and this they
made their churn, while round it, as the strongest tackle
they could think of, they bound the serpent Shesh. And
the gods took hold of the head and the devils took hold of
the tail, and, alternately tugging, they made the mountain
spin round and round until the sea was churned into froth,
and from the churning came up all the treasures of the
deep, and the most precious possessions of man, and last
of all immortality. The gods and the devils scrambled
for the good things, but nothing more is said of the serpent who had been so useful, nor what he got for his
services. Antiquaries in the West incline to think that
he remained in the sea and became the kraken, but the
Nagas believe him to be still under their hills, dispensing
fate by the light of a diamond. When this misconception
is removed from their minds the Nagas may be able to
remark other errors of their beliefs and ways; but
meanwhile they are in utter heathendom, and as delightfully free from misgivings with regard to their methods
of asserting their liberty as are the tigers, rhinoceroses,

elephants, buffaloes, or wild pigs that share their beautiful country with them.

While our disciplined troops were being equipped with scientific weapons, and the machinery of a great Government was slowly set in motion, the naked Nagas were squatting on their hill-sides, taking augury from the flight of jungle-cocks. Our soldiers marched as military science dictated, but the Nagas shaped their course from or towards us at the dictation of their omens—passing deer or falling reeds. On the one side there were Sniders and mountain guns, and on the other spears and daos. So it took little prophesying to foretell that, let the cocks fly as they would, and the reeds fall to the right or to the left, the snake-men had a troubled season before them, and Shesh another sad experience to record on his gem-lit page.

* * * * *

The Turtle.   Much has been written and said about the amiable reptile which men call a turtle ; but many, I regret to say, have approached the subject in a spirit of levity which is very unbecoming. To be flippant about turtles is as intolerable as if one were to be frivolous about aldermen.

Flippancy out of place.   Even in his native waters the turtle is not of a light-hearted kind, for his gestures are solemn and his demeanour circumspect. His spirits never rise to the frolicking point. In captivity the creature assumes a sepulchral deliberation in manner, and his natural sobriety deepens at times into positive dejection. He prowls about his enclosure on tip-toes as if contemplating a burglary, and never betrays any symptoms of alacrity or enthusiasm.

Death, however, gloriously transfigures the turtle. The poor, moping thing which when alive ate even grass apologetically, which seemed always pleading for forbearance and proclaiming itself humble, is at once canonized by the simple process of cooking. The despised worm that yesterday nibbled the herbage at our feet soars to-day a butterfly above our heads. The martyr has become a saint. Festivity and luxury hasten to greet when dead the creature they laughed at when living; and the modest turtle which in the morning was the sport of children is in the evening the favourite of princes. Round it, as round some woodland Oberon, cluster the sprites of mirth and jollity, good living and good fellowship, light and colour, fragrance and flavour ; and when Turtle is the central dish, the lesser planets of the culinary firmament revolve in deferential orbits, confessing that their light is borrowed—that a greater attraction than their own holds the guests in station and regulates the festive board. No wonder, then, that the East believes this creature is an embodiment of the Divinity, and that the world rests upon a tortoise ! The splendid significance of the Vedic legend is not less striking than its beauty, for here we see at once that the alderman keeps up the price of turtle, which keeps up the weight of the earth, and so the alderman himself becomes an avatar of the solar myth. Thus does history work in cycles and a pagan religion stand revealed. A serpent, with its endless coil complete, its head—the earliest of the Hindoo scriptures—swallowing its tail—the Lord Mayor's latest bill of fare—and the Alpha and the Omega is a Menu !

Quid pro Quo ?

It would be a nice point to decide whether the alderman was created for the turtle or the turtle for the alderman. Much is to be said on both sides. It is difficult to imagine either of them preceding the other in point of time, and equally difficult to consider them as eternally co-existent in point of space. Yet they must have been both contemporary and contiguous from the beginning of time, or else we are confronted with the preposterous problem of aldermen apart from turtles. Who knows when either began ; or, if they proceeded from matter at different spots on the earth's surface ? Who can tell us what natural forces first brought them into contact ?

For myself I dare not trust my imagination in such depths of conjecture, but prefer, more comfortably, to avoid the difficulty, and to believe that aldermen and turtles were simultaneous. The primitive alderman, it is certain, could not have eaten up the original turtle, or the species would then and there, in that one disastrous meal, have become extinct. He spared it until it laid eggs, and then he ate it. When he died he bequeathed the secret to his son, who, becoming an alderman in due time, ate turtles likewise, and so on to the present day. The Civic Soup may therefore be added to the many other remarkable survivals of instinct in a species long after the necessity for its exercise has died out.

We, for instance, see the pensive bear dancing in *Force of old Associations.* public places, lifting up its hind feet one after the other in mechanical alternation, and holding its fore paws off the ground altogether, and we forget perhaps at first why it does so. The truth is that dancing is associated in Bruin's memory with the hot plates on which he was taught to dance, and no sooner therefore does he hear the tune played which once was the signal for the fire to be lit beneath him, than by instinct he gets up on his hind legs and keeps moving them one after the other off the surface which he still imagines is being heated. It does not matter to him that neither the country green nor the provincial market-place is fitted up with ovens for baking bears, for the original association of a certain tune with certain hot sensations on the soles of his feet are too strong for him, and he proceeds to dance. In the same way the alderman feeling hungry looks round for a turtle. It is not because this excellent reptile is the only edible thing obtainable, but because hunger, an inherited sensation, is associated in his mind by indissoluble bonds of memory with turtle fat.

Once upon a time, in the age of Diluvia and *How the first Alderman ate the first Turtle.* Catastrophe, the primeval alderman, being unclothed, fled the vertical rays of the sun, and, seeking shelter in the umbrageous swamp, saw there the pristine turtle. Sitting aloof he watched the creature crawling painfully

about, and noted that it was a thing of inconsiderable
agility, and suitable, therefore, to be an easy prey. Being himself of aldermanic proportions, he was averse to
arduous exercise, so he surveyed the turtle pleased.
Anon, he grew hungry, and hunger arousing him to
comparative activity, he circumvented the unsuspecting
turtle, that is to say, he got between it and the water, and
soon made a prisoner of the slowly moving thing. Examination increased his satisfaction, for he found the
turtle carried its own soup tureen on its back, and there
and then, gathering in his simple way a few sticks from
the adjoining brake, this primeval alderman enjoyed the
delights of green-fat soup—calling it, in his barbarous but
expressive dialect, "callipee," and the outer integuments
of more solid meat which he found upon the stomach,
"callipash." So ever afterwards when he felt hungry, and
too lazy to pick acorns, he circumvented a turtle.

Since then, of course, many years have passed. Aldermen now wear clothes, and need not go about catching
their meals, and the umbrageous swamps of a tertiary
Britain are now the site of the City of London ; but the
old instinct, as we perceive, still survives, and the hungry alderman always calls for turtle.

Nor could the civic magnate do better.   Some viands
that have long been traditional for their excellence have
ceased to be paraded on high days, and, to omit the
more recondite, I need only cite the swan, once the
dish of honour at every public feast ; the hog barbecued

the ox roasted whole ; the peacock garnished with his tail and russet pippins ; the sturgeon and the stuffed pike ; the bedizened boar's head. Each had conspicuous merits, and there are still those who maintain that the new meats cannot compare with the old. Let this be as it may, the turtle need never fear rivalry, and the alderman need never dread its extinction. In the seas of Florida alone it swarms in such prodigious quantity that well-authenticated cases are on record of small craft having to heave to until a shoal had passed, while in the remoter corners of the earth it still luxuriates in all its pristine multitudes, unthinned by capture and unmolested by man.

So long, therefore, as the alderman will remain constant to his soup, his soup will never desert him.

It is touching but strange that two species so widely separated, or, at any rate, so distantly connected as the common councilman and the common turtle, should betray this mutual sympathy and confidence.

The latter is rather an ungainly animal, full in the stomach and short-legged, moving on rough ground with great difficulty. It is described in works on natural *Suitability of Turtles* history as having a " short round snout," " a wide mouth," *to Alder-* and a body "very wide across the shoulders." It is *men.* further described as being " very voracious." Yet there is nothing in these traits of person and character to detract from its estimable properties as an article of diet, and so long as it continues to secrete green fat and furnish a reasonable proportion of its callipash to its callipee, the aldermen of London should not quarrel with the turtle either for the shortness of its legs or the rotundity of its body or the gluttony of its appetite.

CHAPTER X.

OF SOME BIRDS.

BIRDS OF PARADISE——THE FOOT-LESS BIRDS: "BIRDS OF GOD"
——HOW AN EMPEROR THOUGHT HE HAD EATEN THE
PHŒNIX AND DIED HAPPY IN CONSEQUENCE——WHITE
CROWS AND OTHERS——THEIR ORIGINAL SIN AND FALL——
THE DIGNITY OF SWANS——BIRDS AND THEIR BARDS——
THE SACRED IBIS——HER GODS DESERTING EGYPT——
PARROTS——IN COURTS OF JUSTICE AND ELSEWHERE——
OSTRICHES AND IRONMONGERY——THEIR LOVE OF WALTZ-
ING AND EXTREME AFFECTION FOR OFFSPRING——HOW TO
PLUCK A SPARROW-CAMEL——ITS MISADVENTURE WITH THE
BAT IN EDEN——AN ACQUISITIVE FOWL——A DIGRESSION
ON THE INDISCRIMINATE COLLECTING OF PROPERTY.

"WOULD you please direct me to some summer isles of Eden, lying in dark-purple spheres of sea?" would surely be a preposterous request to make of an ordinary London policeman?

Yet I confess it seemed to me quite as absurd and incongruous to have to ask one of the keepers in the Zoological Gardens "the way to the Birds of Paradise"

—and I could not for some time make up my mind to do it.

To ask the way to the elephants, to the lions, or to the monkey-house evokes no curiosity from the by-standers, but to inquire the road to the Birds of Paradise turns all heads towards the inquirer, as if he were in search of strange mysteries. Yet the matter-of-fact keepers, who, by daily companionship with them, have come to look familiarly at salamanders, narwhals, and pythons—thinking no more of them than a shopkeeper does of his ordinary stock-in-trade—who live on terms of intimacy with gnus, hippopotami, and condors, and who would not be agitated if introduced to a phœnix or cockatrice, think nothing of the request.

" First to the left, sir, and keep straight on," is the very simple reply.

A couple of hundred yards along a gravel path brings the inquirer to the cages where, amid a strange company of crested birds that sit all green but fly all scarlet, of long-tailed birds that flash about like sunbeams and drop off their perches like falling stars, and strange great crested pigeons of a sleepy feathery blue which might have fluttered straight out of the " Arabian Nights," he find the object of his search—the birds of paradise.

" They're not in colour to-day, sir," apologizes the keeper; and well indeed might he deprecate criticism. Disconsolately dozing on a dead stick sits a long-beaked bird, of a nondescript maroon below and apparently cream-coloured above—a fowl which among a crowd of common ones might pass as a curious specimen, but which in all this aviary of wonders sits alone as calling for no particular admiration.

And yet it has special claims upon attention. *Disappointment on finding them.* The bitterns just beyond are birds of some note, for there are few poets who have not gone to them for a simile; but, those excepted, there is not a fowl—red, green, blue, yellow, or a combination of all—which can command, with all their attractive arts, a fraction of the respect due to this modest bird on the perch.

From time immemorial savages in all countries have gone to the bird-world for their personal ornaments. The plumes of the eagle, the heron, and the egret have been symbols of kingship since the world began, and primitive man has always gone out to battle, whether in America, Africa, Asia, or Polynesia, gaudy with the feathers of birds. It is not strange, therefore, that the exquisite plumes of the Birds of Paradise should have been in great request among the people of the Eastern Archipelago.

When New Guinea was "discovered,", the natives were found wearing the glorious plumage of this bird, and a regular traffic in the skins had been in existence for ages. The prices paid for them were very high, a young female slave being considered a fair equivalent for a complete skin of the emerald bird of paradise.[1] But,

---

[1] I remember reading not long ago of a tripedresser of Hoxton having to appear before the magistrate at Guildhall on one of t

then, there is nothing more beautiful in the created
world than this bird when, as it is described by Lafres-
naye, it expands its marvellous train fan-wise, a halo of
gold and silver, in the centre of which the head glitters
like an emerald, the throat flashing with sparks of ruby
red.   Another species, the "superb bird of paradise,"
orange-chesnut and purple, with wondrous ruffs of soft
plumes, pale yellow and golden green, is hardly less
admirable, while both are eclipsed by the little "king
bird of paradise," maroon and white, with aureoles of
emerald-green and gold springing from its sides and
descending from the back.   No wonder that the old
navigators should have called them the birds of the sun,
and the savages *manuco dewata*, or "birds of God."

"*Birds of God.*"

When Lesson first saw one on the wing, he, a
sober naturalist, was so dazzled by the sight that it did
not occur to him to shoot at "the brilliant meteor," and
the specimen, therefore, escaped him ; while in the works
of Pennant, Wallace, and others the surpassing beauty of
this bird exhausts the vocabulary of ecstatic admiration.

It is, however, emphatically a creature of liberty, space
and sunlight, for if confined it mopes and its lustrous

quaintest charges ever registered.   It was alleged against him that
he was in unlawful possession of "certain property."   Now, this
property was not tripe, or even onions, as might have been supposed,
but *birds of paradise*, eighty-eight of them—a whole forest-full of
birds of paradise !   Was there ever before known such a stock-in-
trade for a tripedresser ?

plumage dulls ; while, if the prison be small, the floating plumes are damaged. In gloomy seasons, even in a wild state, it suffers great diminution of beauty. Nor is it only for its splendour that the feathered gem crouching on its perch in the Zoological Gardens challenges our attention. The naturalist can tell us much about it that is strange. These birds fly in flocks, led by one, whom the natives of Papua—the breeding-place of this splendid family—call the king, and they never fly with the wind. The cascades of plumes that droop from them, the strange ruffs that stand up from their necks and backs, would, if caught by the breeze, bring them to the ground, or drive them headlong, and so they always make way against the wind, and on very gusty days never fly abroad at all. The males are comparatively rare, and every one goes attended by a seraglio of sober-plumaged dames, and, while the latter flit about in the open ground, not shunning observation, their lord, conscious of his fatal gift of beauty, attempts to hide his radiance in secluded glades, or perches himself—but only at sunrise or sunset —on the topmost boughs of the loftiest trees. Of these the birds frequent only certain kinds, thus suicidally indicating their haunts. The traders' agents are not slow to avail themselves of this peculiarity, and the beautiful race, were it not for their polygamous habits, might long ago have been extinct. The weapons used to take them are birdlime or blunt arrows, and to make the latter effectual the hunter has to climb the tree in which the

birds are roosting in the dusk, and shoot them at as close
quarters as possible.

*Heliogaba-
lus' Mis-
take.*
To the student of out-of-the-way lore the bird of paradise is interesting as having for a long time been accepted
as the veritable phœnix. It is a fact that has escaped
Gibbon, but not a more curious historian, that Heliogabalus, having eaten, as he thought, of every living delicacy, awoke one day with keen remorse to the thought
that the phœnix had never been included in his bill of
fare.

It was true that there was only one phœnix at
a time, and that it built its nest of cinnamon, hidden
away somewhere in Arabia; but the Imperial gourmand
was dauntless in pursuit of his side-dish, and the order
went forth throughout the world-wide empire of Rome
that search was to be made for the phœnix, as Cæsar had
a mind to eat it. The zeal of Proconsuls was equal to
the great occasion, and from all quarters of the earth
came strange fowl on trial, each, with some confidence,
affirmed to be "the sacred, solitary bird, That no second
knows, nor third." Heliogabalus ate them all.

But the quest continued, for of every fowl that came
to the Imperial larders a duplicate was in time produced
by some officious Satrap or energetic Legate scouring in
the byways of the earth for the unique thing.

At last one day there came to Rome a bird the
like of which for the glory of its plumage had never
been seen, and its name being given as "the phœnix,"

or " bird of the sun," Heliogabalus ate it, and went to his forefathers contented.

Yet, after all, he had been put off with a crow; for these magnificent creatures are first cousins of that lamentable bird. Perhaps, if Bacon had continued his "Wisdom of the Ancients," he might have found out that when the Latin poets spoke of the crow, punished with blackness for its sins, having once been so beautiful a bird that the artistic Apollo chose it for his own pet messenger, they were concealing a fact of science, and that the bird of paradise is the original crow Before the Fall. At any rate, the legend is widespread, for in *The Original Sin of Crows.* the oldest of the Hindoo books is told the story how the crow, then the favourite of the gods and free of all the Seven Heavens, was guilty of eavesdropping, and how, in punishment for having betrayed the divine counsels, he was driven by Indra from before his throne, condemned to feed on carrion, and all the bravery of his plumage scorched to cinder black. But, whether the original crow or not, the bird of paradise is of the crow family, and shares with them a characteristic defect. For, with all its marvels of plumage, it has to confess to a corvine beak and to the thick, coarse legs and feet of a bird of carrion. The New Guinea natives are accustomed to cut them off, and so, the dense soft plumage concealing the fact of the amputation, these creatures found their way into Europe as " the footless birds."

Poets caught at the beautiful fiction, and "the bird *The footless bird.*

that never rests," the "wind-cradled bird," and other
phrases became current in literature about "that bird of
paradise which," as Berkenhead sings, "hath no feet, but
ever nobly flies." Several illustrious and noble houses,
including that of Savoy, adopted it as their crest, in which
it is always represented legless in mid air, and the
mottoes appended repeat the fiction in twenty different
ways—"Earth is nought to me," "I disdain the earth,"
"Always on high," and so on. This fable necessitated
many others, and Heliogabalus' phœnix was supposed to
hatch its eggs on its back, and, when tired of flying about,
to anchor itself to a tree by twisting its long tail feathers
round a branch. Buffon really believed that it had no
legs, and Linnæus, in deference to the joke, named the
greater emerald birds of paradise—*apoda*. Yet of its
legs, and very ugly ones, any visitor to the aviary in the
Regent's Park may satisfy himself; though when, to use
the keeper's phrase, the birds are "in colour," all will
agree with Lesson that they are miracles of beauty.

*　　*　　*　　*　　*

Small room is left for doubt as to the island of
Cyprus standing sadly in need of British reorganization.
White Crows. The crows there are white ! This is a lamentable irregularity. For many reasons indeed this aberration from a
recognized standard is to be deplored—reasons ornitho-
logical, moral, and general.

Ornithologically, it has been hitherto understood that
a regulation crow was black, so black that a coal

might be reasonably expected to make a white mark
on it ; and this standard of nigritude has received
the approval of men of science and letters from the
very earliest times. Indeed, every child that has a
Noah's ark is aware that the blackest fowls in the whole
aviary are meant for the crows, and it is perfectly intolerable that the Cypriote bird should, as it were, sap
our time-honoured institutions, and, not content with
flatly contradicting all our ornithology, should under-
mine and explode the simple confidence of childhood,
scattering distrust of literature in our nurseries, and
unsettling all the convictions of our infant schools.
Science knows of only five true crows, and they are all
very black ;[2] and, though the family stretches through the
gaudy jays in one direction to the hornbills, and
through the magpies in the other to the splendid birds
of paradise, the actual and veritable crows can be
counted on the fingers of one hand, and be all painted
with the same brushful of Indian ink.

Even here error has crept in, for a much-respected
Dean, one who cannot long escape a bishopric, was on
his own showing convicted of supposing that jackdaws
were young rooks, which when adult were called crows,
and when *very* old indeed ravens. But this confusion of
species, though sufficiently to be regretted, is not so
pernicious as that which would arise if the crows of

---

[2] I am speaking roughly, for I have myself seen in Natal and
the Transvaal, the white-collared crow ; and in India the grey crow.

Cyprus were permitted to continue in irregularity. Our children, we ourselves, would lose one of the few positive facts of science that are now common property, and, once losing hold of this first truth of the blackness of crows, we might slide into interminable errors.

That poets do not speak well of him, and that in fable he seldom takes a creditable place, should not excuse the crow from falling in with the proprieties, and accommodating himself to the *convenances* of ethics and science. There is, of course, an abject depth in the social scale that relieves individuals from the decent necessity of keeping up appearances. But the bird in question affects no such humility, and, indeed, does not, we may easily believe, consider himself as one to be looked down upon. His gestures suggest that he is
puffed up with conceit, and many besides Gay, and Churchill, and Spenser have drawn attention to his "strut." More than this, the literature of all countries has conspired to make the crow satisfied with his circumstances, and even to reflect some dignity upon his antecedents and history. Not only in Greek and Latin, but in Sanskrit and Persian has this bird's origin been invested with a special interest. We all know how Apollo selected the crow for his own, but it is not perhaps so generally known that it was once also the favourite of the Hindu Pantheon, the only fowl free to come and go at the tables of "the gods who hold the earth in their hands." Again, in countries so widely

separated as Norway and Yarkand, Ceylon and North America, we find current the legend that, somewhere, there is "a realm of crows." Hiawatha speaks of the "land of crows and foxes," and so does the Cinghalese Pratya-sataka. Of the Norsemen's hill, Huklebrig, and the Yarkandi city of Karghalik there is equally positive assertion ; and those, therefore, who are "ravished with the reverence of antiquity," may plead for this bird that he has some justification for arrogance, and in the singularity of his traditions an excuse for his obliquities. But those who would thus condone corvine eccentricities should remember that high lineage or noble memories do not alone suffice to perpetuate worth, or the Stuarts would still wear crowned heads, and Emathia not lament for its Universal Monarchy.

The crow therefore cannot, any more than unfeathered bipeds, arrogate a present consequence from past glories, since the world demands for every renewal of its respect *Selfishness of human regard for Animals.* a fresh supply of benefits conferred, and men, at the second generation from the original benefactor, cease to touch their hats to his descendants. A modern traveller has told us of a king in Africa whose crown is made of mud, and has to be remade every morning, each twelve-hours' homage being thus purchased by a fresh coronation. So the "treble-dated bird" must not presume merely upon pre-historic honours for an honourable position in the bird-world of to-day, but to sustain a creditable level of respectability must daily confer new obligations. The cat thus keeps its place in our regards.

It is not because Egypt consecrated it, or because Pope Gregory made a cat a Cardinal, or because, as the Rabbins say, the men of Babel were turned into cats, that we cherish the small quadruped, and make it free of our hearths. Old associations die out in time.

For instance, how many sportsmen in September lower their guns because St. John the Evangelist made a pet of a partridge? When Michaelmas Day comes round, will not the savour of apples and onions overpower our respectful memories of the Capitol, and of the grey goose shafts that glorified the lanes of Poictiers and the field of Creçy?

The crow then can hardly expect exemption, or pretend on the score of antiquated privileges to escape the rigid reform that will follow upon British administration of Cyprus. The moral effect of such exemption might be most embarrassing, for poultry and pigeons could easily, from history and fable, find as sound pretexts for immunity, while the cattle and asses, the sheep and the goats, would have no difficulty in vindicating equal rights to consideration.

Then the lizards, and they are numerous, might, with all propriety, looking to their antecedents, expect official regard ; and it would be hard to discover a reason for excluding black beetles, so precious to Egypt, from equal license. The line must be firmly drawn somewhere, and I do not think the Executive would be exceeding the discretionary powers entrusted to it if the line were drawn at the whiteness of the crows.

*   *   *   *   *

The "peaceful monarch of the lake," as a poet—with the quaint ignorance of bird-life that marks so much of what poets have said of birds—has styled the swan, possesses a most irascible temper, and, indeed, a bear, after a visit to a beehive, would not be less affable to strangers than this bird to those who chance to go near his island home. The preference for islands as breeding-places marks the generalship of the bird, for a swan on shore is, proverbially, a poor creature, but, by giving himself a clear waterway all round his nest, he takes up a strategic position which, for all common enemies, is practically unassailable. A blow from his wing, when the male puts his heart into it, has a force which, to be properly respected, must be experienced. At all times punctilious as to its personal dignity, and ready to resent with promptitude any breach of aquatic etiquette by the commonalty of the waters—the " lower orders " of the goose, duck, and teal kinds—the swan displays an especial irritability during the breeding season. The male at this period never goes far from the nest and its treasures, and every device to tempt him out of sight of his home fails—every device but one, the challenge of a rival or the intrusion of a stranger. Hot pursuit is then his one thought ; and in all the animal world, perhaps, no finer simile for proud

Swans.

Picturesque and poetical birds.

z 2

knightly wrath could be found than the angry swan when, every plume starting with indignation, and the whole body impetuous with eager passion, it drives its way through the water towards the object of its hatred. At idler times the male—known to swan-keepers as "the cob"—cruises round his island citadel, or floats, like some man-of-war on harbour duty, just off the landing-place. The female bird—technically called "the pen"— has equal claims to notice both for personal bravery and parental solicitude. When necessary she joins her lord in battle and pursuit, but, relying as a rule upon his unaided prowess, attends to her domestic duties with exemplary diligence. As soon as the cygnets are hatched she carries them to the water, and in after life, when the young brood encounter difficulties of current or reed, the mother constantly comes to their assistance. Sinking herself till her back is flush with the water, she allows the cygnets to climb upon her, and on this pretty raft conveys them where she wishes them to go.

Every stream upon which swans have colonized is divided by the different colonies into domains, as strictly defined and as jealously defended as the Livingstone River by the cannibal tribes that inhabit its banks. To transgress a frontier is to challenge hostilities; but pursuit, just as with the African savages, extends no further than the neutral line that demarcates the possessions of the pursuer and pursued, save, of course, in those exceptional cases where the insult is deemed expiable by mortal combat alone. Apart, however, from its interesting habits, the swan arrests attention because it is an especial favourite of the poets, and also as a bird about which our legislation has constantly concerned itself. With regard to the first, the nightingale, skylark, *Birds and their Bards* eagle, and dove can alone claim precedence of the swan, for from Homer to Tennyson every poet who has gone to the bird-world for his similes has utilized it. But an acquaintance with natural history and the gift of poetry —except in such marked exceptions as Keats, Shenstone, Tennyson, Longfellow, Gilbert White, and a very few others—have unfortunately been rarely allied ; and, in the case of the swan, only the most salient and least suggestive features have been pressed into service—its whiteness of plumage, the grace of its motion, and its mythical song before death—"the sad dirge of her certain ending"—a myth, by the way, so current in Egypt that this bird stood for music in the hieroglyphic character. Among swans in general, those of the Thames have, from Aldrovandus in prose and Spenser in verse, down to the present day, earned special mention ; but it is only because they were "snowy" or "milk-white," or "silver," or because they were "stately sailing," or else because, "death-divining," they "awakened the inspired strain." The swan, however, I venture to say, admits of a more poetical handling, even without having recourse to fable or to the tales of the old-world mytho-

logies in which swans have such frequent place; for few
birds present, in their circumstances of life and character,
their perilous migrations, desolate but beautiful abodes,
their eagle enemies, their courage and fidelity, so many
points inviting the poet's notice.

*A Royal
Fowl.*   In its other aspect, as a bird of privilege and legislative
note, our national records abound with curious references
to the swan. Cyprus claims to have given our Thames
this feathered grace, for history records how Cœur de
Lion sent them thence in the twelfth century. They
were soon acclimatized, and their possession was everywhere so highly valued that at last our kings created a
royal monopoly in the splendid fowl. It is, therefore,
the sturgeon among birds, and no subject, except by
express grant from the Crown, can claim rights of property in it when swimming on public water. With this
permission the Crown grants a " swan-mark," and on the
river Witham alone ninety-seven different swan-marks
were in existence half a century ago. The theft of a
swan's egg was punished by statute with a year's
imprisonment, together with fine at the royal pleasure;
while for stealing the bird itself the penalty was very
severe. Chief among the liabilities attaching to the
ownership of swans was the provision of plump young
birds for the royal table, whenever demanded, or for the
delectation of the representatives of Majesty when on
circuit or other official business in the neighbourhood.
The recipes for cooking the bird were, of course, numerous

and elaborate, and at all banquets the swan "standard"
held the place of honour. At the present day, however,
they are too highly valued for "the grace they lend the
wave" to find their way often into the poulterers'
market, and as we no longer care to eat them we can
now contemplate them apart from the sideboard, as the
birds which Brahma dignified as his symbol on earth
and his companion in heaven, and which Apollo placed,
crowned, among the stars.

       *   *   *   *   *

How is Egypt fallen ! The ibis, her own sacred bird, has *How is*
migrated to Hungary, and, to the delight of local "sports- *Egypt fallen !*
men," has attempted to found a colony upon the wooded
shores of the Platten See. It may be that its other
breeding-places have been invaded, and that, thus exiled,
it has tried to settle in the country of the Five Rivers ;
but, whatever the reason for its coming, the ibis has
made a great mistake, for the lean Hungarian has
betrayed the fowl's confidence by shooting it on its nest,
and robbing it of its blue egg-treasures. These sportsmen declare that the eggs are good to eat, and that the
flesh of the bird itself is excellent ; and, as the ibis is not
accustomed to being shot at, they find it delightfully easy
to kill. During the daytime the birds wade about singly
or in pairs along the margins of the lake, often remaining
motionless on one spot for half an hour together, and
this is the sportsman's opportunity, for the bird does
not take wing, and, even if startled by the first approach,

is sure to walk only a few paces before it stands still again. It is, however, in the evening that these keen gun-men are in their glory, for the unfortunate birds, returning to their nests, perform in company those pretty evolutions which are characteristic of their tribe, flitting in short flights from point to point along the shore, or joining with outspread wings in a kind of dance, their feet hardly resting on the ground between each step as they go skipping round and round each other, and in and out of the quadrille-like figures which they delight to trace. These evening gatherings give the Hungarian sportsman just such chances as he likes, and we are told that the slaughter of these charming visitors has been immense. We in England are not ourselves free from the reproach of killing feathered strangers that happen by stress of weather to be driven upon our shores, and what might happen if the ibis suddenly appeared in vast flocks upon the Cumberland lakes we would not dare to say. But at any rate, we should not call it " sport " to shoot the visitors, nor, if once noised abroad, would their slaughter be permitted to continue. In Hungary, however, as elsewhere on the Continent, everything eatable, whether furred or feathered, is considered " game," and if the creatures will only stand still or sit down on their nests to be shot at, so much the better for the sportsmen. Yet the ibis, it is a comfort to know, will soon find this out for itself, and next year, when the nesting season comes, it will avoid the Platten See.

Meanwhile, how curiously the advent of this bird to Europe strikes upon the ear and fancy ! The ibis, leaving Egypt for Hungary, the Nile for the Platten See, seems to have removed a familiar landmark from the maps, and the old myth-world seems to have lost another of its few remaining dignities.   Until now the ibis has been a sacred thing, and to harm one in old Egypt was to incur the penalty of death ; yet to-day their eggs are made into omelettes, and their flesh is converted with impunity into stew.   So invincible, said the ancients, was its love of the Nile that it starved itself to death if carried beyond the land which that river waters, yet here we find it of its own accord nesting along the shores of a European lake.

How indeed is Egypt fallen ! Her bird, the ibis, has left *Its Gods* the classic shores of old Nile, deserting the silent temple *deserting the Nile.* courts of Dendera and the untrodden crypts of Thebes, and settled upon the shrub-clad shores of the Platten See. Has then some new sun-god arisen in Egypt, and in old Typhon's shape, hawk-headed and hawk-winged, pursued the moon-bird, the fowl of letters and of wisdom, from the reedy haunts of the hippopotamus and the crocodile ? What was Thoth doing when the ibis, his avatar, spread its pied wings and took flight from the pretty water-nooks where the lotus spreads its broad green leaves? Is his sceptre broken, and is Hermes now a phantom ?

The plumage of the ibis once had the power to startle the monsters of the river from their ambush, and, so Egypt said, to kill them with its basilisk glitter of silver and steel.

But now it would seem the bird flashes along the Nile harmless as the glinting feathers of the dove, unable even to defend itself from intrusion and exile. Once, too, the ibis refused to drink at any wave less pure than that of the sacred Nile, and even there was dainty in its choice, rejecting some pools, sipping at others, and the priests of temples used to watch it, and drink only where the bird drank ; but to-day the prophet fowl is found nesting along the reed-grown skirts of a Hungarian lake.

What holiday, too, the snakes of old Egypt will keep now that the defender of the desert passes has taken wing to Europe. The cerastes, it may be, desperate with broiling upon the Libyan sands, will lead securely into Egypt the vanguard of an invading reptile host, those winged asps and venomous worms with horns that have hitherto never dared to cross the threshold of the sacred land, and, swarming through the defiles which hitherto the ibis had held so well against them, will violate the ruined altars of Memphis and Hermopolis, and revel in the cool and wholesome levels of the Nile !

How will the peasant reckon the rise and fall of the fertilizing river, and who will tell the shore-frequenting things, the birds and lizards and rats, how high the waters will rise, and where their nests may be safe ?

The augur-bird is no longer with them to mark the waxing and the waning moon ; and, unless the spirit of old Egypt has fled, the land is desolate indeed. Her Shekinah has flickered and gone out ; the lustre of her breast-plate is dimmed for ever; the fires of Bubastis are cold; her oracles are dumb, and her gods asleep or dead.

What ails the once potent frog that she sits to-day *Are her* croaking in the sedgy shallows? Has Heka, the *divinities now* goddess of our genesis, come to this, that she should *impotent?* torment the night with idle complainings? It would be more becoming her traditions if she roused herself from her damp couch, and taking counsel with her companion gods, struck new life into mummied Egypt. Overhead still hovers, as of old, the keen-winged divinity of war, but how comes it that, with Thebes a ruin, and the ibis all flying northward, Arueris concerns himself only with chasing little finches? Across the pastures, as in days gone by, stately Osiris paces at the head of the lowing herd, but his "awful front" must have lost its terrors, or why are the fanes of Memphis given up to sacrilege? Who comes here down the river slope, nodding his head so wisely, threading with such precise steps the narrow paths that separate the melon patches from each other—who but Khnum himself, that made the gods, that made men? Yet he seems busy to-day with some lesser thoughts than were wont to occupy him, or why does he frisk in the sight of the woolly flock and foregather for unseemly frolic with his kind upon the margin of the now desolate river? Anubis, forgetful of his high trust, is seen sniffing at a rat-hole, his tail all eloquent of expectation, and, shameless sight, Phtah is chasing Thoth in the hope of sharing a pilfered cucumber!

No wonder then the ibis has left Egypt, now that her other gods behave themselves like mere frogs and hawks, bulls, rams, dogs, and apes.

It may be, however, that the sacred fowl is only obeying some occult influence of nature in thus migrating to the Platten See. Never, or seldom, has it bred in Egypt, but went and came with the ebb and flood of the Nile, and the priests of mystery said therefore that it was self-creative, like the phœnix or the amphisbœna The plumage of the ibis, black and white, represented, they said, the light and shade of the moon, and as its body is the shape of the human heart, and, when standing, its legs form with the ground the mystic triangle, they dignified it with such an accumulation of divine attributes as might have sufficed to make even a god anxious for his responsibilities. Its flesh, now familiar to Hungarian pots and skewers, was considered by the Egyptians as miraculously incorruptible, and so after death the ibises of the temples were mummified with every circumstance of religious pomp, and in the crypts of Thebes and Memphis and Hermopolis they are to be found, some in stone coffins, others in jars, embalmed in numbers. But they have fallen upon profane days, and the Hungarian infidel neither respects them living nor embalms them dead. Yet could they have expected to retain their old honours? The scarabæus beetle, an avatar of the Sun-god, may now be bought in scarf-pins, and the onion, though once held in reverence on the

Nile, receives but scant worship in our kitchens. In the list of monkeys to be seen in Regent's Park, we find both Thoth and Phtah, and Londoners amuse themselves over the vulture and the hawk, the dog and the ape, among the hieroglyphs of Cleopatra's Needle. In such an outraged Valhalla could the ibis hope to retain alone the singularity of its sanctity, or to remain erect in a Pantheon where every other statue had fallen? The times, I fear, were ripe for this crowning desolation of Egypt, and the ibis, by leaving the secret haunts that gave it mystery and the land in which it was held sacred, has precipitated the final ruin.

* * * * *

Two persons disputed the possession of a certain parrot *Parrots.* and brought the matter into a police court. Evidence was so conflicting that the magistrate was puzzled. At last an idea struck the usher of the court and it was acted upon, and Polly, having been duly sworn on a lump of sugar, was set on one side in order that she might state the truth, the whole truth, and nothing but the truth. Now, as it happened, the parrot's position was one of *A parrot* some delicacy, for it had to decide between two bene- *in court.* factors—a trying position for even more intelligent persons than parrots—but it was staunch to its oldest friend, for after thinking the matter over well from all sides, with a good deal of scratching, and, it must be confessed, a certain amount of irrelevant gesture and flippant investigation of plumage, it called the lady who had originally owned it—" mother." This lady had, it appears, allowed it to escape ; had, that is to say, cast this exotic fowl adrift upon the London streets, a prey to a thousand enemies, and incapacitated by long domestication from shifting for itself. There is no large choice of berries growing on lamp-posts, and the parrot, therefore, ran a good chance of starvation, if it went about looking for bread and milk sop, or a varied assortment of edible nuts, on the pavements, so that, humanly speaking, the bird owed the lady a grudge.

A friend in need, however, very soon turned up—for a parrot flashing about in Regent Street was as certain to find a speedy captor as a mermaid combing her hair in the Round Pond would be—and being a boy, and a son, he took it home to his father, who spent eleven shillings on a new cage for the brilliant waif, and otherwise made it comfortable, assuring it against further perils from a vagabond life.

Polly, therefore, had to be ungrateful to one of two friends, and it evidently took her some time and cost her much thought to arrive at her decision.

The Just-ness of its Decision.

For a while the tropical creature stood on one leg thinking, impartially surveying the court, and then proceeded to institute a strict investigation into the condition of its tail feathers. It next satisfied itself, by a superficial examination, of the contents of its water and food pans, and then, having casually tested the quality of a few of the bars of the cage, wiped its beak upon the perch. This concluded its deliberations, and no other argument suggesting itself for consideration, the parrot, after a few inarticulate remarks, no doubt expressive of gratitude to its captor and his parent, and regret at leaving so elegant an abode, confidentially addressed its old friend and possessor by the endearing epithet of "mother." The Court, of course, at once accepted the evidence; the magistrate directed the parrot to be restored, and thus the lady got her own again.

Of course it is impossible to guess at any base motives which may have prompted the bird to a right conclusion; and looking, therefore, merely to the facts before us, it would seem as if the parrot were not such an abandoned person as he has been depicted. It is, of course, as old as the hills that men and women dislike monkeys because the creatures seem to resemble themselves; and "their own defects, invisible to them, seen in another, they at once condemn; and though self-idolized, in every case, hate their own likeness in a brother's face." This postulatory resemblance has borne hard on the monkeys; and from much the same reason it must be that human beings speak, as a rule, so ill of the parrot; for that he has a shabby reputation is beyond doubt. Poets have *Poets sneer* noticed "the Indian bird" only to sneer at his "fine" *at Parrots.* plumage and his "chattering," malevolently classing him with magpies and jays and jackdaws, or else ridiculing him as an indispensable appendage of an old maid's establishment. More than one bard has given the parrot an ode all to itself; but where some pay it no compliments, another author, thinking to invent one, says, "The Queen

of Beauty shall forsake the dove; henceforth the parrot
be the bird of love." Prior apparently did not know
that the parrot holds that place.already; for Waterfield,
the Anglo-Indian poet, tells us how Kama, the love-god,
"hath mounted his parrot that flashed in the sun, and
with blossoms hath pointed his arrows each one;" and up
and down Indian myth and legend will be found scattered
references to the "lory," which the Cupid of the East is
wont to ride. But few, very few poets indeed, have been
in that close sympathy with nature of which they boast;
and turning from the caricatures of Pope and Mallet and
the rest, to the works of naturalists, we find the bird is
not without its virtues. In private life he is monogamous
—like a bishop, " the husband of one wife "—and when
introduced to human society proves himself affectionate
and grateful, while the very fact of his intelligence should
commend him to favour. His brain is larger in comparison, we are told, than any other fowl's, and in this he is
the scholar among birds, not only learning lessons but
seeming to apply his knowledge by the highest form of
reasoning, inductive inference to the varying conditions of life. Is it not on record that a parrot, well

*Their
Scholarship
and Appro-
priateness
of Speech.* known to Anglo-Indian story, learnt so many phrases
of English that it constructed the grammar of the language, and being missed one day was ultimately found
perched on the top of a tamarind tree, teaching all the
parrots of the neighbouring jungle the rudiments of
syntax?

Beyond this neither intelligence nor credulity can go, and it seems tame, therefore, to recur to other familiar varieties of parrot wit. One bird of note, accustomed to ask passers-by what they thought of herself, changed the query of her own accord during the Peel Administration to "What do you think of Sir Robert Peel?" The much-respected citizen is still, I hope, alive and in good health, who, going to woo a widow, was interrupted at a critical moment of his fervent addresses by a voice from the cage at the window, asking in a depressed tone, in sorrow rather than in anger, "Who kissed the cook?" Any popular natural history, such as Cassell's, will be found to abound in delightful anecdotes of parrot character and mimicry: but one of recent occurrence in a London eating-house will be seldom surpassed. The master of the house lay dying—the parrot gravely looking on. "He is dead," said the doctor, "and "—"*Charles, put the shutters up,*" solemnly added the parrot. Perhaps the dim light of the room, and the sudden movement among the company when the worst was announced, misled the bird into thinking it was the usual dispersion at bedtime, but being removed from the chamber he resented the innovation with the remark, in an audible aside, "Lor! what a fuss!"

Immense prices have been given at different times for individual parrots, but it seems almost like a form of the slave trade to hear of the sale and purchase of such a creature as that which Jesse, the naturalist, describes as having seen at Hampton Court. Not only did it answer questions naturally, but inflected the words to suit circumstances, and in its musical ear rivalled the famous parrot of Bristol that, besides saying "everything," sang any popular air it was asked to sing, and if it made a false note stopped and started afresh at the beginning of the bar! These prodigies of memory and mimicry were both "grey parrots," those natives of Western Africa which enjoy, together with the other physical peculiarities of larynx, bill, and tongue that adapt them for this imitation of intelligence, longer lives than most birds, and in their "mortal span" average the length of human existence, and even attain, as men and women occasionally do, the age of a hundred years. With a sagacity which of itself speaks volumes for the brain power of this family of feathered things, the parrots, whether we call them parroquets or lories, macaws, parrots, or cockatoos, have selected as their native countries only the most beautiful parts of the earth, rejecting in each continent such countries as are denied perpetual sunshine and a perennial wealth of fruits, and clustering thickest in those "isles of Eden" which men call Polynesia. Even there, with Paradise all round them, the parrots pick and choose, and as a rule it is only where running water ensures them the richest vegetation and the safest coverts, that these birds of the sun, tulips on wings, flock together for society and food. Man, however, has sometimes also, with a like intelligence, pitched upon the same spots for his home; and the parrots fight hard be- *Beautiful* fore they yield possession, ravaging the invader's crops *—but vandals.* with a vandal wastefulness that embitters the colonists against them. It is little use frightening them away, for they are of a "voracious kind, as often scared as oft return ;" and when they are observed glancing in broad sheets of colour across the sky at sunrise, the owner of the crop, be it grain or fruit, would as soon see a dingy locust cloud approaching as this array of malignant beauty, for they desolate where they cannot feed, and out of pure idleness ruin even the unripe harvests. In their own country, therefore, they have little honour; and it is only when they are caught and caged like some stray sun-flakes from the tropics, in our dull dim houses, that they develope for man's amusement and wonder the talents which, at liberty, they abused to man's injury.

* * * * *

Ostrich-farming as now reduced to a science, with *Ostrich.* its galvanized-wire fencing, English lucerne grass and barley-stacks, and artificial incubators, has, no doubt, given British Africa a valuable source of income, but it has robbed the world of a delightful bird.

All the prophets of Holy Writ adopted as the emblem of *The Ostrich in Holy* scornful pride and gloomy isolation the great fowl which, *Writ.* according to our translators, was the constant companion of the " dragon " of the wilderness, and poets have never tired of drawing similes from the bird that could give the wind a start across the desert and overtake it, that knew no horizons and, a heartless solecism in nature, no maternal love—" silliest of the feathered kind, and formed of God, without a parent's mind." But time is ruthless.

The phœnix, the cockatrice, and the basilisk—all the hybrid things that made nature so exciting in its possibilities to our forefathers—are now relegated to fable and Chinese art; while behemoth and leviathan, the unicorn and the salamander, and a score of seemingly-wondrous creatures, have been reduced by uncompromising classification to whales and crocodiles, antelope and lizards and other realities,—all no doubt most interesting, but, in comparison with their prototypes, very prosaic. The modern ostrich also, has in the same way been disenchanted, and its claims to supernatural properties so long enjoyed, have been formally set aside. It does, it is true, frequent solitudes, but they are solitudes only for men, since " the estridge," albeit there are no dragons now, finds abundant company, feathered and furred, horned and clawed, in the spaces which human beings, and they alone, consider desert and wilderness. Still it is neither proud nor gloomy. Once caught it is easily domesticated, and all its tastes are singularly humble, while in character it is cheerful, if not actually frolicsome. Thus, among the scenes of ostrich life, we are introduced in a recent work to a party at an impromptu afternoon dance. " Beginning with a sort of slow sidling revolution on their toes, and gently beating time with their wings as they revolved,

And in Nature.

Not a commonplace Fowl.

some twenty full-grown birds began waltzing together. As they warmed to the fun, the spirit of it fairly carried the ostriches away, and the revolutions became more and more rapid, until at last all twenty were spinning round at a rate that would have astonished a dancing dervish; and though they swept round and round the enclosure, each waltzer independent of the rest, there were no collisions." We can hardly, therefore, call the ostrich *Maternal Love of the Ostrich.* an unsociable or morose bird; nor, as regards its lack of parental instinct, are the poets more correct than the prophets. As a matter of fact, the hen bird sits patiently enough on her eggs, but the male—a pattern to all fathers—insists on taking his turn, and a great deal more, too, than is fairly due. So far, therefore, from the "sparrow-camel" being wanting in a parent's mind, it has really as much care for its eggs as any other species of bird. As to the speed of the ostrich, Dr. Livingstone gave it as at the rate of twenty-six miles an hour; and the author of "The Great Sahara" sets it down at exactly the same; so that the pace is not actually greater than that of the racehorse or the antelope tribes. Its endurance, however, is prodigious: and if it starts off with a fair wind behind it, "right aft"—to which it holds up its wings—and on ground of its own choosing, no hunter, even riding as men can in the colonies, has a chance of seeing it again; for, after the first spurt, the great bird settles down to its stride, and continues for hours on its course at a reduced, but still formidable, rate.

If the chase is taken up by fresh horsemen placed along
the line of the bird's flight, the ostrich loses heart, and is
fairly run down in the open.

As Poultry.   In its modern aspect, however, the ostriches, stripped
of their historical attributes, become nothing more than
a prodigious species of poultry. Being easily domesticated and very quick in forming attachments, they are
managed with hardly greater difficulty than common
cocks and hens, and certainly with less than the exasperating and volatile guinea-fowl. An ordinary wire-
fencing-suffices to keep the bird from roving, for, in spite
of its length of leg, it can neither step nor jump to any
height ; while its wings are, as a rule, only used to support
it, when the bird is well under weigh and going at its
highest speed, over creeks or streams of water the banks
of which are nearly on a level with each other. Inside
the enclosure they comport themselves as exemplary
farmyard stock should do, contentedly eating the grass
and whatever green stuff is provided, and laying eggs
with punctuality. The eggs have often to be picked up
by stratagem, for the cock, even when not sitting on
them, is always jealously on guard. He has therefore to
be enticed into a separate pen, and the female then submits to the plunder without any violent remonstrance.
Placed in the artificial incubator now coming generally
into use, the eggs hatch in about forty days, the young
ostriches thus brought into the world appearing to be in
every way as healthy as those naturally born. This phrase,

however, requires some explanaion, for in the natural state the chicks are often compelled to come into the world by a method that is at once artificial and severe. The cock, it appears, gets impatient towards the end of the period of proper incubation, and if the young birds do not hatch he breaks the shell himself, and shakes the chick out then and there. The little ones, fortunately, can take care of themselves from the outset.

For the first few days they eat nothing at all. They are too busy thinking and looking about them. But having satisfied their curiosity at last, they prepare at once for the serious duty of supporting life, and set up a mill. This is precisely the fact. The little things, taught by *The Infant* instinct, eat no food until their gizzards are ready, and to *Ostrich.* this end they go about picking up small stones. They do not swallow every pebble they come to, but pick and choose with all the fastidious gravity of experience. Their mills being ready, they begin to provide grist, commencing at first with the softest growths they can find, and, as their machinery gets into good working order, increasing the doses, and becoming less careful in their forage. Nothing comes amiss to them, animate or inanimate, so long as it is on the ground. As a rule, most of their food is grass and the aromatic " karoo " bush, but they will not refuse any vegetable that is not absolutely acrid ; and for a picnic there is no outing they would prefer as a treat to a quiet day in an ironmonger's shop. *Plucking*

When two years old they have feathers fit to pluck, *the Spar-* *row camel.*

and every eight months a crop is taken, the quality and quantity of course increasing with age. The "ripe" feathers, as they are called, are gathered by different processes; but that which promises to become most general is as follows. Having driven as many birds into an enclosure as it will hold, even with their bodies packed tightly against each other, the operator wriggles himself into the crowd. This is attended with some danger, for the plumage, as with all birds, is finest at the breeding season, and the ostriches, therefore, have to be plucked just when they are most ill-tempered. The weakness of the ostrich, however, is in its neck, and if any bird threatens violence it is seized by the neck and sufficiently choked to make it powerless for the time. Supposing no vice to be shown, the operator, armed with an extremely sharp knife with a curved blade, goes from bird to bird, selecting the finest plumes in each, and cutting them off as close to the root as possible. In the general squeezing and hustling the ostriches do not perceive the theft in progress, and the whole flock may be fleeced without a murmur.

Antiquity of wearing Feathers. Fashion has hitherto been singularly constant to ostrich feathers. They were, we know, considered beautiful and desirable before history proper commences, and in the earliest records of every nation of East or West or South are mentioned as ornaments and treasures. In the hieroglyphics of Egypt we find them conspicuous, and Herodotus met tribes in Lybia proud in borrowed plumage. Men, however, were not so chivalrous as now, and they kept all the prettiest things to themselves. Women went about muffled up like chrysalids; but Aristophanes' heroes wore white ostrich plumes in their helmets; and Pliny tells us the Roman male of his day bedecked his person with them. For centuries after this Europe adopted the plume as the special ornament of its princes and nobility; and from head to head the ostrich feathers have travelled, until at last in our day they nod supreme above the coronets of princesses and the crowns of queens. How long the fashion will last it is not for mortal man to guess; but, looking at the broad fact that wherever the ostrich is known and its feathers are attainable there men and women prize them, it would almost seem as if the same sense of beauty and desire to possess the beautiful that has maintained the empire of the diamond will perpetuate the favour shown to the plumage of the ostrich. Upon this point turns the whole value of ostrich farming, for though Mohammedan pilgrims may hang up the egg shells as votive offerings, and Texan officers organize ostrich corps, and the half-wild Boer eat the flesh of the great bird, the industry depends entirely upon the feathers and the fashion for them. At present there seems no diminution of the demand; indeed, the market just now is as brisk as ever; but a word from high places may any day abolish Court plumage, and the arbiters of bonnets lay their ban on feathers. Yet even then there are other worlds to conquer. In India, strangely enough, ostrich feathers are not, and never have been, at all general in the native Courts. The heron, the egret, and the bird of paradise are in possession of the jewelled caps and turbans; but nowhere, perhaps, would a beautiful novelty in personal decoration become at once so popular as in the palaces and harems of the Indian chiefs and princes.

Habits of indiscriminate Feeding. Ostriches have so frequently given extraordinary proof of their immunity from indigestion that men have ceased to be surprised at the museums which are periodically removed from the stomachs of dead specimens. There is still, however, room for a good deal of astonishment and for some reflection. Rash and indiscriminate feeding is visited among the higher orders of creation with painful consequences, and, to say nothing of human beings, the monarchs of the jungle and the plain, the lion and tiger, often suffer in captivity from dyspepsia. In their anxiety to secure as much meat as they can in as short a time as possible, they swallow their food with any foreign matter that may be adhering to it, precipitately, and are consequently very uncomfortable and melancholy. Birds are liable to the same affliction, and there is no mistaking the inconvenience, tending to low spirits, which our caged pets undergo when they have been over-indulging in the pleasures of the table. The " sparrow-camel," however, hardly deserves to be called a bird, and it certainly is not a beast, so that analogies drawn from either order are scarcely applicable. At the

first settlement of the world, according to Oriental tradition, all the creatures upon it were called up by Allah to
be taught their several habits of life and to have their
places on the earth allotted to them. First, the birds
were summoned and they appeared, " the total kind of
birds, in orderly array on wing." But the ostrich, seeing
all the feathered things go flying by, scorned to join them,
and came to the conclusion that he could not be a bird.
In his pride he disregarded the summons, saying to himself, " I perceive I am a beast." It was, however, the
turn of the beasts next, and to the dismay of the ostrich
he found that they had all of them four legs apiece ;
but, remarking that they had no plumes, he recovered
his self-complacency. " It is evident now," said he,
" that I am not a beast either. Beyond doubt, therefore,
I am an angel." So when the beasts had dispersed, the
ostrich found himself all alone—except for the bat. And
Allah, looking out upon the great parade-ground, saw
these two standing together in expectation of a special
summons; but he put a public affront upon them by
pretending not to notice them, and retired without
assigning either of them any fixed place in creation.
The bat has been so ashamed of himself ever since,
that he only goes abroad when it is getting dark, and
the ostrich withdrew into the solitude of the desert.
There it behaves as it likes.

Though manifestly a bird, it has never attempted to
make a nest; and, though not a beast, it lows and roars

like one. It lays eggs like a fowl, but crops the herbage like cattle; wears hair on its back though it has only two legs; and is altogether an irregular and self-opinionated person. That such a creature should go picnicking off an ironmonger's stock-in-trade is, therefore, no more than might be expected from its eccentric habits; and the pretence that it eats tenpenny nails to help its digestion can only be accepted as a discreditable evasion of the truth.

In Rome the other day an ostrich managed to suffocate itself by pushing its neck through between two bars, swallowing a bunch of keys that had been dropped outside, and then trying to get its head back again. The result was that it was choked, and on its stomach being examined for missing property the usual assortment of stones, nails, coins, and beads was discovered, with, however, the interesting addition of a silver medal of the Pope and the cross of an Italian order.

*The Ac-
quisitive-
ness of the
Ostrich.* By whom or when these honourable decorations were "conferred" upon the sparrow-camel, no one knows; but the ostrich, it seems, did its best to show its appreciation of the distinction accorded it, and swallowed both the medal and the order. It had no buttonhole from which to display its honours, but at all events it had a coat—to its stomach—and, as I have said, it did its best. As a surface for display, however, the inside of the stomach cannot be considered better than indifferent, while as a safe for valuables it has the inconvenience that attaches

to the roving "missionary box," which has a mouth but no key.

Anything thrown to it is swallowed at once, for the ostrich prefers to make sure of the article while it can, and to find out its character by subsequent conjecture and experience. There is no hesitation about its conduct, no timid examination of the object offered. The bird has the most complete confidence in its digestive organs, and having done its share by swallowing, leaves its stomach to make its own arrangements. The monkey has none of this generous reliance on Providence, for though it refuses nothing, it will not put anything into its mouth until after having carefully examined it, and then only into a halfway pouch. From this it reproduces the collection at its leisure, and having satisfied itself of each treasure in turn, swallows it beyond recall. But the ostrich never gives a mouthful a second chance. Its stomach has only the retentive faculty, and not, as in the ruminants, the recollective also; so, though it adds to its store with great diligence, it can never reproduce any item of its contents for leisurely discussion. It gobbles up things as monomaniac collectors amass possessions, under an irresistible impulse of aimless acquisition ; and, although *Its Aimless* from its own internal resources it could furnish a dressing *Acquisi- tions.* case or work-basket, or a carpenter's tool chest, or find a key to fit the church door, it makes no use of anything it has got. It must be perfectly well aware, or it might be told by its doctors, that there is little or no nourishment in, say, a double-bladed penknife, and that neither silver watches nor pocket-compasses are valuable for their flesh or bone-making properties. Whether it enjoys a malicious gratification in thus appropriating articles which it cannot utilize, and chuckles over the consciousness of possessing purses and keys, and the crosses and stars of orders of honour, can never be known; but, if it does thus amuse itself, the sparrow-camel must derive, no doubt, an additional pleasure from the fact that it is long-lived, and that those who have seen it swallow their property need never hope to get their own again.

The collecting lunacy. To the ordinary collector of curiosities, the chief pleasure of his collection lies in the fact that he can overhaul and examine it whenever he likes, and can handle and gloat over special treasures; but with the ostrich, once swallowed is for ever swallowed. The money-box can only be rifled by burglarious entrance, and the ostrich, having once assimilated a thing of beauty, robs itself of the joy for ever. Nevertheless, there is a trait in human character that sometimes prompts men to take delight in possessions which they can never enjoy, perhaps never see, and misers not unfrequently hoard their treasures in wells and other places as inaccessible to themselves as to the thieves they dread. When the passion for collecting property in an incoherent and aimless manner gets beyond control, it always ends in absurdity, and sometimes in the police-court. Men, for instance, have been known to hunger greedily after umbrellas—not merely for one at a time, but for whole sheaves of ginghams. One Eddis, dying a few years ago a pauper, was found possessed of a perfect wilderness of umbrellas, hundreds of these being mere skeletons from "the moth and rust," and hundreds more in every condition of mouldy, mushroomy decay, and no small number in excellent preservation. How he came to own so many no one knew, but there can be no doubt that an exceptionally morbific form of umbrella-hunger had seized upon him, and that the unhappy victim had spent his life and means in circumventing the unwary possessors of umbrellas and annexing their property. He had a mission to steal umbrellas, and, with all the doggedness and cunning of a Ghazi, he went about among men gathering in their ginghams, and followed by impotent lamentation as by a shadow. Another well-known kleptomaniac—a duke, too— diligently devoted his declining years to the collection of spoons and forks, and De Quincey tells us that it was the nightly care of a pious daughter, watching over the aberrations of her father, to have his pockets turned out by a confidential valet before he went to bed, and the owners of the purloined articles traced.

Mr. Bryant, the ascetic of Fulham Marshes, again, *The Ascetic of Fulham Marshes.* affords a delightful illustration of this possessive weakness, and of the extraordinary lengths to which "the acquisitive faculty" may lead a man. He was, it seems, the victim of an inordinate propensity for acquiring, quite irrespective of the material acquired and regardless of its quality and nature. Everything was fish that came to his net. Plated goods were carefully hoarded, and so was sawdust. Scaffolding poles and sewing machines, carpets and shavings, sailors' quadrants and old hat-brims, were all welcome alike. Nothing, in fact, was rejected so long as it had substance, and the museum which the police discovered was, therefore, of a very mixed character. He had built for himself in the Marshes a sort of lake-dwelling, a cabin of rough woodwork, raised on timbers above the high-water level, and surrounded by a trench. In this construction he lived a hermit's life, with only a dog to keep him company—and to keep off the water rats— seeing no one, and occupying himself solely in the acquisition of property. Piled all about him were hampers, bags, and old packing-cases, filled not only with rubbish and litter collected, apparently from dust-bins and ditches, but with property of all kinds, watches and books, cutlery and clocks, nautical instruments and several dozens of hats, a few uniforms and sewing machines, several hundredweight of waste paper and some carpets, furniture of different kinds, and odds and ends " too numerous to specify." His bed was composed of old clothes piled upon a box full of old rifles—several cases of gunpowder being also found scattered about— while his heating apparatus consisted of a small stove close to the bed, from which a square pipe made of pieces

of wood roughly nailed together conveyed the smoke
through a hole in the roof. Whether the old man ever
anticipated having to defend his property by force of
arms, and for this reason entrenched his fortalice and
provided himself with the munitions of war, is not
known; but it is probable that the rifles and gunpowder were acquired with no more definite ideas as to
purpose than the sawdust and the old newspapers, while
for the rest no better reason is required than the general
one involved in the notorious strength of this collecting
mania.

What parents, for instance, have not had experience
of the intense activity with which a child amasses its
miscellaneous and worthless treasures? If the little *Children's*
pockets be turned out, the secret drawer or box be over- *"trea-*
hauled, what a wonderful hoard is discovered! As *sures."*
Wendell Holmes says, " Philosophy is puzzled and conjecture and hypothesis alike confounded " in the attempt
to explain the law of selection that presided over the
child's labour; "for when a formal register comes to be
taken of the results of the little creature's busy summer's
days out of doors, the prevailing articles in the procès-
verbal are found to be stones remarkable only for weight
—rusty nails and broken crockery. Doubtless, the
splendid treasure was not secured without incurring
some sense of danger and much labour;" yet the
instinct of possession is one of such immense strength
that childhood forgets its timidity when acquisition is in

prospect. To take another illustration from nature, what could be more intense than "the acquisitive faculty" of the caddis-worm? At first it chooses its bits of stalk with care and exercises judgment in their arrangement; but, its own armament finished, the mania for adding to its store seems to become uncontrollable, and the caddis begins to pile on things at random, reckless of the fact that the more it collects the greater the weight it *The Caddis* has to carry, until at last the victim of ridiculous pos-
worm. sessions can hardly creep under the burden of the rubbish which it has cemented upon its own back. Half the quantity would have sufficed for its protection against its enemies, but the worm's instinct to collect " property," once indulged, carries it on from excess to excess, until the preposterous object, stuck all over with bits of shell and stick, and stone, lumbering along the rough bottom of the pebbly stream, defeats the original intention of security, while adding nothing, we would think, to the pleasure of possession. Yet it does apparently find enjoyment in the process, or why should it do it? By some analogy of taste, perhaps, the ostrich derives in the same way satisfaction from possessions placed beyond its reach, and as it ranges the wilderness the consciousness of having that within it which can never be stolen cheers its solitary reflections. The knowledge of a secret always engenders pride in the possessor. The child is never so proud as when it has hidden something from its nurse and is pressed to dis-

close the place of concealment. It then affects a lofty assumption of sagacity and reserve. The possession of a secret first gives the infant a glimmering of that sense of responsibility which dignifies adult manhood.

A dog, too, when told a secret, becomes at once *Haughti-* haughty ·in his bearing to all who approach him, and *ness of the* *Dog that* when revealing one is unmistakably consumed with pride, *has a se-* for he proceeds to the place of the mystery, as Queen *cret.* Elizabeth danced, " high and composedly," and during the verification of his information walks about stiffly, as if his legs were on wires. This, perhaps, explains the pride which has so often been attributed to the ostrich.

Not that the bird has been fairly treated in tradition or by public report, for there was long a belief that it fed on stones only, except of course when it could get metals, that it treated its eggs with neglect and its young with cruelty, that it was first cousin to the " dragon " and its constant companion, that it was an unclean bird, greedy, vain, and stupid. Nevertheless, its feathers were regarded in ancient Egypt as the emblem of justice and truth, and used by many tribes as the symbol of victory and a sign of high place, just as they now form the badge of our own Prince of Wales. Its plumage indeed has from the first kept the great fowl in repute, for, though often tried as a horse (among others by Arsinoë, the Queen of the Nile) it was found to be a very in- different mount, and it is only therefore as a bird that it continued to command any general respect.

The ostrich, indeed, lays itself open to disrespectful remark by more than one eccentricity of conduct, and by none so conspicuously as its habit of a miscellaneous and preposterous diet. Apart from these, it has some pretensions to honourable regard, for a bird that can step twenty-eight feet at a time and do its mile easily under the two minutes is not a very contemptible fowl, while if beheld at full speed, with all its plumage spread to the favouring breeze, no living object more majestic can be imagined. In captivity, however, it can never be seen to advantage thus scudding under full sail across the sand-oceans it inhabits, and its shabby half-fledged appearance suggests to the visitor only an overgrown fowl of the Cochin-China breed. The knowledge, too that the monstrous fowl's stomach is filled with odds and ends of literature and wearing apparel, hardware, and useful articles generally, and the ridiculous look of anxious acquisitiveness with which it eyes the property of the passer-by, invest it with an unfortunate absurdity.

Not a contemptible Fowl.

CHAPTER XI.

FISHES.

FISH life, so it has been recorded by a man of *The Life of Fishes.*
science, is "silent, monotonous, and joyless."
But is it so? Aquariums are beginning to teach
us differently; yet even without these exponents of sea-
life there would have been room for doubt. Although
the waters of the earth contain within them as many
living things and varieties of life as all the solid land can
show upon its surface and under it, men are accustomed
to lump the inhabitants of the rivers and seas together
contemptuously as "fish." The word itself has come by
some obliquity of reasoning to denominate, whether as
noun-adjective or noun-substantive, an object of doubtful
character or absurd appearance. We disparage a person

or thing by calling it "fishy." One-half of the created life of the world, therefore, is treated as a joke by the other. Beasts are regarded with deference, and birds with admiration, but "fish" are absurdities.

It would be interesting to analyze the process by which this result was arrived at; but for the present the fact must suffice that just as every one whom the Greeks did not happen to be able to understand was called "a barbarian," so original man, puzzled by fish life, loftily dismissed finned things from further discussion as eccentricities. As ichthyology, however, grew into a formulated science, a suspicion of the true majesty of the water-world crept over some thinking minds, and, carrying opinion to the other extreme, actually induced enthusiasts to look upon the solid earth as mere excrescences of the sea, a fortuitous confluence of continental protuberances. Europe, Asia, Africa, and the Americas were mere accidents of the scheme of the universe ; and, as for the islands, they were summarily disposed of as irrelevant archipelagic warts and wens.

Fish ideas opposed to human. This is the view the fish would prefer to see adopted, for to them the interruptions of rock and sand must seem altogether unreasonable and ridiculous. What is more, the interpolation of solid continents in the midst of their spaces, besides marring to a great extent the fine free sweep of water they would have if there were no land, is productive to them of many evils.

It is thence that their chief enemies attack them, and

if land could only be done away with, gulls would have no place to breed in, and would, therefore, become extinct : man himself could not exist—the Deluge showed the fish what an indifferent amphibian he made—and the minor persecutions of fish-hawks and fish-eagles, of kingfishers and otters, would all cease. Man is always trying to reclaim land from the water. Fish would like to see all the water reclaimed from the land. The bones of their ancestors and the shells of preceding generations of molluscs remain to this day on the mountain tops, mementoes to the finny tribes of domains they have lost ; and in every fossil exhumed from the chalk and coal they recognize only melancholy testimony to the waste of broad acres—good sea all run to land.

Meanwhile, circumscribed though their limits are, fishes *Advantage of Sea over land.* have an ample share of the world's surface, and far more than their share of its depth. We, living on dry land, have to content ourselves with the crust of it. Moles, it is true, go a little deeper, and what worms do only worms know. But these exceptions do not disturb the fact that man has to move about on the outside of the ground. He cannot dive down leagues deep under the mould, and swim about subterraneously from one side of the world to the other. Here the fish have manifestly the advantage of us ; for not only is the area of their abode very vast, but its depth also. Nor does this delightful fact debar them from any of the pleasing varieties of landscape which we on the crust of the world enjoy. The sea

floor is as grandly diversified as the surface of the earth,
and its vegetation is varied and superb. Mountain and
valley, forest and plain, are all theirs ; exquisite prospects
of colour, such as on earth are unknown, stretch before
the travelling fish on every side ; and the wonders that it
sees, if written down, would eclipse all earthly fable.
What have all the continents together to compare with an
encounter, a thousand fathoms under the ocean, with a
" school " of whales ? or what would not mankind give in
exchange for a sight of the sea-serpent at home ?

Voices of
Fishes.   It has, nevertheless, been gravely objected to fish life
that it is " silent, monotonous, and joyless." Of its
silence proof is wanting ; and, inasmuch as there are
actually known to science species of fish which indulge
in jews-harps and trumpets and drums, it might be fairly
said that that proof would never be forthcoming.
Musical fishes are a fact of positive knowledge, for not
only can they be heard in shoals thrumming their jews-
harps in unison, but other kinds have been taken in the
very act of trumpeting and drumming. Whether these
noises were elicited from them by the act of capture or
not, does not affect the point at issue, while it puts beyond doubt the property possessed by certain fish of
emitting sounds. Whether this property is exercised
among themselves for mutual diversion is still open to
investigation ; but if frogs croak for company and gnats
sing in chorus, there does not seem sufficient reason for
disbelieving that fishes perform in concert whenever it

pleases them to do so. Against the charge of monotony the proof to the contrary is conclusive and overwhelming. The range of most fish is enormous in extent, and in traversing it what a constant succession of excitement and surprise must the progress of the individual be! To his eyes the sea is thronged with inhabitants, and, look where he will, he is always moving in a crowd. Whether he rises or sinks he finds the waters populous with multitudes of diverse creatures, and every one of them is interesting to him, for those that he cannot eat, eat him. His life, therefore, is one of constant activity, for, except when he foregathers with his equals or his congeners, or when, of his deliberate act, he retires to a sequestered creek for solitude or contemplation, he can divide his days into chasing and being chased.

But among the sea folk there are as many types of life *Sea type* as there are on land, and as many different modes of *of land things.* existence therefore; and with the ancients it was a favourite saying, and one to which Pliny himself, the most delightful of believers, deferentially assents, that in the water might be found anything or everything that was found out of it, and as many more besides. Not only had fishes cognizance of all the forms of life that give terrestrial existence its charm of variety, but they knew of others also that transcended mammalian knowledge. Not only can they indulge themselves in running away from sharks, as we should do from tigers if they swarmed in the streets, in contemplating the whale, the

elephant of the seas, sauntering along through his domain;
or finding diversion and instruction in the winged progress of the flying fish or the tree-climbing of perch, the
buffooneries of sun fish and pipe fish, the cunning artifices of the "angler fish," the electric propensities of
some, the luminosity of others, the venomous nature of
these, or the grotesque appearance of those—not only is
all the variety of experience to be found on the earth to
be found also in the water, but over even a wider range
and in greater diversity. The sea floor is strewn with
marvels, and the rocks are instinct with wonders. The
dark places of the deep hold their ogres and things of
terror, and in the clear water float myriads of translucent
miracles. The animate and the inanimate approach so
closely that the flower-beds of the sea garden are stocked
with vegetables which gradually develope into animals,
and the plants of one day are the protozoa of the next.
There is nothing on earth to correspond to the sponges
and the corals, or the enormous intervening variety of
colourless, organless things that nevertheless subsist and
multiply, content to get through life with a single cell of
matter to serve all purposes.

Does the fish then find no amusement in life, and *are*
scales and mirth incompatible? Looking down upon
fish as a kingdom of the natural world that is only
admitted into it by courtesy as it were, and with reserva-
tions, it is natural that many should be inclined to deny

it the capacity of pleasure. But who that has ever strolled along a river bank and watched the dace or trout contemplative in mid-stream, indolently sucking down the flies, placidly restful, indolent, and fat, can doubt that the creatures are happy? Or who that has ever watched fry darting round the stones in the shallow and obviously at play, has come away believing that life is "joyless" for them?

Yet it is in the rivers, where we know them best, that *Freedom of Fish from domestic Cares.* their dangers and anxieties are really most numerous and pressing; and even there the healthy fish looks the embodiment of easeful, happy existence. In the high seas, where security lies in their very multitude, and where the vast spaces facilitate escape, life is of necessity more careless and less insecure. Of the domestic anxieties the fish escapes nearly all. Having laid its eggs, the mother wanders away, and, even if enemies attack the nursery, what pangs can wring the heart of a parent who has to dissipate her affection and solicitude over three hundred thousand offspring annually? In escaping these anxieties and pains, the fish escapes much that makes other forms of life serious and irksome; and if joy is really, as it has been defined, the absence of sorrow, the fish must be accounted eminently joyful. Sometimes, it is true, an epidemic of self-destruction attacks the finny multitudes, and they rush upon the shore in such myriads that the fishermen tire at last of carting them off, and immense quantities are left on the beach for all who care to help themselves. Such was the case at Walmer not long ago, when the herrings and sprats came shoaling up on the beach in such numbers that they could not all be removed. Everybody and everything was feasting for the time upon them. The gulls came up in flocks, and the carnivora of the sea held high carnival among the demented fish.

Suicides of Fish shoals. But no explanation has been, or can be, offered for the mystery of this vast self-sacrifice, except that Nature, working to her own ends, puts into action now and again such "positive" checks to over-population, and by the periodical immolation of countless lives upon the altars of Order, maintains a proper balance for life. If this be correct, all the doubts so commonly expressed of the failure of species may be dismissed, for economical Nature would never have thus played into the hands of those who are perpetually at war with her. Had herrings and sprats been scarce in the sea, they would never, we may be satisfied, have been so abundant on land. No species, moreover, deliberately works to its own extinction. It might, of course, be whimsically preferred that the shoals which asphyxiated themselves at Walmer were, like the last dodo, wilfully acquiescing in extinction.

That venerable bird, so I have read somewhere, was discovered by a party of travellers gravely promenading in a secluded spot of the island which it inhabited. It had about it all the air of the Last of a Species, and the conscious dignity of being the sole representative of its

Order sat well upon the aged fowl. It had never seen man before. The explorers had never seen a dodo before. There was an instant of mutual surprise— but the bird was the first to get over it. For while the human beings were still flurried and disconcerted, the dodo solemnly pulled itself together, and taking the bearings of the case at a glance, walked up to the explorers and surrendered itself. A string was put round the creature's neck, and the Last of the Dodos led off to the boat of the captors at funeral pace, the primeval one refusing to move faster than a solemn waddle.

There was a dignity about this suicide—for how could a dodo hope to live on board a steamboat?—which, taken in connexion with the fact that the single individual represented in its own person a whole order of birds, brings the event up, in point of importance, to the multitudinous self-sacrifice of the herrings and sprats of Walmer. It points also to the bare possibility of the fact that the said herrings and sprats, finding themselves left alone in the whole of the German Ocean to represent the once innumerable nations of the clypeids, did not think it worth while to continue the farce, and so, to put an end at once to such an absurd misrepresentation of one of the most enormous families of the fish world, came up in a body, and decently performed the Hari-kiri on the Walmer beach.

Other explanations readily offer themselves, but none suffices. It may have been, for instance that, after the fashion of the great vegetable war against man which is recorded in early Hindoo Writ, the herrings and the sprats were the vanguard of the army of a misguided fish-fanatic host attempting the invasion of the solid earth. *A Suggestion in Explanation.* It is written that once upon a time the trees came up and tried to smother man off the face of the globe. They crowded up, kind by kind, in such close forests and with the undergrowth below them in such impenetrable jungle between their serried trunks, that man and all the beasts of the field had to retire before the green flood. From the four continents of the earth the trees came, laying aside for once all frivolous differences as to climate and tastes as to soil, and mustered in an overwhelming phalanx of foliage on the plains of Hindustan. Man was, as nearly as possible, squeezed out of existence in consequence ; but the gods took offence at the conduct of the trees, and as opportunely as any Homeric interposition, smote the banded woods with flame, and thus rescued humanity from being utterly overwhelmed by the vegetables.

Now it was a fish that conveyed to the gods the news of what was then going on, and so the story must be well enough known in submarine society, and it is therefore just possible that the fishes had intended last year a similar invasion. But misdirected enthusiasm has resulted, as it must always do, in miserable failure. The herrings and sprats led the way, but got no further than the water line. As for the rest, the dolphins and narwhals,

the sharks and the sun-fish that were no doubt following, nothing was even seen of them, and it is probable,
therefore, that at the first news of the discomfiture of
the choking sprats they floundered down again into
their obscure abodes. By some of course, those who
hold the dull theory of fish life, it might be surmised
that the fishes, in disgust at the sea, were anxious for a
change, and hoped by their numbers to get on to dry
land, just as the Zulus crossing a rapid stream trust to
the rush of the crowd behind to force the leading ranks
across. Or, again, it may have been that sea life, so far
from being dull, was all too exciting ; that close behind the
thronging sprats was an impi of their voracious enemies,
and that just as the flying-fish, leaping apparently in
sport, leave the water only to baffle the pursuit of the
bonita, so the scaly multitudes that lay heaped upon the
sands may have been flying for life from a combined assault
from the banditti of the sea. But there is little use in
trying to guess the meaning of the wonder, and it is better
to wait, contented with ignorance, till the fish are able to
explain it to us themselves.

Such wholesale suicides are not, however, uncommon
in animal life. In Africa, ants have been seen marching
regiment by regiment, for days together, into a rapidly
running stream, and for days together being swallowed as
fast as they could pour into the water, by crowds of fish.
Butterflies have been known to migrate in immense
clouds from the land, and fly straight out to sea with

nothing but the farther shore of the Pacific or the Atlantic before them, and not the slightest chance of ever reaching it. Rats have been met with, an exodus of myriads, all in a stampede in one direction, resting neither day nor night, with both birds and beasts of prey feeding on them all the way as they went. In the Seychelles some years ago several thousands of turtles conspired to die together on an island in front of the harbour, and unanimously carried out their decision. Such instances might be multiplied by reference to any work on natural history, but the mere enumeration of examples throws no light upon the monstrous hydrophobia that lately seems to have afflicted the fishes of the Channel. It is a pity almost that the sprats took part in so august a phenomenon as the wilful surrender of life by such a multitude of things; but being in it they can now be no more excluded than the sparrow from the leper-cleansing ceremonial of the Mosaic law. How the sparrow got concerned therein, unless by " an accident of translation," has puzzled thinkers from the first, for his presence undoubtedly detracts somewhat from the dignity of so severe a rite.

Adventitious dignity of certain Animals.

In the same way the palm squirrel bears on its undeserving back for ever the impress of the five fingers of the monkey god Hanuman. It was at the time of the Flood, and, to get him across to a place of safety, the beasts and birds made a bridge for the long tailed-deity. A little hole, however, was left unfilled, and the squirrel, which had meanly waited until the bridge was finished to run across safely itself, found itself compelled by the sudden approach of Hanuman to fill the hole, and the god in passing over rested his hand upon the little hypocrite's back, and impressed thereon for ever the sign-manual of his favour. The squirrel, such is its character, now exults impudently in the signal honour, and arrogates to itself, from the accident, an undeserved superiority. But it is not, after all, generous to grudge the sprat the adventitious honour of being concerned, as a principal, in so splendid a sacrifice, for no one should be envious of the dead and least of all, perhaps, of dead sprats.

A fishery exhibition, such as has been recently held, goes far in itself to dispel the theory of the monotony of life in the water, and visitors who went to it, speak of the number of fishy, fishing, and fish-like exhibits as very " surprising." It is, however, a poor compliment to the larger half of the globe to be surprised at the variety of its contents, for, as I have already said, the sea and its ways are just as productive of marvels, beauties, and industries as the solid earth.

Man, as it happens, lives on dry land, and he has, by this accident, therefore, always given most of his attention to soil and stones and the things that grow upon them; but if the whales were to organize an Exhibition, it would no doubt, by a similar selfishness of sympathies, be devoted chiefly to marine objects and pursuits, No committee of narwhals and polar bears, however intelligent and

How Fish might hold an Exhibition.

liberal-minded, could be expected to interest themselves with much enthusiasm in such purely terrestrial exhibits as samples of sugar, piece goods, and so forth. At the same time, I do not deny that they would probably take a sufficiently large view of things to induce them to devote a certain share, a percentage, of their efforts to the illustration of a sphere not altogether their own, and of

Fish Exhibits and Industries.

elements not natural to them as a residence. Thus, the sword-fish would show specimens of small craft which it had perforated and sunk, placing alongside on the shelves the fragments of its own broken snout, and the whales would exhibit vessels of various sorts and sizes, which they had been instrumental in upsetting—for both ramming ships and wrecking them are distinctly marine industries. The walruses and seals and sea lions would make a good display of Arctic Expedition relics, and the sharks produce, from their own resources, a large and varied assortment of human manufactures, fabrics, and tissues of different kinds, and an extensive selection of nicknacks besides, culled at various times from the surface of the seas in the tropics. The collection of harpoons, spears, and hooks of all descriptions that had been carried off in the persons of the different exhibitors would make a peculiarly interesting department of such an exhibition, and from the holds and cabins of different vessels that had foundered the finny things of the sea might bring up and arrange in submarine caves an immense selection of goods to which their relatives had directly contributed either in bone, skin, liver, or blubber.

Indeed, the sea has no reason to depreciate its services to the world, be it social, scientific, or commercial; and a judiciously arranged collection of articles of marine or fluvial origin, found on wrecks by the connexions of those who had given their lives for man, would be replete with interest. From the tiny madrepore, with its stalls of coral jewellery, and trifles of many kinds, to the vast whale with its chandlery store, candle bunches, whalebone, and oil in cans, there would be a multitude of exhibits, of all sorts and sizes, and each would have a tale of wonder to tell.

Nor would it be only the seas that would thus be put *How useful* under tribute, but the lakes and meres also, the rivers and *Fishes could be to* brooks, marshes and pools ; for the hippopotamus would *us.* be there, with sets of artificial teeth made from its tusks and whip-thongs cut from its hide, the beaver and the otter, the manatees and porpoises, turtles and frogs and lizard folk of all sizes from the newt to the crocodile, pearl oysters, shell-fish and crustaceans, and all the nations of the edible sea-things, from the sea-slug, made into birds' nests, that tid-bit of the Chinese, to the sturgeon with his roe in caviare. What a bewilderment of relatives—hermetically sealed, bottled, and boxed—they could produce, and how serviceable their assistance would be in settling such questions as the identity of whitebait, the salmon-disease, the young of many of our

fresh-water fishes, and the domestic secrets of the female
oyster! To the angler such an exhibition would be
invaluable, for who could tell him better than the fish he
angles for the proper instant for striking and the most
killing fly? The subject expands as I proceed, for in
a fishery exhibition, managed by fishes, the virtues and
failings of all known baits, artificial and natural, would
be authoritatively expounded, and the world could never
afterwards dispute as to hook or fly, minnow, spoon or
paste, reel, rod or line, gaff, disgorger or gut, net or night-
line, and all the thousand and one points of tackle and
gear that now give the piscatorial world its topics for
discussion and argument.

*Their
Secrets.*

We should learn, once for all, how and why the oyster
makes its pearls, and we should be set right for ever as
to the existence of the Great Sea Serpent. Ranging
further still, all the wonders of the ancient deep would
be disclosed, the continents that have passed away be
revealed, and their colossal amphibians restored to view.
Were there ever mermaids and Undines, Tritons, and
Nee-ba-naw-baigs, Nereids, Danaids, and sea Satyrs?
Who were the Sirens; and is there any foundation for
the myths of Neptune and Nereus? The fish alone could
tell us. They would inform us, also, where, if anywhere,
the kraken and the anker troll, the great Sea Worm and
the pieuvre are to be found; to what size the cuttle-fish can
grow; and whether dolphins are still amenable to harps.
Nor is this all; for an energetic committee might beat

up for such an exhibition a host of queer exhibitors—the
sea swine and sea devils, sea elephants, cows, horses, and
lions—and make the petrels, the cormorant, the albatross, and all the other ocean birds of story, tell the sad
tale of their metamorphosis. All Hiawatha's acquaintances *Legendary*
of Gitche Gumee, the Big-Sea-Water would be there : *fishes.*
Shingeebis the diver, Ugudwash the great flat fish, and
Mishe Nahma, king of the sturgeons ; the Dagons of
Eastern mythology, a multitude in themselves of wondrous forms : and the myriad of finny things—from the
holy haddock to the tortoise that upholds the Vedic
world—which are known to literature, sacred or profane.
We are still puzzled as to the electricity of the sea and
the galvanic peculiarities of certain congers, rays, and
other marine creatures, nor can we say for certain
whether there are singing fish or not. What was it that
swallowed Jonah, and to what species known or extinct
did the friendly vehicle of Arion belong—the tadpole-
headed and curly-tailed thing which the ancients called
" the dolphin," and crowned king of the seas, symboliz-
ing Neptune by it and adopting it as the hieroglyphic
of celerity? Many pages might be filled with such
queries, but what is the use of asking them, since the
fishes alone can give the answers, and fishes, they say,
are mute ?

It is only characteristic of humanity that man when *Fish*
" exhibiting" sea-things should divide his displays accord- *geography.*
ing to countries. But should they not rather be divided,

as the fishes, if they and not we had the arrangement of it, would certainly divide it according to existing oceans, seas, and rivers and lakes ? With only water-folk on the committee we should see the water-continents and water-countries represented one by one ; should be able to take in at a glance the products and industries of each in turn, and should also view tribe by tribe, the great finned orders that contribute to the welfare of man and the means by which they do it exhibited in mass.

It would be a lesson in humility, and one, perhaps, not altogether undeserved ; for it would seem at present as if man, simply because he himself cannot keep alive under the water, were inclined to disregard the claims of the vast area which is inhabited solely by those that can.

CHAPTER XII.

INSECTS.

 "MOUSE-EATING" spider, such as may be *Nature's*
seen in the Regent's Park collection, can only *carefulness of us in the*
be justified in existing if we consider it to be a *matter of Horrors.*
supreme effort of Nature in the direction of the hideous.
It is a bear-spider, and nearly as hairy, and as ugly as a
nightmare.

Nature makes these efforts to teach us how horrible
she can be when she likes; but she slips her horrors at
us only one by one, and at long intervals, so that the
general impression of her tenderness and grace may not
be too roughly shocked. Her miracles of beauty are
well known, for she places them conspicuously in the

front, scattering butterflies lavishly all over the world, giving her painted favourites, the birds, wings to bring them under the notice of men, and, generally, making her prettiest creatures the commonest. She can, however, work miracles in ugliness also ; but these she hides away from sight, so that men may come upon them by surprise, and thus gradually learn to appreciate the full extent of her powers. While the horse adds a beauty to every road and pasture of the world, the hippopotamus conceals its monstrosity in remote swamps and river-rushes far from human haunts. Birds of delightful song and dainty *Beautiful* plumage brighten every garden and grove ; but the hairy *things com-* apteryx creeps about at night in New Zealand wastes, *mon or* and the dodo, a practical joke rather than a bird, never *large :* waddled beyond the limits of a single island. The harm- *hideous ones* less and pretty " grass snake" and the " green lizards " are *small or* common all over Europe ; but the loathly cerastes is con- *rare.* cealed in Nubian deserts, while the iguana hides itself in the leafy wilderness of the Brazils. In clear common water we find the shapely trout and handsome perch ; but only in the slime of the ocean bed lies the " sea devil." Thus all through nature—beasts, birds, reptiles, and fishes—we find the ugly things made a secret of and the pretty ones displayed ; and in insects also, Nature, to work to the same kind end, uses the same means, for she makes all the common kinds so small that their hideousness is not apparent, and, where size is necessary, puts them out of sight, either in the desert sands or tropical undergrowth, or at the bottom of ponds and running streams. It is fortunate that she does so, for, taking the spiders alone, if they were of large size, they would

> "Mock the majesty of man's high birth,
> Despise his bulwarks, and unpeople earth."

What conceivable system of defences, for instance, *Gigantic* could avail humanity against a creation of spiders as big *spiders.* as sheep? They would float across the sea in the diving bells which they know how to make so well, and swing themselves across rivers as they now do across garden paths. Leaping half a mile at every jump, they could in a night traverse incredible distances, and waking in the morning a whole village might find itself inextricably woven up in a fog of web, every door, gate, and chimney enveloped in a suffocating cobweb of glutinous ropes, with the grim twilight made terrible by the stealthy motions of a gang of bloodthirsty spiders. The monsters would pounce upon the human beings one by one, swathe them in murderous meshes, and sling them up to their tunnel roofs like the men and women of story-books in an ogre's larder. I need not follow the fancy further, for it is evident from even this hint of dreadful possibilities what might be imagined if spiders were as big as sheep and still remained spiders in character and habits.

Yet if they changed their temper with their bulk, and when they became as big as sheep became also as harmless, their presence would be still too horrible to be borne. Their existence would argue the presence among

us of such flies as we should have to attack with shot-
guns, and grasshoppers which we should course with
greyhounds. Our rivers would swarm with dragon-flies
that would buffet boats' crews with the wings of swans,
our trees be munched up like lettuces by anaconda
caterpillars, and wood-lice go about in the bigness of
tortoises. Existence under such circumstances would be
intolerable, and the necessity of spiders to keep down
the insect packs and herds that would otherwise trample
and jostle us out of Great Britain would only increase
the horrors of our condition. The " mouse-eating " spider
in Regent's Park has fortunately been invited to come
among us only as a guest, and not by any means to
naturalize himself here, for his appearance and habits
are abundantly sufficient to make us prefer his continuing
to remain in the Brazils. He is " at home " in Bahia,
and there disports himself (they say) by jumping
upon the backs of little birds, in imitation of his companion the jaguar, sucking out all their blood, and then
playing with their empty skins. As a substitute for the
common or domestic cat, which in these days of cat's-
meat men and careless cooks has considerably lost its
appetite for mice, and thinks it too much trouble to
catch sparrows, it might, perhaps, be usefully acclimatized.

As a Mouse-catcher. But what English household would submit with any
complacency to the domestication of such a creature?
As it is, chairs prove hardly high enough when the aver-

age British spider, which can sit on a threepenny bit, and is afraid of an able-bodied bluebottle, comes near a petticoat; and, if they were any bigger, we should have to keep ladders in every room for the ladies of the household to escape to the roof. The ordinary housemaid, who "never could abide spiders," would go about her occupations with a drawn sword, and scullery-maids plead for the last consolations of religion before entering the cellars. If it were not for this aversion of the sex the mousing spider might be really an acquisition ; for not only could he be depended upon to catch the mice when he got them well into the open, but he could go like a ferret down their holes and chase them about inside the walls. Invaluable, however, as this would be, *Spiders a* the corresponding depreciation of the cat would be *poor substi-* *tute for* deplorable, for the hearth would lose its most comfort- *Cats.* able ornament and "pussy" be banished from nur-series, for no housekeeper would give a spider, how-ever big, a corner by the fire, nor could any one, having seen the abominable creature in Regent's Park, expect children to pet its "kittens."

In behalf of the aversion which I have noticed, it is often contended that such prejudice is " only natural ; " and yet, as a matter of fact, no family of insects probably deserves so well not only our admiration but our respect as the spiders. For one thing, they epitomize for us a large section of the animal world, and present, in their different varieties, a constant series of wonders. Some are the cats, wolves, cheetahs, lynxes, or tigers of the insect creation, as agile as monkeys and as industrious as beavers, carrying parental affection to extravagant lengths, and of an astonishing intelligence ; though without wings they fly through space, like magicians on carpets of their own weaving, and, though dependent on the air, they nest

Spider miracles.

under water. The problems connected with the miracle of their geometric webs, their silk-lined tunnels, diving-bells, and trap-doors fitted with corks or with wafer lids, their leaf-tubes, their gossamer flakes on which they float through the air, are all of delightful interest, while literature is replete with anecdotes of the quaint services rendered to Mahomets and King Davids, Bruces and d'Isjouvals by individuals of this species. Mythology, in its story of Arachne, the Lydian girl who dared to compete with the goddess of artistic needlework, has bequeathed nothing to us that should make us dislike the spider ; while in the infinite service which the latter creatures render us in pursuing by day and night, on every wall and leaf, the enemies of our comfort and gardens, should

Their appalling features.

entitle them to grateful recognition. Nevertheless, they have the misfortune to have inherited prejudices, and to have been selected by Nature for the exhibition of her dexterity in its most grotesque and repulsive aspects. Under the microscope the bristly head of a spider, coroneted with eyes and with an appalling mouth sheathed in plates of horn and garnished with a horrible armature of knives and pincers, is a monstrous object and it is as well, perhaps, for us that the "mouse-eating" spider, whose ill-favoured features are apparent to the naked eye, should live only in Bahia.

Gulliver tells us how intolerable life is where flies are "as big as Dunstable larks," and wasps drone louder than bagpipes, and we are fortunate, therefore, in not having the insect discomforts of Brobdingnag superadded to our own.

*   *   *   *   *

There has lately been discovered a species of ant which deserves to be at once introduced to the attention of all children, servants, and ladies keeping house. No vestry should be ignorant of the habits of so admirable a creature, and sanitary boards of all kinds should without loss of time be put in possession of the leading facts.

This excellent ant, it appears, abominates rubbish. If *Dirt breaks* its house is made in a mess it gets disgusted, goes away, *an Ant's heart.* and never comes back. Dirt breaks its heart.

The insect in question is a native of Colombia, and hatches its eggs by artificial heat, procuring for this purpose quantities of foliage, which, in the course of natural fermentation, supply the necessary warmth. When the young brood is hatched the community carefully carry away the decomposed rubbish that has served its purpose as a hotbed, and stack it by itself at a distance from the nest. The damage which they inflict upon gardens and plantations when collecting the leaves required is so enormous that colonists have exhausted their ingenuity

in devising means for their expulsion or extermination;
but all in vain, for the ant, wherever it "squats," strikes
very firm roots indeed, and neither plague, pestilence,
nor famine, neither fire nor brimstone, nor yet holy water,
can compel it to go away. It takes no notice whatever
of writs of ejectment, and looks upon bell, book, and
candle as mere idle mummeries. The nest may be dug
up with a plough or blown up with gunpowder, soaked
with hot water or swamped out with cold, smothered with
smoke, or made abominable with chemical compounds,
strewn with poison or scattered abroad with pitchforks—
the ants return all the same, and apparently, with a gaiety
enhanced by their recent ordeals. The Inquisition
would have had no chance with them, for all the tortures
of the martyrs have been tried upon them in vain.
Their heroic tenacity to their homesteads would have
baffled the malignity of a Bonner or the persecuting zeal
of an Alva. But where force may fail moral suasion often
meets with success, and this has proved true with the
ants in question. An observant negro, remarking that
the creatures were impervious to the arguments of
violence, and knowing their cleanly habits, suggested
that, if the ants could not be hunted or blown or
massacred off the premises, they might be disgusted
with them. The experiment was made, and with
complete success. The refuse foliage which the ants
had so carefully stacked away in tidy heaps was
scattered over the ground, and some other basketfuls of

rubbish added, and the whole community fled on the instant !

They did not even go home to pack up their carpet bags, but just as they were, in the clothes they stood in, so to speak, they fled from the disordered scene.

Ant habits have always furnished ample material for the moralist, but this, the latest recorded trait of their character, makes a delightful addition to the already interesting history of these " tiny creatures, strong by social league," the " parsimonious" emmet folk. It destroys, it is true, something of their traditional reputation for industry that they should thus abandon themselves to despair rather than set to work to clear away the rubbish strewn about their dwelling-places. It sets them in this respect below the bees, who never seem to weary of repairing damages, and far below the " white ant " of the East, which has an absolutely ferocious passion for mending breaches and circumventing accidents. Nothing beats them except utter annihilation.

The ants of Colombia, however, if they fail in that nobility of diligence which seems to be only whetted by disaster, rise infinitely superior to their congeners in the moral virtues of respect for sanitation and punctilious cleanliness. There is, however, even a more admirable *They resent* psychological fact behind than this, for it appears that *Untidyness next door.* the rubbish which scatters them most promptly is not their own, but their neighbours'. Their own rubbish, it is true, sends them off quickly enough, but the exodus is, if possible, accelerated by employing that from an adjoining nest. To have their own litter lying about makes home intolerable, but that their neighbours should " shoot " theirs also upon them is the very extremity of abomination. Life under such conditions is at once voted impossible, and rather than exist where the next-door people can empty their dust-bins and slop-pails over their walls, they go away headlong. A panic of disgust seizes upon the whole colony, and the bonds of society snap and shrivel up on the instant, like a spider's web above a candle-flame. Without a thought of wife or child, of household gods or household goods, they rush tumultuously from the polluted spot. No pious son stays to give the aged Anchises a lift; none loiters to spoil the Egyptians before he goes ; none looks back upon the doomed city. Forward and anywhere is the motto of the pell-mell flight ; all throw down their burdens that they may run the faster, and shamefully abandon their shields that their arms may not impede their course. Big and little, male and female, old and young, all scamper off alike over the untidy thresholds, and there is no distinction of caste under the common horror of a home that requires sweeping up.

Such a spectacle is truly sublime, for behind the ants there is no avenging Michael-arm, that they should thus precipitately fall into " hideous rout;" no Zulu impi ; no hyæna horde of Bashkirs, as there was after the flying Tartars; no remorseless pursuit of any

kind. Indeed, persecution and fiery trials they confront un-
moved, so there is no element of fear in their conduct.

It. arises entirely from a generous impatience of *A superb*
neighbours' untidy habits, from a superb intolerance of *Intolerance of Dirt.*
dirt. When was such an example ever set, or when will
it ever be followed, by human beings? No single city,
not even a village, is ever recorded to have been abandoned on account of uncleanliness; and yet what a
grand episode in national history it would be, if such
had happened, had the men of Cologne, for instance,
ever gone out into the country-side and all encamped
there, in dignified protest against the "six-and-seventy
separate stinks" of their undrained city! No instance
even is on record of a single householder rushing from
his premises with all his family rather than endure cobwebs and dust; nor, indeed, of a single child refusing to
stay in its nursery because it was untidy. We are still,
therefore, far behind the Colombia ant in the matter of
cleanliness.

In another aspect, perhaps, this impetuous detestation
of dirt is not altogether admirable; for, as I have
noticed, it argues a declension in industry from the
true ant standard. Thus, the very creatures that urge so
headlong a career when the neatness of their surroundings is threatened are marvels of diligence in collecting
the very leaves which afterwards distress them so much.
This assiduity has long been noted. In Cornwall the
busy "murians," as the people call the ants, are still sup-

posed to be a race of " little people," disestablished from the world of men and women for their idle habits, and condemned to perpetual labour ; while in Ceylon the natives say that the ants feed a serpent, who lives under-ground, with the leaves which they pick off the trees, and that, as the reptile's appetite is never satisfied, the ants have to work on for ever. From West to East, there-fore, the same trait of unresting diligence has been re-marked ; and, in one respect, it is no doubt a deplorable retrogression in the Colombia ants that the mere sight of rubbish should thus dishearten them. Yet, looked at from a higher standpoint, their consuming dislike of un-cleanly surroundings is magnificent, for they do not hesi-tate to sacrifice all that is nearest and dearest, to risk even their public character, so long as sufficient effect can be given to their protest and sufficient emphasis laid upon their indignation. Anything short of flight, imme-diate and complete, without condition or reservation, would fail to meet the case or adequately represent their feelings. To them the degradation of submitting to a neighbour's cinders and eggshells seems too despicable to be borne, and rather than live in a parish where the vestry neglects the drains and the dust-bins they abandon their hearths and homes for ever. We human beings cannot all of us afford to show the same superb horror of defec-tive sanitation, but we can admire the ants who do, and can hold them up as models to all slatterns and sluts, parochial or domestic.

* * * * *

Of all the revenges of nature none is more delightful than Sir John Lubbock's recently discovered beetles that live upon locusts. These admirable insects are natives of the classic Troad, and they enter upon the serious duties of life, the consumption of locust eggs, at a very early age. They do not, in fact, even wait until they are beetles, for they begin in their previous grub state, and, insinuating their immature forms into the cases in which the parent locust leaves her eggs to hatch, feed so comfortably inside the weather-tight tent which the locust had provided for the protection of its own young, that they shortly assume a fat and fleshy appearance, very different from their previous attenuated aspect. The mother locust unfortunately does not betray sufficient maternal solicitude to make the sequel satisfactory, for having laid her eggs and, as she thinks, secured them from molestation she takes wing and leaves them to themselves.

How Locusts are served out by Beetles.

Were it otherwise, humanity might derive a malicious consolation from imagining the progenitors of the winged pest returning at some appointed season to see how their nurseries were getting on, and might exult over the dismay and disappointment that would be apparent on the features of the mother when she discovered inside her egg-case a comfortable and fat Lubbock beetle instead of her own interesting colony of juvenile locusts. But this pleasure is denied us, for the winged parents, having fulfilled their destinies, rise to the first passing breeze and are blown away to new pastures where they may ravage and debauch afresh, and they never come back to the scenes of their domestic joys and troubles. The solid fact remains, nevertheless, intact, that whether the mothers of the little locusts ever return or not "to trace beloved lineaments in each infant face," the beetle eats them up and thrives on them. The good that this small creature must do is therefore incalculable, for it is of a very voracious sort; and though the locust is prodigiously prolific the beetle's appetite for its eggs is providentially in proportion. A locust cannot lay too many eggs for the beetle—indeed, the more the better. It may thus be considered an antidote to " the scourge of Allah ;" and though, according to the modern Arabs, the locust bears in the markings upon its wings a statement in excellent Arabic to the effect that it is " the avenging army of the Deity," there is no hint given as to the existence of the beetle which avenges mankind upon the avengers and makes an omelette of all their eggs inside the shells which the careful parents provide. The beetle, however, is an unmistakable fact, and in the Troad in one year is said to have destroyed nearly all the season's brood of locusts, an act of public good which all the ingenuity and industry of man has hitherto failed to effect.

The Chain of Retribution. A popular quatrain tells us how even fleas have " lesser fleas to bite 'em," and that this process of mutual molestation proceeds " ad infinitum." To insect-plagued humanity this reflection must be full of solace.

In human society we have thieves and brigands, burglars and cut-throats, but no one that we know of ever picks a thief's pocket or breaks into a burglar's house. Brigands are never carried away from their afflicted friends to the tops of inaccessible mountains ; and as for cut-throats, it would be absurd to think of their being murdered. There is, of course, the large class of spies, informers, and receivers who prey upon the criminal classes ; but they themselves are so hampered in their plundering that they never inflict upon the original offender any degree of injury commensurate with that which he inflicts upon respectable society. In the insect world, however, these things are very beautifully arranged, for if there are spiders that eat flies, there are also flies that eat spiders.

We human beings, to tell the truth, are too much given to supposing that the insect world from first to last find their destinies in performing some act directly useful or the reverse towards ourselves, whereas it is certain that, if no such animal as man existed, the world would go on as merrily as ever, and not a single insect see its occupation gone. The mosquito would quite as cheerfully amuse itself with an elephant—for this delicate brute is peculiarly sensitive to the mosquito —as it does at present with men and women, while to cockroaches and earwigs it would make no difference if every kitchen and summer-house were destroyed to-morrow.

Is man, then, really an incident in the scheme of nature,
an additional animal, and not at all the essential and all-
necessary ingredient which he supposes ?   The locust, it
is true, ravages his crops, yet not because they are crops,
but merely because they happen to be on the spot where
it comes to feed.   If it alighted on a primeval forest or a
prairie it would ravage in precisely the same way ; and
so in the same way the Lubbock beetle does not eat the
locust's eggs in order to benefit man, but because it likes
locust's eggs.   It probably ate them before man existed,
and would continue to do so even if he ceased to exist.
Meanwhile, that it does benefit man by the opportune
consumption of embryo locusts is beyond· a doubt.

*Insect
Checks to
Insect
Plagues.* Apart, however, from the utility to man of this reciprocal
antagonism of insects, there is, as we have already noted,
a delightful sense of justice cheaply achieved.   While
humanity has been devising scientific schemes for the
amelioration of insect plagues, and fondly imagining
that upon ourselves has rested the burden of keeping the
animal world within proper limits, the insects have themselves taken the matter in hand, and been actively carrying into effect the plans and suggestions which, if left to
us, would never have got beyond the preliminary stages
of consideration.   In the orchard the fruit-farmer watches
with lamentation the depredation of the wasps among
his plums, and his children come crying to him with the
tale of their sufferings, how they picked up a fallen pear
and were stung by the wasp inside.   Yet all this time, so

naturalists tell us, there are wasps that sting wasps and hornets that lie in wait among the tempting fruit to carry off or decapitate the smaller depredators. In the hot summer days flies annoy us, but it is a comfort to know that whenever they sit down on bushes their enemies are on the watch for them, that not only spiders catch and eat them, but winged things of their own kind devour them readily. The cockroach is an abomination in a kitchen, but if he ventures to walk abroad the "pompilus" takes him by the nose and, having stung him senseless, drags him away to some convenient chink that serves it for a larder. The spiders that creep about where they have no business to be and spin threads across pathways, so as to catch the faces of passers-by, are constantly beset by fly foes, who treat them with a delightful contempt, using their fat round bodies to lay their eggs in, and even storing them up like apples to feed the young flies when they are hatched. The caterpillars that destroy our vegetables and work havoc in the flower garden are not the irresponsible tyrants that they seem ; for they go in mortal terror of their lives all day long, not only from other caterpillars that eat them, but from a number of winged creatures that take a truculent delight in their tender bodies. The beetle which we call a cockchafer, and which in France does almost incredible damage, has another beetle told off to it, whose only duty is to hunt and kill it. The wheat fly, snug though it thinks itself, tucked up inside the husks of the grain, is found out by a special fly whose whole work in life is to lay its eggs in the other's body; and even the gall-flies, inside their secret chambers, the clover-fly hidden in the little flower, and the wire-worm underground are each of them the particular objects of pursuit and slaughter to appointed insects. To this complete chain of crime and punishment man can add nothing; but he can, at any rate, take the broad hint which the insects give him, and assist them to indulge their beneficial appetites.

For instance, the locust-beetle is a colonist that many a country would be glad to welcome, and what tenant of a seaside lodging-house would not be grateful for a few specimens of the "reduvius"? This exemplary insect hates the bug with a mortal hatred, though it is its own cousin, and hunts it up and down the furniture with a zest that is very pleasing to contemplate. Morally, of course, it is highly reprehensible, but it saves our species, at any rate, from the poet's stricture that

> "Man only mars kind Nature's plan,
> And turns the fierce pursuit on man."

As a matter of fact, the insect world largely maintains its equilibrium by the cannibalism and constant strife that obtain between creatures of the same *Man not* species; for, as I have shown, caterpillars chase and *the only* eat each other, spiders devour nearly as many spiders as *Criminal* *or Canni-* flies, wasps kill wasps, fleas bite fleas, and bugs destroy *bal in* *Nature.* bugs. Nor are the other serious crimes said to be a special attribute of humanity found absent among the insect folk, for murder, simply for the sake of killing, is not at all infrequent, assassination is constant, and the younger members of one family actually take advantage of the gluttonous habits of their elders to pull them in pieces when they find them lying gorged and helpless— not for food, but simply as a practical joke! Whether these deplorable habits, even though they tend to our own comfort, should excite our admiration or not is a matter for moralists to decide ; but in the meantime it is certainly permitted us to speak appreciatively of arrangements of Nature which place insect-antidotes for insect evils within our reach. It is very sad to think that bug should turn upon brother bug ; but since it is so, let us accept the fact as cheerfully as we can, and carry the "reduvius" with us whenever we have to sleep abroad, and if it has been preordained that little beetles should eat the infant progeny of the locust, it would be unbecoming to question the propriety of the practice. On the contrary, the interesting creatures Sir John Lubbock has now introduced to us deserve the widest possible encouragement.

A misguided fanatic has come forward to announce, as if expecting congratulation, that the white ant of the tropics will thrive in England. He is wisely anonymous, but it passes belief that he should anticipate any enthusiasm for the announcement.

Once upon a time, so it is said, it was proposed

to the people of Abydos that they should establish
a police, but the townsfolk, instantly gathering together
a sufficiency of big pebbles, stoned the would-be reformer out of their city. This they did to show that
they were content with such evils as they already possessed, and did not care to introduce others. I would
not go so far as to say that the Corporation of the
City of London should formally stone out of the City
limits every stranger who came before them with ob-
noxious suggestions, because the indiscriminate application of even the most wholesome correctives may
sometimes lead to their abuse. But it does occasionally happen that exceptional circumstances arise which
seem to call for exceptional treatment, inasmuch as our
ordinary procedure does not meet them. What, for
instance, are we to do with those who would naturalize
the horrors of foreign countries among us, or who
would allow their scientific enthusiasm to betray them into
public exultation over the " success " of experiments in
Criminal acclimatizing such abominable exotics as scorpions,
acclimati-
zation. Colorado beetles, white ants, cobras, and mosquitoes?

All of these have actually in turn been experi-
mented with; and, though there are certain conditions
of Western civilization, hob-nailed boots for one thing,
that act as positive checks to the multiplication of the
species, there has been quite sufficient success to justify
the hope of the misguided individuals who nurture them
that in time they may thrive in our midst. The Colorado

beetle's enormities are of such proportions that he has been formally prosecuted as an enemy of the State, and, with all the pomp of Legislative bell, book, and candle, he has been warned off our shores, while naturalists have been threatened with penalties if they attempt to acclimatize him. The cobra is a criminal of hardly less dignity, and yet it is on record that an enthusiast in serpenti-culture offered to the guardians of the Kensington Gardens a lively family of da capellos, with the suggestion that, if looked after, " they might get on well." The generous offer was promptly declined, and an intimation was conveyed to the would-be donor that any one seen surreptitiously introducing snakes into the rockeries or water-pipes of our public gardens would be instantly prosecuted. Nor was the proposal of breeding white ants received with greater favour. Building societies might, indeed, do worse than introduce this house-devouring insect, but we feel sure that the immorality of such conduct will prevent it from being at all generally followed. Of the other pests we have mentioned, the scorpion has already made himself quite at home among us, and the mosquito has proved beyond doubt its adaptability to our climate. We are content, having these, to invite no more additions to our " common objects of the country ;" and if any one should now hint at tarantulas, centipedes, or other such interesting novelties, the public will probably not forget the people of Abydos.

Scorpions are undesirable, but mosquitoes are altogethe: intolerable. The simple fact that a scorpion can be caught removes much of its terrors. It can be picked up with the tongs, and put at the back of the kitchen fire or a brick can be dropped upon it, and the remains car be kept in spirits of wine. A scorpion is a fact, and therefore assailable. It can be pummelled and kicked into the street. It is in our power to apprehend it and punish it. There is solidity about it, for a scorpion wil sink in water. We can make a parcel of it, and throw i down the sink. It lends itself, being material, to every possible treatment, and invests pursuit, capture, and subsequent destruction with a certain dignity. It i: large enough for a man to protect himself from, and, be fore ladies, to perform prodigies of valour. There i: nothing unmanly in using a stick to a scorpion, nor need anybody be ashamed if found heated in the face and the furniture of the room in disorder, in pursuit of one.

With the mosquito none of this is possible. It is a voice only, but a voice with a proboscis—a phantom with a beak a ghost that bites. It is not to be caught, but if it is there is nothing in the hand worth mentioning. The captor cannot be proud of the residue, for the remain: of a dead ghost are the merest trifle. The meanest o men would not hesitate to throw them away. It is no possible, as with a scorpion, to wait until it settles, and then stamp upon it, for no man can stamp on the nap of his own neck, or permit another to do so. Nor is i of any use to take the fire-irons to the mosquito, or to set a dog upon it. A man would look absurd who went after one with a thick stick, or threw his boots at it.

The insect is, humanly speaking, intangible. It might almost be denied to be matter at all, for our knowledge of it is strictly relative. The victim hears a voice close to his ear, as of some fly whining a monotonous recitative; he feels an itching on the lobe of the ear; he finds a pimple there which he rubs. That is all; and from these phenomena in conjunction he argues the existence of a mosquito in his neighbourhood.

The philosopher asks "What is matter?" and answers himself that it is the name for extension, solidity, divisibility, figure and so forth, conjoined in something. We cannot, he says, think of those properties, apart from something to which they belong, or think of that something without its properties. Mosquitoes might, therefore, be fairly denied corporeal existence, for we know them, as a rule, by their effects only. When they perforate a hole in the skin we argue they have a proboscis which is very sharp at one end, and as they come to us through the air we infer that they have wings; but a proboscis upon wings would be such a preposterous assailant that we gratuitously endow it further with legs and a body and a tail. But it is the height of hypocrisy to affect to regard mosquitoes philosophically. It is all very well to appeal to metaphysics and loftily deny their material existence, or pretend to dismiss them from solid

discussion as being only relative to their effects. Such
treatment of a mosquito does not suffice. It may do fo
" matter " in a lump, but when we come to details, it fails
" I have heard," said the Ettrick Shepherd, " that it i
denied that there are such things as flesh-and-blood men
but I never heard before that the proof of the existence
of ghosts was counted defective." Elephants, rhino
ceroses, and such things may afford subject for philo-
sophical doubt, but the mosquito admits of none. There is
no gainsaying its presence, nor, when it has once settled
upon a man's body, is there any use in pretending that he
does not feel it. Although a mere trifle, as light as air,
it cannot be disregarded. Work must cease before it,
and pleasure in its company is impossible.

The mere passage of the hand through the air blows a
mosquito away, yet this gossamer nothing, this aërial
ephemerid, paralyzes the intellect and turns the human
affections to gall. Asleep or awake, the torment pursues
its victim. The very littleness of the persecutor embitters
life. If the kitchen poker could be of any use, they
might come on by battalions, but there is not enough in
a mosquito to strike. A bushel of scorpions might easily
be disposed of by industrious agility, but even one
mosquito is all too numerous to fight with. Out from
some dark corner the small thing comes in the
twilight, piping a vicious catechism as it flies. It carefully reconnoitres its prey, and settles upon the point
selected as lightly as a shadow. It has taken it half an

hour to make up its mind, and its human foe sits all the time breathless and motionless, while the exasperating sing-song comes and goes, rises and falls, now at one ear, now at another, round behind his head, and then down to the ankles ; but at last it ceases. The mosquito has settled, and the moment for vengeance has arrived. Has it ? The intention is excellent, and the vigour of the blow undeniable, but what is there to show ? A pimple, nothing more—an irritating and unnecessary pimple.

Let other countries, then, keep the rest of their plagues. The mosquito, the chief of small evils, is already acclimatized along our southern coast and in London itself, and nearly every ship that brings a cargo from the Tropics contributes to the number of our scorpions.

For the latter I can admit a certain latitude of commiseration, but for the former there can be none. The *Sympathy with Scorpions possible;* scorpion, child of summer climes, has been accustomed to barefooted races of men and the steamy warmth to be found under luxuriant vegetation. In a thoughtless moment it had crept among some cargo destined for England, and when it next sees light it is on an English wharf. Not a shrub does it find to hide under, and the granite blocks are so closely cemented that there are no cracks of refuge. The air is chill, and the scorpion creeps half-numbed across the cold, wet stones, in the hope of finding shelter ; but suddenly there comes along —how different from the sauntering, bare-footed negro, creole, or Hindoo that he is accustomed to !—a quick-stepping man in hob-nailed boots. He did not even notice that he had put his foot on the scorpion as he passed. The negro, if he had done so, would have leaped up in the air with a shout, and, as the scorpion scuttled down a hole, it would have seen the black man lying on the ground, bellowing out his lamentations. But, with the granite wharf beneath it and the sole of a heavy boot above, the scorpion's interest in its surroundings soon ceases.

With the Mosquito impossible.

But the mosquito's experiences are by no means desperate. Arrived at the wharf it goes ashore, and, seeing the same man in hob-nailed boots sitting on a bench, it perches upon him and makes a meal. We do not, it is true, expose so much bare surface to the mosquito's attack as the races among which it is indigenous, but, on the other hand, we have no artificial defences against its assaults. It does not, therefore, suffer by emigration, nor, if all accounts of its rapid propagation are to be believed, does the difference of climate affect it. When or by whom it was introduced does not now matter, for the fact suffices that it is here.

But any attempt to introduce other pests, reptile or insect, should be taken up at once, not perhaps with all the severity of the townsfolk of Abydos, but, at any rate, with all their promptitude.

AUTHOR'S POSTSCRIPT.

AND now, if I have said anything that either the Beasts or their friends think unkind or unjust, I am sorry for it. Attribute it, Reader, to want of knowledge, not to want of sympathy; and if you would be generous, do not think me too much in earnest when I am serious, or altogether in fun because I jest. The subject of my book is after all only a loaded cork, and however you place it, it insists on turning its lighter end upwards.

الحمد لله

E e

www.ingramcontent.com/pod-product-compliance
Lightning Source LLC
Chambersburg PA
CBHW021330110726
47900CB00005B/1422